Later Years at

Malory Towers

Enid Blyton

Enid Blyton

Later Years at
Malory Towers

EGMONT

EGMONT

We bring stories to life

Upper Fourth at Malory Towers first published in Great Britain 1949
In the Fifth at Malory Towers first published in Great Britain 1950
Last Term at Malory Towers first published in Great Britain 1951

First published as *The Later Years at Malory Towers* in 2014
by Egmont UK Limited
The Yellow Building, 1 Nicholas Road, London W11 4AN

ENID BLYTON ® Copyright © 2013 Hodder & Stoughton Ltd

ISBN 978 1 4052 6908 7

www.egmont.co.uk

55939/3

A CIP catalogue record for this title is available from the British Library

Printed and bound in Great Britain by the CPI Group

MIX
Paper
FSC   FSC® C018306

Upper Fourth at

Malory Towers

Contents

Darrell goes back to school with Felicity

Darrell Rivers was very excited. It was the day to return to Malory Towers, her boarding school – and this time she was taking her young sister Felicity with her.

Felicity stood on the front steps beside her fifteen-year-old sister, dressed in the same brown and orange uniform, feeling excited, too. She was almost thirteen, and should have gone to Malory Towers two terms before, but she had been ill and had to stay at home.

Now it was the summer term, and she was to go with Darrell at last. She had heard so much about her sister's school – the fun they had there, the classrooms over-looking the sea, the four towers in which the two hundred and fifty girls slept, the great swimming-pool hollowed out of the rocks on the shore . . . there was no end to the things that Darrell had told her.

'It's a good thing we're going by train this time, not by car,' said Darrell. 'You'll travel down with the girls then, and get to know some of them. Sally's going by train, too.'

Sally was Darrell's best friend, and had been ever since her first term at Malory Towers almost four years ago.

'I hope I get a friend like Sally,' said Felicity, nervously. 'I'm shyer than you, Darrell. I'm sure I shall never pluck up enough courage to speak to anyone! And if Miss Potts gets cross with me I shall sink through the floor!'

Miss Potts was the first-form mistress, and also the house-mistress for North Tower, the tower to which Darrell belonged, and to which her young sister would go, too.

'Oh, you needn't be afraid of Potty,' said Darrell, with a laugh, quite forgetting how scared *she* had been of her when she was in the first form. 'Dear old Potty – she's a good sort.'

Their father's car drew up at the front door, and the two girls ran down the steps. Mr Rivers looked at them and smiled.

'*Both* off this time!' he said. 'Well, I remember quite well Darrell going off alone for the first time almost four years ago. She was twelve then – now you're fifteen, aren't you, Darrell?'

'Yes,' said Darrell, getting into the car with Felicity. 'And I remember you saying to me, "You'll get a lot out of Malory Towers – see that you put a lot back!"'

'Daddy's said that to me, too,' said Felicity. 'I'm jolly lucky to have an older sister to show me round – though honestly I feel as if I know every corner of Malory Towers already.'

'Now, where's Mother?' said her father, and he hooted the horn. 'Really, this is a dreadful family to collect. If your mother appears in good time, one of you girls is missing, and if you girls are here, your mother is not! We shall miss the train if we don't look out!'

Usually they went all the way down to Cornwall to Malory Towers by car, but this time it was impossible, so Mr Rivers was driving them up to London and seeing them off in the school-train. Felicity had sometimes been to see her sister off by train, and had felt scared of all the girls chattering and laughing on the platform – now this time she was actually going to be one of them! She hugged her tennis-racket to her and thought joyfully of the coming term.

Mrs Rivers came running down the steps, looking very pretty in a simple grey suit with a little blue blouse. Darrell and Felicity looked at her proudly. Parents mattered a lot when you were at boarding school! Everyone wanted to be proud of the way their fathers and mothers looked and spoke and behaved. It was dreadful if a mother came in a silly hat, or if a father came looking very untidy.

'My dear, we were *just* going without you,' said Mr Rivers. 'Now – have we really got everything? Last time we got five miles on the way and then you said you'd forgotten Darrell's night-case.'

'Yes, we've got everything, Daddy,' said Darrell. 'I've checked every single thing – night-cases, with brush and comb, tooth-brush and paste, night-things, health certificate, everything! Tennis-rackets to carry, and our riding-hats! We can't pack those, they're too awkward.'

Felicity glanced round to see if her new riding-hat was there, too. She felt very proud of it.

3

They set off in the car to drive to London. Felicity's heart sank a little as her home disappeared from view. Three whole months before she would see it again! Then she cheered up as Darrell began chatting about the girls.

'I hope Bill will arrive with all her seven brothers on horseback,' she said. 'It's such a sight to see them all galloping up the school drive. Bill was supposed to come in her parents' car the first term she came, but she slipped off, got her horse, Thunder, and came with all her brothers on their horses, too!'

'Bill's real name is Wilhemina, isn't it?' said Felicity, remembering. 'Do even the mistresses call her Bill?'

'Some of them,' said Darrell. 'Not the Head, of course. And Miss Williams, our fourth-form mistress, doesn't either. She's a bit starchy – very prim and proper, but I like her now. I didn't at first.'

It didn't seem long before they were all on the station platform, finding their way between hosts of excited girls to a North Tower carriage. Felicity felt shy and nervous. Oh dear – so many girls, and they all knew one another, and she didn't know anyone. Oh, yes, she did – there was Sally, Darrell's friend, coming towards her, smiling.

'Hallo, Darrell, hallo, Felicity – so you're really coming to Malory Towers at last. Jolly good! Wish I was coming for the first time too, so that I would have years and years of it in front of me, like you. You don't know how lucky you are!'

'I remember someone saying that to *me* on my first day,' said Darrell. 'I was twelve then – now I'm going on for sixteen. Gosh, how old!'

'Yes – and don't forget we'll feel jolly old before this term's out!' said a familiar voice behind Darrell. 'We've all got to work for School Certificate! My hair will be quite grey by the end of term!'

'Hallo, Alicia!' said Darrell, warmly. 'Did you have good hols? Look, this is my young sister, Felicity. She's a new girl this term.'

'Is she really?' said Alicia. 'Well, I must find my cousin then. She's a new girl this term, too. Now where is she? I've lost her twice already!'

She disappeared, and Sally and Darrell laughed. They were sure that Alicia wouldn't bother much about any new-girl cousin! However, she appeared again almost at once bringing with her a twelve-year-old girl, very like her.

'This is June,' she said. 'You might as well make friends with Felicity, June, because you'll see plenty of her this term and for a good many years to come! Though whether Felicity will *want* to see much of you after she knows you well is very doubtful!'

Darrell looked at Alicia to see whether she meant this or not. You never knew with sharp-tongued Alicia! June looked all right, and had a very determined chin and mouth. A bit domineering, Darrell thought – but being in the bottom form of the school didn't give you much chance for that kind of thing. The older girls just sat on you hard if you didn't keep your place.

'Look!' said Alicia, nudging Darrell and Sally. 'There's Gwendoline Mary – come by train instead of car – and staging the same old scene as ever!'

Felicity and June turned to see. They saw a fair-haired girl with large, pale blue eyes, saying good-bye to her mother and her old governess. It was a very sentimental farewell, and a lot of sniffing was going on.

'Gwendoline always does that,' said Alicia in disgust. 'At her age, too! You can forgive a first-former going away from home for the first time – but a fifteen year old, no!'

'Well, it doesn't last long,' said Sally. 'Gwendoline won't even bother to remember to wave to her mother, I'm sure, once she gets into the carriage.'

Sally's mother was talking to Darrell's parents. There were no tears or protestations there! Darrell was thankful that her mother and father were so sensible. She looked at Felicity, and was pleased to see her young sister looking interested and happy.

More girls came up and surrounded Darrell and the others. 'Hallo! Had good hols? I say, is this your young sister? Has she got a temper like yours, Darrell?'

This was from Irene, harum-scarum as usual, her night-case coming undone, and her coat lacking a button already.

'Well – Felicity *has* got a temper,' said Darrell, with a laugh. 'All our family have. I don't expect Felicity will show hers much, though. She'll be too shy her first term.'

'I don't know about that!' said Sally, slyly. 'I seem to remember *you* going off the deep end properly in your first term, Darrell! Who sent me flying to the ground that first half-term – and who gave dear Gwendoline a very hearty scolding in the swimming-pool?'

'Oh, dear – yes, I was dreadful,' said Darrell, and she blushed. 'Really awful. I'm sure Felicity will never do anything like that.'

'My cousin's got a bit of a temper, too,' said Alicia, with a grin. 'She's only got brothers, and you should hear them shout and yell at one another when they disagree.'

'Here's Miss Potts,' said Sally, as the first-form mistress came up with a list in her hand. 'Hallo, Miss Potts, have you collected everyone?'

'Yes, I think so,' said Miss Potts, 'except Irene. Oh, there you are, Irene. I suppose it didn't occur to you to come and report your arrival to me? Thank goodness Belinda is going by car. That's one less scatter-brain to see to. Now, you'd better get into your carriages. There are only four more minutes to go.'

There was a scramble into the carriages. Sally and Darrell pulled Felicity into theirs. 'The new girls are supposed to go with Potty in her carriage,' said Darrell, 'but we'll let you come in ours. Good-bye, Mother, good-bye, Daddy! We'll write on Sunday and tell you all the news.'

'Good-bye!' said Felicity, in rather a small voice. 'Thanks for lovely hols.'

'Thank goodness we haven't got Gwendoline in our carriage,' said Alicia. 'We are at least spared the history of all her uninteresting family, and what happened to them last hols. Even her dogs are uninteresting!'

Everyone laughed. The guard blew his whistle. Doors slammed, and the train moved off slowly. Parents and girls waved madly. Darrell sank back into her seat.

'Off to Malory Towers again!' she said, joyfully. 'Good old Malory Towers!'

Everybody's back again!

The journey was a very long one, but the train arrived at the station for Malory Towers at last. Out poured the girls, complete with night-cases and rackets, and rushed to find good seats in the school coaches that took the train-girls on the last part of their journey.

Felicity was tired and excited. Darrell didn't seem in the least tired, but she was certainly excited. 'Now we shall see the school, and all the rest of the girls,' she said to Felicity, happily. 'Watch for the first glimpse of it when I tell you.'

And so Felicity had the same first glimpse that Darrell had had four years back. She saw a large castle-like building of grey stone rising high on a hill. Beyond was the deep blue Cornish sea, but that was now hidden by the cliff on which Malory Towers stood. Four towers stood at the corners of the building, and Felicity's eyes brightened as she thought of sleeping in one of the towers. She would be in North Tower with Darrell – and it had the best view of the sea! She was very lucky.

'It's lovely,' said Felicity to Darrell, and Darrell was pleased. It was going to be nice to have her sister at school with her. She felt sure that Felicity would be a great success.

Girls who had already arrived by car stood about the drive ready to welcome the train-girls. There were shrieks and squeals of delight as the coaches drove up to the magnificent front entrance, and swarms of girls ran to help down their friends.

'Hallo, Belinda!' shouted Irene, climbing down and leaving behind her night-case. 'Done any decent sketching?'

'Darrell!' called a shy-looking fifteen year old. 'Sally! Alicia!'

'Hallo, Mary-Lou! Anyone put a spider down your neck these hols?' cried Alicia. 'Seen Betty?'

Betty was Alicia's friend, as witty as she was, and as mischievous. She came up and banged Alicia on the back.

'Here I am! You're jolly late – the train must have been even later than usual.'

'There's Mavis,' cried Sally. 'And Daphne – and I say, hallo there, Jean. Seen Bill anywhere?'

'Yes. She came on Thunder as usual and she's in the stable with him,' said Jean, the quiet, shrewd Scots girl, who was now no longer in the same form as Darrell, but was going up. 'She came with the groom, because all her brothers went back to school before we did this term. A very tame arrival!'

Felicity stood unheeded in the general rush and excitement. She hoped that Darrell wouldn't entirely forget her. Alicia had completely forgotten about her cousin June. That youngster now came up to Felicity and grinned. 'Our elders are making a fine noise, aren't they?' she said. 'We're small fry to them. Let's slip off by ourselves, shall we, and make them look for us when they deign to remember we're here?'

'Oh, no,' said Felicity, but June pulled her arm and dragged her away.

'Yes, come on. I know we're supposed to go to Matron and give in our health certificate and our term's pocket-money. We'll go and find her on our own.'

'But Darrell won't like . . .' began Felicity, as she was led firmly away by June.

So it was that when Darrell looked round for her young sister, she was nowhere to be seen!

'Where's Felicity?' she said. 'Blow! What's happened to her? I know how awful you feel when you're new, and I wanted to take her under my wing for a bit. Where in the world has she gone?'

'Don't worry,' said Alicia, unfeelingly. 'I'm not bothering about young June. She can look after herself all right, if I know anything about that young lady. She's got all the cheek in the world!'

'Well, but Felicity hasn't,' said Darrell. 'Dash it, where has she gone? She was here a minute ago.'

'Anyone seen my night-case?' came Irene's voice in a mournful wail.

Nobody had. 'You must have left it in your coach seat,' suggested Darrell, knowing Irene's scatter-brain ways. Irene darted off after the coaches, which were now making their way slowly down the drive. 'Hi, hi!' she yelled. 'Wait a bit!'

'What *is* Irene doing?' said Miss Potts, crossly. 'Irene, come back and stop shouting.'

But Irene had stopped the coach and was climbing up into the one she had ridden in to the school. Miss Potts gaped. Did Irene think she was going home again? She did such mad things that anything was likely with Irene.

But Irene found her night-case, waved it wildly in the air to show the others she had found it, and climbed down again to the drive. She ran back, grinning.

'Got it!' she said, and stood it firmly down on the ground – too firmly, because it at once burst open and everything fell out.

'Oh, *Irene* – why does every case you possess always do that?' said Darrell, helping her to pick everything up.

'I can't imagine,' said Irene, stuffing everything in higgledy-piggledy. 'I have a bad effect on them, I suppose. Come on, let's go and find Matron.'

'I haven't found Felicity yet,' said Darrell, beginning to look worried. 'She can't have gone off with anyone because she doesn't *know* anyone.'

'Well, anyhow, let's go to Matron and hand in our health certificates and money, and ask if she's seen Felicity,' said Sally. 'The drive's pretty well empty now – she's obviously not here.'

So they trailed off to Matron, who had been dealing most efficiently with dozens of girls, health certificates and pocket-money for an hour or more. Darrell was pleased to see her – kindly, bustling, starched and competent.

'Hallo, Darrell! Well, Alicia, turned up again like a bad penny, I see!'

'Mother says you always used to say that to *her* when

she came back each term,' said Alicia, with a grin.

'Yes. She was a bad lot,' said Matron, smiling. 'Not nearly as bad as you, though, Alicia. We'll have to have a talk about "How to Darn" this term, by the way. Don't forget. Aha, Irene, there you are at last. Got your health certificate?'

It was a standing joke that Irene's health certificate always got lost if Irene was given it to bring to Matron. But the last few terms Irene's mother had sent the certificate by post, so it had always arrived safely on the morning of the day that school began.

Irene looked alarmed. Then she smiled. 'You're pulling my leg, Matron,' she said. 'It's come by post as usual.'

'But it hasn't,' said Matron. 'That's the whole point. Plenty of post for me this morning – but no health certificate. It's probably in your night-case, Irene. Go and unpack it and look.'

Darrell was looking round for Felicity, but still she couldn't see her. She really felt very worried and rather cross. Why hadn't Felicity done as she was told, and kept close by her, so that she couldn't lose her in the crowd of girls?

'Matron,' she said, 'you haven't by any chance seen smy little sister, have you?'

'Yes,' said Matron. 'She was here a few minutes ago, and handed in her health certificate. She said you had her money. Nice to have her here, Darrell.'

Darrell was astonished. Felicity had actually gone to Matron and given in her own certificate without waiting to be taken! It didn't seem like Felicity at all – she was so shy.

'Where's she gone now?' she wondered out loud.

'She's gone to have a look at her dormy,' said Matron, and turned to deal with Belinda, who seemed to have lost all her money and was turning out her pockets in despair. 'Belinda! I vow and declare that I'll ask Miss Grayling to put you and Irene into another tower next term. If I have to deal with you two much more I shall go raving mad. Sally, go and see if Irene has found her health certificate yet.'

Sally went off to find Irene in the dormy, and Darrell went off to find Felicity. Sally found Irene sitting mournfully on her bed, the contents of her night-case strewn on the eiderdown – but there was no health certificate there.

'Oh, Irene – you really are a mutt,' said Sally, rummaging round and shaking out the legs of Irene's pyjamas just in case she had put the precious piece of paper there. 'I thought your mother always posted the certificate now.'

'She *does*,' groaned Irene. 'She never fails. She's marvellous like that.'

'Well, all I can say is that she must have given it to *you* to post this time!' said Sally. 'And you must have forgotten.'

A sudden light spread over Irene's humorous face. She slapped Sally on the back. 'Sally, you've got it!' she said. 'That's just what happened! Mother *did* give it to me to post, and I forgot.'

'Well, where did you put it? Left it on your bedroom table at home, I suppose?' said Sally, half-impatient.

'No. I didn't,' said Irene, triumphantly. 'I put it into the lining of my hat, so that I shouldn't lose it on the way to the post – but when I got to the post-office, I just bought some stamps and walked home again. So the certificate should be in my hat-lining still. In fact, I'm sure it is because now I come to think of it, my hat felt jolly uncomfortable all day long.'

It took some time to find Irene's hat, which had rolled under the next bed – but to Irene's joy the envelope with the certificate in was actually still under the lining. She shot off to Matron joyfully with it.

'I put it in my hat to remember to post it,' she explained, 'but I forgot, so it came with me today still in my hat.'

Matron didn't understand a word of this, but dismissed it all as part of Irene's usual irresponsibility, and thankfully took the certificate before Irene could possibly lose it again.

'Did Darrell find her young sister?' she asked Irene.

But Irene didn't know. 'I'll go and find out,' she said, and wandered off again.

Darrell *had* found Felicity. She had found her in the dormy of the first form, with June and several others. June was talking away to everyone as if she was a third-termer, and Felicity was standing by shyly, listening.

'Felicity!' said Darrell, going up to her. 'Why didn't you wait for me? Whatever made you go and find Matron by yourself? You knew I was going!'

'Oh, *I* took her,' said June. 'I thought she might as well

come with me. We're both new. I knew Alicia wouldn't bother herself with me, and I didn't think you'd want to bother yourself with Felicity. We've given in our certificates, but you've got to give in Felicity's money.'

'I know that,' said Darrell, very much on her dignity. What cheek of this new first-former to talk to her like that! She turned to Felicity.

'I do think you might have waited,' she said. 'I wanted to show you your dormy and everything.'

The first evening

Darrell went back to her own dormy to unpack her night-things, feeling puzzled and cross. She had so much looked forward to taking Felicity round and showing her her dormy, her bed and every single thing. How *could* her young sister have gone off with June and not waited for her?

'Did you find Felicity?' asked Alicia.

'Yes,' said Darrell, shortly. 'She'd gone off with that cousin of yours – what's her name – June. It struck me as rather extraordinary. You'd think these youngsters would wait for us to take them round a bit. I know I'd have been glad to have a sister or a cousin here, the first term *I* came.'

'Oh, June can stand on her own feet very well,' said Alicia. 'She's a hard and determined little monkey. She'll always find things out for herself – and as for taking her under my wing, I wouldn't dream of putting anyone so prickly and uncomfortable there! Wait till you hear her argue! She can talk the hind leg off a donkey.'

'I don't like the sound of her much,' said Darrell, hoping that June wouldn't take Felicity under *her* wing. Surely Felicity wouldn't like anyone like June!

'No. She's a bit brazen,' said Alicia. 'We all are! Fault of my family, you know.'

Darrell looked at Alicia. She didn't sound as if she minded it being a fault – in fact she spoke rather as if she were proud of it. Certainly Alicia was sharp tongued and hard, though her years at Malory Towers had done a great deal to soften her. The trouble was that Alicia's brains and health were too good! She could always beat anyone else if she wanted to, without any effort at all – and Darrell didn't think she had ever had even a chilblain or a headache in her life. So she was always very scornful of illness or weakness in any form, as well as contemptuous of stupidity.

Darrell determined to see as much of Felicity as she could. She wasn't going to have her taken in tow by any brazen cousin of Alicia's. Felicity was young and shy, and more easily led than Darrell. Darrell felt quite fiercely protective towards her, as she thought of the cheeky, determined young June.

They all unpacked their night-cases and set out their things for the night. Their trunks, most of them sent on in advance, would not be unpacked till the next day. Darrell looked round her dormy, glad to be back.

It was a nice dormy, with a lovely view of the sea, which was as deep blue as a delphinium that evening. Far away the girls could hear the faint plash-plash of waves on the rocks. Darrell thought joyfully of the lovely swimming-pool, and her heart lifted in delight at the thought of the summer term stretching before her – nicest term in the year!

The beds stood in a row along the dormy, each with its own coloured quilt. At the ends of the dormy were hot and cold water taps and basins.

Irene was splashing in one basin, removing the dust of the journey. She always arrived dirtier than anyone else. No one would ever guess that the scatter-brain was a perfect genius at music and maths, and quite good at her other lessons too! Everyone liked Irene, and everyone laughed at her.

She was humming a tune now as she washed. 'Tumty-tooty-tumpty-tooty, ta, ta, ta!'

'Oh, Irene – don't say we're going to have that tune for weeks,' groaned Gwendoline, who always complained that Irene's continual humming and singing got on her nerves.

Irene took no notice at all, which maddened Gwendoline, who loved to be in the limelight if she possibly could.

'*Irene*,' she began, but at that moment the door opened and in came two new girls, ushered by Matron.

'Girls – here are the Batten twins,' she said in her genial voice. 'Connie – and Ruth. They are fourth-formers and will be in this dormy. Look after them, Sally and Darrell, will you?'

The girls stood up to look at the twins. Their first thought was – how unalike for twins!

Connie was bigger, fatter, sturdier and bolder-looking than Ruth, who was a good deal smaller, and rather shy-looking. Connie smiled broadly and nodded to everyone. Ruth hardly raised her head to look round, and as soon as she could she stood a little way behind her sister.

'Hallo, twins!' said Alicia. 'Welcome to the best dormy in the school! Those must be your beds up there – the two empty ones together.'

'Got your night-cases?' said Darrell. 'Good. Well, if you'd like to unpack them now, you can. Supper will be ready soon. The bell will go any minute.'

'Hope it's good,' said Connie, with a comradely grin. 'I'm frightfully hungry. It's ages since we had tea.'

'Yes – we get a wizard supper the first evening,' said Sally. 'I can smell it now!'

Connie and Ruth put their noses in the air and sniffed hungrily.

'The Bisto twins!' said Alicia, hitting the nail right on the head as usual. Everyone laughed.

'Come on,' said Connie to Ruth. 'Let's hurry. I've got the keys. Here they are.'

She undid both bags and dragged out everything quickly. Ruth picked up a few things and looked round rather helplessly.

'Here. These must be our drawers, next to our beds,' said Connie, and began to put away all the things most efficiently. She took the washing-things to the basin and called Ruth.

'Come on, Ruth. We'd better wash. I'm filthy!' Ruth went to join her, and just as they were towelling themselves dry, the supper-bell went. There was a loud chorus of joy.

'Hurrah! I hope there's a smashing supper. I could do

with roast duck, green peas, new potatoes, treacle pudding and lots of cheese,' said Belinda, making everyone's mouth water.

'What a hope!' said Darrell.

But all the same there was a most delicious supper that first night – cold ham and tomatoes, great bowls of salad, potatoes roasted in their jackets, cold apple pie and cream, and biscuits and butter for those who wanted it. Big jugs of icy-cold lemonade stood along the table.

'My word!' said Connie to Ruth. 'If this is the kind of food we get here, we'll be lucky! Much better than the other school we went to!'

'I hate to undeceive you,' said Alicia, 'but I feel I *must* warn you that first-night and last-night suppers are the *only* good ones you'll get in any term. We're supposed to be jolly hungry after our long journeys to Cornwall – hence this spread. Tomorrow night, twins, you'll have bread and dripping and cocoa.'

As usual Alicia was exaggerating, and the twins looked rather alarmed. Darrell looked round for Felicity. Where was she? She couldn't have her at the Upper Fourth table, of course, but she hoped she would be near enough to say a word to.

She was too far away to speak to – and she was next to that nasty little June! June was talking to her animatedly, and Felicity was listening, enthralled.

Alicia saw Darrell looking across at Felicity and June. 'They've soon settled in!' she said to Darrell. 'Look at young Felicity listening to June. You should hear the tales

21

June can tell of her family! They're all madcaps, like mine.'

Darrell remembered how interesting and amusing Alicia could be when she produced one of her endless yarns about her happy-go-lucky, mischievous family. She supposed that June was the same – but all the same she felt rather hurt that Felicity should apparently need her so little.

Well, if she thinks she can get on by herself, all right! thought Darrell. I suppose it's best for her really – though I can't help feeling a bit disappointed. I suppose that horrid little June will find out everything she needs to know and show Felicity the swimming-pool, the gardens, the stables, and all the things I'd planned to show her.

Felicity badly wanted to go to Darrell after supper and ask her a few things, but as soon as she said she was going, June pulled her back.

'You mustn't!' said June. 'Don't you know how the older ones hate having young sisters and cousins tagging after them? Everyone will be bored with us if we go tailing after Alicia and Darrell. In fact, Alicia told me I'd jolly well better look after myself, because first-formers were such small fry we weren't even worth taking notice of!'

'How horrid of her,' said Felicity. 'Darrell's not like that.'

'They all are, the big ones,' said June in a grown-up voice. 'And why *should* they be bothered with us? We've got to learn to stand on our own feet, haven't we? No – you wait till your sister comes over to you. If she doesn't, you'll know she doesn't want to be bothered – and if she does, well don't make her feel you're dependent on her and want taking under her wing. She'll respect you much more if you stand on your own feet. She looks as if she stood on her own all right!'

'She does,' said Felicity. 'Yes, perhaps you're right, June. I've often heard Darrell speak scornfully of people who can't stand on their own feet, or make up their own minds. After all – most new girls haven't got sisters to see to them. I suppose I shouldn't expect mine to nurse me just because I've come to a new school.'

June looked at her so approvingly that Felicity couldn't help feeling pleased. 'I'm glad you're not a softy,' said June. 'I was afraid you might be. Hallo – here comes Darrell after all. Now, don't weep on her shoulder.'

'As if I should!' said Felicity, indignantly. She smiled at Darrell as she came over.

'Hallo, Felicity. Getting on all right?' said Darrell, kindly. 'Want any help or advice with anything?'

'Thanks awfully, Darrell – but I'm getting on fine,' said Felicity, wishing all the same that she might ask Darrell a few things.

'Like to come and see the swimming-pool?' said Darrell. 'We might just have time.'

Darrell had forgotten that the first-formers had to go to bed almost immediately after supper on the first night. But June knew it. She answered for Felicity.

'We've got to go to bed, so Felicity won't be able to see it tonight,' she said, coolly. 'We planned to go down tomorrow before breakfast. The tide will be in then. I've asked.'

'I was speaking to Felicity, not to you,' said Darrell, in the haughty tones of a fourth-former. 'Don't get too big for your boots, June, or you'll be sat on.' She turned to Felicity and spoke rather coldly.

'Well, I'm glad you're settling down, Felicity. Sorry you're not in my dormy, but only fourth-formers are there, of course.'

A bell rang loudly. 'Our bed-time bell,' said June, who appeared to know everything. 'We'd better go. I'll look after Felicity for you, Darrell.'

And with that the irrepressible June linked her arm in Felicity's and dragged her off. Darrell was boiling with rage. She gazed angrily after the two girls, and was only slightly mollified when Felicity turned round and gave her a sweet and rather apologetic smile.

The brazen cheek of that little pest of a June! thought Darrell. I've never wanted to scold anyone so much in my life.

All together again

Going to bed on the first night was always fun, especially in the summer term, because then the windows were wide open, daylight was still bright, and the view was glorious.

It was lovely to be with so many girls again too, to discuss the holidays, and to wonder what the term would bring forth.

'School Cert to be taken this term,' groaned Daphne. 'How simply horrible. I've been coached for it all the hols, but I don't feel I know much even now.'

'Miss Williams will keep our noses to the grindstone this term,' said Alicia, dolefully.

'Well, *you* don't need to mind,' said Bill. She had spoken very little so far, and the others had left her alone. They knew she got, not homesick, but 'horse-sick' as she called it, the first night or two back at school. She was passionately attached to all the horses owned by her parents and her seven brothers, and missed them terribly at first.

Alicia looked at her. 'Why don't I need to mind?' she said. 'I mind just as much as you do!'

'Well, I mean you don't really need to work, Alicia,' said Bill. 'You seem to learn things without bothering.

I've been coached in the hols, too, and it was an awful nuisance just when I was wanting to ride with my brothers. I jolly well had to work, though. I bet *you* weren't coached in the hols.'

'Mavis, are *you* going in for School Cert?' asked Darrell. Mavis had been very ill the year before, and had lost her voice. It had been a magnificent voice, but her illness had ruined it. She had always said she was going to be an opera singer, but nobody ever heard her mention it now. In fact, most of the girls had even forgotten that Mavis had had a wonderful voice.

'I'm going in all right,' said Mavis. 'But I shan't get through! I feel like a jelly when I think of it. By the way – did you know my voice is getting right again?'

There was a pause whilst the girls remembered Mavis's lost voice. 'Gosh! Is it really?' said Sally. 'Good for you, Mavis! Fancy being able to sing again.'

'I mayn't sing much,' said Mavis. 'But I shall know this term, I expect, if my voice will ever be worth training again.'

'Good luck to you, Mavis,' said Darrell. She remembered that when Mavis had had her wonderful voice they had all thought the girl was a voice and nothing else at all – just a little nobody without an ounce of character. But now Mavis had plenty of character, and it was quite difficult to remember her voice.

I wonder if she'll go back to being a voice and nothing else, thought Darrell. No – I don't think she will. She deserves to get her voice back again. She's never complained about it, or pitied herself.

'I say,' said Mary-Lou's voice, 'who's this bed for, at my end of the room? There are nobody's things here.'

The girls counted themselves and then the beds. 'Yes – that bed's over,' said Darrell. 'Well, it wouldn't have been put up if it hadn't been going to be used. There must be another new girl coming.'

'We'll ask tomorrow,' said Alicia, yawning. 'How are you getting on, twins? All right?'

The two new girls answered politely. 'Fine, thank you.' They had washed, cleaned their teeth, brushed their hair, and were already in bed. Darrell had been amused to see that Connie had looked after Ruth as if she had been a younger sister, turning down her bed for her, and even brushing her hair!

She looked at them as they lay in bed, their faces turned sleepily towards her. Connie's face was plump and round, and her thick hair was quite straight. She had a bold look about her – sort of pushful, thought Darrell. The other twin, Ruth, had a small heart-shaped face, and her hair, corn-coloured as Connie's, was wavy.

'Goodnight,' said Darrell, and grinned. They grinned back. Darrell thought she was going to like them. She wished they had been absolutely alike though – that would have been fun! But they were really very unalike indeed.

One by one the girls got yawning into bed and snuggled down. Most of them threw their quilts off, because the May night was warm. Gwendoline kept hers on. She always liked heaps of coverings, and nobody had ever persuaded her to go without her quilt in the summer.

Miss Potts looked in. Some of the girls were already asleep. 'No more talking,' said Miss Potts, softly. A few grunts were made in reply. Nobody wanted to talk now.

Darrell wondered suddenly if Felicity was all right. She hoped she wasn't homesick. She wouldn't have time to be if June was in the next bed, talking away! What an unpleasant child! thought Darrell. And the cheek she had! It was past believing.

When the bell rang for getting up the next morning, there was a chorus of groans and moans. Nobody stirred out of bed.

'Well – we *must* get up!' said Darrell at last. 'Come on, everybody! Gracious, look at Gwendoline – still fast asleep!'

Darrell winked at Sally. Gwendoline was not fast asleep, but she meant to have a few more minutes' snooze.

'She'll be late,' said Sally. 'Can't let her get into trouble her very first morning. Better squeeze a cold sponge over her, Darrell!'

This remark, made regularly about twenty times every term, always had the desired effect. Gwendoline opened her eyes indignantly, and sat up. 'Don't you dare to squeeze that sponge over me,' she began angrily. 'This beastly getting up early! Why, at home . . .'

'Why, at home, "We don't get up till eight o'clock,"' chanted some of the girls, and laughed. They knew Gwendoline Mary's complaints by heart now.

'Did your old governess make her darling's bed for

her?' asked Alicia. 'Did she tie her bib on her in the morning? Did she feed her sweet Gwendoline Mary out of a silver spoon?'

Gwendoline had had to put up with Alicia's malicious teasing for many terms now, but she had never got used to it. The easy tears came to her eyes, and she turned her head away.

'Shut up, Alicia,' said Darrell. 'Don't start on her too soon!'

Alicia nudged Sally, and nodded towards the twins. Connie was making Ruth's bed for her!

'I can do that,' protested Ruth, but Connie pushed her aside. 'I've time, Ruth. You're slow at things like this. I always did it for you at our other school, and I can go on doing it here.' She looked round at the others, and saw them watching her.

'Any objection?' she asked, rather belligerently.

'Dear me no,' said Alicia in her smooth voice. 'You can do mine for me, as well, if you like! I'm slow at things like that, too!'

Connie didn't think this remark was worth answering. She went on making Ruth's bed. Ruth was standing by, looking rather helpless.

'What school did you come from?' asked Darrell, speaking to Ruth. But before the girl could answer, Connie had replied.

'We went to Abbey School, in Yorkshire. It was nice – but not as nice as this one's going to be!'

That pleased the fourth-formers. 'Did you play hockey

or lacrosse at your other school?' asked Sally, addressing her question to Ruth.

'Hockey,' said Connie, answering again. 'I liked hockey – but I want to play lacrosse, too.'

'Will *you* like lacrosse, do you think?' asked Sally, addressing her question once more to Ruth, wondering if she had a tongue.

And once again Connie answered: 'Oh, Ruth always likes what *I* like! She'll love lacrosse!'

Sally was just about to ask if Ruth ever said a word for herself, when the breakfast-bell rang. The girls hastily looked round the dormy to see if any clothes had been left about, and Alicia hurriedly pulled her quilt straight. Gwendoline was last as usual, moaning about a lost hair-brush. But then Gwen always had a moan! Nobody took much notice of that!

Darrell looked anxiously for Felicity as the girls filed into the big dining-room, all the North Tower girls together. South Tower girls fed in the South Tower, East in the East and so on. Each tower was like a separate boarding-house, with its own common-rooms, dining-rooms and dormies. The classrooms were in the long buildings that joined tower to tower, and so were such special rooms as the lab, the art-room and the sewing-room. The magnificent gym was there, too.

Felicity came in, looking neat and tidy. Miss Potts, seeing her come in, thought how very like she was to Darrell four years ago, when she also had come timidly into the dining-room for her first breakfast.

In front of Felicity was June, looking as if she was at least a third-termer, instead of a new girl on her first morning. She looked about chirpily, nodded at Alicia, who did her best not to see, grinned at Darrell, who stared stonily back, and spoke amiably to Mam'zelle Dupont, who was at the head of the first-form table. The second form were also there, and Darrell and Alicia had the satisfaction of seeing two second-formers push June roughly back when she attempted to sit somewhere near the head of the table.

But nothing daunted June. She merely sat down somewhere else, and said something to Felicity, who grinned uneasily. Something cheeky, I bet, thought Darrell to herself. Well, her form will put her in her place pretty soon – and she'll come up against the second form, too. There are some tough kids in the second – they won't stand much nonsense from a pest like June!

Felicity smiled at Darrell, who smiled back warmly, forgetting for the moment that Felicity had probably gone to see the swimming-pool before breakfast without her. She hoped her little sister would do well in the class tests that day and prove that she was up to standard.

Sally suddenly remembered the empty bed in her dormy, and she spoke to Miss Potts.

'Miss Potts! There's an extra bed in our dormy. Do you know whose it is? We're all back.'

'Oh, yes,' said Miss Potts. 'Let me see – there's one more new girl coming today – what's her name now – Clarissa something – yes, Clarissa Carter. That reminds me

– there's a letter for her already. Here it is, Sally – put it up on her dressing-table for her, will you?'

Gwendoline took the letter to pass it down the table. She glanced at it, and then looked again. The letter was addressed to 'The Honourable Clarissa Carter'.

The *Honourable* Clarissa Carter! thought Gwendoline, delighted. If only she'd be my friend! I'll look after her when she comes. I'll do all I can! Gwendoline was a little snob, always hanging round those who were rich, beautiful or gifted.

Alicia grinned as she saw the girl's face. Gwendoline's going all out for the Honourable Clarissa, she thought. Now we shall see some fun!

5

An interesting morning

The upper fourth were taken by Miss Williams, a scholarly, prim mistress, whose gentleness did not mean any lack of discipline. As a rule the upper fourth were a good lot, responsible and hard working – but this year Miss Williams had sometimes had trouble with her form. There were such a lot of scatter-brains in it!

Still, I think they will all get through the School Cert, thought Miss Williams. They are none of them *really* stupid, except Gwendoline. Daphne is much better since she has had regular coaching in the holidays. Mavis has picked up wonderfully. So has Bill. And though little Mary-Lou is quite sure she will fail, she is quite certain to pass!

Her form did not only consist of the North Tower girls, but of the fourth-formers from the other towers. Betty Hill, Alicia's friend, was one of these. She was as quick-tongued as Alicia, but not as quick-brained. She came from West Tower, and Alicia and she had often groaned because the authorities were so hard-hearted that they would not let Betty join Alicia in North Tower!

Miss Grayling, the Headmistress, had once asked Miss Potts, North Tower's house-mistress, if she should change Betty Hill over to North Tower, as Betty's parents had actually written to ask if she would.

'I can manage Alicia alone,' said Miss Potts, 'or even Betty alone – but to have those two together in one house would be quite impossible. I should never have a moment's peace – and neither would Mam'zelle.'

'I agree with you,' said Miss Grayling. So a letter was sent to Mr and Mrs Hill regretting that it was impossible to find room for Betty in North Tower. Still, Alicia and Betty managed to be very firm friends indeed, although they were in different towers, meeting in class each day, arranging walks and expeditions together – and planning various wicked and amusing jokes and tricks.

The North Tower fourth-formers went eagerly to their classroom after Prayers. They wanted to choose their desks, and to sort out their things, to look out of the window, clean the blackboard, and do the hundred and one things they had done together so often before.

The twins stood and waited till the other girls had chosen their desks. They knew enough not to choose till then. By that time, of course, there were very few desks left – only those for two East Tower girls who were still not back, and for Clarissa Carter, and for themselves.

'We'll sit together, of course,' said Connie, and put her books and Ruth's on two adjoining desks. They were, alas, in the hated front row, but naturally all the other rows had been taken, the back row going first. It was the only row really safe enough for whispering, or for passing a note or two.

Darrell looked out of the window, and wondered if

Felicity had been to see Miss Grayling yet. She must ask her, when she saw her at break. Miss Grayling saw all the new girls together, and what she said to them always impressed them, and made them determine to do their very best. Darrell remembered clearly how impressed she had been, and how she had made up her mind to be one of the worthwhile people of the world.

'I wonder who will be head-girl this term,' said Alicia, interrupting Darrell's thoughts. 'Jean's gone up, so she won't be. Well – I bet *I* shan't be! I never have, and I don't expect I ever will. The Grayling doesn't trust me!'

'I expect Sally will be,' said Darrell. 'She was head of the second when we were in that form, and a jolly good head she made – though as far as I remember, you didn't approve at all, Alicia!'

'No, I didn't,' said Alicia, candidly. 'I thought *I* ought to be head. But I've got rid of silly ideas like that now. I see that I'm not fitted to be head of anything – I just don't care enough.'

Part of this was just bravado, but quite a bit of it was truth. Alicia *didn't* care enough! Things were so easy for her that she had never had to try hard for anything, and so she didn't care. If she had to work jolly hard at lessons, as I have to do, thought Darrell, she'd care all right! We value the things we have to work hard for. Alicia does things too easily.

Gwendoline had chosen a seat in the front row! Everyone was most astonished. Alicia eyed her wonderingly. Could she be sucking up to Miss Williams? No, nobody in the world could do that. Miss Williams simply wouldn't notice it! Then what was the reason for Gwendoline's curious choice?

'Well, of *course*!' said Alicia, suddenly, and everyone gazed at her in surprise.

'Of course *what*?' said Betty.

'I've just thought why dear Gwendoline has chosen that front seat,' said Alicia, maliciously. 'At first I thought she'd gone out of her senses, but now I know!'

Gwendoline scowled at her. She was really afraid of Alicia's sly tongue, and she thought it quite likely that Alicia *had* hit on the correct reason.

But Alicia did not enlighten the class just then. She smiled sarcastically at Gwendoline and said, 'Dear Gwen, I won't give you away – you really have a very *Honourable* reason for your choice, haven't you?'

Nobody could imagine what she meant, not even Betty – but Gwendoline knew! She had chosen a front desk because she knew that the Honourable Clarissa Carter would have to have one there, too – and it would be a very good thing to be next to her and help her!

She flushed red and said nothing, but busied herself with her books. Miss Williams came in at that moment and Gwen rushed to hold the door.

The first day of school was always 'nice and messy' as Belinda called it. No proper lessons were done, but tests were given out, principally to check up on the standard of any new girls. Timetables were made out with much groaning. Irene always gave hers up in despair. Although she was so good and neat at both maths and music, she was hopeless at a simple thing like making out her own timetable from the big class one.

It usually ended in Belinda doing it for her, but as Belinda wasn't much better, Irene was in a perpetual muddle over her timetable, appearing in the wrong classroom at the wrong time, expecting to have a maths lesson in the sewing-room, or a sewing lesson in the lab! All the mistresses had long ago given up expecting either Irene or Belinda to be sane and sensible in ordinary matters.

Irene, with her great gift for music, and Belinda, with her equally fine gift for drawing, seemed to become four year olds when they had to tackle ordinary everyday things. It was nothing for Irene to appear at breakfast-time without her stockings, or for Belinda to lose, most inexplicably, every school book she possessed. The girls loved them for their amusing ways, and admired them for their gifts.

Everyone was busy with something or other that first morning. Darrell made out a list of classroom duties – filling up the ink-pots, doing the classroom flowers, keeping the blackboard clean, giving out necessary stationery and so on. Each of the class had to take on a week's duty, together with another girl, during the term.

Just before break Miss Williams told the girls to tidy up their desks. 'I have something to say to you,' she said. 'It will only take about two minutes, but it is something that I am sure you all want to know!'

'She's going to say who's to be head-girl this term!'

whispered Sally to Darrell. 'Look at Gwendoline! See the look she's put on her face. She really thinks *she* might be!'

It was true. Gwendoline always hoped she might be head of the form, and had enough conceit to think she would make a very good one. Just as regularly she was disappointed, and always would be. Spoiled, selfish girls make poor heads, and no teacher in her senses would ever choose Gwendoline Mary!

'I think probably most of you will know that Jean, who passed School Cert last year, has gone up into the next form,' said Miss Williams. 'She does not need to work with the School Cert form this term. She was head-girl of the upper fourth, and now that she has gone, we must have another.'

She paused, and looked round the listening class. 'I have discussed the matter with Miss Grayling, Miss Potts, Mam'zelles Dupont and Rougier,' said Miss Williams. 'We are all agreed that we would like to try Darrell Rivers as head-girl.'

Darrell flushed bright red and her heart beat fast. Everyone clapped and cheered, even Gwendoline, who always dreaded that Alicia might conceivably be chosen one day!

'I am quite sure, Darrell, that our choice is right,' said Miss Williams, smiling her gentle smile at the blushing Darrell. 'I cannot think for one moment that you would do anything to make us regret our choice.'

'No, Miss Williams, I won't,' said Darrell, fervently. She wished she could go and tell her parents this very minute.

Head-girl of the upper fourth! She had always wanted to be head of something, and this was the first time her chance had come. She would be the very best head-girl the form had ever had.

What would Felicity say? It would be a grand thing for Felicity to be able to say, 'My sister, of course, is head of the upper fourth!' Felicity would be proud and pleased.

Darrell rushed off at break to find Felicity and tell her. But again she had disappeared. How absolutely *maddening*! Darrell only had a few minutes. She rushed round and about and at last found Felicity in the Court, with June. The Court was the space that lay inside the hollow oblong of the building that made up Malory Towers. It was very sheltered, and here everything was very early indeed. It was now bright with tulips, rhododendrons and lupins, and very lovely to see.

But Darrell didn't see the flowers that morning. She rushed at Felicity.

'Felicity! I've got good news for you – I've been made head-girl of the upper fourth!'

'Oh, Darrell! How super!' said Felicity. 'I'm *awfully* glad. Oh, Darrell, I must tell you – I saw Miss Grayling this morning, and she said to me and all the other new girls exactly the same things that she said to you, when *you* first came. She was grand!'

Darrell's mind took her back to her own first morning – standing opposite Miss Grayling in her pleasant sitting-room, hearing her talk gravely to the listening girls. She heard the Head Mistress's voice.

'One day you will leave school, and go out into the world as young women. You should take with you a good understanding of many things, and a willingness to accept responsibility and show yourselves as women to be loved and trusted. I do not count as our successes those who have won scholarships and passed exams, though these are good things to do. I count as our successes those who learn to be good-hearted and kind, sensible and trustable, good, sound women the world can lean on.'

Yes, Darrell remembered those long-ago words, and was very very glad she was beginning to be one of the successes – for had she not been chosen as head-girl that very day, head of the upper fourth, the School Cert form?

'Yes. Miss Grayling's grand,' she said to Felicity.

'And *you're* grand, too!' said Felicity, proudly, to Darrell. 'It's *lovely* to have a head-girl for a sister!'

Clarissa arrives

Gwendoline was keeping a good look-out for the coming of the last new upper-fourth girl, Clarissa. She was about the only girl in the form who had no special friend, and she could see that it wouldn't be much good trying to make friends with the twins, because they would only want each other.

Anyway I don't like the look of them much, thought Gwendoline. They'll probably go all out for games and gym and walks. Why aren't there any nice *feminine* girls here – ones who like to talk and read quietly, and not always go pounding about the lacrosse field or splash in that horrible pool?

Poor lazy Gwendoline! She didn't enjoy any of the things that gave the others such fun and pleasure. She hated anything that made her run about, and she detested the cold water of the pool.

Daphne and Mary-Lou didn't like the pool either, but they enjoyed tennis and walks. Neither of them went riding because they were terrified of horses. Bill, who now rode every day on Thunder before breakfast, scorned Daphne, Mary-Lou and Gwendoline because they wouldn't even offer Thunder a lump of sugar and screamed if he so much as stamped on the ground. She and Darrell and the new twins arranged an evening ride twice a week together, and Miss Peters, the third-form mistress and Bill's great friend, came with them. They all enjoyed those rides on the cliffs immensely.

Felicity was not allowed to go with them because she was only a first-former. To Darrell's annoyance, she learned that the only other good rider in the first form was June, so once again it seemed as if Felicity and June were to be companions and enjoy something together.

It'll end in Felicity having to make June her friend, thought Darrell. Oh, dear – it's an awful pity I don't like June. Felicity likes Sally so much. We ought to like each other's friends. The mere *thought* of having June to stay with us in any holidays makes me squirm!

The North Tower upper-fourth girls paired off very well – except for Gwendoline. Sally always went with Darrell, of course. Irene and Belinda, the two clever madcaps, were inseparable, and very bad for each other. Alicia was the only one who had a friend from another tower, and she and Betty were staunch friends.

Daphne and Mary-Lou were friends, and Mavis hung on to them when she could. They liked her and did not mind being a threesome sometimes. Bill had no special friend, but she didn't want one. Thunder was hers. Bill was better with boys than with girls because, having seven brothers, she understood boys and not girls. She might have been a boy herself in the way she acted. She was the only fourth-former who chose to learn carpentry from Mr

Sutton, and did not in the least mind going with the first- and second-formers who enjoyed his teaching so much. She had already produced a pipe for her father, a ship for her youngest brother, and a bowl-stand for her mother, and was as proud of these as any of the good embroiderers were of their cushions, or the weavers of their scarves.

So it was really only Gwendoline who had no one to go with, no one to ask her for her company on a walk, no one to giggle with in a corner. She pretended not to mind, but she did mind, very much. But perhaps now she would have her chance when the Honourable Clarissa came. How pleased her mother would be if she had a really nice friend!

Gwendoline ran her mind back over the friends she had tried to make. There was Mary-Lou – stupid little Mary-Lou! There was Daphne, who had seemed to be so very friendly one term, and then had suddenly become friends with Mary-Lou! There was Mavis, who had had such a wonderful voice and was going to be an opera singer. Gwendoline would have liked such a grand person for a friend in later life.

But Mavis had fallen ill and lost her voice, and Gwendoline didn't want her any more. Then there had been Zerelda, the American girl who had now left – but she had had no time for Gwendoline!

Gwendoline thought mournfully of all these failures. She didn't for one moment think that her lack of friends was her own fault. It was just the horridness of the other girls! If only, only, only she could find somebody like

43

herself – somebody who had never been to school before coming to Malory Towers, who had only had a governess, who didn't play games, and somebody who had wealthy parents who would ask her to go and stay in the holidays!

So Gwendoline waited in hope for Clarissa's arrival. She imagined a beautiful girl with lovely clothes, arriving in a magnificent car – the Honourable Clarissa! *My* friend, thought Gwendoline, and she imagined herself at half-term saying to her mother and Miss Winter, her old governess, 'Mother, I want you to meet the Honourable Clarissa Carter, my best friend!'

She did not tell any of the girls these thoughts. She knew the words they would use to her if they guessed what she was planning – snob, hypocrite, fraud! Sucking up to somebody! Just like dear Gwendoline Mary!

Clarissa did not arrive till tea-time. Gwendoline was sitting at table with the others, so she did not see her until the Headmistress suddenly appeared with a strange girl.

Gwendoline looked up without much interest. The girl was small and undersized-looking – a second-former perhaps. She wore glasses with thick lenses, and had a wire round her teeth to keep them back. Her only beauty seemed to be her hair, which was thick and wavy, and a lovely auburn colour. Gwendoline took another slice of bread-and-butter and looked for the jam.

The new girl was so nervous that she was actually trembling! Darrell noticed this and was sorry for her. She too had felt like trembling when she first came, and had faced so many girls she didn't know – and here was a poor creature who really *was* trembling!

To Darrell's surprise Miss Grayling brought the girl up to the upper-fourth table. Mam'zelle Dupont was taking tea and sat at the head.

'Oh, Mam'zelle,' said Miss Grayling, 'here is Clarissa Carter, the last new girl for the upper fourth. Can you find a seat for her and give her some tea? Then perhaps your head-girl can look after her when tea is finished.'

Gwendoline almost dropped her bread-and-butter in surprise. Goodness, she had nearly missed her chance! Could this small, ugly girl really be Clarissa? It was, so she must hurry up and put her plan into action.

There was a space beside Gwendoline and she stood up in such a hurry that she almost knocked over Daphne's cup of tea. 'Clarissa can sit by me,' she said. 'There is room here.'

Clarissa, only too glad to sit down and hide herself, sank gladly into the place beside Gwendoline. Alicia nudged Darrell. 'Got going quickly, hasn't she?' she whispered, and Darrell chuckled.

Gwendoline was at her very sweetest. 'Sickly-sweet' was the name given by Alicia to this particular form of friendliness shown by Gwendoline. She leaned towards Clarissa and smiled in a most friendly way.

'Welcome to Malory Towers! I expect you are tired and hungry. Have some bread-and-butter.'

'I don't think I could eat any, thank you,' said Clarissa, almost sick with nervousness. 'Thank you all the same.'

'Oh, you must have *some*thing!' said Gwendoline and took a piece of bread-and-butter. 'I'll put some jam on it for you. It's apricot – very nice for a wonder.'

Clarissa didn't dare to object. She sat huddled up as if she wanted to make herself as small and unnoticeable as possible. She nibbled at the bread-and-butter, but couldn't seem to eat more than a bit of it.

Gwendoline chattered away, thinking how good and sweet she must seem to the others, putting this nervous new girl at her ease in such a friendly manner. But only Mam'zelle was deceived.

The dear kind Gwendoline, she thought. Ah, she is a stupid child at her French, but see how charming she is to this poor plain girl, who shakes with nerves.

'Sucking up,' said everyone else round the table. They said nothing to Clarissa, feeling that it was enough for the new girl to cope with Gwen, without having to deal with anyone else as well. Mary-Lou liked the look of Clarissa, in spite of her thick glasses and wire round her front teeth – but then Mary-Lou always felt friendly towards anyone as timid as herself! They were about the only people she wasn't afraid of.

After tea Mam'zelle spoke to Darrell. 'Darrell, you will take care of Clarissa, *n'est-ce pas*? She will feel strange at first, *la pauvre petite*!'

'Mam'zelle, I'm awfully sorry, but I've got to go to a meeting of all the head-girls of the forms,' said Darrell. 'It's in five minutes' time. Perhaps Sally – or Belinda – or . . .'

'*I'll* look after her,' said Gwendoline, promptly, thrilled that Darrell had to go to a meeting. 'I'll show her round. I'll be very pleased to.'

She gave Clarissa a beaming smile that startled the new girl and made everyone else feel slightly sick. She slipped her arm through Clarissa's. 'Come along,' she said, in the sort of voice one uses to a very small child. 'Where's your night-case? I'll show you the dormy. You've got a very nice place in it.'

She went off with Clarissa, and everyone made faces and grinned. 'Trust our Gwendoline Mary to show a bit of determination over things like this,' said Alicia. 'What a nasty little snob! Honestly, I don't think Gwendoline has altered one bit for the better since she came to Malory Towers!'

'I think you're right,' said Darrell, considering the matter with her head on one side. 'It's really rather strange – I would have thought that being even a few terms here would have made everyone better in some way – and Gwen has been here years – but she's just the same sly, mean, lazy little sucker-up!'

'How has it made *you* better, Darrell?' said Alicia, teasingly. 'I can't say I've noticed much difference in *you*!'

'She was decent to start with,' said Sally, loyally.

'Anyway, I've conquered my hot temper,' said Darrell. 'I haven't flown out in a rage for terms and terms – you know I haven't. That's one thing Malory Towers has done for me.'

'Don't boast too soon,' said Alicia, grinning. 'I've seen a glint in your eye lately, Darrell – aha, yes I have! You be careful.'

Darrell was about to deny this stoutly, when she

stopped herself, and felt her cheeks going red. Yes – she *had* felt her eyes 'glinting', as Alicia used to call it, when she spoke to that pest of a June. Well, she could 'glint' surely, couldn't she? There was nothing wrong in that – so long as she didn't lose her temper, and she certainly wasn't going to do *that*!

'I'll "glint" at you in a minute, Alicia,' she said, with a laugh. 'A head-girl "glint" too – so just you be careful what you say!'

Darrell has a 'glint'

The upper fourth soon began to settle down to its work. Miss Williams was a fine teacher, and was quite determined to have excellent results in the School Certificate exam. Mam'zelle Dupont and Mam'zelle Rougier both taught the upper fourth, but though actually Mam'zelle Rougier was the better teacher, plump little Mam'zelle Dupont got better results because she was friendly and had a great sense of humour. The girls worked better for her than for the other Mam'zelle.

This term there was an armed truce between the two French mistresses. The English mistresses regarded them with great amusement, never knowing from one term to the next whether the two Frenchwomen would be bosom friends, bitter enemies, or dignified rivals.

Miss Carton, the history-mistress, knew that the School Certificate form was well up to standard except for miseries like Gwendoline, who didn't even know the Kings of England and couldn't see that they mattered anyhow. She used her sarcastic tongue on Gwendoline a good deal these days, to try and whip her into some show of work, and Gwen hated her.

The girls grumbled because they had to work so hard

in that lovely summer term. 'Just when we want to go swimming, and play tennis, and laze about in the flowery Court, we've got to stew at our books,' said Alicia. 'I shall take my prep out into the open air tonight. I bet Miss Williams would let us.'

Surprisingly Miss Williams said yes. She knew that she could trust most of the upper fourth not to play about when they were supposed to be working, and she thought that Darrell was a strong enough head-girl to keep everyone up to the mark if necessary. So out they went after tea, and took cushions to sit on, in the evening sun.

Gwendoline didn't want to go. She was the only one, of course. 'You really seem to *loathe* the open air,' said Darrell, in surprise. 'Come on out – a bit more fresh air and exercise would take off some of your fat and get rid of those spots on your nose.'

'Don't make personal remarks,' said Gwendoline, nose in air. 'You're as bad as Alicia – and everyone knows she's been dragged up, not brought up!'

Clarissa, who was with her, looked at Gwendoline in surprise. Gwen had been so sweet and gracious to her that it was quite a shock to hear her make a remark like this. Gwen was quick to see the look, and slipped her arm through Clarissa's.

'If *you're* taking your prep out, I'll take mine, of course,' she said. 'But let's sit away from the sun. I hate getting freckled.'

Betty saw Alicia sitting out in the Court and came to join her. Darrell frowned. Now there would be nonsense and giggling and no work done. Belinda and Irene began to listen to the joke that Betty was telling Alicia, and Irene gave one of her sudden explosive snorts when it was finished. Everyone looked up, startled.

'Oh, I say, that's super!' roared Irene. 'Here, Betty, tell the others.'

Darrell looked up. She was head-girl of the form, and she must stop this, she knew. She spoke out at once.

'Betty, stop gassing. Alicia, you know jolly well we're supposed to be doing our prep.'

'Don't talk to me as if I was a first-former,' said Alicia, nettled at Darrell's sharp tone.

'Well, I shall, if you behave like one,' said Darrell.

'She's glinting, Alicia – look out, she's glinting!' said Irene, with a giggle. Everyone looked at Darrell and smiled. Darrell certainly had a 'glint' in her eye.

'I'm not glinting,' she said. 'Don't be idiotic.'

'I glint, thou glintest, he glints, *she* glints!' chanted Betty. 'We glint, you glint, they glint!'

'Shut up, Betty, and go away,' said Darrell, feeling angry. 'You don't belong to our prep. Go and join your own.'

'I've done it, Miss Glint,' said Betty. 'Shall I help you with yours?'

To Darrell's horror, she felt the old familiar surge of anger creeping over her. She clenched her fists and spoke sharply to Betty again.

'You heard what I said. Clear out, or I'll take the whole of this prep back indoors.'

Betty looked angry, but Alicia nudged her. 'Go on. She's

on the boil already. I'll meet you after we've done prep.'

Betty went, whistling. Darrell bent her red face over her book. Had she been too dictatorial? But what were you to do with someone like Betty?

Nobody said anything more, and prep went peacefully on, accompanied by one or two groans from Irene and deep sighs from Gwendoline. Clarissa sat beside her, working slowly. Gwen copied whatever she could. Nobody could cure her of this habit, it seemed!

After an hour Miss Williams came into the Court, pleased to see the North Tower upper fourth working so peacefully and well.

'Time's up,' she said. 'And I've a message from your games-mistress. The pool is just right now for swimming, so you can all go down there for half an hour, as you had to miss your swim yesterday.'

'Hurrah!' said Irene, and threw her book into the air. It went into the nearby pool, and had to be retrieved very hurriedly. 'Idiot!' said Belinda, almost falling in herself as she tried to fish out the book. 'I suppose you think that's *your* history book you're drowning. Well, it isn't – it's mine.'

'Have we all *got* to go?' Gwendoline asked Miss Williams, pathetically. 'I've been working so hard. I don't feel like swimming.'

'Dear me – can you actually *swim* yet, Gwendoline?' said Miss Williams, with an air of surprise. Everyone knew that Gwendoline could still only flap a few strokes in the water and then go under with a scream.

'Oh, we don't *all* need to go, do we?' said Mary-Lou, who could swim, but still didn't like the water much. Neither did Daphne, and she added her pleas to the others.

'You're all going,' said Miss Williams. 'You are having to work very hard, and these little relaxations are good for you. Go and change at once.'

Thrilled at the thought of an unexpected evening swim, Darrell, Sally and Alicia rushed to the changing-room. Darrell had forgotten her annoyance with Alicia, but Alicia hadn't. Alicia bore malice, which was a pity. So she was rather cool to Darrell who, most unfortunately for Alicia, didn't notice the coolness at all. The others followed, chattering and laughing, with a rather mournful tail composed of Gwen, Daphne and Mary-Lou. Clarissa came to watch. She was not allowed to swim or to play tennis because she had a weak heart.

'Lucky thing!' said Gwendoline, getting into her swimming-costume. 'No swimming, no tennis – I wish *I* had a weak heart.'

'What a wicked thing to say,' said Darrell, really shocked. 'To wish yourself a thing like that! It must be simply horrible to keep on and on having to take care of yourself, and think, "I mustn't do this, I mustn't do that."'

'It *is* horrible,' said Clarissa, in her small shy voice. 'If it hadn't been for my heart I'd not have been taught at home – I'd have come to school like any other girl. It's got much better lately though, and that's why I was allowed to come at *last*.'

This was a long speech for Clarissa to make. Usually

she was quite tongue-tied. As it was, she went red as she spoke, and when she had finished she hung her head and tried to get behind Gwendoline.

'Poor old Clarissa,' said Gwendoline, sympathetically. 'You mustn't do too much, you know. Would you know if you *had* done too much?'

'Oh, yes. My heart begins to flutter inside me – as if I had a bird there or something,' said Clarissa. 'It's awful. It makes me want to lie down and pant.'

'Really?' said Gwendoline, pulling her towel round her. 'Well, you know, Clarissa, I shouldn't be a bit surprised if *I* hadn't a weak heart, too, that nobody knows about. If I try to swim for long I get absolutely panicky – and after a hot game of tennis my heart pumps like a piston. It's really painful.'

'Nice to hear you *have* a heart,' said Alicia, in her smoothest voice. 'Where do you keep it?'

Gwendoline tossed her head and went off with Clarissa. 'Beast, isn't she?' her voice floated back to the others. 'I can't bear her. Nobody likes her really.'

Alicia chuckled. 'I'd love to know what sort of poisonous nonsense Gwendoline Mary is pouring into poor Clarissa's ears,' she said. 'I don't think we ought to let Gwendoline take complete charge of her like this. It's not fair. You ought to do something about it, Darrell. Why don't you?'

Darrell did not like this direct attack. She suddenly realized that Alicia was right – she ought to have made certain that Gwen didn't take such utter and complete charge of the rather weak little Clarissa. She would get all the wrong ideas in her very first term – and the ideas you had at the beginning were apt to stick!

'All right,' she said, in a rather snappy tone. 'Give me a chance! Clarissa has only been here a few days.'

'My dear Darrell, you're glinting again,' said Alicia, with a laugh that provoked Darrell even more. She took hold of herself hastily. Really, she was getting quite touchy!

It was fun down at the pool. The good swimmers had races, of course. Mary-Lou bobbed up and down in the shallow end, swimming a few strokes every now and again. She always got in quickly, even though she hated the water. Daphne was in, too, shivering as usual, but bobbing beside Mary-Lou, hoping that Darrell wouldn't make her join in the racing. Mavis was swimming slowly. She had got over her dislike of the water, but had to be careful not to over-swim, or play too much tennis because of her illness the year before.

Only Gwendoline still stood shivering on the brink. Alicia, Sally and Darrell longed to push her in, but it was too much trouble to get out of the pool.

'If Gwen doesn't get in soon, she won't get in at all,' said Alicia. 'Order her in, Darrell! Go on, put that glint in your eye, and give one of your orders!'

But not even Darrell's shouts persuaded poor Gwendoline to do more than wet her toes. She had got hot sitting in the Court and now the pool felt icy-cold. Ooooh!

It was Clarissa who made her get in. She came running

up to stand beside Gwendoline, slid on a slimy patch of rock, bumped hard into Gwendoline, and knocked her straight into the water!

Splash! In went Gwendoline with a terrible yell of fright. The girls clutched at one another and laughed till they cried. 'Look at poor Clarissa's face,' wept Darrell. 'She's simply horrified!'

'Who did that?' demanded a furiously angry Gwendoline, bobbing up, and spitting out water. 'Beasts, all of you!'

'You're head-girl, aren't you?'

When Gwendoline heard that it was Clarissa who had pushed her in, she didn't believe it. She made her way over to where an apologetic Clarissa was standing.

'Who pushed me in, Clarissa?' she demanded. 'They keep saying it was *you*, the idiots! As if you'd do a thing like that!'

'Oh, Gwendoline. I'm so very sorry but actually it *was* me,' said Clarissa, quite distressed. 'I slipped and fell, and bumped against you – and in you went. Of *course* I wouldn't have done it on purpose! I'm most terribly sorry about it!'

'Oh, that's all right then,' said Gwendoline, pleased to see such a very apologetic Clarissa. 'It did give me an awful shock, of course – and I hurt my foot against the bottom of the pool – but still, it was an accident.'

Clarissa was more apologetic still, which was balm to Gwendoline's wounded feelings. She liked to have the Honourable Clarissa apologizing so humbly. She made up her mind to be very sweet and forgiving, and then Clarissa would think more than ever what a nice friend she was for anyone to have.

But the others spoiled it all. They would keep coming

up and yelling, 'Jolly good push!' to Clarissa, and, 'Well done, Clarissa – you got her in nicely!' and, 'I say, Clarissa, that was a fine shove. Do it again!'

'But I *didn't* push her,' protested Clarissa, time and time again. 'You know I didn't.'

'Never seen such a good shove in my life!' said Alicia, and really, Gwendoline began to be quite doubtful as to whether Clarissa really *had* meant to push her or not! Then unfortunately Clarissa suddenly saw the funny side of all the shouted remarks and began to laugh helplessly. This made Gwen really cross, and she was so huffy with Clarissa that, in great alarm, Clarissa began to apologize all over again.

'Look at the twins,' said Alicia to Sally. Sally looked and laughed. Connie was carefully rubbing Ruth dry, and Ruth was standing patiently, waiting for her sister to finish.

'Why doesn't Connie leave her alone?' said Sally. 'Ruth can do everything for herself – but Connie always makes out she can't. She's too domineering for words!'

'And she's not nearly so good as Ruth is at lessons,' said Alicia. 'Ruth helps her every night, or she would never do the work. She's far behind Ruth.'

'And yet she domineers over her the whole time!' said Darrell, joining in. 'I hate to see it – and I hate to see Ruth putting up with it, too.'

'Speak to her about it,' said Alicia at once. 'Head-girl, aren't you?'

Darrell bit her lip. Why did Alicia keep on and on twitting her like this? She thought that perhaps it was partly envy – Alicia knew she would not really make a good head-girl herself, and envied those who were, and tried to make them uncomfortable. She, Darrell, ought not to take any notice, but she couldn't help feeling annoyed about it.

'You've got a lot on hand now, haven't you?' went on Alicia, rubbing herself dry. 'Looking after young Felicity – seeing that Clarissa doesn't get too much poison from dear Gwendoline, trying to buck up Ruth a bit, and make her stand up for herself – ticking off Betty when she spoils our prep.'

Darrell felt herself beginning to boil again. Then a cool hand was laid on her shoulder, and she heard Sally's calm voice. 'Everything in good time! It's a pity to rush things and spoil them – isn't it, Darrell? You can't put things right all at once.'

Darrell heaved a sigh of relief. That was what *she* ought to have said – in a nice calm voice! Thank goodness Sally had said it for her!

She gave Sally a grateful smile. She determined to look up Felicity a bit more, and try to prise her away from that objectionable June. She would put one of the others on to Clarissa to offset Gwendoline's influence – and she would certainly have a few quiet words with Ruth, and tell her not to let Connie make such a baby of her.

Why, thought Darrell, it's quite absurd – whenever any of us speak to Ruth, Connie always answers for her. I really wonder she doesn't answer for her in class, too!

It was quite true that Ruth hardly ever answered for

herself. Alicia might say to her, 'Ruth, can you lend me that French dicky for a moment,' but it would be Connie who said, 'Yes, here's the dictionary – catch!'

And Sally might say, 'Ruth, don't you want a new ruler? Yours is broken,' but it would be Connie who answered, 'No, thanks, Sally, she can use mine.'

It was annoying, too, to see how Connie always walked a little in front of Ruth, always offered an explanation of anything before her twin could say a word, always did any asking necessary. Hadn't Ruth got a soul of her own – or was she just a weak echo or shadow of her stronger twin?

It was a puzzle. Darrell decided to speak to Ruth the next day, and she found a good chance when both of them were washing painting-jars in the cloakroom.

'How do you like Malory Towers, Ruth?' she asked, wondering if Ruth would be able to answer if Connie wasn't there!

'I like it,' said Ruth.

'I hope you're happy here,' said Darrell, wondering how to lead up to what she really wanted to say. There was a pause. Then Ruth answered politely.

'Yes, thank you.'

She didn't sound happy at all, Darrell thought! Why ever not? She was well up to the standard of work, she was good at all games, there was nothing dislikeable about her – and the summer term was fun! She ought to be very happy indeed!

'Er – Ruth,' said Darrell, thinking desperately that Sally

would be much better at this kind of thing than she was, 'er – we think that you let yourself be – er – well, *nursed* a bit too much by Connie. Couldn't you – er – well, stand on your own feet a bit more? I mean . . .'

'I know what you mean all right,' said Ruth, in a funny fierce voice. 'If anyone knows what you mean, *I* do!'

Darrell thought that Ruth was hurt and angry. She tried again. 'Of course I know you're twins – and twins are always so close to one another, and – and attached – so I quite understand Connie being so fond of you, and . . .'

'You don't understand anything at all,' said Ruth. 'Talk to Connie if you like, but you won't alter things one tiny bit!'

And with that she walked out stiffly, carrying her pile of clean paint-jars. Darrell was left by herself in the cloakroom, puzzled and rather cross.

It's not going to be any good to talk to Connie, I'm sure, thought Darrell, rinsing out the last of the jars. She'd be as fierce as Ruth. She's ruining Ruth! But if Ruth *wants* to be ruined, and made just a meek shadow of Connie, well, let her! I can't see that I can stop her!

She took her pile of paint-jars away, and made up her mind that that particular difficulty could not be put right. You can't drag twins away from each other if they've always been together and feel like one person, she decided. Why, some twins know when the other is in pain or ill, even if they are far apart. It's no good putting those two against me. They must do as they like!

The next thing to do was to ferret out Felicity, and see

how she was getting on. She ought to be more or less settled down now. Perhaps she had made some more friends. If only she had others as well as June, it wouldn't matter so much – but Darrell felt that the strong-minded June would cling like a leech to someone like Felicity, if Felicity had no other friend at all!

So she found Felicity in break, and asked her to come for a walk with her that evening. Felicity looked pleased. To go for a walk with the head-girl of the upper fourth was a great honour.

'Oh, yes – I'd love to come,' she said. 'I don't think June's fixed anything for tonight.'

'What does it matter if she has?' said Darrell, impatiently. 'You can put her off, surely? I haven't seen anything of you lately.'

'I like Miss Potts,' said Felicity, changing the subject as she often did when Darrell got impatient. 'I'm still a bit scared of her – but my work's a bit in advance of the form, really, Darrell, so I can sit back and take things easy this first term! Rather nice!'

'Yes. Jolly nice,' agreed Darrell. 'That's what comes of going to a good prep school – you always find you're in advance of the lowest form work when you go to a public school – but if you go to a rotten prep school, it takes years to catch up! Er – how is June in her work?'

'Brilliant – when she likes!' said Felicity, with a grin. 'She's awfully good fun – frightfully funny, you know. Rather like Alicia, I should think.'

Too like Alicia, Darrell thought to herself, remembering

how wonderful she had thought Alicia in *her* first term at Malory Towers. 'Isn't there anyone else you like, Felicity?' she asked her sister.

'Oh, yes – I like most of my form,' said Felicity. 'They don't seem to like June much, though, and sit on her hard. But she's like indiarubber, bounces up again. There's one girl I like awfully – her name's Susan. She's been here two terms.'

'Susan! Yes, she's fine,' said Darrell. 'Plays lacrosse awfully well for a kid – and she's good at gym, too. I remember seeing her in a gym display last term.'

'Yes. She's good at games,' agreed Felicity. 'But June says Susan's too pi for words – won't do anything she shouldn't, and she thinks she's dull, too.'

'She would!' said Darrell. 'Well, I'm glad you like Susan. Why don't you make a threesome – you and June and Susan? I don't think June's a good person to have for an only friend.'

'Why, you don't even know her!' said Felicity in surprise. 'Anyway, *she* wouldn't want Susan in a threesome!'

A bell rang in the distance. 'Well, see you this evening,' said Darrell. 'We'll go on the cliffs – but don't you go and bring June, mind! I want you to myself!'

'Right,' said Felicity, looking pleased.

But alas, that evening a meeting was called of all the School Certificate girls, and Darrell had to go to it. She wondered if she could possibly squeeze time in for even a short walk with Felicity. No, she couldn't – she had that essay to do as well.

She sent a message to her sister by a second-former. 'Hey, Felicity,' said the second-former, 'compliments from Head-Girl Darrell Rivers, and she says she can't take baby sister for a walky-walk tonight!'

Felicity stared at her indignantly. 'You know jolly well she didn't say that!' she said. 'What *did* she say?'

'Just that,' said the cheeky second-former, and strolled off.

Felicity translated the message correctly and was disappointed.

'Darrell can't go for a walk tonight,' she told June. 'I suppose she's got a meeting or something.'

'I bet she hasn't,' said that young lady, scornfully. 'I tell you, these fourth-formers, like Alicia and Darrell, don't *want* to be bothered with us – and we jolly well won't go bothering them! Come on – we'll go for a walk together!'

9

Gwendoline and Clarissa

Darrell forgot about Clarissa for a day or two, because for some reason the days suddenly became very full up indeed. Head-girls seemed to have quite a lot of duties Darrell hadn't thought of, and there was such a lot of prep to do this term.

Gwendoline now had Clarissa very firmly attached to her side. She sat next to her in class, and offered to help her whenever she could – but this usually ended not in Gwen helping Clarissa, but the other way round!

Their beds were next to each other's at night, for Gwendoline had persuaded soft-hearted Mary-Lou to change beds with her, so that she might be next to Clarissa.

'She's never been to school before, you see, Mary-Lou,' she said, 'and as I hadn't either, before I came here, I do understand how she feels. It's at night you feel things worst. I'd like to be near her just to say a few words till she settles down properly.'

Mary-Lou thought it was extraordinary of Gwendoline to develop such a kind heart all of a sudden, but she felt that it ought to be encouraged anyway – so she changed beds, and to Darrell's annoyance, one night, there was Gwendoline next to Clarissa, whispering away like anything.

'Who told you you could change beds?' she demanded.

'Mary-Lou,' said Gwendoline, in a meek voice.

'But – why in the world did you ask *Mary-Lou*?' said Darrell. 'I'm the one to ask, surely.'

'No. Because it was Mary-Lou's bed I wanted to change over, Darrell,' explained Gwen, still in a meek voice. She saw that Darrell was annoyed, and decided to offer to change back again. Then surely Darrell would say all right, keep next to Clarissa!

'But, of course, if you'd rather I didn't sleep next to Clarissa – though I only wanted to *help* her –' said Gwendoline, in a martyr-like voice.

'Oh, stay there,' said Darrell, who could never bear it when Gwendoline put on her martyr act. So Gwendoline, rejoicing inwardly, did stay there, and was able to whisper what she thought were comforting words to Clarissa at night. She was too far away from Darrell's bed to be heard – and in any case Darrell, usually tired out with work and games, slept very quickly, and heard nothing.

Clarissa thought Gwendoline was really the kindest girl she had ever met – not that she had met many, however! Feeling lonely and strange, she had welcomed Gwendoline's friendliness eagerly. She had listened to endless tales about Gwendoline's uninteresting family, who all seemed to be 'wonderful' according to Gwen, and yet appeared to the listening Clarissa to be uniformly dull!

She said very little about her own family, though Gwendoline questioned her as much as she dared, longing to hear of Rolls Royces and yachts and mansions. But

Clarissa merely spoke of their little country house, and their 'car' – not even 'cars', thought the disappointed Gwendoline.

As Clarissa had a weak heart, and did no games or gym, she hadn't much chance to get together with the other girls. She either had to rest at these times, or merely go to watch, which she found rather boring. So she looked forward eagerly to the times she could be with Gwendoline, who was practically her only companion.

That is, till Darrell really took the matter in hand! Seeing Gwendoline's fair head and Clarissa's auburn one bent together over a jigsaw puzzle one fine evening, when everyone should have been out of doors, she made up her mind that something really must be done!

She went to Mavis. After all, Mavis had no real friend, she just made a threesome with Daphne and Mary-Lou. She could quite well spare some of her time for Clarissa.

'Mavis,' said Darrell, 'we think that Clarissa is seeing a bit too much of darling Gwendoline Mary. Will you try and get Clarissa to yourself a bit and talk to her?'

Mavis was surprised and pleased. 'Yes, of course, Darrell,' she said. 'I'd love to.' Secretly she thought that the small, bespectacled Clarissa was quite well paired off with Gwendoline – but if Darrell thought otherwise, then it must be so! So obediently she went to try to prise Clarissa away from the close-clinging Gwen.

'Come down to the pool with me, Clarissa,' she said, smiling pleasantly. 'I'm not swimming today – but we'll go and watch the others. They want someone to throw in pennies for them to dive for.'

Clarissa got up at once. Gwendoline frowned. 'Oh, Clarissa – you can't go just yet.'

'Why? We've nothing much to do,' said Clarissa, surprised. 'You come, too.'

'No. I feel rather tired,' said Gwendoline, untruthfully, hoping that Clarissa would stay with her. But she didn't. She went off with Mavis, rather flattered at having been asked by her. Clarissa had not much opinion of herself. She thought herself dull and plain and uninteresting, and indeed she certainly appeared so to most of the girls!

Darrell beamed at Mavis. Good old Mavis! She was doing her best, thought Darrell, pleased. But poor Clarissa didn't have much of a time with Gwendoline afterwards!

Gwendoline was rather cold, and gave her very short, cool answers when she returned from the pool. Clarissa was puzzled.

'I say – you didn't really mind my going off with Mavis for a bit, did you?' she said at last.

Gwendoline spoke solemnly. 'Clarissa, you don't know as much about Mavis as I do. She's not the sort of girl your family would like you to be friends with. Do you know what she did last year? She heard of a talent-spotting competition in a town near here – you know, a very *common* show with perfectly dreadful people in it – and she actually went off by herself to sing in the show!'

Clarissa was truly horrified, partly because she knew

that she herself would never have had the courage even to think of such a thing.

'What happened?' she said. 'Tell me.'

'Well – Mavis missed the last bus home,' said Gwendoline, still very solemn. 'And Miss Peters found her lying by the road about three o'clock in the morning. After that she was terribly ill, and lost her voice. She thought she had a wonderful voice before that, you know – thought I can't say *I* ever thought much of it – and so it was a very good punishment for her to lose it.'

'Poor Mavis,' said Clarissa.

'Well, personally I think she ought to have been expelled,' said Gwendoline. 'I've only told you this, Clarissa, because I want you to see that Mavis isn't really the kind of person to make friends with – that is if you were thinking of it.'

'Oh, no, I wasn't,' said Clarissa, hastily. 'I only just went down to the pool with her, Gwen. I won't even do that if you don't want me to.'

Poor weak Clarissa had said just what Gwendoline hoped she would say, and the next time that Mavis came to ask her to go for a short walk with her, she refused.

'Don't bother Clarissa,' said Gwendoline. 'She really doesn't want you hanging round her.'

The indignant Mavis walked away and reported to Darrell that *she* wasn't going to bother about that silly little Clarissa any more! She had better find someone else. What about Daphne?

Daphne came by at that moment and heard her name.

In a fit of annoyance Darrell told her that Mavis had been rebuffed by Clarissa, and that Mavis had suggested that she, Daphne, should have a try. What about it?

'I don't mind having a shot – just to spoil darling Gwendoline Mary's fun,' said Daphne with a grin. So she tried her hand at Clarissa, too, only to be met with excuses and evasions. Gwendoline had quite a bit to tell Clarissa about Daphne, too!

'You see, Clarissa,' said Gwendoline, 'Daphne isn't really *fit* to be at a school like this. You mustn't repeat what I tell you – but a year or two ago Daphne was found out to be a thief!'

Clarissa stared at Gwendoline in horror. 'I don't believe it,' she said.

'Well, just as you like,' said Gwen. 'But she *was* a thief – she stole purses and money and brooches – and this wasn't the only school she'd stolen at, either. When it was found out, Miss Grayling made her come into our common-room and confess everything to us – and we had to decide whether or not she should be expelled. It's as true as I'm standing here!'

Clarissa was quite pale. She looked across the Court to where Daphne was laughing with Mary-Lou. She couldn't believe it – and yet Gwendoline would never, never dare to tell such a lie as that.

'And – did you all say that – you didn't want her expelled?' she said at last.

'Well, *I* was the first to say she should have a chance and I'd stick by her,' said Gwen, untruthfully, for it had been little Mary-Lou who had said that, not Gwen. 'So she was kept on – but as you can see, Clarissa, she wouldn't be a really *nice* friend to have, would she? You'd never feel you could trust her.'

'No. I suppose not,' said Clarissa. 'Oh, dear – I hate thinking nasty things about Mavis and Daphne like this. I hope there are no more nasty tales to tell.'

'Did you ever hear how Darrell scolded me viciously in the swimming-pool, for nothing at all?' said Gwen, who had never forgotten or forgiven this episode. 'I felt ill for ages after that. And you know that girl in the fifth – Ellen? Well, she tried to get hold of the exam papers and cheat by looking at the questions, the night before the exam! She did, really.'

'Don't,' said Clarissa, beginning to think that Malory Towers was a nest of cheats, thieves and idiots.

'And even Bill, that everyone thinks such a lot of, was in awful disgrace last year, through continual deceit and disobedience,' went on the poisonous voice in Clarissa's ear. 'Do you know, Miss Peters had to threaten to send Bill's horse, Thunder, away to her home, because she was so disobedient?'

'I don't want to hear any more,' said Clarissa, un-happily. 'I really don't.'

'Well, it's all true,' said Gwendoline, forgetting her own record of deceit and unkindness, and not even realizing how she had distorted the facts, so that though most of them were capable of simple and kindly explanations, she had presented them as pictures of real badness.

Darrell came up, determined to get Clarissa away from Gwendoline's everlasting whispering. 'Hey, Clarissa,' she called, in a jolly voice. 'You're just the person I'm looking for! Come and help me to pick some flowers for our classroom, will you?'

Clarissa sat as if rooted to the spot. 'Come on!' called Darrell, impatiently. 'I shan't bite you!'

Oh, dear! thought Clarissa, getting up slowly, and remembering Gwen's tale of the scolding Darrell had given her, 'I hope she *doesn't* go for me!'

'Has dear Gwendoline been regaling you with tales of our dark, dreadful deeds?' said Darrell, and then, as she saw Clarissa go red, she knew that she had hit the nail on the head.

Bother Gwendoline! she thought. She really is a poisonous little snake!

10

A day off!

Three or four weeks went by. The School Certificate girls worked very hard indeed, and some of them began to look rather pale. Miss Williams decided it was time to slack off for a bit.

'Go for an all-day picnic,' she suggested. 'Go to Langley Hill and enjoy yourselves.'

Langley Hill was a favourite spot for picnics. It was a lovely walk there, along the cliff, and from the top there was a magnificent view of the countryside and the sea.

'Oh, thanks, Miss Williams! That would be super!' said Darrell.

'Smashing!' said Alicia. This was the favourite adjective of all the first-formers at the moment, often ridiculed by the older girls.

'Langley Hill,' said Clarissa. 'Why, that's where my old nanny lives!'

'Write and ask her if we could go and have tea with her,' said Gwendoline, who didn't like what she called 'waspy picnics' at all. 'It would be nice for her to see you.'

'You always think of such kind things, Gwendoline,' said Clarissa. 'I certainly will write. She will get us a wizard tea, I know. She's a marvellous cook.'

So she wrote to her old nanny, who lived at the foot of Langley Hill. (Thank goodness we shan't have to walk all the way up the hill with the others! thought Gwendoline, thankfully. I really am getting very clever!)

Old Mrs Lucy wrote back at once. 'We're to go to her for tea,' said Clarissa. 'She says she'll have a real spread. What fun!'

'We'd better ask permission,' said Gwendoline, suddenly thinking that Darrell might prove obstinate if the idea was suddenly sprung on her on the day of the picnic. 'Go and ask Miss Williams, Clarissa.'

'Oh, no – you go,' said Clarissa, who was always scared of asking any mistress anything. But Gwendoline knew better than to ask a favour of Miss Williams. Miss Williams saw right through Gwendoline, and might say 'no' just on principle if Gwen went to ask her a favour! She didn't trust Gwendoline any farther than she could see her.

So Clarissa had to go – and with many stammerings and stutterings she at last came out with what she wanted to ask – and handed over her old nanny's invitation.

'Yes. You can go there for tea, so long as you take another girl with you,' said Miss Williams, thinking what an unattractive child Clarissa was, with her thick-lensed glasses and the wire round her teeth. And that dreadful hang-dog expression she always wore made it worse!

The day of the picnic dawned bright and clear, and promised to be lovely and hot.

'A whole day off!' rejoiced Darrell. 'And such a day, too! I vote we take our swimming-things and swim at the foot of Langley Hill. There's a cove there.'

'You'll have to take your lunch with you, but you can have your tea at the little tea-place on top of the hill,' said Miss Williams. 'I've asked the kitchen staff to let you go and help them cut sandwiches and cakes to take with you. Be off with you now – and come back ready to work twice as hard!'

They clattered off, and in half an hour were streaming up the cliff-path on their way to Langley Hill, each girl carrying her share of the lunch.

'I should think we've got far too much,' said Mavis.

'*Do* you? I don't think we've got enough!' said Darrell, astonished. 'But then, my idea of a good picnic lunch is probably twice the size of yours, Mavis! You're a poor eater.'

Gwendoline and Clarissa panted along a good way behind the others. Darrell called to them to hurry up. She was annoyed to see the two together again after all her efforts to separate them.

'Clarissa gets a bad heart if she hurries,' called Gwendoline, reproachfully. 'You know that, Darrell.'

'Oh, Gwen – I hardly ever feel my heart this term,' said Clarissa. 'I believe I'm almost cured! I can easily hurry.'

'Well,' said Gwendoline, solemnly, 'I'm just a *bit* worried about *my* heart, Clarissa. It does funny things lately. Sort of flutters like a bird, you know.'

Clarissa looked alarmed. 'Oh, Gwen – that's just what mine used to do. You'll have to be careful. Oughtn't you to see a doctor?'

'Oh, no, I don't think so,' said Gwen, bravely. 'I hate

going to Matron about anything. She makes such a fuss. And she's quite likely not to believe what I say. She's very hard, you know.'

Clarissa had been to Matron once or twice, and had thought her very kind and understanding. She didn't know that Gwendoline had tried to stuff Matron up with all kinds of tales, term after term, whenever she wanted to get out of anything strenuous, and that Matron now consistently disbelieved anything that Gwendoline had to say. She merely handed out large doses of very disgusting medicine, no matter what Gwen complained of. In fact, Alicia said that she kept a special large bottle labelled 'Medicine for Gwen' on the top shelf of her cupboard, a specially nasty concoction made up specially for malingerers!

'Look at Connie,' said Gwen, as they gradually came nearer to the others. 'Carrying Ruth's bag for her as well as her own! How can Ruth put up with it?'

'Well, they're twins,' said Clarissa. 'I expect they like to do things for each other. Let's catch them up and talk to them.'

But the conversation as usual was carried on by Connie, not by Ruth!

'What a heavenly day for a picnic!' said Clarissa, looking at Ruth.

'Beautiful,' said Connie, and began to talk about the food in the bags she carried.

Gwen spoke to Ruth. 'Did you find the pencil you lost – that silver one?' she asked.

Connie answered for her as usual. 'Oh yes – it was at the back of her desk after all.'

'Ruth, look at that butterfly!' said Clarissa, determined to make Ruth speak. 'Whatever is it?'

'It's a fritillary, pearl-bordered,' answered Connie, before Ruth had even got a look at the lovely thing. Then Gwen and Clarissa gave it up. You just couldn't get Ruth to speak before Connie got her word in.

They had the picnic in sight of Langley Hill, because they were much too hungry to wait till they had climbed up to the top. Gwendoline was very thankful. She was already puffing and blowing.

'You're too fat, that's what the matter with you, Gwendoline,' said Alicia, unsympathetically. 'Gosh, what a wonderful scowl you've put on now – one of your best. A real snooty scowl!'

Belinda overheard and rolled over to be nearer to them. She gazed at Gwendoline, and felt all over herself for her small sketchbook, which was always somewhere about her person.

'Yes – it's a peach of a scowl,' she said, 'a smasher! Hold it, Gwen, hold it! I *must* add it to my collection!'

Clarissa, Ruth and Connie looked surprised. 'A collection of *scowls*?' said Connie. 'I never heard of *that* before!'

'Yes, I've got a nice little bookful of all Gwendoline's different scowls,' said Belinda. 'The one that goes like this' – and she pulled a dreadful face – 'and this one – and this one you must have seen hundreds of times!' She pulled a variety of faces, and everyone roared.

Belinda could be very funny when she liked.

'Oh, quick – Gwen is scowling again!' she said, and flipped open her little book. 'You know, one term I stalked Gwen the whole time, waiting for her scowls, but she got wise to me the next term, and I hardly collected a single one. I'll show you my collection when I get back if you like, Clarissa.'

'Er – well – I don't know if Gwen would like it,' she began.

'Of course she wouldn't,' said Belinda. Her quick pencil moved over the paper. She tore off the page and gave it to Clarissa.

'There you are – there's your darling Gwendoline Mary,' she said. Clarissa gasped. Yes – it was Gwen to the life – and looking most unpleasant, too! Wicked Belinda – her malicious pencil could catch anyone's expression and pin it down on paper immediately.

Clarissa didn't know what in the world to do with the paper – tear it up and offend Belinda – or keep it and offend Gwendoline. Fortunately the wind solved the problem for her by suddenly whipping it out of her fingers and tossing it over the hedge. She was very relieved.

It was a lovely picnic. There were sandwiches of all kinds, buns, biscuits and slices of fruit cake. The girls ate every single thing and then lazed in the sun. Darrell reluctantly decided at three o'clock that if they were going to have tea at the top of Langley Hill, and swim afterwards, they had better go now.

'Oh, Darrell – Clarissa and I have been given

per-mission by Miss Williams to go and have tea with Clarissa's old nanny, Mrs Lucy, who lives at the foot of the hill,' said Gwendoline, in the polite voice she used when she knew she was saying something that the other person was going to object to.

'Well! This is the first I've heard of it!' said Darrell. 'Why ever couldn't you say so before? I suppose it's *true*? You're not saying this just to get out of climbing Langley Hill and swimming afterwards?'

'Of course not,' said Gwendoline, with enormous dignity. 'Ask Clarissa!'

Clarissa, feeling rather nervous of Darrell, produced the invitation from Mrs Lucy. 'All right,' said Darrell, tossing it back. '*How* like you, Gwen, to get out of a climb and a swim! Jolly clever, aren't you?'

Gwendoline did not deign to reply, but looked at Clarissa as if to say, 'What a head-girl! Disbelieving us like that!'

The girls left Gwen and Clarissa and went to climb the great hill. The two left behind sprawled on the grass contentedly. 'I'm just as pleased not to climb that hill, anyway,' said Gwen. 'This hot afternoon, too! I wish them joy of it!'

They sat a little longer, then Gwen decided that she was being bitten by something. She always decided this when she wanted to make a move indoors! So they set off to find Mrs Lucy's cottage, and arrived about a quarter-past four.

The old lady was waiting. She ran out to greet Clarissa,

and petted her as if she was a small child. Then she saw Gwendoline, and appeared to be most astonished that there were no other girls besides.

'But I've got tea for twenty!' she said. 'I thought the whole *class* was coming, Clarissa dear! Oh my, what shall we do? Can you go after the others and fetch them?'

An exciting plan

'You go after them, Gwen,' said Clarissa, urgently. 'I daren't tear up that steep hill. They'll be half-way up by now.'

'No, indeed, Clarissa, I wouldn't dream of *you* racing up that hill, and you only just recovering from that bad heart of yours,' said Mrs Lucy at once. 'I meant this other girl to go.'

Gwendoline was certainly not going to go chasing up Langley Hill in the hot sun, to fetch back people she disliked to enjoy a fine tea. Let them go without!

She pulled rather a long face. 'I will go, of course,' she said, 'but I think there's something a bit wrong with *my* heart, too – it flutters, you know, when I've done something rather energetic. It makes me feel I simply must lie down.'

'Oh dear – that's how I used to feel!' cried Clarissa, sympathetically. 'I forgot you spoke about your heart today, Gwen. Well, it can't be helped. We can't get the others back here to tea.'

'What a pity,' mourned Mrs Lucy, and took them inside her dear little cottage. Set on a table inside was a most marvellous home-made tea!

There were tongue sandwiches with lettuce, hard-boiled eggs to eat with bread-and-butter, great chunks of new-made cream cheese, potted meat, ripe tomatoes grown in Mrs Lucy's brother's greenhouse, gingerbread cake fresh from the oven, shortbread, a great fruit cake with almonds crowding the top, biscuits of all kinds and six jam sandwiches!

'Gracious!' said Gwen and Clarissa, in awe. 'What a spread!'

'Nanny, it's too marvellous for words,' said Clarissa. 'But oh dear, what a waste! And such an expense, too!'

'Oh, now, you needn't think about that,' said Mrs Lucy at once. 'Your sister came to see me yesterday, her that's married, and she gave some money to spend on getting a good spread for you all. So here it is – and only the two of you to eat it. Well, certainly, Clarissa, you did give me to understand in your letter that the whole class were coming.'

'No, Nanny – I said the whole of our form from North Tower were coming for a picnic and could we (that's Gwen and I) come and have tea with you,' explained Clarissa. 'I suppose you thought that "we" meant the whole lot. I'm so very sorry.'

'Sit you down and eat,' said Mrs Lucy. But even with such a wonderful spread the two girls could not eat very much after their very good lunch. Gwen looked at the masses of food in despair.

And then Mrs Lucy had a brainwave.

'Don't you have midnight feasts or anything like that at your school?' she said to Clarissa. 'I remember your sister, her that's married, used to tell of them when *she* went to boarding school.'

'A midnight feast!' said Gwen, remembering the one or two she had enjoyed at Malory Towers. 'My *word* – that's a *super* idea, Mrs Lucy! Could we really have the food for that?'

'Of course you can. Then it will get to the hungry mouths it was made for,' said old Mrs Lucy, her eyes twinkling at the two girls. 'But how will you take it?'

Clarissa and Gwen considered. There was far too much for them to carry by themselves. They would simply *have* to have help. Clarissa was very excited. A midnight feast! She had read of such things – and now she was going to join in one – and provide the food, too!

'I know,' said Gwen, suddenly. 'We have to meet Darrell and the others at half-past five, at the end of the lane down there – the one that leads up from the cove. We will bring some of the girls back here to help to carry the stuff!'

'Good idea,' agreed Clarissa, her eyes shining behind their thick glasses. So, just before half-past five by Mrs Lucy's clock, Gwen and Clarissa slipped along to the end of the lane to meet the others.

But only two were there – and very cross the two were. They were Alicia and Belinda.

'Well! Do you know it's a quarter to six, and we've jolly well been waiting for you two for twenty minutes!' began Alicia indignantly. 'The others have gone on. We've had to wait behind. Haven't you got watches?'

'No,' said Gwendoline. 'I'm so sorry. I'm afraid Mrs Lucy's clock must have been slow.'

'Well, for goodness' sake, put your best foot forward now,' grumbled Alicia.

But Gwen caught at her arm.

'Wait a bit, Alicia. We want you and Belinda to come back to Mrs Lucy's cottage with us. It isn't far.'

Alicia and Belinda stared in exasperation at Gwen. Rapidly she told them about the feast, and all the food left over – and how Mrs Lucy had offered it to them for a midnight feast.

A grin appeared on Alicia's face, and a wicked look on Belinda's. A midnight feast! That would be a fine end to a very nice day. All that food, too! It simply couldn't be wasted.

'Well, it would certainly be a sin to let all that wonderful food go stale,' said Alicia, cheerfully. 'I quite see you couldn't allow that. And I'm sure we could all do with a feast tonight, after our walking, climbing and bathing. We'll go back and help you carry the stuff.'

No more was said about being late. The four of them went quickly back to Mrs Lucy's cottage. She had packed it up as best she could in net bags and baskets. The girls exclaimed in delight and thanked her heartily.

'We'll bring back the baskets and bags as soon as we can,' promised Clarissa. 'My, what a load we've got!'

They had indeed. It was all the four could do to lug it back to Malory Towers. Sally was waiting for them as they came down the cliff-path. 'Whatever *have* you been doing?' she asked. 'Darrell's in an awful wax, thinking you'd got lost or something. She was just about to go and report that you'd all fallen over the cliff!'

Alicia laughed. 'Take a look at this basket,' she said. 'And this bag! Clarissa's old nanny gave us the whole lot for a midnight feast!'

'Golly!' said Sally, thrilled. 'How super! You'd better hide the things somewhere. We don't want Potty or Mam'zelle finding them.'

'Where shall we put them?' wondered Alicia. 'And where shall we have the feast? It would be better to have it out-of-doors tonight, it's so hot. I know! Let's have it down by the pool. We might even have a midnight swim!'

This sounded absolutely grand. 'You go and tell Darrell we're safe,' said Alicia, 'and we four will slip down to the pool, and hide these things in the cubby-holes there where we keep the life-belts and things.'

Sally sped off, and Gwen, Clarissa, Alicia and Belinda swiftly made their way down to the pool. The tide was out – but at midnight it would be in again, and they could splash about in the pool, and have their feast with the waves running over their toes. The moon was full, too – everything was just right!

Alicia packed the food into a cubby-hole and shut the door. Then she and the others went up the cliff-path, but halfway up Alicia remembered that she hadn't locked the door of the cubby-hole she had used.

'Blow!' she said. 'I suppose I'd better, in case anyone

goes snooping round. You go on, you three – and I'll come as soon as I've locked up.'

She went down and locked the cubby-hole, slipping the key into her pocket. She heard footsteps near her as she pocketed the key and turned round hastily.

Thank goodness it was only Betty, her West Tower friend! 'Hallo! What are *you* doing here?' said Betty.

Alicia grinned and told her about the hoard of food. 'Why don't you ask *me* to come along?' said Betty. 'Any objection?'

'No. It's just that Darrell mightn't like it,' said Alicia, hesitating. 'You know that we aren't supposed to leave our towers and join up together at night. That's always been a very strict rule.'

'Well – is there anything to stop me from looking out of my dormy window, hearing something going on at the pool, and coming along to see what it is?' said Betty, with her wicked grin. 'Then I don't see how you can prevent everyone from saying, "Come along and join us."'

'Yes – that's a wizard idea,' said Alicia. 'You do that. Then nobody will know I told you! I'll call out, "Come and join us," and that will make everyone else join in – and Darrell won't be able to say no!'

'Right,' said Betty, and chuckled. 'I could do with a spree like this, couldn't you? Where did you go today? Langley Hill? We went to Longbottom, and had some good fun. I say – I suppose I couldn't bring one or two more West Tower girls with me, could I? After all, it's not like being *invited* if we just pop along to see what the noise is. No one will ever know.'

'All right. Bring Eileen and Winnie,' said Alicia. 'They'll enjoy it. But for goodness' sake don't say I told you, or Darrell will blow my head off! She's taking her head-girl duties very, very seriously!'

'She would!' said Betty, and laughed. 'Well, see you tonight – and mind you're *very* surprised when we appear!'

She sped off and Alicia went to join the others. 'Whatever made you so long?' demanded Belinda. 'We thought you must have thrown a fit and fallen into the pool. You'll be late for supper now if you aren't quick.'

'Have you told Darrell about the food and the midnight feast?' asked Alicia.

'Yes,' said Belinda. 'She looked a bit doubtful at first, and then when we reminded her that the great fifth had had one last term, she laughed and said, "All right! A feast it shall be then!"'

'Good for Darrell,' said Alicia, pleased. 'Did you suggest that down by the pool would be a good place?'

'Yes. She agreed that it would,' said Belinda. 'So we're all set!'

The upper fourth winked at one another so continually that supper-time that Mam'zelle, who was taking the supper-table, looked down at her person several times to see if she had forgotten some article of apparel. Had she lost a few buttons? Was her belt crooked? Was her hair coming down? Then why did these bad girls wink and wink?

But it was nothing to do with Mam'zelle or her clothing or hair – it was just that the girls were thrilled and excited, full of giggles and nudges and winks, enough to drive any mistress to distraction.

Mam'zelle was indulgent. They are excited after their picnic, she thought. Ah, how well they will sleep tonight!

But Mam'zelle was wrong. They didn't intend to sleep at all well that night!

That evening

'For goodness' sake don't let Potty or Mam'zelle guess there's anything planned for tonight,' said Darrell to the others after supper. 'I saw Mam'zelle looking very suspicious. Come into the common-room now, and we'll arrange the details. How gorgeous to have so much food given to us – Clarissa, many thanks!'

Clarissa blushed, but was too nervous to say anything. She was delighted to think that she could provide a feast for the others.

They all went to the common-room and sat about to discuss their plans. 'It's such a terrifically hot evening that it really will be lovely down by the pool,' said Sally. 'There won't have to be any of the usual screeching or yelling though – sounds carry so at night, and although the pool is right down on the rocks, it's quite possible to hear noises from there if the wind is right.'

Alicia was pleased to hear Sally say this. It would make it seem natural for Betty and Eileen and Winnie to come and say they had heard sounds from the pool.

'I and Sally will keep awake tonight,' planned Darrell. 'Then when we hear the clock strike twelve, we will wake you all, and you can get into dressing-gowns and bring your swimming-things. We'd better fetch them from the changing-rooms now, or else we may wake up one of the staff if we rummage about late at night.'

'Is all the food safely down by the pool?' asked Bill, who was very much looking forward to this adventure. It was the first time she had ever been to a midnight feast!

'Yes. Safely locked in the cubby-hole on the left,' said Alicia. 'I've got the key.'

'We'll have a swim first and then we'll feast,' said Darrell. 'It's a pity we haven't anything exciting to drink.'

'I bet if I went and asked the cook for some lemonade, she'd leave us some ready,' said Irene, who was a great favourite with the kitchen staff.

'Good. You go then,' said Darrell. 'Ask her to make two big jugfuls, and leave them in the fridge. We'll fetch them when we're ready.'

Irene sped off. Then Alicia was sent with Mavis to fetch the swimming-things from the changing-room. Everyone began to feel tremendously excited. Clarissa could hardly keep still.

'I wish I hadn't had so much supper,' said Gwendoline. 'I'm sure I shan't feel hungry by midnight.'

'Serves you right for being a pig,' said Belinda. 'You had five tomatoes at supper. I counted!'

'A pity you hadn't anything better to do,' said Gwendoline, trying to be sarcastic.

'Oh, it's wonderful to watch your nice little ways,' said Belinda, lazily. 'No wonder you're getting so fat, the way you gobble everything at meals. Dear me, what a wonderful drawing I could make of you as a nice fat little piggy-wig with blue eyes and a ribbon on your tail.'

Everyone roared. 'Do, do!' begged Sally. Gwendoline began to scowl, saw Belinda looking at her, and hastily straightened her face. She wished she hadn't tried to be sarcastic to Belinda. She always came off badly if she did!

Alicia and Mavis came back, giggling, with the swimming-things. 'Anyone spot you?' asked Darrell, anxiously.

'I don't think so. That pestiferous young cousin of mine, June, was somewhere about, but I don't think she'd spot anything was up,' said Alicia. 'I heard her whistling somewhere when we were in the changing-room.'

Irene came back from the kitchen, grinning all over her face. 'I found the cook, and she was all alone,' she said. 'She'll have two thumping big jugs of lemonade ready for us in the fridge, any time after eleven o'clock tonight. The staff go to bed then, so she says any time after that will be safe for us to get it. Whoops!'

'This is going to be super,' said Alicia. 'What exactly did you say the food was, Clarissa?'

Clarissa explained, with Gwen prompting her proudly. Gwen really felt as if she had provided half the feast herself, and she basked in Clarissa's reflected glory.

'Did you ever have midnight feasts at your last school, Ruth?' asked Darrell, seeing that Ruth looked as excited as the others.

Connie answered for her as usual. 'No. We tried once, but we got caught – and my word we did get a wigging from the Head.'

'I asked Ruth, not you,' said Darrell, annoyed with Connie. 'Don't keep butting in. Let Ruth answer for herself.' She turned to Ruth again.

'Was your last Head very strict?' she asked. Connie opened her mouth to answer for Ruth again, caught the glint in Darrell's eye, and shut it.

Ruth actually answered, after waiting for a moment for Connie. 'Well,' she said, 'I think probably *you* would call her very strict. You see . . .'

'Oh, not *very* strict, Ruth,' interrupted Connie. 'Don't you remember how nice she was over . . .'

'I'M ASKING RUTH,' said Darrell, exasperated.

What would have happened next the form would dearly have loved to know – but there came an interruption that changed the subject. Matron popped her head in and said she wanted Gwendoline.

'Oh, *why*, Matron?' wailed Gwendoline. 'What haven't I done now that I ought to have done? Why do you want me?'

'Just a little matter of darning,' said Matron.

'But I've *done* the beastly darning you told me to do,' said Gwen, indignantly.

'Well, then – shall we say a little matter of *un*picking and *re*-darning?' said Matron, aggravatingly. The girls grinned. They had seen Gwen's last effort at darning a pair of navy-blue games shorts with grey wool, and had wondered if Matron would notice.

Gwendoline had to get up and go, grumbling under her breath. 'I could do her darning for her,' suggested

Clarissa to Darrell. 'I don't play games or do gym – I've plenty of time.'

'Don't you dare!' said Darrell at once. 'You help her too much as it is – she's always copying from you.'

Clarissa looked shocked. 'Oh – she doesn't *copy*,' she said loyally, going red at the idea of her daring to argue with Darrell.

'Don't be such a mutt,' said Alicia, bluntly. 'Gwendoline's a turnip-head – and she's always picked other people's brains and always will. Take off your rose-coloured glasses and see Gwen through your proper eyes, my dear Clarissa!'

Thinking that Alicia really *meant* her to take off her glasses for some reason, Clarissa removed her spectacles most obediently! The girls were about to laugh loudly, when Darrell bent forward in surprise.

'Clarissa! You've got real green eyes! I've never seen proper green eyes before! You must be related to the pixy-folk – people with green eyes always are!'

Everyone roared – but on looking closely at Clarissa's eyes, they saw that they were indeed a lovely clear green, that somehow went remarkably well with her wavy auburn hair.

'My word – I wish I had stunning eyes like that,' said Alicia enviously. 'They're marvellous. How sickening that you've got to wear glasses.'

'Oh, it's only for a time,' said Clarissa, putting them on again, looking rather shy but pleased at Alicia's admiration. 'I'm glad you like my green eyes! Gwendoline thinks it's awful to have green eyes like a cat.'

'If all cats have green eyes, then our dear Gwendoline certainly ought to have them,' said Belinda at once.

Clarissa looked distressed.

'Oh, but Gwendoline has been very kind to me,' she began, and then everyone shushed her. Gwen was coming in at the door, scowling, holding a pair of games shorts and a pair of games stockings in her hands.

'I do think Matron's an absolute *beast*,' she began. 'I spent *hours* darning these last week – and now I've got to unpick all my darns and re-do them.'

'Well, don't darn navy shorts with grey wool, or red stockings with navy wool this time,' said Alicia. 'Anyone would think you were colour-blind.'

Clarissa longed to help Gwen, but after Darrell's remark she didn't like to offer, and Gwen certainly didn't dare to ask for help. The girls sat about, yawning, trying to read, longing for bed because they really felt tired. But not too tired to wake up at twelve and have a swim and a feast.

They didn't take long getting into bed that night. Even slow Gwendoline was quick. Irene was the quickest of the lot, much to Darrell's surprise. But it was discovered that she had absentmindedly got into bed half-undressed, so out she had to get again.

The swimming-things were stacked in someone's cupboard, waiting. Dressing-gowns and slippers were set ready on the ends of each bed.

'Sorry for you, Darrell, and you, too, Sally, having to

keep awake till twelve!' said Irene, yawning. 'Good-night, all – see you in a little while!'

Sally said she would keep awake for the first hour, and then wake Darrell, who would keep awake till twelve. Then each would get a little rest.

Sally valiantly kept awake, and then shook Darrell, who slept in the next bed. Darrell was so sound asleep that she could hardly open her eyes. But she did at last, and then decided she had better get out of bed and walk up and down a little, or she might fall off to sleep again – and then there would be no feast, for she was quite certain no one else would be awake at twelve!

At last she heard the clock at the top of the tower striking twelve. Good. Midnight at last! She woke up Sally and then the two of them woke everyone else up. Gwendoline was the hardest to wake – she always was. Darrell debated whether or not to leave her, as she seemed determined not to wake – but decided that Clarissa might be upset – and after all, it was Clarissa's feast!

They all put on dressing-gowns and slippers. They got their swimming-things out of the cupboard and sent Irene and Belinda for the jugs of lemonade. The dormy was full of giggles and whisperings and shushings. Everybody was now wide awake and very excited.

'Come on – we'll go down to the side-door, out into the garden, and through the gate to the cliff-path down to the pool,' whispered Darrell. 'And for *goodness* sake don't fall down the stairs or do anything idiotic.'

It wasn't long before they were down by the pool, which

was gleaming in the moonlight, and looked too tempting for words. Irene and Belinda had the jugs of lemonade.

'Let's get out the food and have a look at it,' said Sally. 'I'm longing to see it!'

'Alicia! Where's the key of the cubby-hole?' said Darrell.

'Blow!' said Alicia. 'I've left it in my tunic pocket. I'll skip back and get it. Won't be half a minute!'

Midnight feast!

Alicia ran up the cliff-path, annoyed with herself for forgetting the key. She slipped in at the side-door of the tower and went up the stairs. As she went along the landing where the first-form dormy was, she saw a little white figure in the passage, looking out of the landing window.

'Must be a first-former!' thought Alicia. 'What's she out at this time of night for? Little monkey!'

She walked softly up to the small person looking out of the window and grasped her by the shoulder. There was a loud gasp.

'Sh!' said Alicia. 'Good gracious, it's *you*, June! What are you doing out here at midnight?'

'Well, what are *you*?' said June, cheekily.

Alicia shook her. 'None of your cheek,' she said. 'Have you forgotten the scolding I gave you last summer hols for cheeking me and Betty when you came to stay with me?'

'No. I haven't forgotten,' said June, vengefully. 'And I never shall. You were a beast. I'd have split on you if I hadn't been scared. Scolding me as if I was six!'

'Served you jolly well right,' said Alicia. 'And you know what would have happened if you *had* split – Sam and the others would have scolded you, too!'

'I know,' said June, angrily. She was scared of Alicia's brothers. 'You wait, though. I'll get even with you some time!'

Alicia snorted scornfully. 'You could do with another scolding, I see,' she said. 'Now – you clear off to bed. You know you're not supposed to be out of your dormy at night.'

'I saw you all go off with swimming-things tonight,' said June, slyly. 'I guessed you were up to something, you fourth-formers, when I spotted you and somebody else getting swimming-things in the changing-room tonight. You thought I didn't see you, but I did.'

How Alicia longed to scold June – but she dared not raise her voice!

'Clear off to bed,' she ordered, her voice shaking with rage.

'Are you having a midnight feast, too?' persisted June, not moving. 'I saw Irene and Belinda with jugs of lemonade.'

'Nasty little spy,' said Alicia, and gave June a sharp push. 'What we fourth-formers do is none of your business. Go to bed!'

June resisted Alicia's temper, and her voice grew dangerous. 'Does Potty know about your feast?' she asked. 'Or Mam'zelle? I say, Alicia, wouldn't it be rotten luck on you if somebody told on you?'

Alicia gasped. Could June really be threatening to go and wake one of the staff, and so spoil all their plans? She couldn't believe that anyone would be so sneaky.

'Alicia, let me come and join the feast,' begged June. 'Please do.'

'No,' said Alicia, shortly, and then, not trusting herself to say any more, she left June standing by the window and went off in search of the key to the cubby-hole. She was so angry that she could hardly get the key out of her tunic pocket. To be cheeked like that by a first-former – her own cousin! To be threatened by a little pipsqueak like that! Alicia really hated June at that moment.

She found the key and rushed back to the pool with it. She said nothing about meeting June. The others were already in the water, enjoying themselves.

'Pity the moon's gone in,' said Darrell to Sally. 'Gosh, it *has* clouded up, hasn't it? Is that Alicia back? Hey, Alicia, what a time you've been. Got the key?'

'Yes, I'm unlocking the cubby-hole,' called back Alicia. 'Clarissa is here. She'll help me to get out the things. Pity it's so dark now – the moon's gone.'

Suddenly, from the western sky, there came an ominous growl – thunder! Blow, blow, blow!

'Sounds like a storm,' said Darrell. 'I thought there might be one soon, it's so terrifically hot today. I say, Alicia, do you think we ought to begin the feast now, in case the storm comes on?'

'Yes,' said Alicia. 'Ah, here's the moon again, thank goodness!'

The girls clambered out of the water and dried themselves. As they stood there, laughing and talking, Darrell suddenly saw three figures coming down the cliff-path from the school. Her heart stood still. Were they mistresses who had heard them?

It was Betty, of course, with Eileen and Winnie. The three of them stopped short at the pool and appeared to be extremely astonished to see such a gathering of the upper fourth.

'I say! Whatever are you doing?' said Betty. 'We *thought* we heard a noise from the pool! It made us think that a swim would be nice this hot night.'

'We're going to have a feast!' came Alicia's voice. 'You'd better join us.'

'Yes, do – we've got plenty,' said Irene, and the others called out the same. Even Darrell welcomed them, too, for it never once occurred to her that Betty had heard about the feast already and had come in the hope of joining them.

Neither did it occur to her that there was a strict rule that girls from one tower were never to leave their own towers at night to meet anyone from another. She just didn't think about it at all.

They all sat down to enjoy the feast. The thunder rumbled again, this time much nearer. A flash of lightning lit up the sky. The moon went behind an enormous cloud and was seen no more that night.

Worst of all, great drops of rain began to fall, plopping down on the rocks and causing great dismay.

'Oh dear – we'll have to go in,' said Darrell. 'We'll be soaked through, and it won't be any fun at all sitting and eating in the rain. Come on – collect the food and we'll go back.'

Betty nudged Alicia. 'Shall *we* come?' she whispered.

'Yes. Try it,' whispered back Alicia. 'Darrell hasn't said you're not to.'

So everyone, including Betty, Eileen and Winnie from West Tower, gathered up the food hurriedly, and stumbled up the cliff-path in the dark.

'Where shall we take the food?' panted Darrell to Sally. 'Can't have it in our common-room because it's got no curtains and the light would shine out.'

'What about the first-form common-room?' asked Sally. 'That's not near any staff-room, and the windows can't be seen from any other part.'

'Yes. Good idea,' said Darrell, and the word went round that the feast was to be held in the first-form common-room.

Soon they were all in there. Darrell shut the door carefully and put a mat across the bottom so that not a crack of light could be seen.

The girls sat about on the floor, a little damped by the sudden storm that had spoiled their plans. The thunder crashed and the lightning gleamed. Mary-Lou looked alarmed, and Gwen went quite white. Neither of them liked storms.

'Hope Thunder's all right,' said Bill, tucking into a tongue sandwich. Her horse was always her first thought.

'I should think . . .' began Alicia, when she stopped dead. Everyone sat still. Darrell put up her finger for silence.

There came a little knocking at the door. Tap-tap-tap-tap! Tap-tap-tap-tap!

Darrell felt scared. Who in the world was there? And why knock? She made another sign for everyone to keep absolutely still.

The knocking went on. Tap-tap-tap. This time it was a little louder.

Still the girls said nothing and kept quite silent. The knocking came again, sounding much too loud in the night.

Oh dear! thought Darrell. If it gets any louder, someone will hear, and the cat will be out of the bag!

Gwendoline and Mary-Lou were quite terrified of this strange knocking. They clutched each other, as white as a sheet.

'Come in,' said Darrell, at last, in a low voice, when there was a pause in the knocking.

The door opened slowly, and the girls stared at it, wondering what was coming. In walked June – and behind her, rather scared, was Felicity!

'June!' said Alicia, fiercely.

'*Felicity*!' gasped Darrell, hardly believing her eyes.

June stared round as if in surprise.

'Oh,' she said, 'it's you, is it? Felicity and I simply *couldn't* get to sleep because of the storm, and we came to the landing window to watch it. And we found these on the ground!'

She held up three hard-boiled eggs! 'We were awfully surprised. Then we heard a bit of a noise in here and we wondered who was in our common-room – and we thought whoever it was must be having a good old feast – so we came to bring you your lost hard-boiled eggs.'

There was a silence after this speech. Alicia was boiling! She knew that June had watched them coming back because of the storm – had seen them going into the first-form common-room – and had been delighted to find the dropped eggs and bring them along as an excuse to join the party!

'Oh,' said Darrell, hardly knowing what to say. 'Thanks. Yes – we're having a feast. Er . . .'

'Why did you use our common-room?' asked June, innocently, and she broke the shell off one of the eggs. 'Of course, it's an honour for us first-formers to have you upper fourth using our room for a feast. I say – this egg's super! I didn't mean to nibble it, though. So sorry.'

'Oh, finish it if you like,' said Darrell, not finding anything else to say.

'Thanks,' said June, and gave one to Felicity, who began to eat hers, too.

It ended, of course, in the two of them joining in the feast, though Darrell really felt very uncomfortable about it. Also, for the first time she realized that the three girls from West Tower were still there, in North Tower, where they had no business to be! Still, how could she turn them out now? She couldn't very well say, 'Look here, you must scram! I know we said join the feast when we were down by the pool – but we can't have you with us now.' It sounded too silly for words.

Darrell did not enjoy the feast at all. She wanted to send June and Felicity away, but it seemed mean to do that when the feasters were using their common-room, and June had brought back the eggs. Also she felt that Alicia might not like her to send June away. Little did she know that Alicia was meditating all kinds of dire punishments for the irrepressible June. Oh dear – the lovely time they had planned seemed to have gone wrong somehow.

And then it went even more wrong! Footsteps were heard overhead.

14

Things happen fast

'Did you hear that?' whispered Sally. 'Someone is coming! Quick, gather everything up, and let's go!'

The girls grabbed everything near, and Darrell caught up the brush by the fireplace and swept the crumbs under a couch. She put out the light and opened the door. All was dark in the passage outside. There seemed to be nobody there. Who could have been walking about overhead? That was where the first-form dormy was.

June and Felicity were scared now. They shot away at once. Betty, Eileen and Winnie disappeared to the stairs, running down them to the side-door. They could then slip round to their own tower. The others, led by Darrell, went cautiously upstairs to find their own dormy.

A slight cough from somewhere near, a familiar and unmistakable cough, brought them to a stop. They stood, hardly daring to breathe, at the top of the stairs. That was Potty's cough, thought Darrell. Oh, blow – did she hear us making a row? But we really were quite quiet!

She hoped and hoped that Betty and the other two West Tower girls had got safely to their own dormy without being caught. It really was counted quite a serious offence for girls of one tower to meet girls in another tower at night. For one thing there was no way to get from one tower to another under cover. The girls had to go outside to reach any other tower.

What could Potty be doing? Where was she? The girls stood frozen to the ground, waiting for the sign to move on.

'She's in the third-form dormy,' whispered Darrell, at last. 'Perhaps somebody is ill there. I think we had better make a dash for it, really. We can't stand here for hours.'

'Right. The next time the thunder comes, we'll run for it,' said Sally, in a low voice. The word was passed along, and the girls waited anxiously for the thunder. The lightning flashed first, showing up the crouching line of girls very clearly – and then the thunder came.

It was a good long, rumbling crash, and any sound the girls made in scampering along to their dormy was completely deadened. They fell into bed thankfully, each girl stuffing what she carried into the bottom of her cupboard, wet swimming-costumes and all.

No Miss Potts appeared, and the girls began to breathe more freely. Somebody *must* have been taken ill in the third-form dormy. Potty still seemed to be there. At last the upper fourth heard the soft closing of the door to the third-form dormy, and Miss Potts's footsteps going quietly off to her own room.

'Had we better take the lemonade jugs down to the kitchen now?' whispered Irene.

'No. We won't risk any more creeping about tonight,' said Darrell. 'You must take them down before breakfast, as soon as the staff have gone into the dining-room, even though it makes you a bit late. And we'll clear out all the food left over before *we* go down, and hide it somewhere till we can get rid of it. *What* a pity that beastly storm came!'

The girls slept like logs that night, and could hardly wake up in the morning. Gwen and Belinda had to be literally *dragged* out of bed! Irene shot down to the kitchen with the empty jugs. All the rest of the food was hastily put into a bag and dumped into an odd cupboard in the landing. Then, looking demure and innocent, the fourth-formers went down to breakfast.

Felicity grinned at Darrell. She had enjoyed the escapade last night. But June did not grin at Alicia. Alicia's face was very grim, and June felt uncomfortable.

At break Alicia went to find Hilda, the head-girl of the first form. Hilda was surprised and flattered.

'Hilda,' said Alicia, 'I am very displeased with June's behaviour. She is getting quite unbearable, and we fourth-formers are not going to stand it. Either you must put her in her place, or we shall. It would be much better for you to do it.'

'Oh, Alicia, I'm so sorry,' said Hilda. 'We *have* tried to put her in her place, but she keeps saying you'll give us no end of a wigging if we don't give her a chance. But we've given her lots of chances.'

'I bet you have,' said Alicia, grimly. 'Now, I don't know how *you* deal with your erring form-members, Hilda – we had various very good ways when *I* was a first-former – but please do *some*thing – and tell her I told you to!'

'Right. We will,' said Hilda, thankful that she had got

authority to deal with that bumptious, brazen, conceited new girl, June! A week of being sent to Coventry would soon bring June to heel – she loved talking and gossiping, and it would be a hard punishment for her. Hilda went off to call a form meeting about the matter, feeling very important.

June was angry and shocked to hear the verdict of her form – to be sent to Coventry for a week. She felt humiliated, too – and how angry she was with Alicia for giving Hilda the necessary authority! Alicia was quite within her rights to do this. When a member of a lower form aroused the anger or scorn of a higher form, the head-girl of the offender's form was told to deal with the matter. And so Hilda dealt with it faithfully and promptly, and if she felt very pleased to do it, that was June's fault, and not hers. June was certainly a thorn in the side of all the old girls in the first form. It was quite unheard of for any new girl to behave so boldly.

Felicity found that she too had to give her promise not to speak to June. Oh dear – that would be very awkward – but she owed more loyalty to her form than to June. So she gave her promise in a low voice, not daring to look at the red-faced June.

That evening Felicity came to Darrell, looking worried. 'Darrell, please may I speak to you? Something rather awful has happened. Those crumbs we left in the common-room last night, under the couch, were found this morning, and so were two sandwiches. And Potty tackled Hilda and asked her if she'd been having a midnight feast there last night. Potty said she thought she heard something, but by the time she came out of the third-form dormy, where somebody was ill, and went to look in the common-room, it was empty.'

'Gosh,' said Darrell. Then her face cleared. 'Well, what's it matter? Hilda must have been asleep last night, and can't have known anything about it.'

'She *was* asleep – and she told Potty she didn't know a thing about any feast, and that the first form certainly hadn't been out of the dormy last night,' said Felicity. 'Some of them woke up in that storm, but nobody missed me or June, apparently.'

'Well, why worry then?' said Darrell. 'You shouldn't have come along with June last night, you know, Felicity. I was awfully surprised and not at all pleased to see you. You really ought to be careful your very first term.'

'I know,' said Felicity. 'I sort of get carried along by June. Honestly I can't help it, Darrell – she makes me laugh so much and she's so bold and daring. She's been sent to Coventry now, and she's as mad as anything. She knows it's all because of Alicia and she vows she'll get even with her. She will, too.'

'Felicity – do chuck June,' begged Darrell. 'She's no good as a friend. She's a little beast, really. Alicia has told me all about her.'

But Felicity was obstinate and she shook her head. 'No. I like June and I want to stick by her. She's not a little beast. She's fun.'

Darrell let Felicity go, feeling impatient with her little

sister. Anyway, thank goodness Potty hadn't found out anything. She must be jolly puzzled about the crumbs and the sandwiches!

It seemed as if the whole affair would settle down – and then a bombshell came! Felicity came to Darrell again, the next day, looking very harassed indeed.

'Darrell! I must speak to you in private.'

'Good gracious! What's up now?' said Darrell, taking Felicity to a corner of the Court.

'It's June. I don't understand her. She says she's going to go to Potty and own up that she was at the midnight feast,' said Felicity. 'She says I ought to go and own up, too.'

Darrell stared at Felicity in exasperation. These first-formers! 'But if she goes and does that, it's as good as sneaking on *us*,' said Darrell, furiously. 'Where's this little pest now?'

'In one of the music-rooms practising,' said Felicity, alarmed at Darrell's fury. 'She's in Coventry, you know, so I can't speak to her. She sent me a note. Whatever am I to do, Darrell? If she goes to own up, I'll *have* to go, too, or Potty and the rest will think I'm an awful coward.'

'I'll go and talk to June,' said Darrell, and went straight off to the music-room, where the girls practised daily. She found June and burst into the room so angrily that the first-former jumped.

'Look here, June, what's behind this sudden piousness of yours – wanting to go and "own up" – when there's no need for anything of the sort?' cried Darrell, angrily. 'You know you'd get the upper fourth into trouble if you go and split.'

'I shan't split,' said June, calmly, playing a little scale up and down the piano. 'I shall simply own up I was at *the* feast – but I shan't say whose feast. I – er – want to get it off my conscience.'

'You're a little hypocrite!' said Darrell. 'Stop playing that scale and listen to me.'

June played another little scale, a mocking smile on her face. Darrell nearly burst with rage. She pushed June's hand off the piano, and turned her round roughly to face her.

'Stop it,' said June. 'I've had enough of that kind of thing from my dear cousin Alicia!'

At the mention of Alicia's name, something clicked into place in Darrell's mind, and she knew at once what was behind June's pious idea of 'owning up'. She wanted to get even with Alicia. She would like to get her into trouble – and Darrell too – and everyone in the upper fourth – to revenge herself on Alicia's order to Hilda to deal with her.

'You *are* a double-faced little wretch, aren't you?' said Darrell, scornfully. 'You know jolly well if you "own up" – pooh! – that Potty will make enquiries and *I* shall have to own up to the spree in the pool, and the feast afterwards.'

'Oh – worse than that!' said June, in her infuriatingly impudent voice. 'Girls from another tower were there – or was I mistaken?'

'Do you mean to say you'd split on Betty and the others, too,' said Darrell, taking a deep breath, 'just to get even with Alicia?'

'Oh – not *split* – or even *sneak*,' said June, beginning to play the maddening scale again. 'Surely I can own up – and Betty's name can – er – just *slip* out, as it were.'

At the thought of June sneaking on everyone, under the cover of being a good little girl and 'owning up', Darrell really saw red. Her temper went completely, and she found herself pulling the wretched June off the piano-stool and shaking her.

A voice made her stop suddenly.

'DARRELL! Whatever *are* you doing?'

15

A real shake-up

Darrell stared wildly round. Miss Potts stood at the door, a picture of absolute amazement. Darrell couldn't think of a word to say. June actually had the audacity to reseat herself on the piano-stool and play a soft chord.

'June!' said Miss Potts, and the tone of her voice made the first-former almost jump out of her skin.

'Come with me, Darrell,' said Miss Potts. 'And you, too, June.'

They followed her to her room, where Mam'zelle was correcting papers. She gazed in surprise at Miss Potts's grim face, and at the faces of the two girls.

'*Tiens*!' said Mam'zelle, gathering up her papers quickly, and beginning to scuttle out of her room. 'I will go. I will not intrude, Miss Potts.'

Miss Potts didn't appear to have noticed Mam'zelle at all. She sat down in her chair and looked sternly at Darrell and June.

'What were you two doing?'

Darrell swallowed hard. She was already ashamed of herself. Oh dear – head-girl – and she had lost her temper like that! 'Miss Potts – June has something to say to you,' she said at last.

'What have you to say?' enquired Miss Potts, turning her cold eyes on June.

'Well, Miss Potts – I just wanted to own up that I had been to a midnight feast,' said June.

'Hilda said that there had been no midnight feast,' said Miss Potts, beginning to tap on the table with her pencil, always a danger-sign with her.

'I know. It wasn't a first-form affair,' said June smoothly.

'I gather from Darrell's face that it was a fourth-form affair,' said Miss Potts.

Darrell nodded miserably. 'Just the fourth-formers and you, June, I suppose?' said Miss Potts.

'Well – there were a few others,' said June, pretending to hesitate. 'One from my form as well as me. I won't mention her name.'

'Felicity was there,' said Darrell. 'But I take responsibility for that. She didn't mean to come. And Miss Potts – Betty Hill, and Eileen and Winnie were there, too.'

There was a silence. Miss Potts looked very grim.

'Girls from another tower?' she said. 'I think you know the rule about that, don't you, Darrell? And what could you have been thinking about to invite two first-formers as well? Of course – Felicity is your sister – but surely . . .'

'I didn't invite her,' said Darrell. 'And – well – I didn't exactly invite the West Tower girls either.'

'Don't let's quibble and make excuses,' said Miss Potts, impatiently. 'That isn't like you, Darrell. I imagine you were quarrelling with June because she wanted to own up?'

Darrell couldn't trust herself to speak. She nodded. 'I'm sorry I behaved like that,' she said, humbly. 'I thought I'd conquered my temper, but I haven't. I'm sorry I shook you, June.'

June was a little taken-about at this apology, and looked uneasy. But she was very cock-a-hoop and pleased with herself. She was in Potty's good books for 'owning up', she had got Darrell into trouble, and Alicia would get into trouble too and all the others – and she, June, would get off scot-free!

'You can go, June,' said Miss Potts, suddenly. 'I'm not sure I've got to the bottom of all this yet. Darrell had no right to be so rough with you – but as she never loses her temper now unless something very serious makes her angry, I am inclined to take your owning-up with a pinch of salt. You may be sure I shall find out whether you are to be praised or blamed!'

June shot out of the room, scared. Miss Potts looked gravely at Darrell. 'Darrell, you know that you will have to bear the responsibility for allowing girls from another tower into your tower at night, don't you?' she said. 'And I cannot possibly pass over your behaviour to June in the music-room. Whatever provocation you had does not excuse what you did.'

'I know,' said Darrell, miserably. 'I'm not a good head-girl, Miss Potts. I'd better resign.'

'Well – either you must resign, or you will have to be demoted,' said Miss Potts, sadly. 'Sally must be head for the time being – till we consider you can take the responsibility again. If you can't control yourself, Darrell, you certainly can't control others.'

The news soon flew through the school. 'Darrell Rivers has resigned as head-girl! Did you know? There has been a most awful row – something about a midnight feast, and she actually asked girls from another tower – and first-formers as well. Gosh! Fancy *Darrell Rivers* getting into disgrace!'

Felicity heard the news and was filled with the utmost horror. She went straight to June, quite forgetting that she was still in Coventry.

'Did you go and split?' she asked, sharply. 'What has happened?'

Full of glee at all that had happened, June told Felicity the whole thing from beginning to end. 'That will teach the fourth-formers to have a down on me and get me sent to Coventry,' she said. 'I've paid Alicia back nicely – and my word, you should have seen Darrell's face when she was shaking me and Miss Potts came in and saw her. I'm glad she's not head-girl of her form any longer. Serves her right!'

Felicity could hardly believe her ears. She was trembling, shivering all over. June noticed it with surprise.

'What's the matter?' she said. 'You're my friend, aren't you?'

'I was. But have you forgotten that Darrell is my sister?' said Felicity, in a choking voice. June stared at her blankly. In her glee at being top-dog she *had* completely and utterly forgotten that Darrell was Felicity's sister.

'I feel like Darrell – I could shake you, you horrid, two-faced beast!' cried Felicity. 'As it is, I'm going to Hilda to tell her every single thing you've told me – that's not sneaking – that's reporting something almost too bad to be true! Ugh! You ought to be expelled. How could I *ever* have wanted you for my friend!'

And so the friendship between Felicity and June came to a most abrupt end, and was never renewed again. Susan was hunted out by Felicity and gave her the comfort she needed. June kicked herself for forgetting that Darrell was Felicity's sister; but the damage was done. Felicity had seen June in her true colours – and she didn't like them at all!

The fourth form were horrified at all that had happened. One and all they stood by poor Darrell, even Gwendoline coming to offer a few words of sympathy.

But Gwen's sympathy was, as usual, only on the surface. Immediately after she had been to tell Darrell how sorry she was, she was confiding to Clarissa that she really wasn't surprised that Darrell was in disgrace.

'I told you how she shook me, didn't I?' she said. 'And she pushed Sally over once. It'll do her good to be humiliated like this. I never did like Darrell.'

Clarissa looked at Gwendoline with a sudden feeling of dislike. 'Why do you say this when you have just told her you're sorry, and that you'd do anything you could to put things right?' she said. 'I think you're beastly, Gwen.'

And to Gwen's unutterable surprise, the meek, weak Clarissa turned her back on her and walked away! It had cost her a great deal to say this to Gwen, and she was crying as she walked away.

She bumped into Bill, off to ride on Thunder. 'Here, look where you're going, Clarissa. I say, you're crying. Whatever's up?' said Bill, in surprise.

'Nothing,' said Clarissa, not wanting to say anything against Gwen.

Bill only knew one cure for unhappiness – riding a horse! She offered the cure to Clarissa now.

'Come for a ride. It's heavenly out now. You said you were allowed to ride if you wanted to. There's a horse free, I know. Miss Peters is coming, too. She's grand.'

Another time Clarissa would have said no, because it was difficult for her to make up her mind to begin anything fresh, and she had not yet ridden at Malory Towers, although she had been told that she could. But now, touched by Bill's blunt kindliness, and feeling that she wanted to get right away from Gwendoline, she nodded her head.

'All right. I'll change into my jodhpurs quickly. Wait for me.'

And in fifteen minutes' time, to Gwendoline's enormous surprise, Miss Peters, Bill and *Clarissa* swept past her on the cliff, riding fast, shouting to one another as they went. *Clarissa*! Well! She hadn't even known that Clarissa had riding things with her. And there she was, off with that awful Bill and that even more awful Miss Peters! Gwendoline really couldn't understand it at all.

Sally was made temporary head-girl. 'I shall really

share it with you,' she told the subdued Darrell. 'I shall come and ask you everything and take your advice – and I bet it won't be long before you're made head-girl once more. Miss Grayling told me twice I was only temporary.'

Darrell had written to her parents and told them the bad news. They would be sorry and upset, but they had to know. 'I thought I must tell you before you come to see me and Felicity at half-term,' wrote Darrell. 'Please don't say anything about it when you see me, will you, because I shall howl! Anyway, dears, one good thing has come out of all this – Felicity's not friends any more with the horridest girl in her form, but with one of the nicest – Susan, who you saw at the gym display last term.'

Darrell had been very touched by the sympathy given to her by her form. The twins had been very nice, she thought, even though Ruth, as usual, had not said a word, – everything had been said by Connie. And as for Clarissa, she had been almost in tears when she came to Darrell.

'I believe Clarissa's awfully nice, when you can get under her meekness and shyness,' said Darrell to Sally. '*What* a pity she has to wear those glasses! Didn't you think she looked beautiful when she took them off the other day – those deep green eyes, like water in a pool.'

Sally laughed. 'You sound quite poetical,' she said. 'Yes, I like Clarissa now. Gwen doesn't quite know what to think about Clarissa going off riding with Bill, does she? I never knew Clarissa was so fond of horses! She and Bill gabble like anything about all the horses they have ever known – and Gwendoline looks on like a dying duck in a thunderstorm, trying to get a word in.'

'Half-term next week,' said Darrell. 'Oh, Sally, I never dreamed when I was feeling so proud of being made head-girl that I'd lose my position before even half-term came. I'm a terrible failure!'

'Well – plenty of people would like to be the kind of failure *you* are!' said Sally, loyally. 'You may be a failure at the moment – but you're a very *fine* failure, Darrell! You're a lot better than some people who think they're a success.'

16

Gwendoline makes a plan

Half-term would soon be coming! The school was giving all kinds of displays – an exhibition tennis-match played by four of the crack school players – a swimming and diving display – and a dancing display in the middle of the great Court.

'And after that,' said Daphne, gloomily, 'after that – the School Cert exam! I feel awfully depressed whenever I think of it.'

'Think how light-hearted you'll be afterwards!' said Belinda.

'Yes – like you feel after going to the dentist,' said Clarissa. 'You get all gloomy beforehand and then after you've been you feel awfully happy.'

Everyone laughed. They knew that Clarissa had had bad times at the dentist, and they knew that she hated the wire round her front teeth, put there to keep them back. She was hoping she could have it off before long.

'Once I've got rid of that wire and my glasses you won't know me!' she said, and shook back her mass of auburn hair.

She had been riding quite a bit with Bill, and Gwendoline had felt rather out of things. Clarissa rode extremely well, and could apparently manage any horse in the school stables – and had actually been permitted to try Thunder!

Gwendoline found the everlasting horse conversation between the two very trying indeed.

'I once rode a horse who ran away with me and jumped over a hedge before I had even learned how to jump!' Clarissa would begin.

And then Bill would go on. 'Did you really? I bet you stuck on all right. Did I ever tell you about Marvel, my brother Tom's horse?'

Then would follow a long story about Marvel. At the end Gwendoline would try to get a word in.

'I say – Clarissa, do you know where we are going for this afternoon's walk?'

'Not yet,' Clarissa would say. 'Well, Bill, I simply must tell you about my father's old horse that lived to be over thirty. He . . .'

And so the horsy conversation would go on, till Gwendoline felt she could scream. Horses! Horrible great snorting, stamping creatures! How she wished Clarissa had never gone out for that first ride with Bill.

Gwendoline was beginning to be very much afraid of the coming exam. She was backward in her lessons, and because of her habit of picking other people's brains, and of copying their work, her own brains worked very badly when she had to think out something for herself. The exam paper had to be done with her own brains – she couldn't copy anyone's work then – and indeed Gwen knew perfectly well that Miss Williams would see to it that she, Gwendoline, would be seated much too far away from anyone else to copy!

She worried about the exam. She felt uncomfortably that she might possibly be the only person to fail – and what a disgrace and humiliation that would be! Her father would have a lot of hurtful remarks to make, and her mother would cry, and her old governess would look mournful, and say it was all her fault, she ought to have taught Gwen better when she was small. Oh dear – why did these beastly exams matter?

Gwendoline seriously considered the possibility of trying to see the papers beforehand – but that was silly, she knew. They were always locked up. She did not think to herself, 'I am *wrong* to think of such a thing,' she merely thought, 'I am silly to think there would be a chance of seeing them.'

Could she be ill? Could she complain of a sore throat and headache? No – Matron simply *never* believed her. She would take her temperature and say, 'My dear Gwendoline, you are suffering from inflammation of the imagination as usual,' and give her that perfectly horrible medicine.

She thought of Clarissa's weak heart with envy. To have something like that – that prevented you from playing those awful games, and from swimming and climbing up hills – now that was something really worth while having – something sensible. Unfortunately, though, it didn't let you off lessons.

Gwendoline thought about weak hearts for a while, and gradually a plan began to unfold itself in her mind. What about putting it round that her heart was troubling her? She put her hand to where she thought her heart was, and assumed an agonized expression. What should she say? 'Oh, my heart – it's fluttering again! I do wish it wouldn't. It makes me feel so peculiar. Oh, why did I run up those stairs so fast?'

The more she thought about this idea, the better it seemed. Next week was half-term. If she could work up this weak heart business well enough, perhaps her parents would be told, and they would be alarmed and take her away home. Then she would miss School Cert, which began not long after!

Gwendoline's heart began to beat fast as she thought out this little plan. In fact, she felt a little alarmed, feeling it beat so fast with excitement. Suppose she really *had* got one? No – it was only that she was feeling excited about this clever and wonderful idea of hers.

So, little by little, Gwen began to put it about that she didn't feel very well. 'Oh, nothing much,' she told Clarissa and Bill. '*You'll* know what I feel like, Clarissa – my heart sort of *flutters*! Oh, why did I run up the stairs so fast?'

Clarissa was sympathetic. She knew how absolutely sickening a weak heart was. 'Don't you think you ought to tell Miss Williams, or Miss Potts?' she said, quite anxiously. 'Or Matron?'

'No,' said Gwendoline, putting on a pathetically brave face. 'I don't want to make a fuss. Besides, you know, it's School Cert soon. I mustn't miss that.'

If Alicia, Sally or Darrell had been anywhere near, they would have yelled with laughter at all this, but Bill and Clarissa didn't. They listened quite seriously.

'Well, *I* think you ought to say something about it,' said Clarissa. 'If you'd had to go through what *I've* had to – lie up for weeks on end, not do a thing, give up all the riding and swimming I loved – you'd not run any risk of playing about with a groggy heart.'

Gwendoline took to running up the stairs when she saw any of the upper fourth at the top. Then, when she came to the landing, she would put her hand to her left side, droop over the banisters and groan.

'Got a stitch?' Alicia would say, unsympathetically. 'Bend down and touch your toes, Gwendoline. Oh – I forgot – you're too fat to do that, aren't you?'

On the other hand Mary-Lou might say, 'Oh, Gwen, what's the matter? Is it your heart again? You really ought to have something done about it!'

Gwen did not perform in front of either Miss Williams or Miss Potts. She had a feeling that her performance would not go down very well. But she tried it on with Mam'zelle, who could always be taken in.

Mam'zelle was quite alarmed one morning to find Gwen sitting on the top stair near her room, her hand pressed to her heart, groaning.

'*Ma petite*! *Qu'avez vous*? What is the matter?' she cried. 'You have hurt yourself? Where?'

'It's – it's all right, Mam'zelle,' panted Gwendoline. 'It's

– it's nothing – just this awful heart of mine. When I run or do anything energetic – it seems to go all funny!'

'You have the palpitations! You are anaemic then!' cried Mam'zelle. 'Me, I once suffered in this way when I was fifteen! You shall come with me to Matron, and she shall give you some good, good medicine to make your blood rich and red.'

Gwendoline didn't want her blood made 'rich and red' by Matron. It was the last thing in the world she wanted! She got up hastily and smiled weakly at Mam'zelle.

'It's over now! I'm quite all right. It's not anaemia, Mam'zelle – I've never been anaemic. It's just my silly heart. It's – er – it's a weakness in our family, I'm afraid.'

This was quite untrue, but Gwendoline added it because she thought it might convince Mam'zelle it was her heart and not her blood that was wrong! Mam'zelle was very sympathetic, and told Gwen she had better not play tennis that afternoon.

Gwendoline was delighted – but on thinking it over she regretfully decided that she had better play, because she wouldn't possibly be able to convince Sally that her heart had played her up again. Sally simply didn't believe in Gwen's weak heart. So she played. Mam'zelle saw her and was surprised.

The brave Gwendoline! she thought. She plays even though she knows it may bring on the palpitations again! Ah, these English girls, they have the courage and the pluck!

Gwendoline laid a few more plans. She would bring

Mam'zelle up to her parents at half-term, and leave her to talk to them. She was certain that sooner or later Mam'zelle would speak about her heart – and then she, Gwen, would be anxiously questioned by her mother – and if she played her cards well, she would be taken home at once by a very anxious and frightened mother!

Gwen did not stop to think of the pain and anxiety she would give to her parents by her stupid pretence. She wanted to get out of doing the exam, and she didn't mind how she did it. She was quite unscrupulous, and very clever when she badly wanted her own way.

I'm certain Mother will take me home, she thought. I really don't think I need bother about swotting up for the exam. It will be a waste of time if I don't take it. Look at all the others – groaning and moaning every evening, mugging up Latin and French and maths and history and the rest! Well – *I* shan't!

And, to the surprise of everyone, Gwendoline suddenly stopped working hard, and slacked!

'Aren't you afraid of doing frightfully bad papers?' asked Mavis, who was rather afraid of this herself, and was working very hard indeed.

'I shall do my best,' said Gwendoline. 'I can't do more. It's this beastly heart of mine, you know – it does play me up so, if I work too hard.'

Mavis didn't believe in this heart of Gwendoline's, but she was really puzzled to know why the girl was so silly as to waste her time when she ought to be putting in some good hard work preparing for the exam.

But, surprisingly enough, it was Connie who put her finger on the right spot! She had a great scorn for the weak, ineffectual Gwendoline. She was a domineering, strong-minded girl herself, and she could not bear Gwendoline's moaning and grumbling. For some reason or other Connie had been touchy and irritable for the last week or two, and her bad temper suddenly flared out one evening at Gwen.

Gwendoline had come into the common-room and flopped down in a chair. Everyone was swotting hard for the exam as usual, their heads bent over their books.

'I really must *not* carry heavy things again,' began Gwendoline, in her peevish voice. Nobody took any notice except to frown.

'I've had to help Potty with the books in the library,' went on Gwen. 'Great heavy piles! It's set my heart fluttering like anything!'

'Shut up,' said Connie. 'We're working.'

'Well, there's no need for you to be rude,' said Gwen, with dignity. 'If you had a heart like mine . . .'

And then Connie exploded. She got up and went to stand over the astonished Gwendoline.

'You haven't *got* a heart, weak or otherwise! You're a big bundle of pretence! You're making it all up to get out of School Cert. *I* can see through you! That's why you're not working, isn't it – because you're banking on your heart letting you out, in some way or other you've planned? Well, let me tell you this – I don't care tuppence whether you do School Cert or not, or whether you work or not – but I *do* care about my own work! And so do the others. So SHUT UP about your silly heart, and keep away from us with your moanings and groanings till School Cert is over!'

With that Connie went back to her seat, glowering. Everyone was startled – too startled to say a word. They all felt that what Connie said was true.

'You hateful, cruel thing!' said Gwendoline in a trembling voice. 'I hope you fail! And you will, too – see if you don't! You only get decent marks because you're always cribbing from Ruth. We all know that! She'll pass and you won't! I think you're a beast!'

She burst into tears, got up and went out of the room, banging the door so violently that Mam'zelle and Miss Potts, working in their room not far away, wondered whatever was happening.

The girls looked at one another. Alicia made a face. 'Well, I expect Connie's right – though you were a bit brutal, weren't you, Connie?'

'No more brutal than you sometimes are,' said Connie, rather sulkily. 'Anyway, let's get to work again. Some of us are not like you, Alicia – skating lightly over every subject and doing everything well, without bothering. You don't understand how hard some of us find our work. Let's get on.'

There was silence in the room as the girls worked away, reading, making notes, learning by heart. Only Clarissa and Mary-Lou were really troubled about Gwen. Clarissa still believed in her weak heart, and Mary-Lou was always sorry for anyone who cried.

As for Gwendoline, her tears were not tears of sorrow, but of rage. That horrible Connie! If only she could get back at her for her unkind words. How Gwendoline hoped that Connie hadn't spoiled her beautiful plan!

Half-term at last

Half-term came at last. It was a really lovely day, with bright sunshine and a nice breeze. The kitchen staff worked with a will to produce masses of good things for the grand school tea. All the girls were excited about seeing their people.

Gwendoline had quite thought that Clarissa's people were coming, and had planned to introduce them to her mother and father. Then she suddenly heard Bill and Clarissa planning a picnic together on the half-term Saturday!

'Two of my brothers have their half-term at the same time,' said Bill, 'so they're coming with Mother and Daddy. We'll take our lunch up to the top of Langley Hill, shall we, and swim in the cove afterwards, before we come back to the tennis exhibition.'

Gwen listened in astonishment. 'But what will Clarissa's father and mother say to that?' she said. 'Won't they want Clarissa to themselves?'

'They can't come on the Saturday, worse luck,' said Clarissa. 'They may be able to come over on Sunday, though – at least, Mother might be able to, even if Daddy can't. They're dreadfully busy people, you know.'

'So I've asked Clarissa to come with us,' said Bill. 'My family will bring enough lunch for twice as many as we'll be, so we'll have a good time!'

Gwen was jealous. Why, she could have had Clarissa spend the day with *her*, if she'd known.

'Well! You might have told *me* your people couldn't come on Saturday,' she said. 'You know how much I should have liked you to spend your time with *my* people.'

Clarissa looked embarrassed. She had purposely not told Gwen, because she had so much wanted to go with Bill and her brothers – all nice horsey people! But she couldn't explain that to Gwen. So, to make up for her remissness she was extra nice to her, and promised to go and speak to Gwen's people when they arrived.

'You might just *mention* my heart to them,' said Gwendoline. 'I don't really like to make a fuss about it myself – but *you* could just say something, Clarissa.'

'Of course I will,' said Clarissa, who still believed in Gwen's weak heart. 'I think something ought to be done about it.'

So, on half-term Saturday, Clarissa was led up to Mrs Lacey, Gwendoline's mother, and Miss Winter, her gentle and scared-looking old governess. Her father was not there.

Mrs Lacey was talking to another mother. Clarissa sat down on the grass with Gwendoline, waiting till she had finished. Darrell's mother was near, and Darrell introduced her to Clarissa.

Soon Clarissa heard Gwen talking to her mother and

Miss Winter. 'Well, dear,' said her mother, fondly, 'and what has my darling Gwendoline been doing this term? Are you in the exhibition tennis?'

'Well, no, Mother,' said Gwendoline. 'I was almost chosen – but it was decided only to have girls from the fifth and the sixth.'

'How stupid!' said Miss Winter, feeling that Gwen would certainly have been better than any fifth- or sixth-form girl.

'What about your swimming, Gwen?' asked her mother. 'You said in one of your letters that you had won a backstroke swimming race and I *did* think that was clever. Backstroke is *so* difficult. I remember I could never do it at school because the water kept going over my face.'

Clarissa couldn't help hearing this conversation, though she was talking to Mrs Rivers, Darrell's mother. She was horrified. Whatever did Gwen mean by all this?

'No, I'm not swimming today,' said Gwen. 'There's a lot of jealousy, you know, Mother – often the good ones aren't given a proper chance. Still, I don't really mind. I can *dive* almost better than anyone now.'

As Gwen always fell flat on her stomach, hitting the water with a terrific smack whenever she was made to dive, this was distinctly funny – or would have been to Darrell, Sally or Alicia. But it wasn't funny to Clarissa. It was shocking. What terrible lies – real thumping lies! However could Gwen say such things? She was very thankful that she was going out with blunt, straightforward Bill instead of having to be with Gwen and her silly, credulous mother. She saw very clearly why Gwen was as she was – this mother of hers had spoiled her, idolized her, believed every word she said – it was she – and probably that pathetic little governess too – who had made Gwendoline into the silly, conceited, untrustworthy girl she was!

Clarissa felt that she really could *not* go and speak to Gwen's mother, after hearing all Gwen's untruths. She couldn't! Clarissa was meek, and weak in many ways, but she was straight and truthful. She was really shocked now.

She got up to slip away before Gwen could see she was going. But Gwen did see, and pulled her down again, so that she had to smile and say, 'How-do-you-do?' to Gwen's mother and governess.

'I mustn't stop, I'm afraid,' said Clarissa, hurriedly. 'Bill's people have come and I mustn't keep them waiting.'

Gwendoline looked at her meaningly. Clarissa knew what that look meant: 'Say something about my heart.' But alas, she found that she no longer believed in Gwendoline's heart. She was sure that the girl had lied about that now, just as she had lied about the other things a few minutes back.

'And are *you* in the tennis or swimming exhibitions?' asked Mrs Lacey, her large, pale blue eyes, so like Gwen's, looking down at Clarissa's small face.

'No, I'm not, I'm afraid,' said Clarissa.

'You see, *poor* Clarissa has a weak heart,' said Gwen, hastily, seeing a very good opening indeed here for

Clarissa to bring up the subject of Gwen's own heart. But Clarissa didn't say a word.

'Poor child,' said Mrs Lacey. 'What a dreadful affliction for a young girl. Now Gwen has always had such a *strong* heart, I'm glad to say. And doesn't she look well now – so plump and bonny.'

Gwen looked at Clarissa in desperation. This was all wrong! She gave her a sharp nudge. But still Clarissa didn't mention Gwen's weak heart! Gwen glared at her angrily.

Clarissa was now tongue-tied. She sat there, red in the face, her eyes blinking behind their thick glasses, wondering how in the world to get away from Gwen and her silly mother.

Bill came to her rescue with a shout. 'Clarissa! I say, can you come? We're ready!'

'I must go,' said Clarissa, nervously, and got up gladly. 'Good-bye, Mrs Lacey.'

'But, Clarissa!' called Gwendoline after her, dismayed and angry that Clarissa hadn't done what she had said she would do.

'*Who* did you say that girl was?' said Mrs Lacey. 'I didn't catch the name.'

'It's Clarissa Carter,' said Gwen, sulkily. 'Why did she have to rush off like that? Rude, I call it!'

'A most unattractive child,' said Mrs Lacey. 'Very plain indeed. No manners either. Gwendoline, I do hope she isn't a friend of yours.'

'Oh, *no*, Mother!' said Gwendoline, making up her mind that after Clarissa's failure to help her that morning she would never be friendly with her again! 'I don't like her at all. Very plain, as you say – almost ugly – and undergrown, too. Not at all clever, and rather unpopular.'

'I should think so!' said Miss Winter. 'She must have been very badly brought up. When I compare her with Gwendoline – well!'

Gwendoline basked in their approval. She kept a sharp watch for Mam'zelle. Mam'zelle was her only hope now!

The day went by very fast. The tennis exhibition was loudly applauded, and the swimming and diving were exclaimed at in wonder, everyone admiring the crisp, clean strokes of the fast swimmers, and the beautiful diving.

Afterwards the dancing display was held in the amphi-theatre of grass in the centre of the great Court. Mothers and fathers sat on the stone ledges surrounding the big circle, looking for their own girls as they came tripping in, dressed in floating tulle of different colours – and each parent, of course, felt certain that her own child was quite the nicest there!

Clarissa came back after her picnic lunch with Bill and her family. She did not go near Gwen, and would not even look in her direction in case she was beckoned over. But Gwen made no sign – she had finished with Clarissa, the horrid little two-faced thing.

Most unfortunately for Gwendoline, Mam'zelle kept quite out of reach the whole day. She was busy helping the dancing-mistress, dressing the girls, arranging their tulle skirts and wings, thoroughly enjoying herself. Gwendoline had to comfort herself by thinking that she would find it easy to get Mam'zelle the next day. She would ask Mam'zelle to show her mother and Miss Winter the beautiful bedspread she was making. Mam'zelle would certainly love to do that – she was very proud of her bedspread!

'I wish this day wasn't over,' sighed Darrell that night. 'It was lovely – and what a smashing tea!'

She was happy because her mother and father hadn't said a word about her not being head-girl any longer – but each of them had managed to convey to her that they understood all about it, and were backing her valiantly – her father by an extra hard hug, and her mother by linking her arm in Darrell's and holding it very hard as she walked round the towers with her.

Felicity, of course, was mad with joy to see her parents again. 'I love Malory Towers!' she kept saying. 'Thank you for sending me here, Mummy and Daddy. I simply *love* it!'

Before the exam

The next day the girls expected most of their parents again, and could go out with them the whole day long. Clarissa stood at the window, looking out eagerly.

Gwendoline saw her. I suppose she's looking for her mother, she thought. Horrid thing. I shan't even speak to her!

She saw Clarissa suddenly wave in delight. Then she ran from the room and disappeared down the stairs. Gwen looked out to see what her mother was like – and if the car was a grand one.

To her surprise she saw an old car in the drive, and out of it stepped a most ordinary-looking woman. She had on a neat blue suit with a white blouse, and a scarf tied round her grey hair. She wore glasses, and had rather large feet in very sensible-looking shoes.

Well! I don't think much of Clarissa's mother – *or* her car! thought Gwen to herself. Why, the car hasn't even been *cleaned*! And fancy arriving with a scarf tied round her head! My mother would never dream of doing that!

She thought of her own mother with her large flowery hats, her flowery dresses, her flowery parasol, her floating scarves and strings of pearls. She would be ashamed of anyone like Clarissa's mother. She turned away, a sneer on her face, glad that she no longer meant to have Clarissa for a friend.

'What a *lovely* sneer!' said an aggravating voice, and Gwen saw Belinda whipping out her pencil. 'Hold it, Gwen, hold it!'

Gwen made a noise like a dog growling, and went out of the room. Now she must find Mam'zelle and tell her that her mother wanted to see the beautiful bedspread. This went down very well indeed, and Mam'zelle hurried to get it to show 'that nice kind Mrs Lacey'!

Every single girl was out for the whole day, either with her own parents or with someone else's. Miss Grayling was glad that the half-term came just before the School Certificate exam, so that the hard-worked girls might have a little time off to enjoy themselves. They really were working very hard, Miss Williams reported. Except Gwendoline Lacey, of course. *There* was an unsatisfactory girl for you!

By seven o'clock everyone was back – except Gwendoline!

'Where's our dear Gwendoline?' asked Alicia, looking round the supper-table. Nobody knew. Then Mam'zelle, looking rather solemn, enlightened them.

'Poor Gwendoline – she has been taken home because of her bad heart,' said Mam'zelle. 'She has the palpitations so bad, poor, poor child. And will you believe it, when I told Mrs Lacey – ah, the poor woman – about Gwendoline's affliction, she said that the dear, brave child had not complained to her, or said a single word. *Vraiment*, this poor child is to be admired!'

The girls digested this startling information in astonishment. They looked at one another. 'So Gwen's pulled it off after all,' said Sally. 'She'll miss the exam!'

Mam'zelle overheard. 'Yes, she will miss the exam – and how upset she was. "No, Mother," she said, so bravely, "I cannot go home with you – I must do the exam. I did not tell you of my trouble because I could not bear to miss the exam!" That is what she said. With my own ears I heard her.'

The upper fourth felt sick. What a sham! How hateful of Gwendoline to upset her mother like that! And she had got her way after all and would miss the exam. Clever, deceitful, sly Gwendoline!

'You were right, Connie,' said Alicia. '*How* right! Mam'zelle, what's going to happen to our darling Gwendoline Mary then? Isn't she coming back this term? *That* would be too good to be true!'

'I don't know,' said Mam'zelle. 'I know nuzzings more. I am glad I was able to tell Mrs Lacey. Just to think that if I had not taken my bedspread to show her, she would never have known.'

'I suppose *Gwen* asked you to take the bedspread?' said Connie. 'And I suppose one of her palpitations came on whilst you were there, Mam'zelle?'

'I do not understand why you talk in this sneering way, Connie,' said Mam'zelle, surprised. 'You must not be hard. You must have sympathy.'

The girls made various rude noises, which surprised Mam'zelle very much. Why these poohs and pahs and pullings of faces? No, no, that was not kind! Mam'zelle pursed up her lips and said no more.

'Well,' said Darrell, in the dormy that night, 'Gwen's got away with it all right – but fancy Mam'zelle falling for all that. Mam'zelle Rougier wouldn't. She sees right through Gwendoline – just like Miss Williams does!'

'All the same – she's lucky, getting out of the exam,' groaned Belinda. 'Wish I could! It's going to be awful to swot and swot all this week, after such a lovely half-term. And then – next Monday, the exam! I'm surprised you can't all hear my heart going down with a plop into my bedroom slippers!'

It was very hard to swot in such lovely weather. Alicia longed for a game of tennis. Darrell longed for the swimming-pool. Clarissa longed to go and laze in the flowery Court and watch the goldfish jumping. Belinda wanted to go out sketching. Irene became plagued with an enchanting tune that begged to be put down on paper – but poor Irene had to turn her back firmly on the lilting melody, and do pages and pages of French translation.

There was a lot of touchiness and irritability that week. The twins were on edge, especially Ruth, though she had less to fear in the exam than Connie, who was not nearly so well up to standard. Irene was touchy because she wanted to get at her beloved music and couldn't. Darrell was irritable because she was too hot. Mavis was hot and bothered because she thought she was going to have a sore throat – just as her voice seemed about to get right too!

Only Alicia seemed really cheerful and don't-carish, and this attitude infuriated the others at times. Alicia was always the one to finish her work first and go off to swim. She could do her work and whistle an irritating little tune all the time, which nearly drove the others frantic. She laughed at their earnest faces, and their heartfelt groans.

'It's not worth all this amount of misery,' she would say. 'It's only School Cert. Cheer up, Connie – don't look like a dying duck over that French.'

Connie flared up as she had done with Gwendoline. She banged her book down on the table and shouted. 'Be quiet! Just because things are easy for you to learn, you sneer at others who aren't so lucky! Wait till you have a bad headache and have to learn pages of French poetry. Wait till your mind goes fuzzy because you're tired and want to sleep, and you know you mustn't. Wait till you have a bad night and have to think of things to say in a composition. Then you won't be quite so hard and don't-carish and sneering, and you'll shut up that awful whistling, too!'

Alicia was startled. She opened her mouth to retaliate, but Sally spoke first.

'Connie doesn't really mean all that,' she said in her quiet, calm voice. 'We're all over-working and we're irritable and touchy. We'll be all right when the exam is over. After all, it's an important exam for us, and we're all taking it seriously and doing our best. Let's not squabble and quarrel when we want to save ourselves up for next week.'

Darrell looked at Sally in admiration. How did she always know the right thing to say? She had certainly poured oil on the troubled waters very successfully, because Connie spoke up at once.

'I'm sorry I said all that, Alicia. I *am* over-working and I'm touchy.'

'It's all right,' said Alicia, rather taken aback by this swift apology. 'Sorry about my whistling – and if anyone wants any help, they've only got to ask me. I'll share these envied brains of mine with anyone!'

After this there was peace. Alicia shut her book quietly and crept out. The others worked on in silence. Would they ever, ever know all they ought to know for the exam? Why hadn't they swotted more during the year? Why hadn't they done this and that and the other? In fact their thoughts were almost exactly the same as every other exam-class's thoughts the week before the exam!

The week went by, and the girls worked more and more feverishly. Miss Williams forbade any work to be done on the Sunday before the exam, and there were deep groans.

And then came a surprise. Gwendoline arrived back at Malory Towers!

She came back on the Saturday, just before supper, looking subdued and tearful. She had a short interview with Miss Grayling, and then was sent to join the others, who had just gone in to their supper.

'Why, GWEN!' said Mavis, in astonishment, seeing her first. 'We thought you weren't coming back.'

'Ah, here is Gwendoline back again,' said Mam'zelle. 'And how is the poor heart?'

'All right, thank you,' mumbled Gwen, slipping into her seat, and trying to look as if she was not there.

The girls saw that she had been crying and tried not to look at her. They knew how horrid it was to have people looking at red eyes.

'Jolly lucky you'll be, next week,' said Sally, trying to make light conversation. 'Whilst we're all answering exam papers, you'll be lazing away in the Court, doing what you like!'

There was a little pause. 'I've got to go in for the exam,' said Gwen, in a choking voice. 'That's why they've sent me back. It's too *bad*.'

To the girls' dismay, Gwendoline's tears began to fall fast into her plate of salad. They looked uncomfortably at one another. Whatever had happened?

'Better not say any more,' whispered Darrell. 'Don't take any notice of her. Poor Gwen!'

19

The exam week

Nobody ever knew what exactly had happened to Gwen. She was much too hurt and ashamed to tell anyone the story. So she said nothing, but went about subdued and red-eyed the whole weekend.

Everything had gone so well at first! Her frightened mother had taken her straight home after Mam'zelle had mentioned Gwen's strange heart flutterings and palpitations. She had made her lie down and rest, and she and Miss Winter had fussed over her like a hen with one chick. Gwendoline had loved every minute, and had at once produced the languid ways and the feeble voice of the invalid.

She was rather pleased to know that her father was away and not likely to be back at all that week. By that time Gwen hoped she would be established as a semi-invalid, would miss all the exam, and might then gradually get better, once the exam danger was over.

The doctor came and listened solemnly to Gwen's mother's frightened explanations. 'I'm *so* afraid it's her heart that's wrong, Doctor,' she said. 'The games are *very* strenuous at school, you know.'

The doctor examined Gwen carefully. 'Well, I can't find

anything wrong,' he said. 'Nothing that a week's rest won't put right, anyway. She's a bit fat, isn't she – she could do with a bit of dieting, I should think.'

'Oh, but Doctor – there *must* be something wrong with the child's heart,' insisted Mrs Lacey. 'Miss Winter and I have been very troubled to see how she loses her breath, and can hardly get up to the top stair when she goes to her bedroom.'

'Well – why not get another opinion then?' said the doctor. 'I should like you to satisfy yourself about Gwendoline.'

'I'll take her to a specialist,' said Mrs Lacey, at once. 'Can you recommend one, Doctor?'

The doctor could and did, and on Wednesday the languid invalid was carefully driven up to London to see the specialist recommended. He took one quick glance at Gwendoline and sized her up at once.

He examined her very carefully indeed, with so many 'hums' and 'hahs' that Gwendoline began to feel frightened. Surely she hadn't *really* got something the matter with her? She would die if she had!

The specialist had a short talk with Mrs Lacey alone. 'I will think over this, and will write to your doctor full details and let him know the result of my considerations. In the meantime, don't worry,' he said.

On Friday the doctor got a letter from the specialist, and it made him smile. There was nothing wrong with Gwendoline's heart, of course, in fact nothing wrong anywhere at all, except that she was too fat, and needed very much more exercise. 'Games, and more games, gym, walks, no rich food, no sweets, plenty of hard work, and no thinking about herself at all!' wrote the specialist. 'She's just a little humbug! Swimming especially would be good for her. It would take some fat off her tummy!'

The doctor had to paraphrase all this considerably, of course, when he telephoned the news to Mrs Lacey that there was nothing the matter with Gwen. 'I should send her back to school at once,' he said. 'It's not good for the girl to lie about like this.'

Gwen was angry and miserable when she heard all this. She laid her hand to her heart as if it pained her. 'Oh, Mother!' she said. 'I'll go back if you say so – but give me one more week – I feel so much better for the rest.'

Mrs Lacey promised Gwen that she should not go back for another week or more. Gwen was satisfied. So long as she missed the exam, she didn't mind!

Then her father arrived home, anxious because of his wife's letters and telephone calls about Gwen. Gwen lay on the couch and gave him a pathetic smile. He kissed her, and enquired anxiously what the specialist had said.

'What! *Nothing* wrong,' he said in astonishment. 'I'll go round and see the doctor. I'd like to see the specialist's letter myself. I shall feel more satisfied then.'

And so it came about that Gwen's father actually read the candid letter – saw that Gwen was called a 'little humbug' – knew very clearly indeed that once more his daughter had tried a little deception – a cruel deception, that had caused her parents much anxiety – and all because she had merely wanted to get out of working for the exam.

What he said to Gwendoline the girl never forgot. He was angry and scornful and bitter – and at the end he was sad. 'You are my only child,' he said. 'I want to love you and be proud of you, like all parents. Why do you make it so hard for me to be proud of you, and to love you, Gwendoline? You have made your mother ill with this, and you have made me angry and disgusted – and very sad.'

'I won't do it again,' sobbed Gwendoline, terrified and ashamed.

'You must go back to school tomorrow,' said her father.

'Oh no, Daddy! I can't! It's the exam,' wailed Gwendoline. 'I haven't done any work for it.'

'I don't care. Go in for it just the same, fail and be humiliated,' said her father. 'You have brought it all on yourself. I am telephoning Miss Grayling to apologize for taking you away, and to give her the specialist's instructions – games, more games, gym, walks – and most of all, swimming!'

Swimming! The one thing Gwen detested most of all. She dissolved into tears again and wept the whole of the evening and the whole of the way down to Cornwall the next day. What had she done to herself? She hadn't been so clever after all! It had all ended in her having to take the exam without working for it, and in having to go in for games more than ever – and probably swim every single day in that nasty cold pool! Poor Gwen. People do

148

often bring punishment on themselves for foolishness – but not often to the extent that Gwendoline did.

The exam began. Everyone was jittery – even Alicia, curiously enough. Day after day the work went on, whilst the bright July sun shone in through the open windows, and the bees hummed enticingly outside. The girls were glad to rush off to the swimming-pool after tea each day – then back again they went to swot up for the next day's exam.

Something curious had happened to Alicia. She didn't understand it. The first day she sat and looked at the questions, feeling sure they would be easy for her. So they were. But she found that she could not collect her thoughts properly. She put her hand up to her head. Surely she wasn't beginning a headache!

She struggled with the questions – yes, *struggled* – a thing the quick-witted, never-at-a-loss Alicia had hardly ever done before! She looked round at the others, puzzled – goodness, how could they write so quickly? What had happened to her?

Alicia had seldom known a day's illness. She was strong and healthy and clever. She really could not imagine why this exam was so difficult. She could not go to sleep at night, but lay tossing and turning. Had she been over-working? No – surely not – the others had worked far harder than she had, and had envied her for not having to swot so much. Well, *what* was it then?

Gosh, thought Alicia, trying to find a cool place on her pillow, I know what it must feel like now, to have slow brains like Daphne, or a poor memory like Gwendoline. I can't remember a thing – and if I try, my brains won't work. They feel as if they want oiling!

The others noticed that Alicia was rather quiet and subdued that week, but as they all felt rather like that, they said nothing. Quite a few of them went about looking very worried. Ruth looked white and drawn, Connie looked anxious, Gwendoline looked miserable, Daphne was almost in tears over the French – what a collection they were, thought Miss Williams – just like every other School Certificate form she had ever known, when exams were on. Never mind – it would be all behind them next week, and they would be in the highest spirits!

She glanced at one or two of the papers when they were collected. Darrell was doing fine! Gwendoline would be lucky if she got quarter marks! Mary-Lou was unexpectedly good. Connie's was poor – Ruth's was not good either. How strange! Ruth was usually well up to standard! It was doubtful if she would pass, if she completed the rest of her papers badly. And Alicia! Whatever in the world had happened to *her*? Bad writing – silly mistakes – good gracious, was Alicia playing the fool?

But Alicia wasn't. She couldn't help it. Something had happened to her that week and she was frightened now. It must be a punishment to me for always laughing and sneering at people who aren't as quick and clever as I am, she thought, in dismay. My brains have gone woolly and slow and stupid, like Gwen's and Daphne's. I can't remember a thing. How horrible! I'm trying so hard, too, that my head feels as if it's bursting. Is this what the others feel sometimes, when I laugh at them for looking so serious over their work? It's horrible, horrible, horrible! If only my brains would come back properly! I'm frightened!

'Is anything the matter, Alicia?' said Darrell, on the last day of the exam. 'You look all out.'

Alicia never complained, no matter what went wrong with her. 'No,' she said. 'I'm all right. It's just the exam.'

She sat next to Darrell for the exam. At the end of the last paper, Darrell heard a slight noise. She looked up and gave a cry. Alicia had fallen forward over her papers!

'Miss Williams! Alicia's fainted!' she called. Matron was called, and as soon as Alicia came round again, looking bemused and strange, she was taken to the san. Matron undressed her – and cried out in surprise.

'You've got *measles*, Alicia! Just *look* at this rash – I never saw anything like it in my life! Didn't you notice it before?'

'Well – yes – but I thought it was just a heat-rash,' said Alicia, trying to smile. 'Oh, Matron – I'm so glad it's only measles. I thought – I really thought my brains had gone this week. I felt as if I was going potty, and I was awfully frightened.'

Alicia felt so thankful when she got into bed and rested her aching head against the cool pillow. She felt ill, but happy. It was only measles she had had that awful week! It wasn't that her brains had really gone woolly and stupid – it wasn't a punishment sent to her for sneering at the others who were slower than herself – it was just – measles.

And with that Alicia fell asleep and her temperature began to go down. She felt much better when she awoke. Her brains felt better, too!

'I'm afraid you'll have no visitors or company this week, Alicia,' said Matron. 'Just your own thoughts!'

Yes – just her own thoughts. Thankfulness that she wasn't going to be slow and stupid after all – shame that she had been so full of sneers and sarcastic remarks to others not so clever as herself – sadness because she knew she must have done terrible papers, and would surely fail. She would have to take School Cert all over again! Blow!

Well, thought Alicia, her brains really at work again, as her strong and healthy body began to throw off the disease, well – I'd better learn my lesson – I shan't be so beastly hard again. But I honestly didn't know what it was like to have slow brains. Now I do. It's awful. Fancy having them all your life and knowing you can't alter them. I'll never sneer at others again. Never. At least, not if I can remember it. It's a frightful habit with me now!

It was indeed. Alicia was going to find it very hard indeed to alter herself – but still, she had taken the first important step – she had realized that there was something to alter! She would never be quite so hard again.

The exams were over at last! The girls went quite mad and the mistresses let them! The swimming-pool was noisy and full, the tennis-courts were monopolized by the upper fourth, the kitchen staff were begged for ice-creams and iced lemonade at every hour of the day – or so it seemed! Girls went about singing, and even sour-faced Mam'zelle

Rougier smiled to see them so happy after the exam.

Gwendoline wasn't very happy, of course. Miss Grayling had taken her father's instructions seriously, and Gwen was having more games, more walks – and more swimming – than she had ever had before. But it was no good complaining or grumbling. She had brought it all on herself – it was nobody's fault but her own!

The Connie affair

'Now we can have a good time for the rest of the term,' said Darrell, pleased. 'No more swotting – no more long preps even, because Miss Williams says we've done enough. We'll enjoy ourselves!'

'It ought to be a nice peaceful end of term, with no horrid happenings,' said Sally. 'When Alicia comes back, it will be nicer still.'

Sally was wrong when she said there ought to be a nice peaceful end of term, with no horrid happenings – because the very next day the Connie Affair began.

It began with quite small things – a missing rubber – an essay spoiled because a page was missing, apparently torn out – a lace gone from one of Connie's shoes.

Nobody took any notice at first – things always *were* missing anyhow and turned up in the most ridiculous places – and pages did get torn out of books, and laces had a curious habit of disappearing.

But the Connie Affair didn't end there. Connie was always in trouble about something! 'Now my French poetry book has gone!' she complained. 'Now my cotton has gone out of my work-basket.' Now this and now that!

'But, Connie – how is it that so many things happen to

you lately?' said Darrell, puzzled. 'I don't understand it. It's almost as if somebody was plaguing you – but who could it be? Not one of us would do silly, idiotic things like this – sort of first-form spite!'

Connie shook her head. 'I can't think who's doing it,' she said. 'I suppose it *is* someone. It can't be a series of accidents – there are too many of them.'

'What do *you* think about it, Ruth?' asked Darrell – but Connie answered first.

'Oh, Ruth can't think who does it, either. It's very upsetting for her, because twins are always so fond of one another. She's sweet, too – keeps on giving me her things when I lose mine.'

'Well, it's certainly most extraordinary,' said Darrell. 'I'm very sorry about it, it's a horrid thing to happen in the *fourth* form!'

The girls talked about the Connie Affair, as they called it, and puzzled about it. One or two of them looked at Gwendoline, wondering if she had anything to do with it.

'Don't you remember how Connie flared out at Gwen and put her finger on Gwen's weak spot – when she was putting over that nonsense about her heart?' said Daphne. 'And you know – Gwen *has* done these nasty tricks before. Don't you remember? She did them to Mary-Lou when we were in the second form.'

'Give a dog a bad name and hang him,' quoted Darrell. 'Just because Gwen did once do things like this, and got a bad name for it, doesn't mean we ought to accuse her of the same thing now. For goodness' sake wait a bit before we decide anything.'

'There speaks a head-girl,' said Irene.

Darrell flushed. 'I'm not head-girl,' she said. 'Wish I was. But seriously, it really is jolly strange, all this business. The things are so very *silly*, too – Connie's ink-pot was stuffed up with blotting-paper this morning, did you know?'

'Well!' said Belinda. 'How petty!'

'Yes – most of the things are petty and spiteful and quite futile,' said Darrell. 'You don't suppose they'll get any worse, do you? I mean – stop being petty and get harmful?'

'Let's hope not,' said Mavis. 'Here are the twins. Hallo, Connie – anything more to report?'

'Yes – somebody's cut my racket handle,' she said, and showed it to them. 'Just where I grip it! Mean, isn't it?'

'You can use mine, Connie. I told you,' said Ruth, who was looking very distressed. 'You can use anything of mine.'

'I know, Ruth – but supposing your things get messed up, too?' said Connie. 'I'd hate that.'

'It's all very, very strange,' said Irene, and hummed a new melody she had just composed. 'Tooty-tooty-tee!'

Mavis sang to it – 'It's all – very – strange! It's all – very – strange!'

'I say!' said Darrell. 'Your voice is coming back! That's just how you *used* to sing, Mavis! It is, really.'

'Yes, I know,' said Mavis, her face red with pleasure. 'I've tried it out when I've been alone – though that's not often here! – and *I* thought it had come back, too. Let me sing a song for you, and you can all tell me if you think I've got my voice back!'

She sang a song that the lower school had been learning. The girls listened spellbound. Yes – there was no doubt about it, Mavis's lovely, low, powerful voice had come back again – better than ever. And this time it was owned by a Somebody, not a Nobody, as it had been before!

'We shall once again hear you saying, "When I'm an opera singer and sing in Rome and New York and . . ."' began Darrell. But Mavis shook her head.

'No, you won't. You know you won't. I'm not like that now. Or am I? Do say I'm not!'

'You're not, you're not!' said everyone, anxious to reassure a girl they all liked.

Darrell clapped her on the back.

'I'm *so* glad, Mavis. That almost makes up for this horrid Connie Affair. You'll be able to have singing lessons again next term.'

For a day or two it seemed as if the Connie Affair was at an end. Connie did not report any more strange happenings. Then she came to the common-room almost in tears.

'Look!' she said, and held up her riding-whip. It was one she had won at a jumping competition and was very, very proud of.

The girls looked. Someone had gashed the whip all the way down, so that in places it was almost cut through. 'I had it out riding this afternoon,' said Connie, in a trembling voice. 'I came home and took my horse to the stable . . .'

'You took two horses,' said Bill. 'Yours and Ruth's, too. I saw you.'

'I took the horses to the stable,' said Connie, 'and left my whip there. When I went back to look for it, I found it like this!'

'Anyone in the stables?' said Darrell.

'No. Nobody at all. Bill had been there, of course, and June and Felicity had, too – and I and Ruth. Nobody else,' said Connie.

'Well, *one* of those must have done it,' said Darrell. 'But honestly I can't believe any of them *did*. Ruth and Bill certainly wouldn't. My sister Felicity wouldn't even think of such a thing. And I feel pretty certain June wouldn't either, much as I dislike that cheeky little brat.'

'Anyway, both the first-formers had gone by the time I'd stabled the horses,' said Connie. 'You didn't see them when we left, did you, Ruth?'

'No,' said Ruth.

'Did you notice anyone else at *all* when you were grooming your horse, Ruth?' asked Darrell, puzzled.

'She didn't even groom her horse,' Connie answered for her. 'I always do that. She stood there, looking at all the other horses, and would have seen anyone slinking round.'

Everyone was puzzled. Ruth went out of the room and came back with her own whip, a very fine one. 'You're to have this, Connie,' she said. 'I'm so upset about all these things happening. I insist on your taking my whip!'

'No, no,' said Connie. 'I don't mind taking things like rubbers and shoe-laces – but not your beautiful whip.'

That evening Darrell was alone with Bill. She was worried and puzzled. 'Bill,' she said, 'are you *sure* there was nobody else in the stable but you and the twins this afternoon? I suppose – er – well, Gwendoline wasn't there, was she?'

'No,' said Bill.

'I hated to ask that,' said Darrell, 'but it *is* just the kind of thing Gwen would do.'

'It's her own fault if we think things like that of her,' said Bill.

'Why does Connie groom Ruth's horse for her?' asked Darrell. 'Is Ruth so lazy? She's always letting Connie do things!'

'No. She's not lazy,' said Bill. 'She's just strange, I think – a shadow of Connie! Well, I must go and give Thunder a lump of sugar, Darrell. See you later.'

She went out and left Darrell thinking hard. A curious idea had come to her mind. She fitted one thing into another, like a jigsaw puzzle – she remembered all the unkind things that had been done to Connie, and she remembered also all the kind things that Ruth had done to try and put right the unkind things. She remembered also a strange look she had seen on Ruth's face that evening when Connie had refused Ruth's whip.

A kind of frightened, half-angry look, thought Darrell. Just as if she'd apologized to Connie, and the apology had been refused.

And then something clicked in her mind and she suddenly saw who the spiteful person might be that played all these petty tricks on Connie.

What am I to do about it? wondered Darrell. I can't tell anyone in case I'm wrong. It's got to be stopped. And I'm half afraid of going and tackling anyone to get it stopped. But I must! It's serious.

She got up and went in search of Ruth. Yes, it was Ruth she wanted, and Ruth she must tackle!

Darrell puts things right

Where was Ruth? She wasn't in the common-room or the dormy or the classroom. Where could she be?

'Anyone seen Ruth?' asked Darrell, when she met any girls in her search. Nobody had. But at last a second-former said she thought she had seen Ruth going into the gardeners' shed by the stables.

Darrell sped off to look. She came to the shed where the gardeners kept their tools, and stopped outside the door to try and think what she was to say.

As she stood there, she heard a curious sound. Some-body was certainly in the shed – and the sound was like a kind of groan. Darrell pushed open the door quietly and looked in.

Ruth was there, right at the back, sitting on some sacks. In her hand she held the cut and broken riding-whip, which she had obviously been trying to mend.

She didn't see Darrell at first. She put her hand over her face and made another sound – either a groan or a sob, Darrell didn't know which.

'Ruth,' said Darrell, going in. 'Ruth! What's the matter?'

Ruth leaped up in fright. When she saw it was Darrell she sat down on the sacks again, and turned her face away, still holding the broken whip.

'Ruth,' said Darrell, going right up to the girl, 'why did you spoil that lovely whip of Connie's?'

Ruth looked up quickly, amazement and dismay on her face. 'What do you mean?' she said. 'I didn't spoil it! Who said I did? Who said so? Did Connie?'

'No. Nobody said so. But I know you did,' said Darrell. 'And it was you who did all the other horrid things, wasn't it? Took this and that, hid things, and broke things, anything you could get hold of that belonged to Connie.'

'Don't tell anyone,' begged Ruth, clasping Darrell's hand tightly. 'Please don't. I won't do it again, ever.'

'But Ruth – why did you *do* it?' asked Darrell, very puzzled. 'Anyone would think that you hated your twin!'

Ruth slapped the broken whip against the sacks. She looked sulky. 'I *do* hate her!' she said. 'I always have done – but oh, Darrell, I love her, too!'

Darrell listened to this in surprise. 'But you can't love a person and hate them at the same time,' she said, at last.

'You can,' said Ruth, fiercely. 'You *can*, Darrell. I love Connie because she's my twin – and hate her because – because – oh, I can't tell you.'

Darrell looked for a long time at Ruth's bent head, and saw the tears rolling off her cheeks. 'I think I know why you hate Connie,' she said at last. 'Isn't it because she's so domineering – always answering for you, doing things for you that you'd rather do yourself – pushing herself in front of you – as if she was at least two years older?'

'Yes,' said Ruth, rubbing her wet cheeks. 'I never get a

chance to say what *I* think. Connie always gets in first. Of course, I know she must have a better brain than I have, but . . .'

'She hasn't,' said Darrell, at once. 'Actually she ought to be in the lower fourth, not in the upper. I heard Miss Williams say so. They only put her with you in the upper class because you were twins, and your mother said you wouldn't like to be separated. Connie only keeps up with the form because you help her so much!'

There was a silence. Darrell thought about everything all over again. How very strange this was! Then a question arose in her mind and she asked Ruth at once.

'Ruth – why did you *suddenly* begin to be so beastly to Connie? You never were before, so far as I noticed. It all seemed quite sudden.'

'I can't tell you,' said Ruth. 'But oh – I'm so miserable about it.'

'Well, if *you* won't tell me, I shall go and ask Connie,' said Darrell, getting up. 'Something's gone awfully wrong, Ruth, and I don't know if I can put it right, but I'm going to have a jolly good try.'

'Don't go to Connie,' begged Ruth. 'I don't want you to tell her it was me that was so beastly all the time. And oh, Darrell, I was so *sorry* for Connie, too, when I saw how upset she was at losing her things. It's dreadful to hate somebody and make them unhappy, and then to know you love them, and try to comfort them!'

'I suppose that's why you kept giving Connie your own things,' said Darrell, sitting down on a tub. 'Strange business, this! First you hate your twin and do something to upset her, like spoiling the riding-whip she loved – and then you love her and are sorry – and come to give her your own riding-whip! I could see you were upset when she didn't take it.'

'Darrell – I *will* tell you why I hated Connie so much lately,' said Ruth, suddenly, wiping her eyes with her hands. 'I feel I've got to tell someone. Well – it was something awful.'

'Whatever was it?' said Darrell, curiously.

'You see – Connie adores me, and likes to protect me and do everything for me,' began Ruth. 'And so far we have always been in the same class together. But Connie was afraid she would fail in School Cert and felt sure I would pass.'

'So you would,' said Darrell. 'And Connie would certainly fail!'

'Well – Connie thought that if she failed and I passed, I'd go up into the lower fifth next term, and she would have to stay down in the upper fourth and take the exam again another term,' went on Ruth. 'And that would mean she wouldn't be with me any more. So she asked me to do a bad paper, so that I would fail, too – and then we could still be together!'

Darrell was so astonished at this extraordinary statement that she couldn't say a single word. At last she found her tongue.

'*Ruth*! How wicked! To make you fail and feel humiliated when you could so easily pass! She *can't* love you.'

'Oh, but she does – too much!' said Ruth. 'Anyway, I said I *would* do a bad paper – somehow I just can't help doing what Connie wants, even if it's something horrid like that – so I *did* do a bad paper – and then afterwards I hated Connie so much for making me do it that I did all these horrible things to her!'

Poor Ruth put her face in her hands and began to sob. Darrell went and sat on the sacks beside her and put her strong comforting arm round Ruth's shoulders.

'I see,' she said. 'It's all very peculiar and extra-ordinary, but somehow quite understandable. It's because you're twins, I expect. Connie should have been your elder sister, then it wouldn't have mattered! You could have loved each other like ordinary sisters do, and you'd have been in different forms, and things would have been all right. Cheer up, Ruth. It's all been frightening and horrible to you, but honestly I can see quite well how it all happened.'

Ruth looked up, comforted by Darrell's simple explanation. She pushed her hair back and sniffed.

'Darrell, please, please don't tell Connie I did all those things,' she said. 'I'm awfully sorry now that I did. She wouldn't understand, and she'd be awfully upset and unhappy. I couldn't bear that.'

'Yes – but you can't go on like this – being bossed by Connie, and being just an echo for her,' said Darrell, sensibly. 'I don't see any way of stopping it except for us to tell her. I'll come with you if you like.'

But Ruth began to sob so much when Darrell

suggested this that Darrell had to give up the idea. A distant bell sounded and she got up. 'You'd better go and bathe your eyes,' she said kindly. 'I'll try and think of some way to put things right without telling Connie – but it's going to be difficult!'

Ruth went off, sniffing, but much comforted. Darrell rubbed her nose hard, as she often did when she was puzzled. 'There's only one thing to do!' she said. 'And that's to tell Miss Williams. *Something's* got to be done!'

So that evening, after supper, Miss Williams was astonished to find Darrell at her door, asking for an interview. She wondered if Darrell had come to beg to have her position as head-girl restored to her. But it wasn't that.

Darrell poured out the strange story of the twins. Miss Williams listened in the greatest amazement. The things that could go on in a school that nobody knew about, even though the girls concerned were under her nose all day long!

'So, you see, Miss Williams,' finished Darrell, 'if Ruth can't bear Connie to be told, everything is as bad as before! They'll both fail the exam, they'll both stay down in the upper fourth, instead of going up next term, and poor Ruth will go on being domineered over, and will hate and love Connie at the same time. It must be horrible.'

Very horrible, thought Miss Williams, horrified. And very dangerous. Things like this often lead to something very serious later on. She did not say this to Darrell, who sat earnestly watching her, waiting for some advice.

'Darrell, I think it was very clever of you to find this out,' said Miss Williams, at last. 'And you have acted very wisely all through. I do really feel very pleased with you.'

Darrell went red and looked pleased. 'Can you think how to put things right?' she asked. 'Oh, Miss Williams, *wasn't* it a pity that Ruth did a bad exam paper! If she hadn't, things would have got right of themselves – the twins would have been in different forms.'

'Darrell,' said Miss Williams after a pause, 'what I am going to say now is between you and me. I glanced at all the exam papers before sending them up – and Ruth didn't do quite as bad a one as she thought! In fact, I feel pretty certain she will scrape through.'

'Oh, *good*!' said Darrell, delighted. 'I never thought of that. So they'll be in different forms next term after all, then!'

'I think so,' said Miss Williams. 'That will give Ruth a chance to stand on her own feet and develop a personality of her own, instead of being Connie's shadow – and Connie will have to stop domineering over her – it will all disappear naturally and gradually, which is the best thing that could happen in this curious case.'

'Won't Connie know anything then?' asked Darrell. 'Won't she have to be told?'

'That will be Ruth's business, and no concern of anyone else's,' said Miss Williams. 'Some day, when the right time comes, she may choose to confess to Connie – and perhaps they will even laugh at it all. Keep an eye on Ruth for me, will you, Darrell, for the rest of the term?

You're in her confidence now and I shall trust you to see that nothing else goes wrong between the twins.'

'Oh, I will,' said Darrell, pleased to be asked this. 'I'd love to. I like Ruth.'

'And Darrell – I shall make you head-girl again in two days' time,' said Miss Williams. 'And this time I shall be very, very proud of you!'

'Ping!'

Everyone was delighted when Miss Williams announced in her quiet voice, two days later, that Darrell was once more to be head-girl of the form. 'Thank you for taking on the position temporarily,' she said to Sally. 'But I am now convinced that Darrell deserves to be promoted again.'

'Why, Darrell? Why has Miss Williams put you back as head this week?' asked Belinda and the others, after class. But Darrell didn't tell them, of course. Miss Williams hadn't actually said that it was because of her trying to put right the affair of the twins – but she knew that it was. She had really acted like a responsible head-girl then.

No more spiteful things were done to Connie, and gradually the Connie Affair, as it was called, was forgotten. Ruth seemed to forget her dislike and resentment, and was very sweet to Connie. Next term, thought Darrell, things will be quite all right – they'll be in different forms, and Ruth can go ahead with her good brains, and Connie can work at her own pace and keep her hands off Ruth.

The term was slipping away fast now. Alicia was better, and fortunately no one else had caught measles from her. Most of the upper fourth had already had them, which was fortunate. Alicia groaned because she felt sure she had failed – and would have to take the School Certificate all over again. She was to come back to school a week before breaking-up. The girls were very pleased. They had all missed Alicia's quickness and sense of fun. Gwendoline was perhaps the only one who didn't want her back. Poor Gwen – she had already lost some of her fat, through having to play so much tennis and go for so many walks, and swim – or try to – each day! But she certainly looked healthier, and her spots were rapidly going.

Clarissa amazed the class one day by coming back from a visit to the dentist and the optician looking completely different! 'I haven't got to wear glasses *any* more!' she announced. 'And that awful wire's been taken from my front teeth. Do you recognize me, girls?'

'Hardly!' said Darrell, and Belinda got out her pencil to make a sketch of this different and most attractive Clarissa!

She stood laughing in front of them – her deep green eyes flashing round, and her white teeth no longer spoiled by an ugly wire. Her wavy auburn hair suited her eyes, and she looked unusual and somehow distinguished.

'You'll be a beauty one day, Clarissa,' said Belinda, her artist's eye seeing Clarissa at twenty-one, lovely and unusual in her colouring. 'Well, well – talk about an ugly duckling turning into a swan!'

Clarissa was now fast friends with Bill, much to the girls' amusement. Nobody had ever thought that the boyish Bill, who seemed only to care for her horse Thunder, and for Miss Peters (but a good way behind Thunder!), would make a friend in her form. But she had, and the two chattered continually together, always about horses, and rode whenever they could. Gwendoline didn't care. Since she had seen Clarissa going off at half-term with the dowdy-looking elderly woman in the old car, she had taken no further interest in her.

Gwendoline wanted a grand friend, not somebody ordinary, whose people didn't even clean their old car when they came at half-term! So Gwen was once more alone, with no one to talk or giggle with, no one to call her friend.

'We ought to do something to celebrate Alicia coming back,' said Belinda. 'She's coming tomorrow.'

'Yes! Let's do something,' said Darrell, at once.

'Something mad and bad,' said Betty, who was in the Court with the others.

'A trick!' said Irene. 'We haven't played a trick for two whole terms. Think of it! What are we coming to? We must be getting old and staid.'

'Yes, let's play a trick,' said Sally. 'After all, the exams are over, and we worked jolly hard – we deserve a really good laugh!'

'What trick shall we play?' asked Mavis. 'Betty, didn't you bring anything back this term? Last term you brought back that awful spider that could dangle from the ceiling like a real one – but we never got a chance of using it. Gosh, I'd like to have seen Mam'zelle's face if we had managed to let it down over her desk!'

Everyone giggled. 'I didn't bring it back with me this

171

term,' said Betty, regretfully. 'I stayed with Alicia in the hols and one of her brothers bagged it. But I tell you what I *have* got!'

'What?' asked everyone, getting thrilled.

'I haven't tried them yet,' said Betty. 'They're awfully odd things. They're little grey pellets, quite flat. One side is sticky, and you stick it to the ceiling.'

'What happens?' asked Irene.

'You have to dab each pellet with some kind of liquid,' said Betty, trying to remember. 'At least, I *think* that's right – and then, according to the instructions, a strange bubble detaches itself slowly from the pellet, floats downwards, and suddenly pops – and makes a pinging sound.'

Everyone listened in delight. '*Betty*! It's too marvellous for words!' said Irene, thrilled. 'Let's play the trick tomorrow, to celebrate Alicia's coming back. We'll have to get the step-ladder to put some of the pellets on the ceiling. Let's do it when Mam'zelle takes us. She's always fun to play tricks on.'

So, with much secrecy, the step-ladder was hidden in the cupboard outside the upper fourth classroom, and just before morning school, three flat grey pellets were quickly fixed to the ceiling where, quite miraculously, so it seemed to the girls, they stuck very tightly indeed, and could hardly be seen at all.

Betty brushed each one over quickly with the liquid from a small bottle sent with the pellets. Then the ladder was bundled into the cupboard again, just as Mam'zelle's high heels were heard tip-tapping down the corridor.

Daphne flew to hold the door open, and the others stood ready in their places.

'*Merci*, Daphne,' said Mam'zelle, briskly. 'Ah, Alicia – it is very, very good to see you back. You have had a bad time with your measle?'

'Well, actually I didn't mind my measle very much, after the first day,' said Alicia, with a grin. She was looking very well now.

'It is good that no one got the measle from you,' said Mam'zelle, sitting down at her desk.

'I had a measle last year,' said Irene, and this was the signal for everyone to talk about when they had a measle, too. Mam'zelle had to bring the talk to an end, because it showed signs of getting very boisterous.

'We will have no more measly talk,' she said, firmly, and wondered why the girls laughed so much at this.

They took quick, surreptitious glances at the ceiling every now and again, longing to see the new trick at work. Alicia had heard all about it, of course, and was thrilled with their novel way of celebrating her return. She had suggested that everyone should pretend they could not see the bubbles, or hear the 'ping' when they exploded.

'Mam'zelle will think she's gone crackers,' she said. 'I know I should if I saw bubbles that pinged round me when nobody else did!'

'Today I go through the questions that you answered on the exam paper,' said Mam'zelle, smiling round. 'You will tell me what you put and I will say if it was good or no.'

'Oh, *no*, Mam'zelle,' protested Alicia. 'We had to do the exam – let's forget it now it's over. Anyway, I did such a frightful paper, I've failed, I know. I can't bear to think of the exam questions now.'

Irene nudged Belinda. One of the grey pellets was beginning its performance. A small grey bubble was beginning to form up on the ceiling. It grew a little bigger, became heavy enough to detach itself, and floated gently down into the air. All three pellets had been placed just above the big desk belonging to Miss Williams, where Mam'zelle was now sitting.

With bated breath the girls watched the bubble slowly descend. It looked as if it was about to fall on Mam'zelle's head, decided not to, and skirted round her hair, near her left ear. When it got there, it burst suddenly, and a curious sharp, very metallic 'ping' sounded.

Mam'zelle almost jumped out of her skin. '*Tiens*!' she said. '*Qu'est-ce que c'est que ça*? What was that?'

'What was what, Mam'zelle?' asked Sally, innocently.

'A ping – *comme ça*!' said Mam'zelle, and pinged again. 'Ping! Did you not hear a ping, Sally?'

'A ping? What exactly do you mean, Mam'zelle?' asked Sally, putting on a puzzled look that made Darrell want to cry with laughter. 'You don't mean a *pong*, do you?'

'Perhaps she means a ping-pong,' suggested Irene, and began to giggle. So did Mavis. Darrell frowned at them.

'I sit here, and suddenly in my ear there comes a *ping*!' said Mam'zelle. 'I feel it on my ear.'

'Oh, I thought you meant you *heard* it,' said Sally.

Last week of term

By this time, of course, the girls were almost helpless with laughter. Tears were pouring down Darrell's cheeks and Sally was holding her sides, aching with laughter. Irene appeared to be choking and Alicia and Betty were holding on to each other helplessly.

Mam'zelle rushed to Miss Williams. She was taking a class in the second form, and was amazed at Mam'zelle's sudden entrance.

'Miss Williams! I beg you to come with me to your classroom,' Mam'zelle besought the astonished Miss Williams. 'It goes "ping" and it goes "pong" – right in my ears – yes, and down by my foot.'

Miss Williams looked astounded. Was Mam'zelle off her head? What was all this ping and pong business? The second form began to giggle.

'Mam'zelle, what exactly do you mean?' asked Miss Williams, rather crossly. 'Be more explicit.'

'In your classroom there are pings and pongs,' said Mam'zelle again. 'The girls do not hear them, but I do. And I, I do not like it. Miss Williams, come, *je vous prie*!'

As it looked as if Mam'zelle was about to go down on her knees, Miss Williams got up hurriedly and went with her to the upper fourth. The girls had recovered a little and were on the watch to see who might be coming. One or two more bubbles had floated down and burst with sharp pings, and another was just about to descend.

'Sssst! It's Miss Williams,' said Mavis, suddenly, from the door. 'Straighten your faces.'

With difficulty the girls pulled their faces straight, and stood up as Miss Williams entered with Mam'zelle.

'What is all this?' asked Miss Williams, impatiently. 'What is it that Mam'zelle is complaining of? I can't make head or tail of it.'

'It is a ping,' wailed Mam'zelle, beginning to despair of making Miss Williams understand.

'I think Mam'zelle has noises in her ears,' said Alicia, politely. 'She hears pings and pongs, she says.'

A bubble fell near Mam'zelle and burst. 'Ping!'

Mam'zelle jumped violently and dug Miss Williams unexpectedly in the ribs with her finger. 'There it comes again. Ping, it said!'

'Don't poke me like that, Mam'zelle,' said Miss Williams, coldly, whereupon another bubble burst, and yet another, and two pings sounded almost together. Miss Williams began to look puzzled.

'I go,' said Mam'zelle, and took a step towards the door. 'I go. There is something ABOMINABLE in this room!'

Miss Williams firmly pulled Mam'zelle back. 'Mam'zelle, be sensible. I heard the noise, too. I cannot imagine why the girls do not hear it.'

The girls suddenly decided they had better hear the

next ping – so, when it came, they all called out together.

'Ping! I heard it, I heard it!'

'Silence,' said Miss Williams, and the girls stopped at once – just in time for a bubble to descend on Mam'zelle's nose and explode with an extra loud ping.

Mam'zelle shrieked. 'It was a bobble! I saw a bobble and it went ping.'

Miss Williams began to think that Mam'zelle really must be mad this morning. What was this 'bobble' now?

And then Miss Williams herself saw a 'bobble' as Mam'zelle called it. The bubble sailed right past her nose, and she gasped. It pinged beautifully on the desk and disappeared.

Miss Williams looked silently up at the ceiling. Her sharp eyes saw the three flat pellets there – and saw a bubble forming slowly on one. She looked back at the girls, who trying not to laugh but not succeeding very well, gazed back innocently at her.

Miss Williams' lips twitched. She didn't know what the girls had done, nor exactly what the trick consisted of – but she couldn't help feeling that it was very ingenious – yes, and very funny, too, especially when played on someone like poor Mam'zelle Dupont, who could always be relied on to take fright at anything unusual.

'Mam'zelle, take your class out into the Court to finish the lesson,' she said. 'There will be no pings there. And if I were you, I would give the cleaner instructions to take a broom and sweep the ceiling before you next take a class in this room.'

This last suggestion reduced Mam'zelle to a state of such astonishment that she could only stand and stare after Miss Williams' departing figure. Sweep the *ceiling*! Was Miss Williams in her right mind?

The class began to giggle again at Mam'zelle's astounded face – and then as another ping sounded Mam'zelle plunged for the door. '*Allons*! We go to the Court,' she said. 'We have been much disturbed. Come now, we will leave behind these bad pings and pongs and go to do some work.'

The story of the pellets and their pings flew through the school and made every girl gasp and laugh. There were so many visitors to the upper-fourth form room that Miss Williams grew quite cross.

She stood a broom by the door. 'Anyone else who comes can sweep the ceiling six times,' she said. 'And let me tell you, it's not as easy as it looks!'

'Oh – that *has* done me good,' said Alicia that night. 'I've never laughed so much in my life. Mam'zelle's face when that first bubble pinged! I nearly died!'

'Miss Williams was rather a sport about it, wasn't she?' said Darrell. 'She spotted the trick all right, and wanted to laugh. I saw her lips twitching. I'll be sorry to leave her form and go into the fifth.'

'Yes – next term most of us will be up in the fifth,' said Sally. 'Goodness, how strange it will seem to be so far up the school.'

'I've liked this term,' said Darrell, 'although it had its horrid bits – like when I lost my place as head-girl.'

'I was glad when you got it back again,' said Ruth, speaking suddenly on her own, as she had done several times lately. She looked affectionately at Darrell. She had had a great admiration for her ever since Darrell had put things right for her – and had not told Connie. Miss Williams had quite casually told Ruth that although she had been disappointed in her exam paper, she thought probably she had passed all right – and that if Connie didn't, she hoped Ruth wouldn't very much mind her twin being left down in the fourth, whilst she, Ruth, went up into the fifth.

So it looked as if things would be better next term. Connie would soon get over the separation and, after all, they would continually see each other in the dormy and at meal-times.

The last few days of the term flew by. The breaking-up day seemed to come all at once. The usual pandemonium broke out. Mistresses began to feel as if they were slowly going mad as girls whirled past them, shouting and calling, and trunks were hurled about, night-cases lost, rackets strewn all over the place, and an incessant noise raged in every tower.

The train-girls went off first, and were loudly cheered as the coaches moved off down the drive. 'Write to us! See you next term! Be good if you can! Hurrah!'

Darrell went to find Felicity, who seemed to be continually disappearing. She found her exchanging addresses with Susan. June had gone with the train-girls, and Darrell had noticed that Felicity had not even bothered to wave good-bye to her. So *that* friendship was finished with. Good! Darrell still thought of June with dislike, but now that her little sister was no longer dragged around by June, but was standing on her own feet, she had lost the desire to scold June hard!

'Felicity! As soon as I find you and stand you by the front door, you disappear again,' said Darrell. 'Daddy will be here soon with the car. For goodness' sake come with me and don't leave me again. Where's your riding-hat? You've got to take it home with you in case you go riding in the hols.'

'It was here a minute ago,' said Felicity, looking round. 'Oh, no, look – that pest of a Katie has got it – what an ass she looks – her head's miles too big for it. Katie! KATIE! Give me my RIDING-HAT!'

'Felicity! Is there any *need* to yell like that?' said Miss Potts as she hurried by, almost deafened.

'Oh, Potty, I haven't said good-bye to you, Potty!' yelled Felicity. Darrell felt quite shocked to hear Felicity call her form-mistress Potty.

'Felicity!' she said. 'Don't call her that.'

'Well! You told me that everyone was allowed to on the last day of term,' said Felicity. 'POTTY!'

Belinda came by with Irene's music-case. 'Anyone seen Irene? She wants her music-case and I've just found it.'

She disappeared and Irene came along, groaning. 'Where's my wretched music? I put it down for a moment and some idiot has gone off with it.'

'Belinda's got it. Hey, Belinda, BELINDA!'

Mam'zelle came walking by with her fingers in her ears and an agonized expression on her face. 'These girls! They have gone mad! I am in an asylum. Why do I teach mad girls? Oh, this noise, it goes through my head.'

'Mam'zelle! MAM'ZELLE! Good-bye. My car's come.'

'*Au revoir*, Mam'zelle. I say, is she deaf?'

'Hurrah! There's our car. Come on, Irene.'

Clarissa came by, excitement making her green eyes gleam. She looked very pretty. 'Mummy's come,' she shouted to Bill. 'Come and see her. She wants to know if you can come and stay with me in the hols. Bill, come and see my mother!'

Gwendoline went out at the same time as Bill and Clarissa. Drawn up by the great flight of steps was a magnificent limousine, gleaming and shining. Leaning out was a charming, auburn-haired woman, beautifully dressed. A most distinguished-looking man sat beside her.

'Mother!' shrieked Clarissa. 'You've come at last. This is Bill. You said you'd ask her to stay in the hols!'

Gwendoline gaped in amazement to see this gleaming car, and such parents – parents to be really proud of! But – how could they be Clarissa's? Hadn't Gwen seen her dowdy grey-haired mother come and fetch her one Sunday at half-term, in an old car?

'Good-bye, Gwen,' said Clarissa, seeing her standing near, but she did not offer to introduce the girl to her mother.

'I thought that was your mother who came to take you out at half-term,' said Gwen, unable to stop herself from looking surprised.

'Oh, no – that was my dear old governess,' said Clarissa, getting into the car. 'Mother couldn't come, so Miss Cherry popped over in her old car to take me out instead. Fancy thinking she was my *mother*!'

Gwen's car was just behind, and Mrs Lacey was looking out and waving.

'Gwen! How are you? Oh, you *do* look well! Who was that pretty, attractive child that just went away in the beautiful limousine. Is she in your form?'

'Yes,' said Gwen, kissing her mother.

'Oh, I *do* hope she is a friend of yours,' said her mother. 'Just the kind of girl I'd like.'

'You saw her at half-term,' said Gwen, sulkily. 'And you *didn't* like her. That's Clarissa Carter.'

Darrell and Felicity looked at each other and giggled. How sorry Gwen must be that she didn't get Clarissa's friendship! As it was, it was Bill who was going to spend most of the holidays with Clarissa, and not Gwen. Poor Gwen as usual wouldn't be asked anywhere.

'There's our car!' cried Felicity suddenly. She caught Mam'zelle round the waist. 'Good-bye, dear Mam'zelle. See you next term!'

'Ah, dear child!' said Mam'zelle, quite overcome at Felicity's sudden hug. She kissed her soundly on each cheek and everyone grinned at Felicity's startled expression.

'Good-bye!' cried Darrell, waving to the rest of the girls. 'See you in September. Look out, Belinda, you're treading on somebody's hat!'

'It's mine, it's mine,' shrieked Felicity, in anguish.

'Take your great foot off it, Belinda.'

'You teach your young sister to be polite to her elders!' called Belinda, as Darrell and Felicity went headlong down the steps, almost knocking over poor Matron.

'Good-bye, Matron! Good-bye, Miss Williams! Good-bye, Potty! Hallo, Mother! Daddy, you look fine! Hurrah, hurrah, it's holidays!'

And into the car piled the two girls, shouting, laughing, happy and completely mad. They leaned out of the window.

'Good-bye! Happy hols! See you soon again! Good old Malory Towers – we'll come back in September!'

In the Fifth at

Malory Towers

Contents

Going back

'Felicity! Look – there's Malory Towers at last!' cried Darrell. 'I always look out for it at this bend. This is where we catch a glimpse of it first.'

Felicity gazed at the big square-looking building of grey stone standing high up on a cliff by the sea. At each corner was a rounded tower.

'North Tower, East Tower, South Tower, West Tower,' said Felicity. 'I'm glad we're in North Tower, overlooking the sea. Are you glad to be going back, Darrell?'

'Yes, awfully. Are you?' asked her sister, still with her eyes glued to the gracious building in the distance.

'Yes, I am really. But I do hate saying good-bye to Mummy and Daddy, and the dogs and the cat, and . . .'

'The robin in the garden and the six hens and the ducks and the goldfish and the earwigs on the veranda!' finished Darrell, with a laugh. 'Don't be such a goose, Felicity. You know quite well that as soon as you set foot in the grounds of Malory Towers you'll love being there!'

'Oh yes, I know I shall,' said Felicity. 'But it's quite a different world from the world of home. And it's a bit difficult suddenly going from one to the other.'

'Well, all I can say is – we're lucky to have two such

marvellous worlds to live in!' said Darrell. 'Home – and Malory Towers! Look, who's that in that car?'

Felicity leaned out to see. 'It's June,' she said. 'June – and Alicia, her cousin.'

Darrell snorted. She didn't like the first-former June. 'Don't you go and get friendly with that sly, brazen little June again,' she warned Felicity. 'You know what happened last term. You stick to Susan.'

'I'm going to,' said Felicity. 'You needn't tell me things like that. I'm not a new girl now. I'm in my second term.'

'Wish I was!' said Darrell. 'I hate to think that every term the day I leave comes nearer.'

'Well, it's the same for me,' said Felicity. 'Only I don't bother about it yet with so many terms in front of me. I say – fancy you being a fifth-former this term! In the fifth at Malory Towers – gosh, it does sound grand. And me only a first-former.'

'Yes. You first-formers do seem babies to me now,' said Darrell. 'Absolute kids! It's funny to think how I looked up to the fifth-formers when I was in the first, and hardly dared to speak to one; and if one spoke to me I almost fell through the ground. I don't notice anything like that about *you*, young Felicity!'

'Oh, well – I suppose it's because you're my sister,' said Felicity. 'I'm not falling through the ground just because you address a few words to me – no, not even if you are made head-girl of the fifth!'

'Well, I shan't be,' said Darrell. 'I had my share of responsibility last term when I was head of the upper fourth. Anyway, I'd like to sit back and take a bit of a rest from responsibility this term. Last term was pretty hectic, what with being head-girl, and having to go in for School Certificate, too!'

'But thank goodness you passed!' said Felicity, proudly. 'And with all those credits, too! Did everyone in the upper fourth pass, do you know?'

'Not Gwen. Nor Alicia,' said Darrell. 'You remember she got measles during the exam? And Connie, Ruth's twin, didn't pass either. She'll be left down in the fourth, thank goodness. Now Ruth will be able to say a few words on her own!'

Connie and Ruth had both been in the upper fourth the term before, and the girls had often felt cross because Connie never gave Ruth a chance to speak for herself, but always answered for her. She looked after Ruth as if she were a baby sister, not a girl of her own age, nearly sixteen! Now, with Connie in a form below, Ruth would have a chance of being herself instead of Connie's shadow. That should be interesting.

'Here we are – sweeping into the drive!' said Felicity. 'Mother – do look at Malory Towers. Isn't it super?'

Her mother turned round from the front seat of the car and smiled at the two enthusiastic faces behind her.

'Quite super, as you call it,' she said.

'In fact, smashing!' said Mr Rivers, who was at the wheel. 'Isn't that the right word, too, Felicity? It's the word I seem to have heard you use more than any other these holidays.'

3

The girls laughed. 'The lower school call everything smashing or smash,' said Darrell, in rather a superior voice.

'And the upper school are too la-di-da for words!' began Felicity, eager to retaliate. But nobody heard because Mr Rivers came to a stop near the great flight of steps, and immediately they were all swamped in crowds of excited girls running here and there from cars and coaches. The train-girls had just arrived in the coaches that brought them from the station, and there was such a tremendous noise of yelling and shouting and hooting of car horns that it was impossible to hear what anyone said.

'DARRELL!' screamed somebody, putting an excited face in at the window. 'Good! I hoped you wouldn't be late. Sally's here somewhere.'

The face disappeared, and another one came. 'FELICITY! I thought it was you. Come on out!'

'Susan! I'm just coming!' shouted Felicity, and leaped out so suddenly that she fell over a pile of lacrosse sticks and almost knocked over a tall girl standing nearby saying good-bye to her people.

'Felicity Rivers! Look where you're going,' said a wrathful voice, and Felicity blushed and almost fell through the ground. It was Irene speaking, Irene who was now a fifth-former. Darrell grinned to herself. Aha! Felicity might cheek one fifth-former, her own sister – but she was still in awe of the big girls after all!

'Sorry, Irene,' said Felicity in a meek voice. 'Frightfully sorry.'

Darrell jumped out too and was immediately surrounded by her friends.

'Darrell! I'll help you in with your things!'

'Hallo, Darrell, did you have good hols? I say, you passed your School Cert. jolly well. Congratulations!'

'Darrell Rivers! You never answered my letter last hols! And I wrote you pages!'

Darrell grinned round at the laughing faces. 'Hallo, Alicia! Hallo, Sally! Irene, you nearly made my people fall out of the car when you screamed in at the window just now. Hallo, Belinda! Done any good sketching in the hols?'

Mrs Rivers called out from the car, 'Darrell! We shall be going in a few minutes, dear. Tell Sally to come and have a word with me.'

Sally was Darrell's best friend, and her mother was a great friend of Mrs Rivers. She came up to the car and Mrs Rivers looked at her with approval. Sally had once been such a prim, plain little first-former – now she had blossomed out into a pretty, bonny girl, sturdy and dependable, with very nice manners.

Mrs Rivers had a few words with her and then looked round for Darrell, who was still talking away to a crowd of her friends. Felicity was nowhere to be seen.

'We must go now,' she said to Sally. 'Just tell Darrell and Felicity, will you?'

'Darrell! You're wanted!' shouted Sally, and Darrell turned and ran to the car. She was already half-lost in the world of Malory Towers.

'Oh, Mummy – are you going? Thanks for the most lovely hols. Where's Felicity?'

Felicity was not to be found. So thrilled was she at being back and hearing the excited voices of her friends that she had gone off with them without another thought! Darrell went to look for her.

'Anyone seen Felicity?'

Plenty of people had but nobody knew where she was. Blow her! She's gone up to her dormy, I suppose, to see what bed she's got this term, thought Darrell, and sped up to find her. But she wasn't there. Darrell went down again and out to the car.

'I can't find her anywhere, Mummy,' she said. 'Can you wait a bit?'

'No, we can't,' said Mr Rivers, impatiently. 'I've got to get back. Tell Felicity we waited to say good-bye. We must go.'

He gave Darrell a hug and then she hugged her mother, too. Mr Rivers put in the clutch and the car moved slowly off.

There was a shriek behind him. 'Daddy! Don't go without saying good-bye!' Felicity had appeared from nowhere. 'You were going without saying good-bye. You were!'

'I was,' said her father, with a grin exactly like Darrell's. 'Can't wait about for girls who forget their mother and father a quarter of a minute after arriving.'

'I didn't forget you, of course I didn't,' protested Felicity. 'I just wanted to go and see our form-room. It's all been

done up in the hols and looks super. Good-bye, Daddy.'
She gave him a bear-hug that almost knocked off his hat.

She ran round to the other side and gave her mother a hug, too. 'I'll write on Sunday. Give my love to the gardener, and the dogs, and . . .'

The car was moving! She and Darrell stood waving as the car made its way slowly down the crowded drive. Then it moved out of the gate with other cars, and was gone.

Felicity turned to Darrell with shining eyes. 'Isn't it fun to be back again? Did you feel like that your second term, Darrell? I'm not nervous or shy any more as I was last term. I belong now. I know everyone. It's smashing!'

She tore up the steps at top speed and collided with Mam'zelle Dupont.

'*Tiens*! Another mad girl! Felicity, I will not have you . . .'

But Felicity was gone. Mam'zelle's face broke into a smile as she gazed after her. 'These girls! Anyone would think they were glad to be back.'

More arrivals

The first day of term and the last day were always exciting. Nobody bothered about rules and regulations, everyone talked at the top of their voices, and as for *walking* down the corridors or up the stairs, well, it just wasn't done, except by the staid sixth-formers and the mistresses.

It was fun to go and see what bed you had in the dormy, and whose bed was next to yours. It was fun to go and peep into your classroom and see if it looked any different. It was fun to say how-do-you-do to all the mistresses, and especially to tease Mam'zelle Dupont. Not Mam'zelle Rougier, though, the other French mistress. She was as sharp as Mam'zelle Dupont was simple, and as irritable as the other was good-tempered. Nobody ever teased Mam'zelle Rougier.

Darrell went to look for the rest of her friends in the fifth form. Fifth form! How grand it sounded! She was actually in the fifth now, with only one more form to go into. Oh dear – she was certainly getting very grown-up.

Alicia and Sally came up, with Irene and Belinda. 'Let's go and see our new classroom,' said Darrell. 'The fifth! My goodness!'

They all went along together. The new classroom was an extremely nice one, high up and overlooking the cliff. Down below was the blue Cornish sea, as blue as corn-flowers today, the waves tipped with snowy white.

'I say – this is a wizard room, isn't it?' said Alicia, looking round. 'Lovely windows and view – nice pictures – and all done up in cream and green.'

'Any new girls, does anyone know?' asked Darrell, leaning out of the window and sniffing the salty sea air.

'There's someone called Maureen coming,' said Irene. 'I heard about her. The school she was at shut down suddenly, when the Head died – and she's coming here. I don't know anything about her, though.'

'I suppose *you're* coming into the fifth, Alicia?' said Sally. 'I mean – I know Connie's been left down in the fourth because she didn't pass her School Cert. – and you didn't either, because you had the measles. But surely you won't be left down?'

'Oh no. I'm up all right!' said Alicia. 'Gosh, I wouldn't have come back if I hadn't been put up with the rest of you. Miss Grayling wrote to Mother and said I could pass School Cert. on my head any time I liked – and I could go up into the fifth with you, and work for School Cert. on the side, so to speak.'

'Anyone left down with us from the old fifth form?' asked Darrell.

'Yes – Catherine Gray and Moira Linton,' said Irene, promptly. There were groans from the others.

'Oh, I *say* – two of the worst of them!' said Sally. 'I

never did like Moira – hard, domineering creature! Why has she been left down?'

'Well, actually she's a year young for the sixth,' said Irene, 'so they said she'd better stay down a year – but personally I think she was so unpopular that they just dropped her thankfully and went on without her!'

'What about Catherine?' asked Sally.

'She hasn't been well,' said Irene. 'Worked herself too hard, or something. She's pretty pious, isn't she? I don't really know much about her. She's one of those girls that don't make much impression from a distance.'

'Well, as far as we're concerned, that's like three new girls, then,' said Darrell. 'Catherine, Moira and Maureen. Who'll be head-girl?'

'You or Sally,' said Irene, promptly.

'No. I don't think so,' said Darrell. 'I imagine it will have to be either Catherine or Moira – after all, they've been fifth-formers for ages. It wouldn't be fair to put an ex-fourth-former over them at once.'

'No. You're right,' said Alicia. 'Gosh, I hope it isn't Moira, then. She does love to get her own way! Did you hear how she set all the second-formers a long poem to learn last term, to go and say at Monitors' Meeting, just because one of them wrote a poem about her, and nobody would own up to it? Every single one of them had to learn 'Kubla Khan'. They did howl about it!'

'Yes. I remember now,' said Darrell. 'Oh well, I dare say we shall manage Moira all right.'

'If you don't lose your temper with her too often!'

said Irene, with a sly grin. Darrell's hot temper was well known. She had tried to conquer it for terms and terms, and just when she prided herself on really having got the better of it at last, out it came again.

Darrell looked ruefully at the others. 'Yes. I'll have to be careful. I lost it really well last term, didn't I, Alicia, with that brazen young cousin of yours, June? I hope she behaves better this term!'

'She came to stay with us in the hols,' said Alicia. 'I've got three brothers, you know – and when June actually dared to disobey Sam, he gave her the choice of doing all his chores or running round our paddock twenty times each day!'

'And which did she choose?' asked everyone.

'Oh, running round the paddock, of course,' said Alicia. 'And Mother was awfully surprised to see her going round and round it each day like that. She thought she was training for sports or something! Sam stood and watched her, grinning like anything. So she *may* be better this term!'

'She can do with a lot of improvement!' said Darrell. 'I say – what in the world's that?'

It was the sound of thunderous hooves out in the drive somewhere – so thunderous that the noise even came round to the back of Malory Towers and was heard in the classroom where the five girls stood listening.

'*I* know! It's old Bill back – and her brothers have brought her as usual – all on horseback!' cried Belinda, rushing out of the room. 'Come along – let's go into the art-room and look out of the window. We can see the drive from there.'

They were soon leaning out of the high window. They saw a sight which they had already seen two or three times before, and were never tired of!

Wilhelmina, called Bill for short, had arrived on her horse, Thunder – and accompanying her were six of her seven brothers, all on horseback, too. What a sight they were, six well-grown boys, ranging from seventeen down to ten, with Bill, their sister, in the midst.

'Whoa there! Now then, quiet, quiet!'

'Thunder! We're here!'

'Bill, here's your case.'

Clippity-clop, clippity-clop went the hooves of the seven grand horses, curvetting about the broad drive. 'Hrrrrrrrumph!' said one of them, and then all seven neighed together.

'Bill, where can we let the horses drink?' came the deep voice of the seventeen-year-old brother.

'Follow me,' said Bill, and the six brothers trotted up the drive and round a corner, following the girl sitting so straight on her magnificent horse, Thunder.

'Gosh!' said Alicia. 'What a horde of brothers. Where's the seventh?'

'Gone into the army,' said Sally. 'My word – I wish *I* had seven brothers.'

'Well, I've got three and that's more than enough,' said Alicia. 'No wonder Bill's more like a boy than a girl.'

'Here they come again!' said Irene. 'Belinda, where's

your sketch-book – do draw them all!'

Belinda had already got out her sketch-book which was always somewhere about her person. Her swift pencil sketched in horse after horse, and the others watched in admiration. Oh, to have a gift like Belinda's! She could draw anyone and anything.

The seven horses seemed to know that Bill and Thunder were to be left behind. They lifted their heads and whinnied softly. Bill leaned over and stroked the noses of those nearest to her.

'Good-bye, Moonlight. Good-bye, Starlight. Good-bye, Snorter. Good-bye, Sultan . . .'

'She's paying a lot more attention to the horses than to her brothers!' said Alicia, with a grin. 'That's Bill all over, of course – horse-mad!'

'Well, her brothers are as bad!' said Sally. 'Look – yelling good-bye to Thunder but not to Bill!'

'Off they go,' said Darrell, envying Bill her brothers. 'Look at Thunder, trying to follow them. He doesn't want to be left behind!'

Bill was left alone in the drive with the impatient Thunder, who thought he should go with his comrades; he reared and curvetted in annoyance at being made to go the other way, up the drive instead of down.

The six horses and brothers disappeared in a clatter of hooves and a cloud of dust. Bill, looking rather solemn, made Thunder take the path to the stables. She hated being parted from the many horses that her family owned. But now that she had settled down well at Malory Towers, and was allowed to bring her horse, she would not have given up boarding school for anything.

Another clatter of hooves, this time coming *up* the drive, made Bill rein in her horse, and look round. The five up in the art-room yelled to her.

'Bill! BILL! Here comes Clarissa – and she's on her horse, too!'

Sure enough, up the drive came a beautiful little horse with white socks, tossing his pretty head and showing off. Clarissa Carter rode him. She had been a new girl the term before, a plain, bespectacled little thing with an ugly wire round her front teeth. But now she had no wire and no spectacles, and she galloped up, her auburn hair flying in the wind, and her green eyes shining.

'Bill! Bill! I've brought Merrylegs! Isn't he sweet? Oh, do let him see Thunder. They'll love one another.'

'Two horse-mad creatures,' said Alicia, with a laugh. 'Well, Bill never had a friend till Clarissa came – so they'll have a fine time together this term, talking about horses and riding them, feeding them and grooming them . . .'

'Scrubbing their hooves and brushing their tails!' added Irene. 'Gosh, those galloping hooves have given me an idea for a new tune – a galloping tune – like this!'

She hummed a galloping, lilting melody – 'Tirretty-tirretty-tirretty-too . . .'

'Dear old Irene – she's not horse-mad, she's music-mad,' said Belinda, putting away her sketch-book. 'Now we shall have nothing but galloping tunes for the next few weeks! Come on, tirretty-too!'

And she galloped her friend out of the room at top speed. 'Tirretty-tirretty-tirretty-too. Oh – *so* sorry, Miss Potts – we never saw you coming!'

Supper-time

All but the new girls were well settled in by the evening. Matron had received health certificates and pocket-money from the lower school, and health certificates but no money from the upper school, who were allowed to keep their own without having to ask Matron for it.

'Did Irene's health certificate arrive all right?' asked Darrell, remembering how almost every term Irene's certificate was mislaid.

Sally laughed. 'Oh, somebody put an envelope in Irene's case, marked "Health Certificate", and she thought her mother had put it there instead of sending it by post – so she took it to Matron, of course, and said, "Here you are, Matron – I've really remembered it at last!"'

'And what was inside it?' asked Darrell.

'A recipe for Bad Memories,' chuckled Sally. 'I forget how it went. Take a cupful of Reminders, and a spoonful of Scoldings – something like that. You should have seen Matron's face when she saw it. Irene was dumbfounded, of course. She would be! However, it didn't matter because Matron had got her certificate by post.'

'Irene's such a scatter-brain, for all her cleverness,' said Alicia. 'So is Belinda. There must be something about art and music that makes people with those gifts perfectly idiotic over ordinary things. If Irene *can* lose something, she does. And if Belinda *can* forget something, she forgets it! Do you remember how she came down to breakfast once without her blouse on?'

'There's the gong for supper,' said Darrell, thankfully. 'I'm awfully hungry. Hope there's as super a supper as usual – we always have such a good one on the first night! I'm glad I haven't got to fuss round Felicity this term – she's not a new girl any more. She can stand on her own feet.'

They went down into the big dinning-room to supper. Sally absent-mindedly walked towards the fourth-form table, and Darrell pulled her back.

'Idiot! Do you want to sit with those kids?' she hissed. '*Here's* the fifth-form table!'

They took their places, and saw three girls already there, two old fifth-formers, and one new girl. Catherine and Moira nodded to them, and Catherine gave them a beaming smile. Moira didn't. She was tight-lipped and looked as if the cares of the whole school rested on her shoulders!

The new girl, Maureen, smiled at them brightly. She was a fluffy, rather untidy-looking girl, with a big mouth, a large nose and rather uneven teeth that stuck out a little and made her look rabbity.

'I'm Maureen Little,' she said, in a light, friendly voice. 'I hope you won't mind having me at Malory Towers!' She gave a little giggle.

'Why should we?' asked Darrell, surprised. 'We heard your old school had closed down. That was bad luck.'

'Yes,' said Maureen, and looked pensive. 'It was such a marvellous school, too – you should have seen the playing fields! And we had two swimming-pools, and we were allowed to keep our own pets.'

'Well, I expect you'll find Malory Towers isn't too bad,' said Alicia, joining in.

'Oh *yes*,' said the girl, smiling again, and showing her rabbit-teeth. 'I'm sure it's *wonder*ful. That's why my mother chose it. She said that next to Mazeley Manor – that was my old school, you know – Malory Towers was the best.'

'Dear me – that *was* nice of her,' said Alicia in her smooth voice. 'I don't seem to have heard of Mazeley Manor. Or was it the school whose girls always failed in the School Cert.?'

Maureen flushed. 'Oh *no*,' she said. 'It couldn't have been. Why, quite half of us passed. I passed myself.'

'Very clever of you,' said Alicia, and Darrell nudged her. What a pity for Maureen to get on Alicia's wrong side so soon! She was just the type that irritated the sharp-tongued Alicia. Alicia winked at Darrell but Darrell frowned. It wasn't fair to tease a new girl so soon. Give her a chance!

But Maureen didn't give herself a chance! 'I must be friendly!' she said to herself. 'I must keep my own end up, I must im*press* these girls!'

So she chattered away in a light, airy voice, and didn't seem to realize that new girls should be seen and not heard! It was only when the others very pointedly began to talk to one another, turning away from her until she found that no one at all was listening to her, that she stopped.

In the first form if any new girl behaved like that the first-formers would have pointed out at once that she'd better keep her mouth shut before somebody sat on her. But the fifth-formers were not quite so crude. They merely ignored her, hoping she would see that she was behaving stupidly and making a bad start.

'Are we all back?' said Darrell, looking round the table. 'Ah, there's Mavis. How's the voice, Mavis? I hope it's quite all right now!'

Mavis nodded. She had a beautiful voice, which she had lost for a few terms, but which was now back in all its beauty. She looked happy.

'And there's Mary-Lou – and Daphne – and Ruth – hallo, Ruth! How's your twin?'

'All right. You know she's been left down in fourth form?' said Ruth. 'It'll be strange without her. I've always had her, no matter what school or form I've been in. I hope she won't miss me too much.'

'Oh, she'll soon find someone else to look after and speak up for, just as she used to do to you!' said Alicia. 'You were her little shadow, Ruth – now this term we'll be able to see what you're really like yourself. We didn't know before!'

'Oh!' put in Maureen. 'Is Ruth a twin? There were twins at my old school, and they were so . . .'

Well, it simply wasn't *done* for a new girl to speak out of turn like this, and to Maureen's surprise everyone at the table began talking at once, so that nobody could possibly hear what she said. Mam'zelle Dupont, who was at the head of the table, was sorry for her. She liked the fluffy type of girl, and she spoke comfortingly to Maureen.

'They are excited, you see, at being back again. You will soon be their friends, *n'est-ce pas*? Tomorrow they will – what do you call it – they will take you to their chests and you will be one of them. What a pity dear Gwendoline isn't back yet. Now, you would like her, Maureen. She has golden hair, like you, and . . .'

Alicia caught part of this and winked at Sally. 'I bet Gwendoline would be just the person for Maureen,' she said. She raised her voice and spoke to Mam'zelle.

'What's happened to dear Gwendoline Mary, Mam'zelle? She's the only one not back.'

'She only came back from France today,' said Mam'zelle. 'She comes to us tomorrow. The dear child – she will be able to talk to me about my beloved country. We shall gobble together about it.'

'*Gabble*, Mam'zelle, you mean,' said Sally, with a giggle.

'Oh, *I've* been to France, too,' said Maureen, delighted.

'Then you and Gwendoline and Mam'zelle can all gobble about it together,' said Irene. 'Nice trio you'll make, gobbling away about *la belle France*!'

'Don't be an ass, Irene,' said Moira's voice. 'Remember you're in the fifth form now, not the fourth.'

'Oh – thanks most awfully for reminding us, Moira,' said Alicia, in her smoothest voice. 'I say – it must be *frightful* for you to have to live with *us* – awful come-down to pig it with old fourth-formers instead of queening it in the sixth.'

'Moira and I don't mind a bit,' said Catherine, with such an air of pouring oil on troubled waters that the old fourth-formers couldn't help nudging one another. 'After all, *somebody* has to be left down sometimes – and it's always a help, don't you think, when an old member of the form can help new ones to carry on the tradition.'

'*Ah ça – c'est bien dit*!' said Mam'zelle. 'Very well said, Catherine.'

But nobody else thought so. 'Hypocrite!' muttered Alicia to Irene. 'Who wants Catherine to help us? She couldn't teach a cat to drink milk! Gosh, if she's going to be as pi as that I shall resign from the fifth and go up into the sixth!'

Irene did one of her explosive snorts, and Catherine looked astonished. 'Do tell us the joke,' she said, with a beaming smile.

'Joke over,' said Alicia, also with a beaming smile. Darrell winked at Sally. It was easy to see that there was going to be some fun that term. She glanced at Moira who was frowning glumly.

'Want to collect a few more scowls for your notebook, Belinda?' said Darrell, softly. Belinda glanced at Moira too and nodded. She had pursued Gwendoline once for a whole term, collecting her scowls, drawing them one after another in what the girls came to call her 'Gwendoline Collection'. Now here was another person with a wonderful selection of scowls for Belinda!

Bill and Clarissa were happily talking horses together, unheedful of anyone else at the table. 'I wonder they

21

don't whinny to one another!' said Alicia, exasperated. 'Bill! Clarissa! Do you think you're in the stables still?'

'Oh – sorry,' said Clarissa, looking round with shining green eyes. 'I forgot where I was for a minute. But it's so nice to be back with Bill again and talk horses.'

'Ah, this horse-talk! I do not understand it!' chimed in Mam'zelle. 'Me, I would not go near a horse – great, stamping creatures.'

'You really *must* come and let Thunder take a lump of sugar from the palm of your hand one day!' said Bill, with an impish grin. 'Will you, Mam'zelle?'

Mam'zelle gave a small squeal. 'Always you say that to me, Bill! It is not kind. I will not let your great horse tread on my foot with its paws.'

'Hooves, Mam'zelle, hooves,' said Bill, quite shocked at Mam'zelle calling them paws.

'Shaking its hair all over me,' went on Mam'zelle, conjuring up a fearsome picture of a stamping, head-shaking, rearing creature!

'Shaking its *mane*,' corrected Bill. 'Oh, Mam'zelle, you're awful about horses. I shall drag you out to Thunder and give you a lesson on all his different parts!'

'This horrible Bill!' said Mam'zelle, turning her eyes up to the ceiling. 'Why must I teach her French when all she wants to learn about is horses? Why do you laugh, girls? I would not make a joke about so serious a thing!'

'Oh – it's good to be back again, isn't it?' said Darrell to Sally. 'I never laugh anywhere like I do at school, never!'

Night and morning

Darrell found time that first evening to make sure that her young sister Felicity was not being whisked off by June, Alicia's thirteen-year-old cousin in the first form. To her relief she saw that Felicity was arm-in-arm with Susan, her friend of the term before.

June was standing alone, on the edge of the little crowd of first-formers. She had a most determined look on her face, and Darrell wondered what she was thinking of. She is certainly planning *something*, thought Darrell. Well, so long as she leaves Felicity out of her plans, she can do what she likes! How I do dislike that child!

The fifth-formers went to bed a quarter of an hour after the fourth-formers. It was grand having just fifteen minutes more. They chattered as they undressed, and speculated on all sorts of things in the coming term.

'I shall miss having Miss Williams to teach us,' said Sally, who had liked the fourth-form mistress very much. 'I wonder if . . .'

The dormitory door opened and a face looked in. It was Connie, Ruth's twin.

'Ruth! Are you all right?' she said. 'It's odd not being with you. Are you managing all right? Did you find your . . .'

'*Connie*!' exploded Alicia. 'What do you mean by coming into the fifth dormy when you're jolly well supposed to be in bed? Clear out.'

Connie stood in the doorway obstinately. She was a great one for arguing. 'I only just came to see if Ruth was all right,' she said. 'We've never been parted before, and . . .'

'Clear out!' yelled everyone, and Irene brandished her hair-brush fiercely, almost knocking Belinda's eye out.

But still Connie held her ground. Her eyes searched Ruth's face, which was also wearing an obstinate look. 'Ruth,' began Connie, urgently. 'Do say something. Don't stand there like that. I only just came to . . .'

'Clear out!' said Ruth, and everyone stood silent in astonishment. Nobody had expected that. Ruth had been such a shadow that, even when she had begun to assert herself a little the term before, no one had ever thought she could possibly order Connie about.

'I know you're my twin and we've always been together,' said Ruth, in an unnecessarily loud voice. 'But I'm in the fifth now and you're in the fourth. You can't come tagging after a fifth-former, you know that. Leave me alone and clear out!'

Only Ruth could defeat Connie, and make her go. Connie gaped, then turned and went without a word. Ruth sat down suddenly on her bed.

'Good for *you*!' said Darrell, warmly. 'You'll have to stand up for yourself a bit, Ruth, or you'll have Connie pestering you again and again.'

'I know,' said Ruth in a small voice. 'But I'm – I'm

awfully fond of her, you know – I hated saying that. But she would never take any notice of anyone else. And after all – I can't let her hang on to the fifth, can I? Poor Connie.'

'Not "poor" at all,' said Darrell. 'And don't you believe it. She's got the cheek of a dozen! She won't give up easily, either – she'll keep on trying to tag on to you and to us.'

'Quite right,' said Alicia, in a voice not loud enough for Ruth to hear. 'Connie's so thick-skinned she wants a whole lot of shouting at before she feels or understands what we're getting at!'

'I've got a sister like that in the fourth,' said Moira, unexpectedly joining in. 'A tough nut if ever there was one. She's like a rubber ball – if you sit on her and squash her flat she bounces back to shape again immediately. Awful kid.'

'What's her name?' said Darrell. 'Oh, wait a bit – is it Bridget?'

'Yes,' said Moira. 'She and Connie would make a pair!'

'Well, let's hope Connie and she will get together!' said Alicia. 'Nice pair they'd make – rub each other's corners off a bit!'

Soon they were all in bed. Darrell was next to Maureen. She said goodnight to the new girl, and to Sally who was on the other side of her, and shut her eyes. Her bed was harder than at home but she knew she would soon get used to that. She threw off her quilt after a bit. It was such a warm night. She heard a sniff from the next bed.

Gosh – it can't be Maureen sniffing like any new first-former, thought Darrell, in surprise. She turned over and listened.

'Sniff, sniff!' Yes, there it was again.

'Maureen! What on earth's the matter?' whispered Darrell. 'Surely you're not a first-night sniffer? At *your* age?'

Maureen's voice came shakily to Darrell. 'I'm always like this at first. I think of Mummy and Daddy and what they're doing at home. I'm sensitive, you know.'

'Better get over being sensitive, then,' said Darrell, shortly. In her experience people who went round saying that they were sensitive wanted a good shaking up and, if they were lower school, needed to be laughed out of it.

'But you can't help being it, if you are,' sniffed Maureen.

'Oh, I know – but you *can* help talking about it!' said Darrell. 'Do go to sleep. I can't bear to hear you sniffing as if you wanted a hanky and haven't got one.'

Maureen felt that Darrell was very unkind. She wished there was someone in the bed the other side of her – someone more sympathetic. But the bed was empty. It was Gwendoline's, and she hadn't yet come back.

Darrell grinned to herself in the darkness. If only they could wish Maureen on to Gwen! Maureen was very like Gwen to look at, and had the same silly weak nature, apparently. How marvellous if they could push her on to Gwen, and see what happened!

'You wait till Gwendoline Mary comes back tomorrow,' said Darrell wickedly to Maureen. 'She's just your sort. She's sensitive, too. I'm sure she'll understand all you feel. She hates first nights still. You look out for her tomorrow,

Maureen, she's just your sort, I should think.'

Sally, who was in the next bed, listening, gave a little snort of laughter. How mad Gwen would be to have someone else like her in the form, someone who thought themselves too wonderful for words, and who wanted admiration and sympathy all the time! How wicked of Darrell to be pushing Maureen on to Gwen already – but how altogether suitable!

'No more talking,' said Moira's voice, out of the darkness. 'Time's up now.'

The old fourth-formers resented this sudden command. Moira wasn't head-girl – not yet, anyway! Nothing official had been said about it. Nobody said any more but there were various 'Poohs' and 'Pishes' from several beds. Still, they were all tired, and nobody except Maureen really wanted to keep awake.

There were a few more sniffs from Maureen's bed and then silence. Irene began to snore a little. She always did when she lay on her back. Belinda, who was in the next bed, leaned over and gave her a hard poke to make her turn over. Irene obediently shifted on to her side without even waking up. Belinda had got her well-trained by now!

Connie actually appeared at the door again in the morning, looking belligerent and obstinate.

'You *still* there?' said Alicia. 'Been standing there all night long, I suppose, wondering if Ruth was having a nice beauty sleep or not!'

'There's no rule against my coming here in the morning to ask a question, is there?' said Connie. 'Don't be so beastly, Alicia. I've only come to give Ruth a pair of stockings that got into my case.'

'Thanks,' said Ruth, and took them. Connie straightened one or two things on Ruth's dressing-table. Ruth immediately put them crooked again. 'It's no good, Connie,' she said. 'Leave me alone. I'm in the fifth now, I tell you.'

'I never thought you'd crow over me if I was left behind,' said Connie, looking suddenly bewildered.

'I'm not. Do go away,' said Ruth, in a low voice, knowing that everyone in the room was intensely interested in this little battle, although most of the girls were pretending not to notice. Darrell had managed to stop Alicia from interfering. Let Ruth manage the fight herself!

Moira suddenly spoke. 'Will you take this book to my sister Bridget?' she said, in her abrupt voice. She held out a small book. 'She's in the fourth, too – came up from the third this term. I expect you've spoken to her already.'

'Yes, I have,' said Connie. 'I'll give her the book.'

She took it, and went out of the room without another look at Ruth. Darrell glanced at Ruth. She was looking rather miserable. What a shame it was that Connie should force her into such a difficult position! How could anyone be as thick-skinned as that twin!

The breakfast-bell went. Maureen gave a wail. 'Oh, I say – is that the bell again? I was thinking I was still at Mazeley Manor – the bell didn't go till much later! I shall be late!'

'We're going to hear rather a lot about Mazeley

Manor, I'm afraid,' said Darrell in Sally's ear, as they went downstairs.

'Perhaps Gwen will hear it all instead,' said Sally. 'That's your plan, isn't it? The thing is – will Gwen be in the fifth? *She* failed the School Cert., too, you know. She may be kept down in the fourth with Connie.'

'Oh no – surely not!' said Darrell. 'She's too old. She's above the average age even of the fifth, by a few months. After all, Connie's well below it – so it doesn't much matter for her.'

They asked Mam'zelle at breakfast-time about Gwen.

'Will she be in the fifth with us?' said Darrell.

'Yes, yes,' said Mam'zelle. 'Of course! It is true she failed, the poor child, in this terrible examination of yours – but she was ill. Yes, she had a bad heart, poor Gwendoline.'

The fifth-formers nudged one another. Gwen's bad heart! Gwen had produced a heart that fluttered and palpitated, in order to get out of doing the exam – but nobody had believed in it except Mam'zelle. And Gwen had had to do the exam after all, and had failed.

'Well, heart or no heart, apparently she's in the fifth with us,' said Alicia. '*Dear* Gwendoline Mary – *what* a treat to have her back with us today!'

Miss James has good news

The fifth went to their classroom just before nine o'clock. They rejoiced in the glorious view. Darrell flung the windows wide and let in the golden September air.

'Heavenly!' she said. 'I hope we shall be allowed to swim still. I bet the pool down in the rocks is just perfect now.'

Maureen looked alarmed. 'Surely you're not allowed to swim in the winter term!' she said. 'Why, at Mazeley Manor we . . .'

'It must have been a wonderful place,' said Alicia, in her smooth voice.

'Oh yes – we used to . . .' went on Maureen.

'*So* sad it had to shut down,' interrupted Irene.

'Yes, very sad,' agreed Maureen, delighted at this sudden interest and sympathy. 'You see, all of us were very . . .'

'You must find Malory Towers very second-rate after such a marvellous place,' put in Belinda, also sounding very sympathetic.

'Still, we'll do our best,' Sally assured her. Maureen began to feel doubtful about all these interruptions, kind as they seemed. Perhaps she had better say no more till she had found her feet a little. These girls seemed so different from the ones at dear Mazeley Manor.

'What's our new form-mistress, Miss James, like?' said Darrell to Catherine and Moira. 'You've been taught by her for some terms – is she all right?'

'Easy-going to a point,' said Moira. 'Then look out! She changes from sweet to sour in the twinkling of an eye – and it's bad for you if you don't notice the change-over immediately. Still, Jimmy's not a bad sort.'

'She's James when she's sour, and Jimmy when she's sweet,' explained Catherine, with her beaming smile. 'Actually she's rather a dear.'

'Oh, Catherine thinks heaps of people are "rather-dears", and "dear-old-souls" and even "pet lambs",' said Moira. 'She never speaks evil of anyone, do you, Catherine? And if ever you want anything done, Catherine will do it for you – she just loves to run around for other people.'

Catherine blushed. 'Don't be silly, Moira,' she said, but a look of anxiety came into her eyes. Was Moira pulling her leg – sneering at her just a little? The others didn't wonder about it – they knew! Moira was not praising Catherine – she was sneering. Moira would probably never praise anyone whole-heartedly.

The girls had chosen their desks. The favoured ones at the back of the room went to the two old fifth-formers, of course, Moira and Catherine, and to Darrell and Sally, who had each been head-girl for a time the term before. Irene and Belinda also had back desks.

There were other girls in the room now, girls also

in the fifth but from other Towers – Tessa and Janet and Penelope, Katie and Dora and Gladys – girls the North Tower fifth-formers knew by name and sight, but not nearly as well as they knew their own Tower girls, of course. The girls of all the Towers mixed for lessons and games, but were quite separate afterwards, each going to their own Tower for meals, leisure and sleeping.

'Sssssst!' said someone. 'Jimmy's coming!'

And in came Jimmy, or Miss James – a tall, spare woman of about fifty, whose curly grey hair framed a scholarly face with kind but shrewd hazel eyes.

'Sit,' she said, and the class sat, shuffling their feet, moving their chairs a little, shifting books and papers. Miss James waited until there was complete silence.

'Well, once more I have a new class,' she began, her shrewd eyes resting first on one girl and then on another. 'Only three of you, I think, were in my form last term, and they, for various good reasons, have not gone up into the sixth, but are still with me. They will, of course, be a great help in getting the form into my ways.'

The girls looked to see who the third old fifth-former was. Oh – it was little Janet. Well, she was miles too young to go up into the sixth, of course! She had only been put into the fifth a year ago because she had passed her School Certificate so absurdly early. She still looked like a fourth-former, thought Darrell, not even like a fifth-former!

Janet looked pleased to be left down. She was scared of the sixth form. Moira scowled. She hated being left behind. Catherine beamed. Yes – yes, she would help all she could.

Miss James could depend on her, of course she could. She tried to catch the mistress's eye, but for some reason Miss James steadfastly looked in the other direction.

Catherine kept her beaming smile on for some time, hopefully gazing at Miss James. But the mistress left the subject and began on something else. Catherine had to switch off the smile. Her cheek muscles were beginning to ache!

'Darrell is to be head of fifth-form games,' said Miss James. 'Sally is to help her. You realize, Darrell, don't you, that head of fifth-form games means taking on the training of some of the younger players for the lower teams of the school? That will take up some time, but you will have Sally to help you.'

Darrell glowed. How lovely to be able to pick out some of the young first- and second-formers and lick them into shape for the third and fourth games teams of Malory Towers. Suppose she and Sally made the teams so good that they won all their matches, home and away! What a record that would be! Darrell went off into a day-dream in which she saw some well-turned out, smart lower-school teams winning match after match.

I'll train Felicity, of course, she thought. She's quite good already. I can make her first class. And Susan's good as well. And I'll lick that young June into shape, too. My word, she'll have to toe the line now. I shan't stand any nonsense from *her*! And there's Harriet in the second form and Lucy in the second, too . . .

She missed the next few things that Miss James said,

she was so lost in her dream of first-class lacrosse teams.

'You all worked very hard last term,' said Miss James. 'Practically all of you in this form passed, and passed well, in the School Cert. exam. Those who didn't, failed because of some understandable reason, and will have another chance later on. They will be specially coached for it, and will have to leave the usual lessons of this class for a time until the exam is over.'

Alicia sighed. It wouldn't be this term, of course – but she hated the idea of having to leave the others and have special coaching. Blow! Why did she have to have measles right in exam week last term?

'Now, as you all had a hard term last term, I don't intend to work you hard *this* term,' said Miss James, and a sigh of relief went all round the room like a small breeze. 'I mean – I shall not set you lengthy preps to do, nor push you hard – but there will be other things to take up your time. I want the fifth to produce the Christmas entertainment this year, for instance.'

That made everyone sit up. Produce the Christmas entertainment! My word! That would be fun. What about a play? Or a pantomime? Or a ballet? All kinds of thoughts ran through the girls' minds, and they glanced at one another in delight.

'You will do it all on your own, except for any advice you may need from Mr Young, the music-master, or Miss Greening, the elocution coach,' went on Miss James, pleased at the pleasure shown by the girls. Ah, when they got up into the fifth, how they liked to do things on their own, with no interference from anyone! Quite right, too – if they didn't learn to handle affairs and stand on their own feet now, they never would!

'You will choose your own producers,' said Miss James. 'I should have at least two, for the work will be too much for one. The more you do on your own the better I and Miss Grayling, the Head, will be pleased – but we shall, of course, be glad to give you any advice or help if you need to ask for it.'

Every girl in the class at once fiercely determined not to ask one single piece of advice. The Christmas Show, whatever it was, should be theirs and nobody else's.

'It shall be the best one ever done at Malory Towers!' vowed Darrell.

We'll get the parents to come and what a surprise they'll have! thought Sally.

What a chance! thought Alicia, and her agile mind began to run over all kinds of ideas at once. She longed for the first meeting. If only they would make her one of the producers! She could organize well. She could plan and she could be more resourceful than anyone. She knew she could!

They all longed for break, so that they could discuss the ideas put into their heads by Miss James. Irene was in the seventh heaven of delight – if they did a pantomime, *would* they let her write the music? The music for a whole pantomime – why, that would give her more scope than she had ever had before!

Mavis was also dreaming delightfully. Would she be

able to do some of the singing, if they did a play or a pantomime? She was allowed to practise her singing properly this term, and had a special singing-master of her own, who came to the school to teach her. Oh, if only she could sing the principal songs!

Break came at last. The fifth-formers rushed off in a crowd, gathering in a corner of the grounds, all talking at once.

'We'll have to have a proper meeting,' said Darrell. 'Oh gosh – I do feel thrilled – to be told we can do the Christmas entertainment all on our own – and to be told I'm games captain and responsible for the picking and training of the lower-school kids for their teams! Why – I shan't have time for any work at all!'

'Well, we've learned how to work by now,' said Sally. 'If we haven't, we never will! We've got other things to learn now, I suppose – how to plan things on our own, and carry them out – and how to work together in them properly – things like that.'

'Oh! Do you suppose Jimmy's planned all this just to make us learn a whole lot of *other* things, then?' said Daphne.

'Quite likely,' said Alicia. 'But what does it matter? If we're learning something by producing a pantomime, well, let's learn it by all means! I'm all for it!'

'We have to choose a committee,' said Moira, taking charge. Sally, Darrell and Alicia felt a momentary annoyance. They had been so used to leading everything in the fourth form that they found it difficult to recognize

Moira's authority. Still, she was head-girl. She had the right to take charge, and she was perfectly capable of it – there was no doubt about that at all.

The girls could all feel the impact of a hard and dominating personality in Moira – much the same as they felt in Alicia, who was also hard and strong in character. But Alicia had a sense of humour, which was quite lacking in Moira – that made all the difference in the world!

Alicia could say something biting – and yet it would produce a laugh because of the way she said it. She was bright and lively, too, which Moira was not. Well, it took all sorts to make a world, and there was a place for the Moiras and Gwens and Maureens, thought Darrell, and for the Sallies and Irenes and Belindas as well.

'Only *they're* so much nicer to know!' Darrell said to herself.

'We'd better choose a committee of seven or eight,' went on Moira. 'And we'll choose it in the usual way – each of us writes the names of the girls they'd like to have on the committee and we'll put them all into a box. Then we take them out, open them, count them, and see who's got the most votes. We'll do that tonight.'

Oh, I *hope* I'm on the committee! thought Darrell. And Alicia hoped the same. Alicia badly wanted to have a finger in this pie. She felt perfectly sure she could run the whole show, if only she was allowed to!

6

Half an hour in the sun

'When's dear Gwendoline Mary coming back?' asked
Alicia, as they all lay out in the sun after their dinner at a
quarter to two that day. It was so warm and sunny that it
was like summer. All the girls had found warm places out
of doors, and the grounds were full of little companies of
girls happily sunning themselves.

'Gwen? Oh, she's arriving at tea-time,' said Darrell.
'*Dear* Gwendoline Mary! Would you think she's what
Catherine would call a "pet lamb"?'

'I could think of much more suitable names than that,'
said Belinda, busy drawing Mavis, who had gone to sleep
with her mouth open.

'Is Gwendoline nice?' asked Maureen. 'She *sounds* nice,
to me.'

Darrell winked at Alicia.

'Nice? Oh, you'll love her!' she said. '*So* sympathetic
and ready to listen! So interesting to talk to – and the tales
she tells about her family and her dogs and her cats – well,
you could listen for hours, Maureen.'

'Is she fond of sports?' asked Maureen, who quite
definitely wasn't. 'At Mazeley Towers we didn't do games
unless we wanted to. I mean – they weren't compulsory,

as they are here – *such* a mistake, I think.'

'Oh, Gwen hates games,' said Alicia. 'But because she's fat she has to do them as much as possible and walk miles, too.'

'Poor Gwendoline!' said Maureen, sympathizing deeply with the absent fifth-former. 'We shall have a lot in common, I can see. Has she – has she a special friend, do you know? Of course – that's a silly question, I know – a girl like that's bound to have a special friend. But I just thought – you know, I'm rather one on my own – it would be so *nice* to find someone here who wasn't already fixed up with a companion for walks – and talks.'

'Let me see,' said Alicia, blinking up at the sky. '*Has* Gwendoline Mary a friend?'

Everyone appeared to think very deeply.

'Well – perhaps not a *special* friend,' said Irene, with a small snort of laughter. 'Let us say she's a little-friend-of-all-the-world, shall we?'

'Ah – you've just hit the nail on the head,' said Darrell, trying not to giggle. 'I think she'd like Maureen, don't you?'

'She'll love her,' said Belinda, with the utmost conviction. 'Wake up, Mavis, and see how beautiful you look when you're asleep.'

'Beast!' said Mavis, taking a look at Belinda's comical sketch of her lying asleep with her mouth open. Maureen took a look as well.

'That's quite a clever drawing,' she said. 'I can draw, too. I was one of the best at Mazeley Manor. I must show you my sketches sometime, Belinda. They're very much the same style as yours.'

Belinda was about to say something short and rude when Irene frowned at her, and then spoke in a sickly-sweet tone to the unsuspecting Maureen.

'I suppose you can sing, too, can't you – and can you compose?'

'Oh, I can sing,' said Maureen, pleased with all this attention. 'Yes, I had special lessons at Mazeley Manor. The singing-master said I had a most unusual voice. And I've composed quite a few songs. Dear, dear – you mustn't make me talk about myself like this!'

She gave her silly little laugh. Everyone else wanted to laugh, too. How could anyone be so idiotic?

'Were there many girls at your last school?' asked Sally, wondering how in the world any school could turn out somebody like Maureen.

'Oh no – it was a very very *select* school,' said Maureen. 'They picked and chose their girls very very carefully.'

'You'll have to tell Gwen all these things,' said Alicia, earnestly. 'Won't she, girls? Gwen will be *so* interested. And don't you think it would be nice for dear Gwendoline to have someone like Maureen for a friend? I mean – I feel she's made of, er – finer stuff than we are – and I'm sure Gwendoline Mary would appreciate that.'

Maureen could hardly believe that all these wonderful remarks applied to her. She gazed round half suspiciously, but the girls all looked at her with straight faces. Irene had to look away. She felt certain one of her terrific snorts was coming.

'Gwen's always lonely when she comes back,' went on Alicia. 'Then's the time to talk to her, Maureen. We'll tell her about you, and you can make friends.'

'Thank you very much,' said Maureen, basking in what she thought was universal appreciation of herself. 'I really hardly think the girls at Mazeley Manor could be nicer than you!'

Irene snorted loudly and somehow turned it into a cough and a sneeze.

Maureen looked a little suspicious again, but at that moment Mam'zelle Dupont descended on them, smiling. She sat down on the grass, first looking for ants, earwigs and beetles. She was terrified of them. She beamed round amicably. The girls smiled back. They liked the plump, hot-tempered, humorous French mistress. She was not like Mam'zelle Rougier, bad tempered all the time – if she got into a temper, she blew up, certainly – but it didn't last long.

'Ah – you are all basketing in the sun,' she said, much to the surprise of everyone.

'Oh – you mean *basking*, don't you, Mam'zelle?' said Darrell, with a squeal of laughter.

'Yes, yes – this lovely sun!' said Mam'zelle, and she wriggled her plump shoulders in enjoyment. In a moment or two, however, she would feel afraid of getting a freckle, and would retire into the shade!

'And you, *ma petite* Maureen – you are settling down

here nicely, are you not?' asked Mam'zelle, kindly, seeing Maureen next to her. 'Of course, you will be missing your old school – what name is it, now – ah, yes – your Measley Manor, is it not?'

A shout of laughter deafened her.

'Oh, Mam'zelle – you're priceless!' almost wept Belinda. 'You always hit the nail on the head!'

'The nail? What nail?' asked Mam'zelle, looking all round as if she expected to see a nail suspended in the air somewhere. 'I have hit nothing. Do not tease me now. It is too hot!'

She turned to Maureen again. 'They interrupt their kind old Mam'zelle,' she said, smiling down at the fluffy-haired Maureen. 'I was asking you about your lovely Measley Manor.'

This time it was too much. Maureen's look of offended disgust with Mam'zelle and with the laughing girls made them roll on the grass in an agony of mirth. Mam'zelle was astonished. What had she said that was so funny?

'All I ask is about this lovely . . .' she began again, in bewilderment. Nobody stopped laughing. Maureen got up and walked off in a huff. How hateful to laugh at such a horrid name for her old school – and did Mam'zelle *really* mean to call it that? Was *she* poking fun at her, too? Maureen seriously began to doubt if all the nice things said to her were meant.

'Oh dear,' said Darrell, sitting up and wiping the tears from her eyes. 'You're a pet, Mam'zelle! Girls, in future, we refer to *Measley* Manor as soon as Maureen trots out her horrible soppy school again. We'll soon cure her of that.'

'I wish Gwen would hurry up and come,' said Sally. 'I'm longing to see those two together. Maureen's so like Gwen in her ways – it'll be like Gwen looking into a mirror and seeing herself, when she knows Maureen!'

'Now, now – play no treeks on Maureen,' said Mam'zelle. She meant tricks, of course. 'Poof! It is hot. I shall grow a freckle on my nose. I feel it! I must sit in the shade. Poof!'

'We're going to have a nice term, Mam'zelle,' said Darrell. 'Games, plenty of them – and we fifth-formers are doing the Christmas entertainment! We shan't have much time for French, I'm afraid.'

'*Méchante fille*!' said Mam'zelle at once, fanning violently and making herself much hotter. 'Bad girl, Darrell. You will have plenty of time for French. And no treeks. No treeks this term. There will be NO TIME for treeks.'

'Why don't *you* play a treek, Mam'zelle?' asked Alicia, lazily. 'We give you full permission to work as hard as you like at playing a treek on us.'

'Oh yes – as many tricks as you like!' said Sally, joyfully.

'But we'll see through them all,' said Mavis.

'Ah – if I played you a treek it would be *superbe*!' said Mam'zelle, pronouncing it the French way, '*Superbe*! *Magnifique*! *Merveilleuse*! Such a treek you would never have seen before.'

'We dare you to, Mam'zelle,' said Alicia at once.

'Me, I am not daring,' said Mam'zelle. 'I think of a treek

perhaps, yes – but I could not do it. I have not your dare.'

The bell rang for afternoon school. Everyone got up. Alicia hauled Mam'zelle to her feet so strongly that she almost fell over again. 'You have too much dare,' she told Alicia, crossly. 'Always you have too much dare, Alicia!'

Gwendoline arrives

Gwendoline came back just before tea, by car. The news flew round. 'Dear Gwendoline Mary's back! Come and see the fond farewells!'

Gwen's farewells were a standing joke at Malory Towers. There were always tears and fond embracings, and injunctions to write soon, that went on for ages between her and her mother and her old governess, Miss Winter, who lived with them.

Faces lined the windows overlooking the drive. Gwendoline got out of the car. Her mother and Miss Winter got out, too. Her father, who was driving, made no move. He had got very tired of Gwendoline in the holidays.

'Out come the hankies!' said Alicia, and out came Gwen's and her mother's and Miss Winter's. And dear me, out came the hankies of all the wicked watchers at the windows above!

'Now we pat our eyes!' went on Alicia, and sure enough the eye-patting went on down below – and above too, as everyone sniffed and wiped their eyes.

Irene, of course, gave the show away with one of her explosions. The four below looked up in surprise and saw the watching girls, all with hankies to their eyes.

Mr Lacey roared. He held on to the wheel and laughed loudly. 'They're putting up as good a show for you, Gwen, as you're putting up for them!' he cried. The girls at the window disappeared as soon as they saw that they had been seen. They felt a little uncomfortable. Mrs Lacey might complain of their bad manners now! It would be just like her.

'Mother, get back into the car,' said Gwendoline, exasperated. She hadn't known she was being watched at all. She did so love these little farewell scenes – and now this one was spoiled! Her mother and Miss Winter were almost hustled back, without another tear or hug.

'I don't like that behaviour, Gwendoline,' said Mrs Lacey, offended at the conduct of the girls. 'I've a good mind to write to Miss Grayling.'

'Oh *no*, Mother!' said Gwendoline, in alarm. She never liked being brought to Miss Grayling's notice at all. Miss Grayling had said some very horrid things to her at times!

'It's all right, Gwen. I shan't let her,' said her father, dryly. 'For goodness' sake, say good-bye now, and go in. And mind – if I hear any nonsense about you this term you'll have me to reckon with, not your mother. You were bad and foolish last term, and you suffered for it. You will suffer for it again, if I hear bad reports of you. On the other hand, no one will be more pleased than I shall to have a good report of you. And I've no doubt I shall.'

'Yes, Daddy,' said Gwendoline, meekly.

'How unkind you are just as we're leaving Gwen,' said

Mrs Lacey, dabbing her eyes again. 'Good-bye, darling. I shall miss you so!'

Gwendoline took a desperate look up at the windows. Gracious, was Mother going to begin all over again?

'Good-bye,' she said, curtly, and shut the car door. Immediately her father put in the clutch and the car moved off. Without even turning to wave Gwen marched up the steps with her lacrosse stick and nightcase. Her trunk had been sent on in advance.

Maureen had not seen the fond farewells. She did not see Gwen till tea-time. Gwen took her case up to the dormy and was thankful to find it empty. She looked at herself in the mirror. She wasn't fat any more – well, not *very*, she decided. All those hateful walks had taken away her weight. And now she had to face a term with heaps of games and walks – but, thank goodness, no swimming!

The tea-bell went. Gwen quickly brushed her fluffy golden hair, so like Maureen's, washed her hands, pulled her tie straight, and went downstairs.

She walked into the dining-room with the last few girls. She caught sight of her form at the fifth-form table. They waved to her.

'Hallo! Here's dear Gwendoline Mary again!'

'Had good hols?'

'You went to France, didn't you? Lucky thing.'

'You're a day late – you've missed a lot already!'

'Said good-bye to your people?'

Gwendoline felt pleased to be back. Of course, it *was* nice to be at home with her mother and Miss Winter and be waited on hand and foot, and be fussed over – but it was fun at school. She made up her mind to be sensible and join in everything this term. So she smiled round very amiably.

'Hallo, everyone! It's nice to be back. You'll have to tell me all the news. I only got back from France yesterday.'

'Ah – *la belle France*!' put in Mam'zelle. 'We must have some chest-to-chest talks about *la belle France*.'

Gwen looked surprised. 'Oh – you mean heart-to-heart talks, Mam'zelle. Yes, that would be lovely.'

'Gwendoline, there's a new girl,' said Alicia, in a suspiciously smooth voice. 'Let me introduce her – you'll like her. This is Maureen. And this is Gwendoline Mary. A bit alike to look at, aren't they, Mam'zelle?'

'*C'est vrai*!' agreed Mam'zelle. 'Yes, it is true. Both so golden – and with big blue eyes. Ah yes, it is a true English beauty, that!'

This gratified both Gwen and Maureen immensely, and made them look with great interest at each other. They shook hands and smiled.

'I've kept a place for you,' said Maureen, shyly, making her eyes big as she looked at Gwen. Gwen sat down and looked to see what there was for tea. She was hungry after her long car-ride.

'Have some of my honey,' said Maureen, eagerly. 'We keep bees, you know – and we always have *such* a lot of honey. We have hens, too. So we have plenty of eggs. I brought some back with me. I hope you'll share them with me.'

Gwendoline rather liked all this. Dear me, she must have made quite an impression on the new girl, although she had only just arrived!

'The others have been telling me all about you,' gushed Maureen. 'How popular you seem to be!'

This didn't ring quite true, somehow, to Gwendoline. She hadn't known she was as popular as all that. In fact, though she didn't admit it frankly to herself, she knew quite well she was probably the least popular of all the girls in the form!

Maureen chattered away merrily, and Gwen listened, not so much because she wanted to, as because she was so busy tucking in. At this rate, thought the amused Alicia, Gwendoline would put on more fat than games and gym and walks would take off!

'You'll be pleased to hear we haven't got to work quite so hard this term, Gwen,' she told her. 'More time for games and gym. You'll like that.'

Gwendoline gave Alicia one of her looks, as she called them. Alas, they never impressed Alicia. It wasn't safe to argue with Alicia, or contradict, or try to say something cutting. Alicia was always ten times as quick at answering back and a hundred times as cutting as anyone else.

'We'll have the committee meeting at half-past five,' announced Moira. 'That seems to be the best time. You'll be coming, Gwendoline, won't you – have you heard about the Christmas Entertainment Committee yet?'

Gwendoline hadn't, so she was duly enlightened. She was pleased. She saw herself at once in one of the chief parts of whatever play or pantomime was chosen. She would loosen her sheet of golden hair – what a pity it wasn't curly. She would look lovely, she knew she would!

Exactly the same thoughts were going through Maureen's mind. She too would like one of the chief parts – and she too would play it with her golden hair loose. She felt she would like to confide her thoughts to Gwendoline.

'When I was at Mazeley Manor,' she began. Belinda interrupted at once.

'Oh yes – have you told Gwen about Measley Manor?'

Maureen frowned. 'You know it's Ma*zeley*,' she said, with dignity. 'Mam'zelle just didn't know how to pronounce it, that's all, when she said it.'

Mam'zelle caught her name mentioned. She turned, with her wide smile. 'Ah – you want to talk about Measley Manor again, your dear old school, *n'est-ce pas*? You have not yet told Gwendoline about Measley Manor?'

Maureen saw the girls grinning and gave it up. She went on talking to Gwen, who was astonished at all this by-play which she didn't, of course, understand.

'At my old school we did a pantomime,' said Maureen. 'It was the *Sleeping Beauty*. I had to have my hair loose, of course. You *have* to have someone with golden hair for those parts, don't you?'

Gwen agreed heartily. She was very proud of her golden hair, and only wished she was allowed to wear it loose round her face at school, as she did at home.

'The prince was grand,' went on Maureen. 'I really

must tell you all about the play. You're so interested in plays, aren't you? Well . . .'

And till long past tea-time Maureen went on and on interminably with her long and boring tale of what happened in the play at her last school. Gwendoline couldn't stop her or get rid of her. Maureen was just as thick-skinned and slow at taking a hint as she was!

'Gwen's met her match at last,' said Darrell to Sally.

'I say, look at Bill – and Clarissa, too – all dressed up in riding things. Don't they *know* the committee meeting's in about ten minutes?'

Sally called to them. 'Hey, you two! Where do you think you're going?'

'To have a look at Thunder and Merrylegs,' said Bill.

'But didn't you *know* there's a committee meeting on almost at once?' said Darrell, exasperated.

'No. Nobody told us,' said Clarissa, looking startled. 'It wasn't up on the notice-board.'

'Well, we've been talking about it ever since this morning, and except for Maureen and Gwen, who discussed golden-haired beauties in plays, we've talked about nothing else all tea-time,' said Darrell. 'Where are your ears? Didn't you hear a word of it?'

'Not a word,' said Bill, seriously. 'I'm so sorry. Of course we'll come. Have we time just to go and see Thunder and Merrylegs first? We must have been talking about something else, Clarissa and I, and not heard the rest of you.'

'You were whinnying away to each other,' said Sally. 'I

suppose you've got horses on the brain again. No, don't go down to the stables now – you certainly won't be back till the end of the meeting if you do. I know you two when you disappear into the stables. You're gone for ever!'

Clarissa and Bill walked off to the fifth-form common-room with a good grace. Perhaps there would be time afterwards to go to the stables.

'Come on,' said Sally to Darrell. 'Let's go and round up all the others. I'm longing for this committee.'

Meeting at half-past five

The whole of the fifth form was soon collected in the North Tower common-room. The girls sat on chairs, lounged on the couches, or lay on the floor-rugs. They talked and shouted and laughed. Moira came in and went straight to the table. A big chair had been put behind it.

Moira banged on the table with a book.

'Quiet!' she said. 'The meeting is about to begin. You all know what it's about. It's to choose a committee to handle the organization of the Christmas entertainment, which we, the fifth form, are to undertake.'

'Hear hear,' said somebody's voice. Moira took no notice.

'I think the whole form should also be asked to discuss and choose what kind of entertainment we shall do,' she said.

'Punch and Judy Show!' called someone.

'Don't be funny,' said Moira. 'Now, first of all we'll get down to the business of choosing the committee. I asked Catherine to cut out the slips of paper to use. Where are they, Catherine?'

She turned to where Catherine was sitting next to her. Catherine handed her a sheaf of slips.

'Here they are. I did them all as soon as you told me

you wanted them. And here's a box. I got it out of the cupboard in the fifth-form room. And I've collected enough pencils for everyone to use. And look . . .'

'All right, all right,' said Moira. 'That's all we shall want. Now, who'll give out the paper slips? You, Mary-Lou?'

Mary-Lou was perched up on the top of a small cupboard, swinging her legs. She made preparations to climb down.

'No, no – don't you bother, Mary-Lou,' said Catherine, at once. 'I'll give them out.' And before anyone could stop her she was going round the room, handing everyone a slip of paper and a pencil.

'Everyone got a slip?' asked Moira. 'Look, Mavis hasn't got one, Catherine.'

'*So* sorry I missed you out!' said Catherine, in an apologetic voice. She always apologized if she could. 'Here you are.'

'Now,' said Moira, 'I think we'll have eight people on this committee – because there will be a lot of work to be done. We shall want someone to represent the art side, for instance – someone for the music side – and so on. I must be one of the committee, as I am head-girl, so you need not vote for me, of course. That means you need only put down seven names.'

'Well, I don't know that I *should* have voted for Moira,' said Alicia to Irene, in a low voice. 'Too bossy for my taste. We shall all have to salute her when we meet her soon!'

Everyone was soon busy scribbling down names. Maureen was at a loss because she knew so few.

Gwendoline prompted her, and Moira soon noticed it.

'Gwendoline! Don't tell Maureen names to put down. That simply means *you* have two votes instead of one. I forgot that Maureen is new. We shall have to leave her out of this for the moment.'

The papers were folded over and put into the box that Catherine took round. Then, while the rest of the girls chattered, Moira and Catherine took out the slips, jotted ticks beside the names of the girls chosen, and counted them up.

Moira rapped on the table. 'Silence, please! We've got the results now. These are the names of the girls with most votes: Alicia, Mavis, Irene, Belinda, Darrell, Janet – and Sally and Betty tie.'

Janet and Betty were girls from other houses who were in the fifth form. Betty was Alicia's best friend, as clever and witty as she was, and very popular.

'Well, there you are,' said Moira. 'As Sally and Betty have tied, we'd better have them both in, making a committee of nine, instead of eight.'

'I'll take on the music side,' said Irene.

'And I'd like to take the art side – any decorations and so on,' said Belinda.

'I draw very well,' whispered Maureen to Gwen. 'I could help with that. Shall I say so?'

'No,' said Gwen, who couldn't draw anything, and didn't particularly want this new girl to shine.

'I'll take on the costumes,' said Janet, who was extremely clever with her needle, and made all her own dresses. 'I'd love to help with those.'

'Good,' said Moira, approvingly.

'Could I – do you think I could help with the *singing* part of it?' said Mavis, hesitatingly. 'I don't want to push myself forward – but if there's to be any singing – you know, choruses and all that – I could train them. I've had such a lot of training myself I think I'd know how to set about it.'

'Right. That's a good idea,' said Moira.

'And if there's any solo-work, you can sing it yourself!' called Darrell. 'Your voice is lovely now.'

Mavis flushed with pleasure. 'Oh well – I'll see. There might not be any,' she said. 'It depends what we do, doesn't it?'

'That leaves Alicia, Darrell, Sally and myself for general things – the organization,' said Moira, who was certainly able to handle a meeting well, and make it get on with things. 'We'll have to work together smoothly, efficiently – and amicably.'

She glanced at Alicia, as she spoke, a quick, rather hostile glance, a mere flick of the eyes. But Alicia caught it and noted it. That word 'amicably' was meant for her. All right – she would be amicable just as long as Moira was – and not a moment longer!

'Well, now that we've got the members of the committee settled, we'll get on with the next thing,' said Moira. 'What kind of entertainment shall we give?'

'Pantomime!'

'No – a play – a humorous play! Let's do *A Quiet Weekend*!'

'A variety show!'

'A ballet! Oh, do let's do a ballet!'

The last suggestion was from a girl who was a beautiful ballet dancer. She was cried down.

'No, no – that's too one-sided. We can't all dance!'

'Well, let's have something that everyone can be in, and *do* something in.'

'Well, it had better be a pantomime, then,' said Moira. 'We can have songs, dances, acting and all kinds of side-shows in that. A pantomime never sticks to its story – it just does what it likes.'

After some more shouting and discussion a pantomime was decided on, and for some reason or other *Cinderella* found more favour than any other pantomime idea.

Gwen and Maureen immediately had visions of themselves as perfect Cinderellas, loose hair and all. Maureen turned to Gwen.

'How I'd love to act Cinderella,' she murmured. 'At my last school I . . .'

'Let's see now – what was your last school?' asked Belinda at once.

Poor Maureen didn't dare to say the name. She turned her back on Belinda. 'At my last school I was once Cinderella,' she said. 'I was a great success. I . . .'

Gwen didn't like this kind of thing at all. She began to think Maureen very boring and conceited. Why, *she* had been about to say what a good Cinderella *she* would make! She didn't consider that Maureen, with her weak, silly, rabbit-mouthed face would make a good leading lady at all.

'We'll choose Cinderella for our pantomime story then,' said Moira. 'We will write the whole thing ourselves. Darrell, you're good at essays – you can draft it out.'

Darrell looked enormously surprised. 'Draft it out – draft out a whole *pantomime*!' she exclaimed. 'Oh, I couldn't. I wouldn't know how to begin.'

'You've only got to get the script of one or two other pantomimes to see how to set about it,' said Moira. 'Can you write verse – and words for songs? We'll have to have those, too.'

Darrell wished fervently she wasn't on the committee at all. Why, this was going to be Real Hard Work – just as she thought she was going to have a nice slack term, too. She opened her mouth to protest, but Moira had already finished with her. She was now speaking to Irene.

'Can you get on with the music as soon as we've got the words?' she asked. 'Or perhaps you prefer to write the music before you get the words and have them fitted afterwards?'

'I'll work in my own way, thank you,' said Irene, perfectly politely, but with a steady ring in her voice that said, 'Keep off! Where music is concerned I'm going to do as I like.' She looked straight at Moira. 'You can safely leave it to me. Music's my job, it always has been and it always will be.'

'Yes, but I must know how you're going to set about it – what kind of tunes you'll write, and so on,' said Moira, impatiently. 'We can't leave things like that in the air.'

'You'll have to as far as I'm concerned,' said Irene. 'I don't know what tunes I'm going to write till I hear them in my head. Then I'll catch them and write them down. And I don't know *when* I'll hear them either, so don't tell me to sit down at ten each morning and listen for them!'

Catherine tried to pour oil on troubled waters once more. She loved doing that. 'Well, after all – when you're dealing with a *genius*,' she began. 'You can't make rules for geniuses, can you? Moira doesn't quite *understand*, Irene.'

'Don't apologize for anything *I* say,' said Moira, scowling at Catherine. 'What do you mean – I don't quite *understand*! I've done this kind of thing often enough. Didn't I run the show last year, and help to run it the year before that?'

Catherine put on a saintly expression. 'Yes, of course, Moira. Don't put yourself out. I shouldn't have said a *word*! I'm sure Irene understands?'

She gave Irene such a sweet smile that everyone felt quite sick. *Did* Catherine have to make herself quite so humble?

The meeting had to come to an abrupt end because the supper-bell went. 'Good gracious – how the time flew!' said Maureen.

'And now we shan't have time to go to the stables,' mourned Bill, dismally.

'We'll call a short committee meeting tomorrow, same time,' said Moira, gathering up her things. 'We'll tie up any loose ends then.'

She swept efficiently out of the room, almost as if she were a mistress!

'Gosh! We'll have to mind our Ps and Qs now,' said Daphne, with a comical look. 'What *have* we done to have Moira wished on us this term!'

The balloon trick

The first week of term always went very slowly indeed. The next week slipped away faster, and then the weeks began to fly. But now it was still only the first week, with a lot of planning and time-tables to make, and settling-in to be done.

Darrell found herself very busy indeed. She had to attend committee meetings for the Christmas entertainment. She had to read through two or three pantomime scripts, and decide how to draft out her own version of *Cinderella*. She found Sally an enormous help here, and discovered that two heads are decidedly better than one.

She was also in charge of the games, and had to draw up practice times for the lower school, and to do a little coaching to help the games-mistresses. They consulted with her as to the best players to pick out for matches in the lower school, and Darrell enjoyed feeling important enough to argue with them about the various girls.

'But you *can't* have Rita,' she would say. 'I know she's good – but she simply won't turn out for practice. She'll go to pieces in a match.'

'Well, what do you think of Christine, then?' the

games-mistress would say. 'She's so small, I don't like to pick her.'

'But she runs like the wind!' Darrell would reply. 'And she's so keen. She's just waiting for a chance!'

Yes, Darrell had a lot to do, and she was always busy and always interested in her jobs. The lower school adored her, and vied to win an approving word from her. Felicity was very proud of her fifth-form sister.

'Everyone thinks you're super,' she told Darrell. 'You should see the way they turn out for practice now – on even the most disgusting days! I say – *have* I got a chance to get into one of the match-teams some day, Darrell? You might tell me.'

'I can only say that if you go on as you are doing you won't be able to *help* getting in,' said Darrell, and Felicity gave a whoop of joy.

June was passing and gave her a sour look. She spoke to Gwyneth, the girl with her. 'Talk about favouritism! You'll see Darrell choosing her young sister before anyone else and putting her into the team.'

Darrell heard and was over beside June at once. 'June! How *dare* you say a thing like that about a fifth-former! Just you wait a minute!'

She fished out the Punishment Book that all the fifth-formers were allowed to have and wrote down June's name in it. She wrote something beside it, tore it out and gave it to June.

'There you are – a little hard work will keep you quiet, and teach you to guard that nasty tongue of yours!'

June took the paper sulkily. She glanced at it. Darrell had written:

'Learn three sonnets of Shakespeare's, and say them to me or one of the other fifth-formers before Tuesday.'

June scowled. 'I can't do this,' she said. 'I've got something to learn for Alicia this week. I can't do both.'

'I'm afraid you'll have to,' said Darrell. 'I suppose you cheeked Alicia again. Well, we won't have it. If you don't learn manners now, and respect for your elders, you never will. You say those sonnets to me before Tuesday!'

She went off with Felicity. 'June's awful,' remarked Felicity. 'If only she wasn't so frightfully funny sometimes, I honestly would never speak to her. Nor would Susan. But she plays such idiotic tricks. She's playing one tomorrow on Mam'zelle Dupont.'

'What is it?' asked Darrell, with interest. 'I shouldn't have thought there were any tricks left to play on poor old Mam'zelle.'

'Well, there are – and June plays them,' said Felicity. 'And when I see Mam'zelle's face I laugh till I cry.'

'Yes, I know – I've laughed till I've ached too, sometimes,' said Darrell, remembering some of the jokes she and her form had played at times. 'What's June playing at tomorrow?'

'Oh, Darrell,' said Felicity, beginning to giggle as she thought of it. 'She's got a kind of flat balloon arrangement – well, she's got four, in fact. And you put one under your blouse at the back and another in your front, and another under your skirt at the back, and the last one in front.'

Darrell chuckled. 'Go on. I can guess what happens.'

'Well, June showed us,' said Felicity, beginning to laugh helplessly. 'All the balloons are joined together by little tubes – and there's an inflator you press to fill them and a deflator you pull out to empty them. When she pressed the inflator she swelled up, you see, and she looked simply *frightful*. Oh, dear – I laughed so much I couldn't sit in my chair.'

Darrell laughed, too. 'Well, that's a new trick, certainly! I wish we'd had it when *we* were in the first form. Where does June get these tricks from? Alicia always got them from her brothers.'

'Oh, June gets advertisement booklets sent her from the firms that make conjuring tricks and funny tricks,' said Felicity. 'I think she must spend all her pocket-money on them.'

'It wouldn't be a bad idea to have a spot of conjuring in our pantomime,' said Darrell, thoughtfully. 'Alicia is awfully good at conjuring. Yes – I'll put a conjuror into the pantomime – it shall be Alicia! If you can borrow that book – or however many she's got – from June, I'd like to look through them.'

'Right. But I won't tell her *you* want it,' said Felicity. 'You'll be mud to her now, after giving her those sonnets to learn. June's doing the trick tomorrow morning at twelve in French *Dictée*, Darrell. You're not free by any chance, are you? If so, couldn't you come along with some message for Mam'zelle, or something, and see June swell up? You'll know when it's happening because I expect we'll shriek with laughter.'

Darrell pondered. She had put that period aside to get on with the draft of the pantomime. Until she had worked out the characters they could not be chosen, so it was important to get on with it. But how could she resist the chance of slipping down to see Mam'zelle's face?

'Well, I'll come if I can,' she promised.

But when twelve o'clock came next morning Darrell was called to talk to Matron about some missing socks. Matron always went into matters of this sort very thoroughly indeed, and it was twenty minutes before Darrell was free.

I wonder what's happened down in the first form? she thought, feeling rather guilty at her interest in something such babies did. I wonder if the trick's been played?

It had. June, who always had to sit in one of the front desks, so as to be under every mistress's eye, had inflated herself very successfully indeed. She did it gradually, so that when Mam'zelle kept looking at her to see that she was getting on with the dictation, she did not at first notice anything.

However, she certainly began to seem a little on the plump side after a bit. Mam'zelle pondered over it: 'That child, June – she gets fat. Maybe a little fat will do her good. She is too restless – a truly difficult girl. Now, *fat* girls are not usually difficult – an interesting point.'

She glanced at June again and got rather a shock. Why, the child was positively bloated! She stared at June fixedly. One or two of the girls felt such a desire to laugh that it was agony to keep their faces straight.

June wrote steadily on. 'June!' said Mam'zelle, sharply. 'Are you holding your breath?'

June looked innocently at Mam'zelle. 'Holding my breath?' she said, with wide eyes. 'No. Why should I? But I will if you want me to, Mam'zelle. I can hold it for a long time.'

She blew out her cheeks and held her breath. The inflator worked marvellously. She swelled visibly, and Mam'zelle stared in alarm.

'No, no – let out your breath, June. You will burst. What is happening to you?'

June let out her breath with a loud hissing noise, and at the same time pulled the deflator. She deflated at once – and it looked exactly as if it was because she had let out her breath. Mam'zelle was most relieved to see her become her right size again.

'It was rather nice, holding my breath like that,' said June, foreseeing a very nice little game of holding her breath and inflating herself, and letting it out and deflating at the same time.

To Mam'zelle's horror she breathed in again, blew out her cheeks and held her breath – and visibly, before Mam'zelle's alarmed gaze, she inflated till she looked really monstrous. Mam'zelle started up from her seat.

'Never have I seen such a thing!' she said, wildly. 'June, *je vous prie* – I beg you, do not hold your breath in this manner. You will burst.'

The whole class burst at that moment. It was

impossible to hold their laughter in any longer. June let out her breath and deflated rapidly.

'Don't, don't, June!' gasped Felicity, rolling about in her chair. 'Oh, don't do it again.'

But June did, and Mam'zelle watched wildly while she swelled up once more. 'Monstrous!' she cried. 'June, I beg of you once more. Do not hold your breath again. See how it swells you up, poor child.'

And then something went wrong with the deflator! It wouldn't work. June pulled it frantically, but it wouldn't deflate the fat balloons under her clothes. She sat there, pulling wildly at the string fastened to the deflator. It came off!

Mam'zelle was almost in tears. 'This poor June! Children, children, how can you laugh? It is no laughing matter. I go, to get help. Matron must come. Be still, June. Do not burst.'

She hurried out, wringing her hands. June looked decidedly alarmed. 'I say! The beastly thing's gone wrong. I can't let Matron see me like this. I'd get an awful wigging. What can I do?'

Darrell had just arrived at the door at the moment that Mam'zelle rushed out, looking frantic. She had pushed by Darrell without even seeing her. Darrell looked in at the open door.

She saw the monstrous June. Felicity saw Darrell as an angel in disguise. 'Darrell! The deflator's gone wrong! Mam'zelle's gone to get Matron. Quick, what can we do?'

'Get a pin, idiot,' said Darrell. 'Stick it into June and

she'll go pop and subside. Then you'd better get her out of that arrangement quickly, because Matron will certainly do some exploring.'

A pin was produced. Felicity dug it into the four swellings and they each went off with a loud *pop*! June became her own size and shape at once. She began to pull everything out, frantically and wildly. She was frightened now.

She got the rubber balloons out at last and put them into her desk, just as footsteps were heard down the corridor. Darrell slipped out, finding it difficult not to dissolve into laughter. How she would have loved to see Mam'zelle's face when she first saw June swelling up!

Mam'zelle was alone, looking rather subdued. She hurried by Darrell and came to the first form. She went in and gazed at June.

'Ah – so – you are flat now! I told Matron about you and she laughed at me. She said it was a treek. A TREEK! What is this awful, horrible, *abominable* treek? I will find it. I will seek it. I will hunt for it in every desk in the room. Ahhhhhhhh!'

Mam'zelle looked so fierce as she stood there that nobody dared to say a word. June began to wish she had left the balloons in her clothes. If Mam'zelle did look in her desk she would certainly find them.

Mam'zelle found them. She lifted up the lid and saw the rubber balloons at once, flat and torn. She picked them out and shook them in June's face. 'Ah, now you can hold your breath again, you bad, wicked June! Hold your breath and listen to what I have to say! You will learn for me one hundred lines of French poetry before Tuesday. Yes, one hundred lines! Does that make you hold your breath, you bad girl?'

It certainly did. June already had two lots of English lines to learn – now she had a hundred French ones to add to the lot. She groaned.

Mam'zelle rummaged further in the desk. She took out some booklets and looked at them.

'New treeks. Old treeks. Treeks to play on your friends. Treeks to play on your enemies,' she read. 'Aha! These I will take from you, June. You shall do no more treeks this term. These I will confiscate, and I do not think you shall have them back. No!'

She put the booklets with her books on the desk and, very grim and determined, went on with the French *Dictée*. The class soon recovered and longed for the last bell to go, so that they might laugh once again to their heart's content.

Mam'zelle said a sharp good morning when the bell went, and went off with the rubber balloons, the booklets about tricks, and her own books. She sat down in the room she shared with Miss Potts, the house-mistress of North Tower.

'You look hot and bothered, Mam'zelle,' said Miss Potts, sympathetically.

'Ah – this June – she swells up like a frog – under my eyes!' began Mam'zelle, fiercely, swelling up too. Then she saw Miss Potts's astonished look, and she smiled suddenly.

She opened her mouth and laughed. She rolled in her seat and roared.

'Oh, these treeks! One of these days I too will play a treek. It shall be *superbe, magnifique, merveilleuse*. Ha, one day I too will play a treek!'

In the common-room

Darrell told Alicia about June's idiotic trick. Alicia laughed. 'It's in the family, isn't it! I and my brothers are trick-mad, and now June, my cousin, is going the same way. It's a pity we're in the fifth. I feel it wouldn't be very dignified to play any of our tricks now.'

Darrell sighed. 'Yes, I suppose you're right. Growing-up has its drawbacks, and that's one of them. We have to be dignified and give up some of our silly ideas – but oh, Alicia, I *wish* you could have seen June all blown up – honestly it was as good as any of *your* tricks!'

'It's a pity that cousin of mine is such a hard and brazen little wretch,' said Alicia. 'I don't actually feel she's afraid of *anything* – except perhaps my brother Sam. The odd thing is she simply adores him, though he's given her some first-class scoldings, and won't stand a scrap of nonsense from her when she comes to stay.'

'You can't seem to *get* at her, somehow,' said Darrell. 'I mean – she doesn't seem to care. Well – she's a bit like you, you know, Alicia – though you're a lot better now!'

Alicia went rather pink. 'All right. Don't rub it in. I know I'm hard, but you won't make me any better by telling me! You've probably not noticed it but I *have*

71

tried to be more sympathetic with fools and donkeys! Of course, not being either yourself you've had no chance of seeing it.'

Darrell laughed. She slipped her arm through Alicia's. 'You're a bit of a donkey yourself,' she said. 'But there's one thing about you that sticks out a mile – and that is your absolute straightness – and I don't feel that about June. Do you? I feel it about my sister Felicity – you could trust her anywhere at any time – but not June. There's something sly about her as well as hard.'

'Well, we'll have to lick her into shape while we're still at Malory Towers,' said Alicia. 'We've got two more years to do it in – and then off we go to college – leaving kids like June and Felicity behind to carry on!'

June arrived in the fifth-form common-room on Tuesday evening to say her lines to Alicia and Darrell. She looked very sulky. The girls, who were most of them busy with odd jobs such as darning, making out lists, re-writing work, writing letters home and so on, looked up as June strode into the room.

'Don't you know that a lower-school kid knocks before she comes in?' said Moira.

June said nothing, but glowered.

'Go out, knock and wait till you're told to come in,' ordered Moira, in her dictatorial voice. June hesitated. She detested being ordered about.

Moira felt in her pocket for her little Punishment Book, and June fled. She didn't want any more lines!

'I never knew anyone who so badly needed licking into

shape,' said Moira, grimly. 'Little toad! I know she's your cousin, Alicia, but she's no credit to you!'

'I can't say your sister Bridget is much credit to *you* either,' retorted Alicia. She didn't particularly want to defend June, but she resented Moira's high and mighty manner. Let her look after her own bad-mannered sister!

'June's knocked twice already,' said Catherine. 'Oughtn't we to say "come in"?'

'When I say so,' said Moira. 'Do her good to wait.'

June knocked again. 'Come in,' said Moira, and June came in, red and furious. She went to Darrell and silently gave her the book out of which she had learned her lines.

'Repeat them to me,' said Darrell. June gabbled them off without a single mistake. Darrell looked at her. She really was very like Alicia – and she had Alicia's marvellous memory, too. No doubt it had taken June only about five minutes to memorize those poems.

She went to Alicia, and gabbled off what she had learned for her, again with no mistake. 'Right,' said Alicia. 'You can go – and if you don't want to spend the whole of this term learning lines, try to be more civil to your elders.'

June scowled. Belinda whipped out her pencil.

'Hold it!' she said to the surprised June. 'Yes – just like that – mouth down, brows frowning, surly expression. Hold it, hold it! I want it for my Scowl Book. It's called "How to Scowl" and it's really interesting. You should see some of the scowls I've got!'

Moira and Gwendoline, who knew they had contributed to this unique book, immediately scowled with

73

annoyance, and then straightened their faces at once in case Belinda saw them. Blow Belinda! One couldn't even scowl in peace with her around.

June stood still, scowling even more fiercely. 'Done?' she said at last. 'Well, I wish you joy of all your scowls – I'll be willing to come along and offer you a good selection any time you like. It's an easy thing to do when any fifth-former is around.'

She stalked off, feeling in her pocket for the lines she had learned for Mam'zelle. They hadn't really taken her very long. Thank goodness for a parrot memory! June had only to read lines through once, saying them out loud, to know them. Others with less good memories envied her tremendously. It didn't seem fair that June, who tried so little, could do such good work, and that they, who tried so hard, very often only produced bad or ordinary work!

'Blow!' said Irene, suddenly, putting down her pencil. She had been composing a little galloping tune, the one that had been in her head for some time after she had heard the galloping hooves of the horses in the drive. 'I'm just nicely in the middle of this tirretty-too tune – and I've just remembered it's my turn to do the flowers in the classroom. I ought to go and pick them before it's quite dark.'

'Let *me* go,' said Catherine, putting down her darning. 'I'll be pleased to do it for you. You're *such* a genius, Irene – you just go on with your tune. I'm only an ordinary mortal – no gifts at all – and it's a pleasure to do what little I can.'

She smiled her beaming smile, and Irene felt slightly sick. Everyone was getting tired of Catherine and her martyr-like ways. She was always putting herself out for someone, offering to do the jobs nobody else wanted to do, belittling herself, and praising others extravagantly.

'No thanks,' said Irene, shortly. 'It's my job and I must do it.'

'How like you to feel like that!' gushed Catherine. 'Well – I'm quite busy darning Gwendoline's stocking, so if you *really* wouldn't like me to do the flowers for you, I'll . . .'

But Irene was gone. She slammed the door and nobody except Catherine minded. They all felt like slamming the door themselves.

'I do think Irene might have said thank you,' said Catherine, in rather a hurt voice. 'Don't you, Maureen?'

Maureen felt that everyone was waiting to pounce on her if she dared to say 'yes'. Irene was so very popular. She was hesitating how to answer when the door opened and Irene came back.

'Someone's done the flowers!' she said.

'Yes – now I come to think of it, I saw Clarissa doing them,' said Mavis.

'What on earth for?' demanded Irene. 'Gosh – I hope people aren't going to run round after me doing my jobs! I'm still perfectly capable of doing them.'

'Well,' said Darrell, suddenly remembering, 'it's Clarissa's week, idiot. Your week is next week. You looked it up this morning.'

'Gosh!' said Irene again, with a comical air of dismay. 'I'm nuts! I go and interrupt my own bit of composing, and rush off to do a job I'm not supposed to do till next week. Anyway – it gave dear Catherine a chance to make one of her generous offers!'

'That's not kind of you, Irene,' said Catherine, flushing. 'But never mind – I do understand. If I could compose like you I'd say nasty things sometimes, I expect! I do understand.'

'Could you stop being forgiving and understanding long enough for me to finish my tune?' said Irene, in a dangerous voice. 'I don't care if you "understand" or not – all I care about at the moment is to finish this.'

Catherine put on a saintly face, pressed her lips together as if stopping herself from retorting, and went on darning.

There was a knock at the door. Irene groaned. 'Go away! Don't come in!'

The door opened and Connie's face peered round. 'Is Ruth here? Ruth, can you come for a minute? Bridget is out here. We've got rather a good idea.'

'I don't like Bridget,' said Ruth, in a low voice. 'And anyway I'm busy. So's everyone else here.'

'But, Ruth – I've hardly seen you this week,' protested Connie. 'Come on out for a minute. By the way, I've mended your roller-skates for you. They're ready for you to use again.'

Irene groaned. Darrell groaned, too. She was trying to draft out the third act of the pantomime.

'Either tell Connie to go, or go yourself,' said Irene. 'If

not, *I'll* go! I'll go and sit in the bathroom and take this with me. Perhaps I'll get a few minutes' peace then. Tirretty-tirretty-too. Yes, I think I'll go.'

She got up. Connie fled, thinking Irene was going to row her. Ruth looked round apologetically, but said nothing.

'It's all right,' said Darrell, softly. 'Keep Connie at arm's length till she leaves you in peace, Ruth – and don't worry about it!'

But Catherine had to be silly about it, of course. 'Poor Connie,' she said. 'I really can't help feeling sorry for her. We oughtn't to be *too* hard on her, ought we?'

The weeks go on

Now the days began to slip by more quickly. Two weeks went – three weeks – and then the fourth week turned up and began to slip away, too.

Everything was going well. There was no illness in the school. The weather was fine, so that the playing-fields were in use every day, and there was plenty of practice for everyone. Work was going well, and except for the real duds, nobody was doing badly. Five lacrosse matches had already been won by the school, and Darrell, as games captain for the fifth, was in the seventh heaven of delight.

She had played in two of the matches, and had shot both the winning goals. Felicity had gone nearly mad with joy. She had been able to watch Darrell in both because they were home matches. Felicity redoubled her practices and begged Darrell for all the coaching time she could spare. She was reserve for the fourth school-team, and was determined to be in it before the end of the term.

The plans for the Christmas entertainment were going well, too. So far no help had been asked from either Mr Young, the music-master, or Miss Greening, the elocution mistress. The girls had planned everything themselves.

Darrell had been amazed at the way she and Sally had

been able to grasp the planning of a big pantomime. At first it had seemed a hopeless task, and Darrell hadn't had the faintest idea how to set about it. But now, having got down to it with Sally, having read up a few other plays and pantomimes, and got the general idea, she was finding that she seemed to have quite a gift for working out a new one!

'It's wonderful!' she said to Sally. 'I didn't know I *could*. I'm loving it. I say, Sally – do you think, do you *possibly* think I might have a sort of gift that way? I never thought I had any gift at all.'

'Yes,' said Sally, loyally. 'I think you *have* got a gift for this kind of thing. That's the best of a school like this, that has so many many interests – there's something for everybody – and if you *have* got a hidden or sleeping gift you're likely to find it, and be able to use it. There's your way of scribbling down verse, too – I never knew you could do that before!'

'Nor did I, really,' said Darrell. She fished among her papers and pulled out a scribbled sheet. 'Can I read you this, Sally? It's the song Cinderella is supposed to sing as she sits by the fire, alone. Her sisters have gone to the ball. Listen:

'By the fire I sit and dream
And in the flames I see,
Pictures of the lovely things
That never come to me,
That never come to me,
Ah me!

79

Carriages, a lovely gown,
A flowing silver cloak –
The embers move, the picture's gone,
My dreams go up in smoke,
My dreams go up in smoke,
In smoke!'

She stopped. 'That's as far as I've got with that song. Of course, I know it's not awfully good, and certainly not poetry, only just verse – but I never in my life knew I could even put things in rhyme! And, of course, Irene just gobbles them up, and sets them to delicious tunes in no time.'

'Yes. It's very good,' said Sally. 'You do enjoy it all, too, don't you? I say – what *will* your parents think when they come to the pantomime and see on the programme that Darrell Rivers has written the words – and the songs, too!'

'I don't know. I don't think they'll believe it,' said Darrell.

Darrell was not the only member of the fifth form enjoying herself over the production of the pantomime. Irene was too – she was setting Darrell's songs to exactly the right tunes, and scribbling down the harmonies as if she had been composing all her life long – as she very nearly had, for Irene was humming melodies before she was one year old!

The class were used to seeing Irene coming along the corridor or up the stairs, bumping unseeingly into them, humming a new tune. 'Tumty-ta, ti-ta, ti-ta, tumty-too.

Oh, sorry, Mavis. I honestly didn't see you. Tumty-ta, ti-ta – gosh, did I hurt you, Catherine. I never saw you coming.'

'Oh, that's *quite* all right,' said Catherine, gently, patting Irene on the arm, and making her shy away at once. 'We don't have geniuses like you every . . .'

But Irene was gone. How she detested Catherine with her humble ways, and her continual air of sacrificing herself for others!

'Tumty-ta, ti-ta,' she hummed suddenly in class, and banged her hand down on the desk. 'Got it! Of course, that's it! Oh, *sorry*, Miss Jimmy – er, James, I mean, Miss James. I just got carried away for a moment. I've been haunted by . . .'

'You needn't explain,' said Miss James, with a twinkle in her eye. 'Do you think you've got that particular tune out of your system now, and could concentrate, say for half an hour, on what the rest of the class are doing?'

'Oh yes – yes, of course,' said Irene, still rather bemused. She bent over her maths book, pencil in hand. Miss James was amused to see one page of figures and one page of scribbled music, when the book was given in – both excellent, for Irene was almost as much a genius at maths as at music. She insisted that the two things went together, though this seemed unbelievable to the rest of the class. Maths were so dull and music so lovely!

The words of the pantomime progressed fast, and so did the music. It was essential that they should because there could be no rehearsing until there was something to rehearse!

Belinda was busy with designs for scenery and costumes. She, too, was extremely happy. Her pencil flew over the paper each evening and every moment of free time – she drew everything, even the pattern on Cinderella's apron!

Little Janet waited eagerly as the designs grew and were passed on to her. She too was eager and enthusiastic. She turned out the enormous trunks of dresses and tunics and costumes of all periods, used by other girls at Malory Towers in terms gone by. How could she alter this? How could she use that? Oh, what a wonderful piece of blue velvet! Just right for the Prince!

Little Janet had always been ingenious, but now she surpassed herself. She chose all the material and stuff she needed, with unerring taste – she sorted out dresses and costumes that could be altered. She ran round the school pressing all the good needle-workers into her service. She begged Miss Linnie, the quiet little sewing-mistress, to help her by allowing some of the classes to work on the clothes and decorations.

'I would never have thought that little mouse of a Janet had it in her to blossom out like this!' said Miss Potts to Mam'zelle. 'What these children can do if they're just given a chance to do things on their own!'

Another person who was working hard, though in quite a different direction, was Alicia! Alicia, who never worked really hard at anything, because she had good brains and didn't need to. But now she had something to do that, brains or no brains, needed constant hard work and practice.

Alicia was to be the Demon King in the pantomime – and he was to be an enchanter, a conjuror who could do magic things! Alicia was to show her skill at conjuring, and she meant to be as good a conjuror on the school stage as any conjuror in a London pantomime.

'Well – I didn't dream that Alicia's ability for playing silly tricks and doing bits of amateur conjuring to amuse her friends would make her work as hard as *this*,' said Miss Peters, the third-form mistress, shutting the door of one of the music-rooms softly.

She had heard peculiar sounds in there – sounds of pantings, sounds of something falling, sounds of sheer exasperation, and she had peeped in to see what in the world was going on.

Alicia was there, with her back to her, practising a spot of juggling! Yes, she was going to juggle, as well as conjure – and she had an array of coloured rings which she was throwing rapidly up into the air, one after another, catching them miraculously.

Then she would miss one, and click in exasperation. She would have to begin all over again. Ah – Alicia had found something that didn't need only brainwork – it needed patience, practice, deftness, and then patience all over again.

'Why did I ever say I'd be the Demon King!' groaned Alicia, picking up the rings for the twenty-second time and beginning again. 'Why did I ever agree to do conjuring and juggling? I must have been mad.'

But her pride made her go on and on. If Alicia did a

thing it had to be done better than anybody else could possibly do it. The fifth form were most intrigued by this new interest of Alicia's. It was such fun to see her suddenly pick up a pencil, rubber, ruler and pen, and juggle them rapidly in the air, catching them deftly in one hand at the finish!

It was amusing to see her get up to find Mam'zelle's fountain-pen, and pick it apparently out of the empty air, and even more amusing to see her gravely abstract an egg from Mam'zelle's ear.

'Alicia! I will not have such a thing!' stormed Mam'zelle. 'Oh, *là là*! Now you have found a pencil in my other ear. It is not nice! It makes me go – what do you call it – duck-flesh.'

'Goose-flesh, Mam'zelle,' said Alicia, with one of her wicked grins. 'Dear me – has your fountain-pen gone again? It's up in the air as usual!' And she reached out her hand and picked it once more from the air.

No wonder the class liked Alicia's new interest. It certainly added a lot more enjoyment to lessons!

12

Gwendoline Mary and Maureen

Two girls were anxiously waiting for Darrell to finish the pantomime. They were Gwendoline and Maureen. Each of them saw herself in the part of Cinderella. Each of them crept away to the dormy on occasion, let her golden hair loose, and posed in front of the dressing-table mirrors.

'I look exactly right for Cinderella,' thought Gwendoline Mary. 'I'm the *type*, somehow. I could sit pensively by the fireside and look really lovely. And as the princess at the ball I'd be wonderful.'

She wrote and told her mother about the coming pantomime. 'Of course, we don't know *yet* about the characters,' she said. 'Most of the girls would like me to be Cinderella – they say I *look* the part. I don't know what *you* think, Mother? I'm not conceited, as you know, but I can't help thinking I'd do it rather well. What does Miss Winter think?'

Back came two gushing letters at once, one from her delighted mother, one from her old governess, worshipping as ever.

DARLING GWEN,

Yes, of course you must be Cinderella. You would be

85

absolutely right. Your hair would look so lovely in the firelight. Oh, how proud I shall be to see you sitting there pensive and sad, looking into . . .

And so on and so on. Miss Winter's letter was much the same. Both of them had apparently taken it completely for granted that Gwendoline would have the chief part.

Moira came barging into the dormy one day and discovered a startled Gwendoline standing in front of her mirror, her hair all round her face, and a towel thrown over her shoulders for an evening cloak.

'Gosh – what *do* you think you're doing?' she said, in amazement. 'Washing your hair or something? Are you mad, Gwen? You can't wash your hair at this time of day. You're due for French in five minutes.'

Gwendoline muttered something and flung the towel back on its rack. She went bright red. Moira was puzzled.

Two days later Moira again came rushing into the dormy to see if the windows were open. This time she found Maureen standing in front of *her* mirror, her hair loose down her back in a golden sheet, and one of the cubicle curtains pinned round her waist to make a train.

Moira gaped. Maureen went pink and began to brush her hair as if it was a perfectly ordinary thing to be found with it loose, and a curtain pinned to her waist.

Moira found her voice. 'What do you and Gwen think you're doing, parading about here with your hair loose and towels and curtains draped round you?' she demanded. 'Have you both gone crackers? Every time I come into this dormy I see you or Gwen with your hair loose and things draped round you. What are you up to?'

Maureen couldn't possibly tell the scornful practical Moira what she was doing – merely pretending to be a beautiful Cinderella with a cloud of glorious hair, and a long golden train to her dress. But Moira suddenly guessed.

She laughed her loud and scornful laugh. 'Oh! I believe *I* know! You're playing Cinderella! Both of you pretending to be Cinderella. What a hope you've got! We'd never choose rabbit-teeth to play Cinderella.'

And with this very cutting remark Moira went out of the room, laughing loudly. Maureen gazed at herself in the mirror and tears came to her eyes. Rabbit-teeth! How *horrible* of Moira. How frightfully cruel. She couldn't help her teeth being like that. Or could she? Very guiltily Maureen remembered how she had been told to wear a wire round her front teeth to force them back – and she hadn't been able to get used to it, and had tucked it away in her drawer at Mazeley Manor.

Nobody there had said anything about it. Nobody had bothered. Mazeley Manor was a free-and-easy school, as Maureen was so fond of saying, comparing it un-favourably with Malory Towers, and its compulsory games, its inquisitive Matron and determined, responsible house-mistresses.

If I'd been *here* when the dentist told me to wear that wire round my teeth, Matron and Miss Potts would both have made me do it, even if I didn't want to, she thought. And by now I'd have nice teeth – not sticking-out and ugly.

And for the first time a doubt about that wonderful school, Mazeley Manor, crept into Maureen's mind. Was it so good after all to be allowed to do just as you liked? To play games or not as you liked? To go for walks or not at your own choice? Perhaps – yes perhaps it *was* better to *have* to do things that were good for you, whether you liked them or not, till you were old enough and responsible enough to choose.

Maureen had chosen not to wear the wire when she should have done – and now she had been called Rabbit-Teeth, and she was sure she wouldn't be chosen as Cinderella. She did up her hair rather soberly, blinking away a few more tears, and trying to shut her lips over the protruding front teeth.

She forgot to unpin the curtain, and went out of the room, thinking so deeply that she didn't even feel it dragging behind her. She met Mam'zelle at the top of the stairs.

'*Tiens*!' said Mam'zelle, stopping in surprise. '*Que faites-vous*, Maureen? What are you doing with that curtain?'

Maureen cast a horrified look at her 'train' and rushed back to the dormy. She unpinned it and put the curtain back into its place. Feeling rather subdued she went downstairs to find Gwen.

Gwen was getting very very tired of Maureen. The new girl had fastened on to her like a leech. She related long and boring stories of her people, her friends, her old school and especially of herself. She never seemed to think that Gwen would like to talk too.

Gwen sometimes broke into the middle of Maureen's boring speeches. 'Maureen, did I ever tell you about the time I went to Norway? My word, it was super. I stayed up to dinner each night, and I was only thirteen, and . . .'

'I've never been to Norway,' Maureen would interrupt. 'But my aunt went there last summer. She sent me a whole lot of postcards. I'll find them to show you. You'll be interested to see them, I'm sure.'

Gwen wasn't interested. She was never interested in anything anyone else ever showed her. In fact, like Maureen, she wasn't interested in anything except herself.

The only time that Maureen ever really listened to her was when she told unkind tales of the others in the form. Then Maureen would listen with great interest. 'I wouldn't have thought it of Darrell,' she would say. 'Good gracious, did Daphne really do that? Oh, I say – fancy *Bill* being so deceitful!'

Gwen was forced to play games and not only that, but to take part in a lot of practices. She was made to do gym properly, and never allowed to get out of it by announcing she didn't feel too well. She had to go for every walk that was planned, fuming and furious.

It was June that enlightened Maureen about all this assiduous attendance at games, gym and walks. She told her gleefully the history of Gwen's weak heart the term before.

'Gwen wanted to get out of the School Cert. exam, so she foxed and said she'd a weak heart that fluttered like a bird!' grinned June. 'Her mother took her home. And then it was discovered Gwen was pretending and back she came just in time for the exam – and ever since she's been made to go in for games and gym like anything. She's a humbug!'

June had no right to say all this to a senior, and Maureen had no right to listen to her. But, like Gwen, she loved a bit of spiteful gossip, and she stored the information up in her mind, though she said nothing to Gwen about it.

The two girls were forced to be together a great deal. Almost everyone else in the form had their own friend. Moira had no particular friend, but went with Catherine, who was always at anyone's disposal. So Gwen and Maureen, being odd ones out, had to walk together, and were left together very often when everyone else was doing something.

Gwen grew to detest Maureen. Horrid, conceited, selfish creature! She hated the sound of her voice. She tried to avoid her when she could. She made excuses not to be with her.

But Maureen wouldn't let her go. Gwen was the only one available to be talked to, and boasted to, and on occasion, when she had fallen foul of Miss James, to be wailed to.

Maureen thought she could draw as well as Belinda – or almost as well. She thought she could sing beautifully – and, indeed, she had an astonishingly powerful voice which, alas, continually went off the true note, and was flat. She was certain she could compose tunes as well as

Irene. And she even drove Darrell to distraction by offering to write a few verses for her.

'What are we to do with this pest of a Maureen?' complained Janet, one evening. 'She comes and asks if she can help me and then if I give her the simplest thing to sew, she goes and botches it up so that I have to undo it.'

'And she had the sauce to come and tell me she didn't like some of my chords in the opening chorus of *Cinderella*,' snorted Irene. 'I ticked her off. But she won't *learn* she's not wanted. She won't learn she's no good! She's so thick-skinned that I'm sure a bullet would bounce off her if she was shot!'

'She wants a lesson,' said Alicia. 'My word – if she comes and offers to show me how to juggle, I'll juggle her! I'll juggle her all down the corridor and back again, and down into the garden and on to the rocks and into the pool!'

'Gwen's looking pretty sick these days,' said Belinda. 'She doesn't like having a double that clings to her like Maureen does. I wonder if she knows how like her Maureen is. In silliness and boringness and conceitedness and boastfulness and . . .'

'Oh, I say,' said the saintly Catherine, protesting. 'Aren't you being rather unkind, Belinda?'

Belinda looked at Catherine. 'There are times to be kind and times to be unkind, dear sweet Catherine,' she said. 'But you don't seem to know them. You think you're being kind to me when you sharpen all my pencils to a pin-point – but you're not. You're just being interfering. I don't *want* all my pencils like that. I keep some of them blunt on purpose. And about this being unkind to Maureen. Sometimes unkindness is a short-cut to putting something right. I guess that's what Maureen wants – a dose of good hard common sense administered sharply. And that's what she'll get if she doesn't stop this silly nonsense of hers.'

Catherine put on her martyr-like air. 'You know best, of course, Belinda. I wouldn't dream of disagreeing with you. I'm sorry about the pencils. I just go round seeing what I can do to help, that's all.'

'Shall I show you how you look in your own thoughts, Catherine?' said Belinda, suddenly. Everyone listened, most amused at Belinda's sudden outburst. She was usually so very good-natured – but people like Maureen, Gwen and Catherine could be very very trying.

Belinda's pencil flew over a big sheet of paper. She worked at it for five minutes, then took up a pin. 'I'll pin it to the wall, girls,' she said. 'Catherine will simply *love* it. It's the living image of her as she imagines herself.'

She took the sheet to the wall and pinned it up. The girls crowded round. Catherine, consumed with curiosity, went too.

It was a picture of her standing in a stained-glass window, a gleaming halo round her head. Underneath, in big bold letters Belinda had written five words:

OUR BLESSED MARTYR, ST CATHERINE

Catherine fled away from the shrieks of delighted laughter. 'She's got what she wanted!' said Darrell. 'Catherine, come back! How do you like being a saint in a stained-glass window?'

A plot – and a quarrel

Before that week had ended Darrell was ready with the whole pantomime, words and all. Most of the music had been written, because Irene almost snatched the words from Darrell as she finished them.

'Quite a Gilbert and Sullivan,' said Moira, rather sneeringly, speaking of the famous comic-opera pair of the last century. She was feeling rather out of things. Until the pantomime was written, she could not produce it, so she had nothing to do at the moment. And Moira disliked having nothing to do. She liked running things, organizing things and people, dominating everyone, laying down the law.

She was not a popular head-girl. The fifth-formers resented her dictatorial manner. They disliked her lack of humour, and they took as little notice of her as they could.

Moira chafed under all this. 'Do buck up with this pantomime, Darrell and Sally,' she said. 'I wish I'd undertaken to write it myself now, you're so slow.'

'You *couldn't* write it,' said Darrell. 'You know you couldn't. You hardly ever get good marks for composition.'

Moira flushed. 'Don't be cheeky,' she said.

Catherine spoke up for her, using a sweet and gentle

voice. 'I'm sure Moira only let you and Sally do it to give you a chance,' she said. 'I'm sure she could have done it very well herself.'

'There speaks our blessed martyr, Saint Catherine,' put in Alicia, maliciously. 'Dear Saint Catherine. She deserves the halo Belinda gave her, doesn't she, girls?'

Catherine frowned. Belinda called out at once. 'Hold it, Catherine, hold it! No, don't smile in that sickly sweet manner, let me have that frown again!'

Catherine turned away. It was too bad that she should be laughed at when all the time she was trying to be kind and self-sacrificing and really *good*, poor Catherine thought to herself. She glanced at the wall. Blow! There was yet another picture of her up there, with a bigger halo than ever!

Catherine regularly sneaked into the common-room when it was empty, and took down the pictures that Belinda as regularly drew of her. But always there was a fresh one. It was absolutely maddening. This one showed her sharpening thousands of pencils, and if anyone looked carefully at the big halo they could see that it, too, was made of sharpened pencils set closely together.

It's enough to make anyone furiously angry, thought Catherine. I wonder I don't lose my temper and break out, and call people names. Well – I *try* to like them all, but it's very very difficult.

The fifth form decided they must deal with Maureen as well as with Catherine. 'Better show them both exactly where they stand before we begin rehearsing,' said Alicia.

'We can't be bothered by interferers and whiners and saints when once we're on the job. Now – how shall we deal with Maureen?'

'The trouble with *her* is that she's so full of herself – thinks she can do everything better than anyone else, and is sure she could run the whole show,' said Darrell. 'She's so jolly thick-skinned there's no doing anything with her. She's too vain for words!'

'Right,' said Alicia. 'We'll give her a real chance. We'll tell her to draw some designs to help Belinda – we'll tell her to sing one or two songs to help Mavis. We'll tell her to compose one or two tunes to help Irene – and write one or two poems to help Sally. Then we'll turn the whole lot down scornfully, and she'll know where she stands.'

'Well – it sounds rather *drastic*,' said Mary-Lou.

'It does, rather,' said Sally. 'Can't we tell her to do the things – and let her down not *too* scornfully?'

'Yes. We could pretend she wasn't being serious – she was just pulling our legs when she brings the tunes and verses and things,' said Darrell. 'And we could pat her on the back and clap and laugh – but not take them seriously at all. If she's got any common sense she'll shut up after that. If she hasn't, we'll have to be a bit more well – *drastic*, as Mary-Lou calls it.'

Everyone was in this plot except Gwen and Catherine. The girls were afraid one of the two might tell tales to Maureen if they knew of the plan. Moira approved of it, though she thought it not whole-hearted enough. She would have liked the first idea, the 'drastic' one.

Maureen was told to submit verses, tunes and designs. Also to learn two of the songs in case she could improve on Mavis's interpretation of them.

She was so gratified and delighted that she could hardly stammer her thanks. At last, at last she was coming into her own. Her gifts were being recognized! How wonderful!

She rushed straight off to tell Gwen. Gwen could hardly believe her ears. She listened, green with jealousy. To ask *Maureen* to do these things! It was unbelievable.

'Aren't you pleased, Gwen? I can do them all better than the others, can't I?' cried Maureen, her pale-blue eyes shining brightly. 'At last the others are beginning to realize that I *did* learn something at Mazeley Manor.'

'You and your Measley Manor,' said Gwen, turning away. Maureen was shocked. Had *Gwen*, Gwen her friend, actually said 'Measley'? She must have misheard. She took Gwen by the arm, chattering happily.

But Gwen was strangely unfriendly. She was so jealous that she could hardly answer a word.

Maureen worked hard. She produced two lots of verses, two tunes, and a variety of designs for costumes. She learned the two songs that Darrell had given her, going alone into a fifth-form music-room, where she let her loud voice out to such an extent, and so much off the note, that the girls in the next music-rooms listened, startled and amazed.

It was not only a loud voice, but it was not true in pitch – it kept sliding off the note, and going flat, like a gramophone just about to run down. It made the astonished girls in the rooms nearby shiver down their spines. Whoever could it be, yowling like that?

Bridget, Moira's fourth-form sister, went to have a look. Gracious, it was a fifth-former yowling in there – who was it – Maureen Little! Bridget grinned and went to find Connie. The two of them had become friends, and Connie was gradually leaving Ruth to herself, coming less and less to ask for her company.

The two fourth-formers peered into the square of glass window set in the door of the practice-room where Maureen was singing.

'Hear that?' said Bridget, maliciously. 'Wonderful, isn't it? Let's both go into the room next door and yowl too. Come on. It's empty now. If a fifth-former's allowed to do that, so are we!'

So the two of them went next door and made such a hullabaloo, pretending to be a couple of opera singers, that everyone in the corridor was startled.

Only Maureen, lost in her loud voice, soaring to higher and louder heights, heard nothing. Her door suddenly opened and Moira came in.

'MAUREEN! Shut up! We can even hear you in the common-room!'

Maureen stopped abruptly. Then, from the next room rose more yowls. Moira hurried there, amazed. *Now* what was going on?

Connie stopped as soon as she saw Moira. But Bridget, who cared nothing for her sister's anger, sang on vigorously, altering the words of her song at once.

'OHHHHHHH! Here is MOIRA! HERE – is SHE-EE.'

'Bridget! Stop that at once!' said Moira, angrily. But Bridget didn't stop.

'HERE – is SHEE-EEE!' she repeated.

'Did you hear what I said?' shouted Moira.

Bridget stopped for breath. 'I'm not making nearly such a noise as Maureen,' she said. 'And anyway I keep on the note and she doesn't. If a fifth-former can yowl away like that, why can't we?'

'Now don't you start being cheeky,' began Moira, going white with annoyance. 'You know I won't stand that. Connie, go out of the room. I advise you not to make close friends with Bridget. You'll only get yourself into trouble.'

Connie went, scared. If it had been Ruth with her, in trouble, she would have stayed and stuck up for her – but Bridget was different. She always stood up for herself. She faced Moira now.

'*That's* a nice thing to tell anyone about your sister, Moira,' she said. 'Washing your dirty linen in public! Telling somebody I'm not fit to make friends with.'

'I *didn't* say that,' said Moira. 'Why can't you behave yourself, Bridget? I'm ashamed of you. I'm always hearing things about you.'

'Well, so am I about you,' said Bridget. 'Who is the most domineering person in the fifth? You! Who is the most unpopular head-girl they've ever had? You! Who didn't go up with the old fifth form because nobody could put up with her? You!'

'*Oh*!' cried Moira, whiter still with rage. 'You're

unbearable. I shall report you to Miss Williams, yes, and Connie too. And I shall report you every single time I find you doing something you shouldn't. *I* know how you sneak out of your dormy at night to talk to the third-formers. *I* know how you get out of the jobs you ought to do. *I* hear things too!'

'Sneak,' said Bridget.

It was a very ugly sight, the two sisters standing there, shouting at one another. Moira was trembling now and so was Bridget. Moira had to keep her hands well down to her side, she so badly wanted to strike her sister. Bridget kept well out of the way. She always came off worst in a struggle.

There was a pause. 'You'll be sorry if you do report me about this afternoon,' said Bridget at last. 'Very sorry. I *warn* you. Go and report Maureen! She'll expect it of the domineering Moira! But just remember – I've *warned* you – you'll be sorry if you report *me*.'

'Well, I shall,' said Moira. 'It's my duty to. Fourth-formers aren't allowed in these practice-rooms, you know that.'

She turned and left the room, still trembling. She went to find Miss Williams, the fourth-form mistress. If she didn't report those two straight away, while she was furious, she might not do it when her anger had died down.

Miss Williams was rather cool about the affair. She wrote down the two fourth-form names Moira gave her, and nodded. 'Right. I'll speak to them.'

That was all. Moira wished she hadn't said anything.

She felt uncomfortable now about Bridget's threats. How could Bridget make her sorry? Bridget was so very fierce sometimes, and did such unaccountable things – like the time when she had broken every single one of Moira's dolls, years ago, because Moira had thrown one of Bridget's toys out of the window.

Yes, Moira felt decidedly uncomfortable as she walked back to the common-room. Bridget would certainly get back at her if she could!

The plot is successful

Maureen had been rather scared at Moira's sudden arrival in the practice-room. She had heard the angry voices in the next room too, when Moira had left her, and had been even more scared. It didn't take much to scare Maureen! She slipped hurriedly out of the room and went off to the classroom to put the finishing touches to her designs. She was to show them to the others that evening.

She saw Gwen's sour face as she walked into the common-room with her sheaf of designs, and sheets and sheets of music and verses. Oh, Maureen had been very busy! If Mam'zelle and Miss James had known how hard she had been at work they would have been most surprised. Neither of them had any idea that Maureen had it in her to work at all.

'*What* they taught at Mazely Manor I really do not know,' Miss James said to the other teachers each time she corrected Maureen's work.

'Self-admiration – self-esteem – self-pity,' murmured Miss Williams, who taught one lesson in the fifth form, and had had quite enough of Maureen.

'But not self-control,' said Miss James. 'What a school! It's a good thing it's shut down.'

Everyone was in the common-room waiting for Maureen, though neither Gwen nor Catherine knew the little plot that was being hatched by the rest. Maureen beamed round. '*Now* you're going to see something,' she said, gaily, and laughed her silly little laugh. 'It was always said at Mazeley Manor that I was a good all-rounder – don't think I'm boasting, will you – but honestly, though I say it myself, I *can* do most things!'

Maureen was surprised to hear some of the girls laughing quite hilariously.

'You're such a *joker*, Maureen,' said Alicia, appreciatively. 'Always being really humorous.'

This was a new idea to Maureen. Nobody had ever called her humorous before. She at once went up in her own estimation.

'Now,' she said, 'I'll show you the designs first. This is for Cinderella's ball costume – I've gone back to the sixteenth century for it, as you see.'

Shrieks of laughter came from everyone. 'Priceless!' said Darrell, pretending to wipe her eyes. 'How *can* you think of it, Maureen?'

'A perfect scream,' said Mavis, holding up the crude drawing, with its poor colouring. 'What a joke! I didn't know you'd such a sense of humour, Maureen.'

Maureen was puzzled. She hadn't meant the drawing to be funny at all. She had thought it was beautiful. She hurried on to the next one – but the girls forestalled her and picked up the sheets, showing them round to one another with squeals of laughter.

'Look at this one! I never saw anything so funny in my life!'

'Good enough for *Punch* magazine. I *say* – look at the baron's *face*! And what *is* he wearing?'

'This one's priceless. Gosh, Maureen really is a humorist, isn't she?'

Then Irene picked up the sheets of music. 'Hallo! Here are the tunes she has written! I bet they'll be priceless, too. I'll play them over.'

She went to the common-room piano, and with a very droll expression on her face she played the tunes, making them sound even sillier than they were.

Everyone crowded round the piano, laughing. 'Isn't Maureen a scream! She can do funny drawings and write ridiculous tunes too!'

Maureen began to feel frightened. Were the girls really in earnest about all this? They seemed to be. Surely – surely – they couldn't *really* think that all her lovely work was so bad that it was funny? They must be thinking it was funny on purpose – perhaps they thought she meant it to be!

She turned to find Gwen. Gwen would understand. Gwen was her friend, she had told Gwen everything – how good she was at drawing, music and singing, how hard she had worked at all this, how pleased she was with the results.

Gwen was looking at her and it wasn't a nice look. It was a triumphant look that said, 'Ah – pride comes before a fall, my girl – and what a fall!' It was a look that said,

'I'm glad about all this. Serves you right.'

Maureen was shocked. Gwen laughed loudly, and joined in with the others.

'Frightfully funny! Priceless, Maureen! Who would have thought you could be so funny?'

'Now sing,' said Mavis, and thrust one of the songs into her hand. 'Let's hear you. You've such a wonderful voice, haven't you, so well-trained. I'm sure it must be a great joy to you. Sing!'

Maureen did not dare to refuse. She gazed at the music with blurred eyes and sang. Her loud voice rose, even more off the note than usual. It shook with disappointment as the girls began to clap and cheer and laugh again.

'Ha ha! Listen to that! Can't she have a *comic* part in the play, Darrell, and sing it? She'd bring the house down. Did you ever hear such a voice?'

Maureen stopped singing. Tears fell down her cheek. She gave one desperate look at Gwen, a look begging for a word of praise – but none came.

She turned to go out of the room. Catherine ran after her. 'Maureen! Don't take it like that. The girls don't *mean* anything!'

'Oh yes we do,' said Darrell, under her breath. 'We've been cruel to be kind. Catherine *would* say a thing like that.'

'Don't touch me!' cried Maureen. '*Saint* Catherine – coming all over pious and goody-goody after you've laughed at me with the rest! Ho – SAINT!'

Catherine shrank back. Nobody smiled, except Gwen. Mary-Lou looked upset. She couldn't bear scenes of any sort. Bill looked on stolidly. She got up.

'Well, I'm going riding,' she said. 'There's half an hour of daylight left. Coming, Clarissa?'

Bill's stolidness and matter-of-fact voice made everyone feel more normal. They watched Bill and Clarissa go out of the room.

'Well – I don't somehow feel that was quite such a success as we hoped,' said Sally. 'Actually I feel rather low-down.'

'So do I,' said Darrell. 'Maureen *is* a conceited ass, of course, and badly needed taking down a peg – but I'm afraid we've taken her down more pegs than we meant to.'

'It won't hurt her,' said Gwen, in a smug voice. 'She thinks too much of herself. I can't *think* why she's attached herself to me all these weeks.'

Alicia couldn't resist this. 'Like calls to like, dear Gwen,' she said. 'Deep calls to deep. You're as like as two peas, you and Maureen. It's been a sweet sight to see you two together.'

'You don't really mean that, Alicia?' said Gwen, after a surprised and hurt silence. 'We're not *really* alike, Maureen and I. You've let your tongue run away with you as usual.'

'Think about it, dear Gwendoline Mary,' Alicia advised her. 'Do you babble endlessly about your dull family and doings? So does Maureen. Do you think the world of yourself? So does Maureen. Do you think you'd be the one and only person fit to be Cinderella in the play? So does Maureen.'

Gwen sprang to her feet and pointed her finger at Moira. 'Oh! Just because you found me with my hair down in the dormy the other day, and a towel round my shoulders you went and told the others that I wanted to be Cinderella!'

'Well, I didn't realize it until I caught Maureen doing exactly the same thing,' said Moira. '*Both* of you posing with your hair loose and things draped round you! Alicia's perfectly right. You're as like as two peas. You *ought* to be friends. You're almost twins!'

'But – I don't *like* Maureen,' said Gwen, in a loud and angry tone.

'I'm not surprised,' said Alicia's smooth voice, a whole wealth of meaning in it. '*You* should know what she's like, shouldn't you – seeing that you're almost twins!'

Gwen went stamping out of the room, fuming. Darrell drummed on the table with a pencil. 'I'm not awfully pleased about all this,' she said, in rather a small voice. 'Too much spite and malice about!'

Gwen suddenly put her head in at the door again and addressed Moira.

'I'll get even with you for telling the girls about me and Maureen in front of the glass!' she said. 'You'll see – I'll pay you back, head-girl or no head-girl!'

Moira frowned and Belinda automatically reached for her pencil. A very fine scowl! But Darrell took the pencil away with a beseeching look.

'Not this time,' she said. 'There's too much spite in this room this evening.'

'All right – Saint Darrell!' said Belinda, and Darrell had to laugh.

Moira came over to her. 'Let's change the subject,' she said. 'What about the house-matches? Let's have a look at the kids you've put in.'

Darrell got out the lists. Moira, as head-girl, took an interest in the matches in which the fifth-formers played, and because she liked games, she was interested too in the lower-school players. It was about the only thing that she and Darrell saw eye-to-eye about. Soon they were deep in discussion, weighing up the merits of one player against another.

'This match against Wellsbrough,' said Darrell. 'Next week's match, I mean, with the fourth team playing Wellsbrough's fourth team. I've put young Susan in – and I'd *like* to put my young sister, Felicity in. What do you think, Moira?'

'Good gracious, *yes*,' said Moira. 'She's absolutely first-class. Super! Runs like the wind and never misses a catch. She must have been practising like anything!'

'She has,' said Darrell. 'I just hesitated because – well, because she's my sister, and I was a bit afraid I might be showing favouritism, you know.'

'Rot!' said Moira. 'You'd be showing yourself a bad captain if you didn't stick the best kids into the team! And I insist on your putting Felicity in!'

Darrell laughed. She was pleased. 'Oh, all right, seeing

that you insist!' she said, and wrote Felicity's name down. 'Gosh, she'll be pleased.'

'How's June shaping?' called Alicia. 'I've seen her practising quite a bit lately. Turning over a new leaf do you think?'

'Well – not really,' said Darrell. 'I mean – she practises a lot – but when I coach her she's as off-hand as ever. Never a word of thanks, and always ready to argue. I can't put her into a match-team yet. She simply doesn't understand the team spirit – you know, always plays for herself, and not for the side.'

'Yes, you're right,' said Moira. 'I've noticed that, too. Can't have anyone in the team who isn't willing to pull their weight.'

Darrell glanced curiously at Moira. *How* much nicer Moira was over this games question than over anything else! She was fair and just and interested. She forgot to be domineering and opinionated. What a pity she was head of the form – she might have been so much nicer if she had had to knuckle down to someone else.

'Could you take the lists down for me and put them up on the sports board?' she said to Moira. 'I've got a whole heap of things to do still.'

Moira took the list just as Catherine hurried to offer to take it. '*I'll* take it,' said Catherine, who seemed to think it was only right she should be a doormat for everyone.

'No thanks, Saint Catherine,' said Moira, and Catherine went red with humiliation. She had done so much for Moira, been so nice to her, taken such a lot of donkey-work off her shoulders – and all she got was that scornful, hateful name – Saint Catherine. She gave Moira an unexpectedly spiteful look.

Darrell saw it and shivered impatiently. I don't like all this spitefulness going about, she thought to herself. It always boils up into something beastly. Fancy the saintly Catherine giving her beloved Moira such a poisonous look!

Moira went down with the lists. She pinned the list of names for the fourth team up first, heading it, TEAM FOR WELLSBROUGH MATCH. Immediately a crowd of excited first-formers swarmed round her.

'Felicity! You're in, you're in!' yelled somebody, and Felicity's face glowed happily.

'So's Susan. But you're not, June,' said another voice. 'Fancy – and you've been practising so hard. Shame!'

'Oh well – what do you expect – Darrell would be *sure* to put her sister in,' said June's voice. She was bitterly disappointed, but she spoke in her usual jaunty manner.

Moira heard. 'June! Apologize at once! Darrell shows no favouritism at all. She was half-inclined to leave Felicity out. *I* insisted she should be put in. Apologize immediately.'

'Well,' began June, defiantly, ready to argue, but Moira was insistent.

'I said, "Apologize". You heard me. Do as you're told.'

'I apologize,' said June, sulkily. 'But I bet it was you who missed *me* out!'

'I told Darrell that I wouldn't have anyone in the match-team who didn't play for the team and not for themselves,' said Moira, curtly. 'You don't pull your weight. You practise and practise – and then in a game all you want to do is to go your own way, and blow the others! Not *my* idea of a good sportsman. Think about it, June.'

She walked off, not caring in the least what the first-formers thought of her outspokenness. June said nothing. She looked rather odd, Susan thought. She went up to her.

'It was mean to say all that in front of us,' she began. 'She should have . . .'

'What does it matter?' said June, suddenly jaunty again. 'Do you suppose I care tuppence for Moira, or Darrell or Alicia – or *any* of those stuck-up fifth-formers?'

Grand meeting

A grand meeting was called to discuss the pantomime, the casting of the characters, and the times of rehearsal. Darrell had finished her writing, and Irene had completed the music. Everything was ready for rehearsal.

All the fifth-formers attended the meeting in the North Tower common-room. It was very crowded. A fire burned in the big fire-place, for it was now October and the nights were cold.

Moira was in the chair. Catherine – rather a quiet and sulky Catherine, not quite so free with her beaming smile – was at her left hand, ready to provide her with anything she wanted. The committee sat on chairs on each side of the table.

Moira banged on the table with a book, and shouted for silence. She got it. People always automatically obeyed Moira! She had that kind of voice, crisp and curt.

The meeting began. Darrell was called upon to explain the pantomime and the characters in it. She was also asked to read the first act.

Very flushed and excited she gave the listening fifth-formers a short summary of the pantomime. They listened with much approval. It sounded very good.

Then, stammering a little at first, Darrell read the first act of the pantomime, just as she had written it, dialogue, songs, stage directions and everything. There was a deep silence as she read on.

'That's the end of the act,' she said at last, raising her eyes shyly, not absolutely certain if she had carried her listeners with her or not.

There was no doubt about that a second later. The girls stamped and clapped and cheered. Darrell was so pleased that she felt hot with joy, and had to wipe her forehead dry.

Moira banged for silence.

'Well, you've all heard what a jolly good play Darrell and Sally have got together,' she said. 'Darrell did most of it – but Sally was splendid too. You can tell it will bring the house down if we can produce it properly.'

'Who's going to produce it?' called Betty.

'I am,' said Moira, promptly. 'Any objections?'

There were quite a lot of doubtful faces. Nobody really doubted Moira's ability to produce a pantomime – but they did doubt her talent for getting the best out of people. She rubbed them up the wrong way so much.

'I think it would be better to have *two* producers,' said somebody.

'Right,' said Moira, promptly. She didn't mind how many there were so long as she was one of them. She meant to be the *real* producer, anyway. 'Who do you want?'

'Betty, Betty!' shrieked half the fifth-formers. It was obviously planned. Moira frowned a little. Betty! Alicia's laughing, careless, clever friend.

'Yes – let Betty,' said Alicia, suddenly. She felt that she wouldn't be able to work happily with Moira alone for long. But two producers would be easier. She could consult with Betty all the time!

Betty grinned round and took her place on one of the committee chairs. 'Thanks,' she said. 'I'll produce the goods all right!'

'Now to choose the characters,' said Moira. 'We have more or less worked them out. I'll read them.'

Gwendoline and Maureen held their breath. *Was* there any hope of being Cinderella? Or even the Fairy-Godmother? Or the Prince?

Moira read the list out.

'Cinderella – *Mary-Lou*.'

There was a gasp from Mary-Lou, Gwen and Maureen – of amazement from Mary-Lou and disappointment from the others.

'Oh – I *can't*!' said Mary-Lou.

'You *can*,' said Darrell. 'We want someone sort of pathetic-looking – a bit scary – someone appealing and big-eyed – and it has to be someone who can act and someone who can sing.'

'And you're exactly right for the part,' said Sally. 'That's right – make your eyes big and scared, Mary-Lou – you're poor little Cinderella to the life!'

Everyone laughed. Mary-Lou had to laugh, too. Her eyes began to shine. 'I never thought you'd choose me,' she said.

'Well, we have,' said Darrell. 'You can act very well and

you've a nice singing voice, though it's not very loud.'

'The Prince – *Mavis*,' said Moira. Everyone knew that already. The Prince had a lot of singing to do and Mavis would do that wonderfully well. Her voice was beautiful again, and Irene had written some lovely tunes for her to sing to Darrell's words. Everyone clapped.

'The Baron – *Bill*,' said Moira, and there was a delighted laugh.

'Oh *yes*! Bill stamping about in riding-breeches, calling for her horse!' cried Clarissa in delight.

'Fairy-Godmother – *Louella*,' said Moira. Everyone looked at Louella who came from South Tower, and had a tall, slim figure, golden curls and a good clear voice.

'Hurray!' shouted all the South Tower girls, glad to have someone from their tower in a good part.

'Buttons – the little boots – *Rachel*,' went on Moira. 'Rachel can act jolly well and she's had the same part before, so she ought to do it well.'

'Who are the Ugly Sisters?' called a voice.

Gwen's heart suddenly gave a lurch and sank down into her shoes. Ugly Sisters! Suppose *she* had been chosen to be one? She couldn't, couldn't bear it. She saw Alicia gazing at her maliciously and felt sure she *had* been chosen.

She simply couldn't bear it. She got up, saying she didn't feel very well, and went towards the door. Alicia smiled. She could read Gwen's thoughts extremely well. Gwen was going because she was afraid her name would be read out next as one of the Ugly Sisters.

'Your heart worrying you again?' called one of the

West Tower girls to Gwen, and everyone laughed. Gwen disappeared. She made up her mind not to go back till the meeting was over.

Maureen was also worried about the same thing. She thought about her rabbit-teeth. Moira might think she was *made* for an Ugly Sister. Why, oh why hadn't she been sensible and had her teeth straightened when she had a chance? She drew her upper lip over them to try and hide them.

'Ugly Sisters – *Pat* – and *Rita*!' said Moira, and there was an instant roar of approval from the girls.

Pat and Rita looked round humorously. They were twins, and certainly not ugly – but they had upturned comical noses, eyes very wide-set, and hair that flew out in a shock. They were comical, good at acting, and would make a splendid pair of Ugly Sisters.

'Thanks, Moira!' called out Rita. 'That suits us down to the ground – right down to our big ugly feet!'

'Demon King – *Alicia*!' said Moira, and again there was a great roar of approval, led by a delighted Betty.

Moira beamed round, looking quite pleasant. 'Alicia's going to do juggling and conjuring as well as leap about the stage like a demon,' she said. 'I can't think of anyone else who could be a demon so successfully.'

More shrieks of approval. Miss James, not far off, wondered what in the world was happening. It sounded as if about fifty thousand spectators at a football match were yelling themselves hoarse.

'Jolly good casting!' called somebody. 'Go on!'

'Well, now we come to the servants and courtiers and so on,' said Moira. 'That means the rest of you. There's a part for everyone, even though it may be small.'

'What about Darrell?' called a voice.

'Darrell's written the play and will help in the producing,' said Moira. 'Sally will help her too. They won't be in it because their hands will be full. We're going to ask Pop if he'll do the electricity part – he'll love it.'

Pop was the handyman of the school, very much beloved, and quite invaluable on these occasions.

'It all sounds jolly good,' said Winnie. 'When are the rehearsals?'

'Every Tuesday evening, and on Friday evenings too for those who want an extra one,' said Moira. 'And the parts will be sent out to everyone tomorrow. For goodness' sake learn them as quickly as you can. It's hopeless to keep reading them when we rehearse – you can't act properly like that.'

'You forgot to say that Irene's done the music and Belinda the decorations and Janet's doing the costumes,' said Darrell.

'No, I hadn't,' said Moira, quickly. 'I was coming to that. Anyway, everyone knows it. By the way, we'll be glad of any help for Janet in making the costumes. Anyone good with their needle will be welcomed. Janet will give out the work if you'll be decent enough to ask her for it.'

More clapping. Then a spate of excited talk. This was going to be the best pantomime ever! It would make the whole school sit up! It would bring the house down.

'There's never been a show before where the girls wrote the songs and words and music themselves,' said Winnie. 'My word – won't the Grayling open her eyes!'

A bell went somewhere and everyone got up. 'We'll be at rehearsal! We'll learn our parts! Mavis, what about the singing? Are you going to train the chorus?'

Chattering and calling they all went to their own Towers. Darrell sighed happily and put her arm through Sally's.

'This is about the most exciting thing I've ever done in my life, Sally,' she said. 'You know – I shouldn't be surprised if I don't turn out to be a writer, one of these days!'

16

Felicity's first match

Felicity came to see Darrell the next day about the match with Wellsbrough School. She looked with bright eyes at her fifth-form sister.

'I *say*! Fancy me playing in the fourth school team! I thought perhaps I might by the end of the term, with luck – but next *week*! Thanks awfully for putting me in, Darrell.'

'Well, actually – it was Moira who insisted on putting you in,' said Darrell. 'I wanted to – and yet I just wondered if I was thinking favourably of you because you were my sister, you know. Then Moira said you must certainly go in, and in you went.'

'June's awfully disappointed she's not in,' said Felicity. 'She's been practising like anything, Darrell. She pretends she doesn't care, but she does really. I wish she wouldn't say such awful things about you fifth-formers all the time – she really seems to have got her knife into you. It's horrid.'

'She'll get over it,' said Darrell. 'We don't lose any sleep over young June, I can tell you!'

'Will you be able to come and watch the Wellsbrough match?' asked Felicity, eagerly. 'Oh do. I shall play ever so much better if you're there, yelling and cheering.'

'Of course I'll come,' said Darrell. 'And I'll yell like anything – so just be sure you give me something to yell for!'

The first-formers prayed for a fine day for their match. It was to be at home, not away, and as it was the first time they had played Wellsbrough fourth team, they were really excited about it.

The senior school smiled to see the 'babies' so excited. They remembered how they, too, had felt when they had the delight of playing in an important match for the very first time.

'Nice to see them so keen,' said Moira to Darrell. 'I think I'll get my lacrosse stick and go and give them a bit of coaching before dinner. I've got half an hour.'

'I'll fetch your stick,' said Catherine at once, in her usual doormat voice.

'No thanks, Saint Catherine,' answered Moira. 'I'm still able to walk to the locker and reach my own stick.'

The day of the match dawned bright and clear, a magnificent October day. The trees round the playing fields shone red and brown and yellow in their autumn colours. The breeze from the sea was salty and crisp. All the girls rejoiced as they got up that morning and looked out of the window. Malory Towers was so lovely on a day like this.

The happiest girls, of course, were the small first-formers, excited twelve-year-olds who talked to one another at the top of their voices without stopping. How they ever heard what anyone else said was a mystery.

Miss Potts, the first-form mistress, was lenient that

morning. So was Mam'zelle, who was always excited herself when any of her classes were.

'Well, so today is your match?' she said to the first form. 'You will play well, *n'est-ce pas*? You will win all the goals. I shall come to watch. And for the girl that wins a goal . . .'

'*Shoots* a goal, Mam'zelle,' said Susan.

'Shoots! Ah yes – but you have no gun to shoot a goal,' said Mam'zelle, who never could learn the language of sports. 'Well, well – for the girl who *shoots* a goal I will say, "No French prep tomorrow"!'

'But, Mam'zelle – that's not fair!' cried a dozen voices. 'We're not *all* in the match – only Felicity and Susan and Vera.'

'Ah, I forgot,' said Mam'zelle. 'That is so. Then what shall I say?'

'Say you'll let us *all* off French prep for the rest of the week if we win!' called Felicity.

'No, no,' said Mam'zelle, shocked. 'For one day only I said. Now, it is understood – if you win your match no French prep for you tomorrow!'

'You're a peach, Mam'zelle,' called a delighted first-former.

'*Comment*!' said Mam'zelle, astonished. 'You call me a *peach*. Never have I . . .'

'It's all right, Mam'zelle – it's a compliment,' said Felicity. 'Peaches are wizard.'

Mam'zelle gave it up. 'Now – we will have our verbs,' she said. 'Page thirty-five, *s'il vous plaît*, and no more talking.'

The Wellsbrough girls arrived at twenty past two in a big coach. They were rather older than the Malory Towers team, and seemed much bigger. The Malory Towers girls felt a little nervous. The two captains shook hands and the teams nodded and smiled at one another.

The games-mistress blew her whistle and the teams came round her. The captains tossed for ends.

The teams took their positions in the field. Felicity gripped her lacrosse stick as if it might leap from her hand if she didn't. She put on a grim expression that made everyone who saw it smile.

Her knees shook just a little! How she hoped nobody could see them. It was silly to be nervous in a match – just the time *not* to be!

'Good luck,' whispered Susan, who was not far off. 'Shoot a goal!'

Felicity nodded, still looking grim.

Darrell and Moira and Sally were together, watching. Most of the other fifth-formers were there, too, because many of them helped the younger ones and were interested in their play. A good sprinkling of the other forms were also there. Wellsbrough was a splendid school for sport and usually sent out first-class match-teams.

'Your small sister looks pretty fierce,' said Sally to Darrell. 'Look at her! She means to do and dare all right!'

The match began. The ball shot out down the field, and the girls began to race after it, picking it up in their nets, throwing it, catching it, knocking it out again, picking it up, tackling one another and making the onlookers yell with excitement.

The Wellsbrough team shot the first goal. It went clean into the net, quite impossible to stop. The twelve-year-old goal-keeper was very downcast. One to Wellsbrough!

Felicity gritted her teeth. Wellsbrough had the lead now. She shot a look at Darrell. Yes, there she was, never taking her eyes off the ball. Felicity longed to do something really spectacular and make Darrell dance and cheer with pride. But the Wellsbrough team was tough, and nobody could do anything very startling. Always there was a Wellsbrough girl ready to knock the ball out of a Malory Towers lacrosse net as soon as it was there!

And always there was a Wellsbrough girl who seemed to be able to run faster than any of the home team. It was maddening. Felicity and Susan became very out of breath and panted and puffed as they tore down the field, their hearts beating like pistons!

And then Susan shot a goal! It was most unexpected. She was tearing down the field, far from the goal, with two Wellsbrough girls after her, and Felicity running up to catch the ball if Susan passed it.

Susan took a quick glance round to see if Felicity was ready to catch it. A Wellsbrough girl ran up beside Felicity, a tall girl who would probably take the ball instead of Felicity, if it was passed. Blow!

On the spur of the moment Susan flung the ball at the distant goal. It was a powerful throw, and the ball flew straight. The goal-keeper rushed out to catch it – but she missed, and the ball bounced right into the very middle of the net!

Cheers rang out from the spectators. Darrell yelled too. Then she turned to Moira.

'A very lucky goal. Those far throws don't usually come off – but that one did. One all!'

It was almost half-time. One minute to go. The ball came to Felicity and she caught it deftly in her net, jumping high in the air for it.

'Good!' yelled everyone, pleased to see such a fine catch. Felicity sped off with it and passed to Rita. She didn't see a big Wellsbrough girl running up to her and collided heavily. Over she went on the ground and felt an agonizing pain in her right ankle. It was so sharp that she couldn't get up. Things went black around her. Poor Felicity was horrified. No, no, she mustn't faint! Not on the playing-field in the middle of the match! She couldn't!

The whistle went for half-time. Felicity heaved a long shaky sigh of relief. Five minutes' rest. Would her ankle be all right?

She wasn't going to faint after all! She sat there on the grass, pretending to fiddle with her lacrosse boot till she felt a little better. Susan came running up.

'I say – you went over with a terrific wallop. Did you hurt yourself?'

'Twisted my ankle a little,' said Felicity. She looked very white and Susan was alarmed. The games-mistress came up.

'Twisted your ankle? Let's have a look.'

She undid the boot quickly and looked at Felicity's foot, pressing it and turning it.

'It's an ordinary twist,' she said. 'Horribly painful when it happens, I know. You'd better come off and let your reserve play.'

Felicity was almost in tears. Darrell came running up. 'Has she twisted her ankle? Oh, she often does that. Her right ankle's a bit weak. Daddy always tells her to bandage it fairly tightly – round the foot just here – and walk on it immediately, not lie up.'

'Well, I'm agreeable to that if Felicity can stand on it all right, and run,' said the mistress. 'It's up to her.'

Susan brought Felicity a lemon quarter to suck. She began to feel much better and colour came back into her cheeks. She stood up, testing her ankle gingerly. Then she smiled.

'It's all right. It will be black and blue tomorrow, but there's nothing really wrong. In a few minutes' time it will be better.'

The games-mistress bound the foot up tightly, and Felicity put on her boot again. The foot had swollen a little but not much. Chewing her lemon, Felicity hobbled about for a minute or two, feeling the foot getting better and better as she went.

'Nothing much wrong,' reported the games-mistress. 'A nasty twist – but Felicity's a determined little character, and where another girl would moan and make a fuss and go off limping, she's going to go on playing. It won't do the foot any harm – probably do it good.'

The whistle went again, after a little longer half-time to give Felicity a chance to recover. The girls took their places, all at the opposite ends this time.

Susan was a marvel that second half. She saved Felicity all she could, and leaped about and ran like a mad March hare! Everyone cheered her.

Felicity's foot ceased to hurt her. She forgot about it. She began to run again, and made another wonderful catch that set all the spectators cheering. She tackled a Wellsbrough girl and got the ball away. She ran for goal.

'Shoot!' yelled everyone. 'SHOOT!'

But, before she could shoot, the ball was knocked out of her net and a Wellsbrough girl was speeding back down the field with it. She passed the ball on, and it was caught and passed again, and shot straight at the Malory Towers goal.

'Save it, save it!' yelled everyone in agony. The goal-keeper stood there like a rock. She made a wild slash with her lacrosse stick and miraculously caught the hard rubber ball, flinging it out to a Malory Towers girl at once.

'No goal, no goal!' sang the girls in delight. 'Well saved, Hilda, well saved!'

'Looks as if it's going to be a draw,' said Moira, glancing at her watch. 'Only two minutes more. Felicity's limping just a bit again. Plucky kid to run on as she did.'

'She's got the ball!' cried Darrell, clutching Moira in excitement. 'Another marvellous catch! My word, practice does pay! She catches better than anyone. Look, she's kept it!'

Felicity was running down the field with the ball. She was tackled by a Wellsbrough girl, dodged, turned herself right round and passed to Susan. Susan caught it and immediately passed it back to Felicity, seeing two of the enemy coming straight at her. Felicity nearly didn't catch it, because it was such a high throw, but by leaping like a goat she got it into the tip of her net, and it ran down safely.

Then off she went, tearing down the field, her face set grimly.

'SHOOT!' yelled the girls. 'SHOOOOOOOOOOOT!'

And she shot, just as the stick of an enemy came crashing down to get the ball from her. The ball shot out high in the air, and the goal-keeper rushed out to get it.

She missed it – and the ball bounced and ran slowly and deliberately into a corner of the goal, where it lay still as if quite tired out with the game.

'GOAL!' yelled everyone, and went completely mad. Moira, Sally and Darrell swung each other round in a most undignified way for fifth-formers, Bill and Clarissa did a kind of barn-dance together, and as for the lower school, they began a most deafening chant that made Mam'zelle put her hands to her ears at once.

'Well – done – Felici-TEEEEEE! Well – done – Felici-TEEEEEE!'

The whistle went for time. The teams trooped off, red in the face, panting, laughing and happy. Felicity was limping a little, but so happy and proud that she wouldn't have noticed if she had limped with *both* feet!

Darrell thumped her on the back. 'You got the winning

goal, my girl! You did the trick! Gosh, I'm proud of you!'

Moira thumped her, too. 'I'm glad we p it you into the team, Felicity! You'll be there for the rest of the term. You've got team-spirit all right. You play for your side all the time.'

June was just nearby. She heard what Moira said, and felt sure she was saying it so that she might hear. She turned away, sick at heart. *She* might have been playing in the match – she might even have shot that winning goal. But Felicity had instead. June couldn't go and thump Felicity on the back or congratulate her. She was jealous.

Felicity was too happy to notice little things like that. She went off with her team and the Wellsbrough girls to a 'smashing' tea. Anyone seeing the piles of sandwiches, buttered and jammy buns, and slices of fruit cake piled high on big dishes would think that surely it would need twenty teams to eat all that!

But the two teams managed it all between them quite easily. What fun it all was! What a noise of shouting and laughter and whole-hearted merriment.

School's smashing, thought Felicity, munching her fourth jammy bun. Super! Wizard!

Half-term

Rehearsals began. A Tuesday and a Friday came, and another Tuesday – three rehearsals already!

'I think it's going well, don't you?' said Darrell to Sally. 'Little Mary-Lou knows her part already – she must have slaved at learning it, because Cinderella has almost more to say then anyone.'

'Yes – and she's going to look the part *exactly*,' said Sally. 'Who would ever have thought that timid little Mary-Lou, who was scared even of her own shadow when she was in the lower school, would be able to take the principal part in a pantomime now!'

'Shows what Malory Towers does to you!' said Darrell. 'Still, I suppose any good boarding school does the same things – makes you stand on your own feet, rubs off your corners, teaches you common-sense, makes you accept responsibility.'

'It depends on the person!' said Sally, with a laugh. 'It doesn't seem to have taught dear Gwendoline Mary much.'

'Well, I suppose there must be exceptions,' said Darrell. 'She's about the only one that has come through school with us who doesn't seem to have learned anything sensible at all.'

'It was a shock when we told her she and Maureen might be twins!' said Sally. 'She really saw herself then as others see her. Anyway, I think she is better than she was – especially since she's had to go in for games and gym properly.'

'She doesn't like being a servant in the play,' said Darrell, with one of her wide grins. 'Nor does Maureen. They've neither of them got a word to say in the play, and not much to do either – but as they both act so badly, it's just as well!'

'It's an awful blow to their pride,' said Sally. 'I say – Bill's going to be good, isn't she? She's the surly baron to the life as she strides about the stage in her riding-boots, and slaps her whip against her side!'

Yes – the play was really going quite well. The fifth-formers were almost sorry that it was half-term weekend because it meant missing a rehearsal that Friday. Still, it would be lovely to see their people again. Darrell had a lot to tell her parents – and so had Felicity.

Felicity's ankle had certainly been black and blue the next day, and she showed it off proudly to the first-formers. What a marvel to shoot a goal when you had an ankle like that! Felicity was quite the heroine of the lower school.

Half-term came and went, all too quickly. Darrell's father and mother came, and had to listen to two excited girls both talking at once about pantomimes and matches.

'We're rehearsing well, and my words sound fine, and you should see Mary-Lou as Cinderella,' cried Darrell at the top of her voice.

'And when I shot the winning goal I simply couldn't believe it, but there was such a terrific noise of cheering and shouting that I had to,' shouted Felicity, at the same time as Darrell. Her mother smiled. What a pair!

Four of Bill's brothers came to see her, and her mother as well, all on horseback! It was the boys' half-term, too, and Bill rode off happily, taking Clarissa with her. What a lovely way to spend half-term, thought Clarissa, riding all day long, and having a picnic lunch and tea!

Gwendoline watched her go jealously. If she had been sensible last term she could have been Clarissa's friend. But she hadn't been sensible – and now she was stuck with that awful Maureen!

The dreadful thing was that Maureen's parents couldn't come at the last moment, so Maureen had no one to go out with. She went to tell Gwen.

'Oh, Gwen – are you taking anyone out with you? My parents can't come. I'm so bitterly disappointed.'

Gwen stared at her crossly. This *would* happen, of course. Now she would have to have Maureen tagging about with her all day long.

She introduced Maureen to her mother and Miss Winter, her old governess, with a very bad grace.

'Mother – this is Maureen. Her parents haven't come today, so I said she could come with us.'

'Of course, of course!' said Mrs Lacey at once. As usual she was dressed in far too fussy things, with veils and scarves and bits and pieces flying everywhere. 'Poor child – what a shame!'

Maureen warmed to Mrs Lacey. Here was someone she could talk to easily. She gave her silly little laugh.

'Oh, Mrs Lacey, it's *so* kind of you to let me come with you. It's my first term here, you know – and really I don't know *what* I'd have done without dear Gwendoline. She's really been a friend in need.'

'I'm sure she has,' said Mrs Lacey. 'Gwendoline is always so kind. No wonder she is so popular.'

'And do you know, the girls say Gwen and I *ought* to be friends, because we're so alike,' chattered Maureen, tucking the rug round herself in the car. 'We've both got golden hair and blue eyes, and they say we've got the same ways, too. Aren't I lucky to have found a twin!'

This was the kind of conversation that both Miss Winter and Mrs Lacey understood and liked. Miss Winter made quite a fuss of Maureen, and Gwen didn't like that at all.

Gwen hoped that Maureen would say nice things about her as she was taking her out for the day. But Maureen didn't. Maureen talked about herself the whole time. She described her home, her family, her dogs, her garden, all the holidays she had ever had, and all the illnesses. Gwen couldn't get a word in, and after a time she fell silent and sulked.

What a bore Maureen is! How silly! How selfish and conceited! thought Gwen, sulkily. What a silly affected laugh.

Her mother made a most terrifying remark at lunch-time. She beamed round at both girls. 'You know, except that Maureen's teeth stick out a little, you two are really *very* alike! You've got Gwen's lovely way of chattering all about your doings, Maureen – and even your laugh is the same – isn't it, Miss Winter?'

'Yes, they really might be sisters,' agreed Miss Winter, smiling kindly at the delighted Maureen. 'Their ways are exactly the same, and even their voices.'

Gwen felt quite sick. She could hardly eat any dinner. If her mother and Miss Winter, who really adored her, honestly thought that that awful, boring, conceited Maureen was exactly like her, then she, Gwen, must be a really appalling person too. No wonder she wasn't popular. No wonder the girls laughed at her.

That day was a really terrible one for Gwen. To sit by somebody who was supposed to be like her, to hear her own silly laugh uttered by Maureen, to listen to her everlasting, dull tales about herself, and see her own shallow, insincere smile spread over Maureen's face was a horrible experience.

I shall never forget this, thought poor Gwen. Never. I'll be jolly careful how I behave in future. And I'll alter my laugh straight away. Do I *really* laugh like that? Yes – I do. Oh, I do feel so ashamed.

'Gwen's very quiet,' said Miss Winter, at last. 'Anything wrong, Gwen?'

'Oh, poor Gwen – she's so disappointed because she's not been chosen for Cinderella,' said Maureen, swiftly.

'Well, so were you!' retorted Gwen. '*You* thought you were going to be. Moira said so!'

'Girls, girls! Don't talk like that to one another,' said Mrs Lacey, shocked. 'Why – I quite thought Gwen was to be Cinderella!'

'Yes – you said in your letter that most of the girls wanted you to be,' said Miss Winter. 'Why didn't they choose you, Gwen? You would have made a fine Cinderella! It's a shame.'

'For the same reason they didn't choose Maureen, I suppose,' said Gwen, sulkily. 'They didn't think we were good enough.'

'Well, of course, I couldn't *possibly* expect to be chosen – it's only my first term,' said Maureen, quickly.

'You *did* expect to be!' said Gwen.

'Oh no, Gwen dear,' said Maureen, and laughed her silly laugh. It grated on Gwen's exasperated nerves.

'I shall go mad if you laugh that laugh again,' she said, savagely.

There was a surprised silence. Maureen broke it by laughing again and Gwen clenched her fists.

'Poor Gwen!' said Maureen. 'Honestly, Mrs Lacey, it *was* a shame they didn't choose her – it really did upset her. And when we go to rehearsals it's maddening for Gwen to see Mary-Lou as Cinderella, while she's only a servant, and says nothing at all – not a single word in the whole of the play!'

'Darling!' said Mrs Lacey, comfortingly, to the glowering Gwen. 'I'm *so* sorry! I don't like to see Mother's girl sad.'

'*Stop* it, Mother,' said Gwen. 'Let's change the subject.'

Mrs Lacey was very hurt. She turned away from this

unusually surly Gwen, and began to talk to Maureen, being extra nice to her so as to show Gwen that she was very displeased with *her*. Miss Winter did the same, and Maureen blossomed out even more under this sunshine of flattery and rapt attention. Poor Gwen had to listen to more and more tales of Maureen's life, and to hear her silly laugh more and more often!

The day came to an end at last. Maureen thanked Mrs Lacey and Miss Winter prettily, tucked her arm into Gwen's, and went off, waving.

'I'll look after Gwen for you!' she called back.

'Well, *what* a charming child – and *what* a nice friend she'd make for Gwen,' said Mrs Lacey, driving off. 'It's a pity Gwen's so upset about that Cinderella business. Maureen must have been just as disappointed.'

'Yes. I'm afraid dear Gwen's not taking that very bravely,' said Miss Winter. 'Never mind, she has that nice child Maureen to set her a good example.'

'I think we ought to ask Maureen to stay for a week or two in the Christmas holidays,' said Mrs Lacey. 'It would be so nice for Gwen.'

Poor Gwen! If she had heard all this she would have been furious. She was to get a great shock when her mother's letter came, telling her she had invited Maureen to stay for a week in the holidays.

She pulled her arm away from Maureen's as soon as the car drove out of sight. She turned on her.

'Well – I hope you've enjoyed spoiling my whole day, you beast! Telling your awful tales, and laughing your awful laugh, and sucking up like anything. Ugh!'

'But, Gwen – they said I was so like you,' said Maureen, looking puzzled. 'They liked me. How can I be so awful if I'm exactly like you?'

Gwen didn't tell her. It was a thing she really couldn't bear to think about.

The dictator

The days began to fly after half-term. Darrell and Sally got fits of panic quite regularly whenever they thought of the pantomime being performed to the parents at the end of term.

'We'll NEVER be ready!' groaned Darrell.

'No. We never imagined there'd be so much to do,' said Sally, seriously.

'If only everyone knew their parts like Mary-Lou and Mavis,' said Darrell. 'Louella drives me mad. She forgets the words of her songs every single time. I wish we hadn't chosen her to be the Fairy-Godmother now.'

'Oh, she'll be all right on the night,' said Sally. 'She was like that in the play she was in last year – never knew a word till the last night, and then was quite perfect.'

'Well, I only hope you're right,' groaned Darrell, amusing the steady Sally very much. Darrell went down into the dumps easily over her precious pantomime. Sally was very good for her. She refused to think anyone was hopeless, and was always ready with something comforting to say.

'Alicia's marvellous, isn't she?' she said, after a pause, looking up from the work she was doing.

'Yes. She's a born demon,' said Darrell, with a giggle. 'I get quite scared of her sometimes, the way she leaps about the stage and yells. And her conjuring is miraculous.'

'So is her juggling,' said Sally. 'And she's practised that demon-sounding voice till it really sounds quite uncanny.'

Daphne joined in with a laugh. 'Yes – and when she suddenly produces it in French class, the amazement on Mam'zelle's face is too good to be true.'

'Alicia's a scream,' said Darrell. 'She'll be the best in the show, I think.'

There was a little silence. 'There's only one thing that *really* worries me,' said Darrell, in a low voice. 'And that's Moira. She's not hitting it off with Betty at all – or Alicia either. She's bossing them too much.'

'Yes. She can't seem to help it,' said Sally. 'But it's idiotic to be bossy with people like Betty and Alicia. After all, Betty's co-producer, and Alicia's a terrific help to them.'

Darrell was right to worry about Moira. Moira was intensely keen on getting the whole pantomime perfect, and made everyone work like slaves under her command. The girls resented it. Louella purposely forgot her words in order to annoy Moira. Bill purposely came in at the wrong side each time to make her shout. And Moira couldn't see that she was handling things in the wrong way.

She was a wonderful organizer, certainly. She had gone into every detail, worked out every scene with Darrell, proved herself most ingenious, and given very wise advice.

But she did it all in the wrong way. She was aggressive and opinionated, she contradicted people flatly, and she found fault too much and praised too little.

'You're a dictator, Moira,' Bill informed her at one rehearsal. 'I don't take kindly to dictators. Nor does anyone else here.'

'If you think you can produce a first-class pantomime without giving a few orders and finding a few faults, you're wrong,' said Moira, furiously.

'I don't,' said Bill, mildly. 'I never said I did. But you can do all that without being a dictator. You sit up there like a war-lord and chivy us all along unmercifully. I quite expect to be sent to prison sometimes.'

'Let's get on,' said Darrell, afraid that Moira was going to blow up. Arguing always wasted so much time. 'We'll take that bit again. Mavis, begin your song.'

Mavis sang, and a silence fell. What a lovely voice she had, low and pure and sweet. That would make the audience gasp! It wasn't often that a schoolgirl had a voice like that.

We shall miss her when she leaves, and goes to study music and singing at the College of Music, thought Darrell. Mavis's song came to an end, and she stepped back to let Buttons come on and do her bit.

Yes, rehearsals were hard work, but they were fun, too. Sally and Darrell began to feel more confident as time went on. Darrell surprised herself at times, when she suddenly saw something wrong with the lines of the play, and hurried to alter them.

I know just what's wrong and what's right now, she thought, as she scribbled new lines. I adore doing this pantomime – feeling it's mine because I wrote it all. I want to do a play next. *Could* I write one – perhaps just a short one for next term? Shall I ever, ever be a well-known playwright?

Gwen was a sulky actor. She hated being stuck at the back in the chorus, dressed as a servant, with nothing to say or do by herself. Maureen was much more cheerful about it. She drove Gwen nearly mad by some of the things she said.

'Of course, *I* don't mind having such a small, insignificant part,' she said. 'But it's different for you, Gwen. You've been here for years, and I've not been even one term. You *ought* to have had a good part. I couldn't expect one.'

Gwen growled.

'I shall write and tell your mother you are *awfully* good as a servant,' went on Maureen. 'I do think it's so kind of her to ask me to stay. Won't it be fun to be together so much, Gwen, in the hols?'

Gwen didn't answer. She was beginning to be a little afraid of Maureen. Maureen was silly and affected – but she had a cunning and sly side to her nature, too. So had Gwen, of course. She recognized it easily in Maureen because it was in herself too. That was the dreadful part of this forced friendship with Maureen. It was like being friends with yourself, and knowing all the false, silly, sly things that went on in your own mind.

Gwen did try to alter herself a bit, so that she wouldn't be like Maureen. She stopped her silly laugh and her wide, false smile. She stopped talking about herself too.

To her enormous annoyance nobody seemed to notice it. As a matter of fact, they took so little notice of her at all that if she had suddenly grown a moustache and worn riding-boots they wouldn't have bothered. Who wanted to pay any attention to Gwen? She had never done anything to make herself liked or trusted, so the best thing to do was to ignore her.

And ignore her they did, though poor Gwen was doing her best to be sensible and likeable now. She had left it a bit too late!

Two more weeks went by, and then suddenly a row flared up at a rehearsal. It began over a very silly little thing indeed, as big rows often do.

Alicia took it into her head to evolve a kind of demon-chant whenever she appeared or disappeared on the stage. She only thought of it a few minutes before rehearsal, and hadn't time to tell Darrell or Sally, so she thought she would just introduce the weird little chant without warning.

And she did. She appeared with her sudden, surprising leaps, chanting eerily, 'Oo-woo-la, woo-la, riminy-ree, oo-woo-la . . .'

Moira rapped loudly. The rehearsal stopped. 'Alicia! What on earth's that? It's not in the script, as you very well know.'

'Of course I know,' said Alicia, annoyed as always by Moira's unnecessarily sharp tone. 'I hadn't time to ask Darrell to put it in. I only thought of it just now.'

'Well, we can't insert new things now,' said Moira, coldly. 'And in any case it's not for you to suggest extraordinary chants like that. If we'd wanted one we'd have got Darrell to write one in.'

'Look here, Moira,' said Alicia, losing her temper rapidly, 'I'm not a first-former. I'm . . .'

Darrell interrupted hastily. 'Moira, I think that's really a good idea of Alicia's. What do you think, Betty? I never thought of a chant like that for the demon – but it does sound very demon-like, and . . .'

'Yes,' said Betty, anxious to go against Moira, and back up her friend Alicia. 'Yes. It's a jolly fine idea. We'll have it.'

Moira went up in smoke at once, in a way that a demon king himself might have envied!

She stood up, glowering. 'You only say that, Betty, because you're Alicia's friend, and . . .'

'Shucks,' said Betty, rudely.

Moira went on without stopping. 'And Darrell only says it because she always backs up Alicia, too. Well, I'm chief producer, and I'm going to have my way over this. There'll be no demon-chant. Get on with the rehearsal.'

Alicia was white. 'I'm not performing any more tonight,' she said, in a cold and angry voice. 'You're quite stealing the performance yourself, aren't you, Moira? Wonderful demon queen you'd make, with that look on your face!'

It was so exactly what Moira did look like that there were quite a lot of guffaws. Alicia walked off the stage. Darrell was petrified. Sally took charge.

'Who's on next? Come on, Bill.'

Bill came on the wrong side as usual, determined to flout Moira, too. She stalked in, her hands in her breeches' pockets. She always wore riding things when she rehearsed. She said it made her feel more baronial!

'BILL! You know perfectly well you don't come in that side,' shouted Moira, who also knew perfectly well that it was just Bill's way of showing that she sided with Alicia. Bill stood there like a dummy.

'Go back and come in the right side,' ordered Moira, harshly.

'No. I'm going riding,' said Bill. Quite simply and mildly, just like that! She walked off, humming, and Moira heard her calling to Clarissa.

'Clarissa! Come on! I'm not feeling fit for acting tonight. I want to do something energetic!'

'This is silly,' said Betty. 'Everyone walking off. Let *me* take charge, Moira. You're rubbing them up the wrong way tonight.'

Moira shoved her roughly aside. She had a wicked temper when she was really roused, the same kind of temper as her sister Bridget, who liked to smash things up if she really felt mad!

'I'm going on,' she said, between her teeth. 'Once we let things get out of hand, we're done for. We'll take the servants' chorus.'

The chorus came on, giggling and ready to play up Moira if they could. They all resented her hard ways, even though they admitted that she could get things done and done well.

Moira picked on Gwen and Maureen at once.

'You two! You're not singing! Oh no, you're not! So don't say you were. You're pretty awful every time, and you'd better pull your socks up now, or you won't even be in the chorus. I'll get some third-formers instead.'

'I say! Do shut up, Moira,' said Betty, in a low tone. 'You know you'll never do much with those two, and certainly not if you go for them like that.'

Moira took not the slightest notice. 'Did you hear what I said, Gwen and Maureen?' she called. 'Come out in front and sing by yourselves, so that I shall see if you *do* know the words.'

Gwen hesitated. She longed to cheek Moira, or walk off as Bill had done. But she was afraid of Moira's sharp tongue.

'Very well, then – stop where you are and sing there,' said Moira, suddenly realizing that she couldn't very well go and drag Gwen and Maureen to the front by main force. 'Music, Irene!'

Irene, looking very glum and disgusted, played the servants' chorus. Gwen's reedy voice piped up and Maureen mumbled the words, too.

'Stop,' said Moira, and the music stopped. 'You don't know the words and you don't know the tune – and it is about the seventh rehearsal. You're the worst in the whole play, both of you.'

Gwen and Maureen were furious at being humiliated like this in front of everyone. But still they dared not answer Moira back. They were both little cowards when it came to anything like that. They stood mute, and Gwen felt the usual easy tears welling up in her eyes.

Needless to say the rehearsal was not a success. Everyone sighed with relief when the supper-bell went. Moira went off scowling. Many of the girls sent scowls after her in imitation.

'Beast,' said Daphne. 'She gets worse!'

'She's worried because she has so many rehearsals to take, and so much to do,' said Darrell, trying to stop the general grumbling. It made things so difficult if the girls didn't come willingly and cheerfully to rehearsal. It was *her* pantomime, *her* masterpiece – she couldn't let their resentful feelings for Moira spoil it all.

'*Saint* Darrell!' called Betty, in delight. Darrell grinned.

'I'm no saint!' she said. 'I'm as hot and bothered as everyone else. But what's the good of messing up the show just because we've got a producer who can't keep her temper?'

'Let's chuck her out,' suggested somebody. 'We've got Betty – and there's you and Sally and Alicia at hand to help. We don't need Moira now the donkey-work is done.'

'We can't possibly chuck her out,' said Darrell, decidedly. 'It would be mean after she's got it more or less into shape. I do honestly think she's irritable because she's so interested in getting it perfect, and every little thing upsets her. Give her another chance!'

'All right,' agreed everyone. 'But only ONE more chance, Darrell!'

19

The anonymous letters

Darrell spoke to Moira rather nervously about the failure of the last rehearsal.

'We all know you're a bit overworked because you've done so much for the show already,' she began.

'Oh, do be quiet. You sound like Saint Catherine,' said Moira, with a glance at the nearby Catherine. 'She's already tried to make a hundred silly excuses for me. I hate people who suck up. I wasn't angry because I was tired or overworked. I was angry because people like Alicia and Bill and Gwen and Maureen were defiant and rude and silly and lazy and didn't back me up. Now you know.'

'Well, look, Moira – for goodness' sake be more understanding and patient next time,' said Darrell, holding tight on to her own temper. She felt it suddenly rising up. Oh dear! It would never do for two of them to get furious!

'Will you let me get on with my French or not?' asked Moira, in a dangerous voice. Darrell gave it up.

The next rehearsal was a little better but not much. Darrell had insisted on writing in Alicia's chant, and Moira had frowned but said very little. After all, the script *was* Darrell's business. Moira didn't find any fault with either Alicia or Bill this time. She didn't need to. Both were admirable and knew their parts well. Bill, at Darrell's request, came on the stage from the right side, and all was well.

But other things went wrong. Other people came in for criticism and blame, the courtiers were ordered to sing their song four times, the servants didn't bow properly, or curtsy at the right moment, Buttons was talking when she shouldn't be!

Moira didn't lose her temper, but she was unpleasant and hard. She fought to keep herself in hand. She was head-girl of the fifth. She was chief producer of the show. She had done all the donkey-work and licked things into shape. She meant to have her own way, and to have things as she liked – and she wasn't going to say please and thank you and smile and clap, as that idiot of a Betty did!

There was a lot more grumbling afterwards. Darrell and Sally began to feel panicky. Suppose the pantomime went to pieces instead of getting perfect?

And then another horrid thing began. It was the coming of the anonymous letters – spiteful, hateful letters with no name at the end!

Only one girl in the form got them – and that was Moira. She got the first one on a rehearsal day. She slit open the envelope and read it in the common-room. She exclaimed aloud in disgust.

'What's up?' said Darrell. Moira threw the letter across to her. 'Read that,' she said.

Darrell read it and was horrified. This was the letter:

IF ONLY YOU KNEW WHAT PEOPLE REALLY THINK OF THE HEAD-GIRL
OF THE FIFTH! BAD-TEMPERED, UNJUST, BOSSY — IF YOU LEFT AT THE
END OF THE TERM IT WOULDN'T BE TOO SOON FOR

    ME

'What a disgusting thing,' said Darrell, in dismay. 'Who could possibly have written it? It's all in printed capitals, to hide the writer's own handwriting. Take no notice of it, Moira. The only place for anonymous letters is the fire.'

Moira tossed the note into the fire, and went on with her work. Nobody could tell if she was upset or not – but everyone wondered who had written such a horrible letter.

The next one arrived the following day. There it was, on top of Moira's pile of books, addressed in the same printed writing.

She opened it, unthinking.

SO YOU GOT MY FIRST LETTER. I HOPE YOU ENJOYED IT. WOULDN'T
YOU LOVE TO KNOW WHAT THE GIRLS SAY ABOUT YOU? IT WOULD
MAKE YOUR EARS BURN! YOU'VE CERTAINLY GOT THE DISTINCTION
OF BEING THE MOST UNPOPULAR GIRL IN THE SCHOOL — BUT WHO
WANTS THAT DISTINCTION? CERTAINLY NOT

    ME

'Here's another of them,' said Moira, in a casual tone, and gave it to Darrell and Sally. They read it, dismayed by the spite that lay behind the few lines.

148

'But, Moira – *who* can it be?' said Darrell. 'Oh dear – it's horrible. Anonymous letters are always written by the lowest of the low, I feel – and it's awful to think there's someone like that at Malory Towers.'

'*I* don't care,' said Moira. But she did care. She remembered the spiteful words and worried over them in bed. She worried over the rehearsals, too. She badly wanted them to go as well as they had done at first – but poor Moira always found it very difficult to give up her own opinions and ways. She couldn't alter herself – she expected everyone else to adapt themselves to *her*. And they wouldn't, of course.

'Don't open any more notes,' said Sally to Moira, seeing her look rather white the next day. 'You know which they are – chuck them in the fire. You can tell by the printing on the envelope what they are.'

But the next one wasn't in an envelope. It was stuffed in Moira's lacrosse locker down in the changing-room. It was actually inside her right boot! She took it out, and saw immediately what was written, for the note this time had no envelope.

WHAT'S A DICTATOR? ASK MOIRA. DON'T ASK –

ME

Just that and no more. Moira crumpled up the note fiercely. This horrible letter-writer! She knew just what to say to hurt Moira most.

She told Darrell. She didn't really want to tell anyone,

but somehow she felt she must put a brave front on the matter, and by telling about the letters and making them public she felt that would show the writer she didn't care.

She laughed as she showed Darrell the note. 'Quite short this time,' she said. 'But not exactly sweet!'

'Oh! It's *hateful*!' said Darrell. 'We *must* find out who it is. We *must* stop it. I've never, never known such a thing happen all the time I've been at Malory Towers. Poisonous, malicious letters! Moira, why aren't you more upset? I should be absolutely miserable if I got these! Even if I knew they weren't true,' she added, hurriedly.

'You needn't add that,' said Moira, with a faint smile. 'They *are* true, actually. More than one of you have called me a dictator, you know – and bossy and bad-tempered.'

Darrell stared at her in horror. 'Moira – you wouldn't think *I* did it, would you? Or Sally? Or Alicia – or . . .'

Moira shrugged her shoulders and turned away. Darrell stared after her in dismay. She turned to Sally.

'We *must* find out who it is. We can't have Moira suspecting every one of us! Gosh, what will the rehearsals be like if this kind of thing goes on?'

The fourth note didn't get to the person it was intended for. It was certainly slipped, unfolded, into a book on Moira's desk – but the book happened to be one that Miss Potts had lent Moira about play-production. And having finished with it, Moira handed it back to Miss Potts without discovering the anonymous note inside.

So it was Miss Potts who found it. It slipped out to the

floor in the room she shared with Mam'zelle. She picked it up and read it.

ARE YOU WORRYING ABOUT THESE NOTES? THERE ARE PLENTY MORE TO COME! I'VE GOT QUITE A FEW MORE NAMES TO CALL YOU, AND ADJECTIVES THAT WILL SUIT YOU. HOW ABOUT THE DEMON QUEEN? YOU LOOK LIKE A DEMON SOMETIMES. A DOMINEERING, BOSSY, SCOWLING, GLOWERING ONE, TOO. AT LEAST, THAT'S HOW YOU APPEAR TO

ME

Miss Potts was amazed at this note. She read it over again. Who was it meant for? She turned it over and saw a name printed on the back. MOIRA!

'Moira!' she said. 'So somebody slipped it into the book I lent her. An anonymous note – and a particularly spiteful one. Who in the world is low enough to think out things like these?'

She examined the writing. It gave her no clue, because all the letters were in capitals, very carefully done. Miss Potts frowned as she stood there. Like all decent people she thought that anonymous letter-writers were either mad or cowardly. They didn't dare to say what they thought openly – they had to do it secretly and loathsomely.

She sent for Moira. Moira told her about the other notes. 'Have you any idea at all who sent these?' asked Miss Potts.

Moira hesitated. 'Yes. But I'm not sure about it, so I can't say.'

'Go and get Darrell, and Sally, too,' said Miss Potts,

thinking she could probably get more out of them. 'This has got to be stopped. Once a person of this sort gets away with a thing like this there's no knowing what they'll do next.'

Sally and Darrell came. They read the note. Darrell looked sick. 'Horrible,' she said.

'Who has written them?' demanded Miss Potts.

All three girls looked away. 'Well?' said Miss Potts, impatiently. 'This is not a thing to be backward about, is it? Don't you agree that it must be stopped?'

'Oh *yes*,' said Darrell.

'Well, then – if you have any idea who has written them, tell me,' said Miss Potts. 'I can then go and tackle them at once.'

'Well – you see – it might be one of quite a number of people,' said Darrell.

'A *number* of people?' said Miss Potts, disbelievingly. 'Are you trying to tell me that there are a *number* of people who hate Moira enough to write her notes like this?'

There was a silence. Miss Potts clicked in exasperation. 'Has Moira so many enemies? And why? I have had no complaints of her as head-girl. Why do you think so many people hate Moira?'

This was very awkward and most embarrassing. Darrell and Sally didn't know what in the world to say. Moira came to their rescue. She was pale, and looked strained.

'*I'll* tell you who it might be, Miss Potts!' she said. 'It might be Gwen. It might be Maureen. It might even be Alicia.'

'NO!' said both Sally and Darrell together.

Moira went on. 'It might be Catherine. It might be – it might be Bridget.'

'*Bridget* – do you mean your sister in the fourth?' asked Miss Potts, amazed.

Moira nodded, looking miserable. She wouldn't look at Sally or Darrell. Miss Potts turned to them. 'What do you think of all this?' she demanded.

'Well – it *could* be any of those except Alicia,' said Darrell. 'Alicia *does* feel angry with Moira because of something that happened at a rehearsal – but Alicia's not underhanded. If she wanted to tell Moira all those things she'd say them out loud, probably in front of everyone, too! It's certainly not Alicia.'

'I agree with you,' said Miss Potts. 'We can certainly rule out Alicia. That still leaves four people that Moira thinks detest her enough to write these notes. Moira – it's rather dreadful to feel you have four people around you that might regard you with such bitter feelings, isn't it? What *can* you have been doing to arouse them?'

Moira said nothing. She knew perfectly well why all four had cause to hate her. She had sneered at Gwen and Maureen unmercifully, and had humiliated them too, on the stage at last week's rehearsal. She had called Catherine a doormat and sneered too at her, for her annoying self-sacrificing ways, and had shoved her to one side, in spite of all the hundreds of things Catherine had done for her.

As for Bridget – well, there never had been any love lost between the sisters. Bridget hated her, she was sure of it. And hadn't Bridget threatened her not so long ago? What had she said? 'I warn you, Moira, you'll be sorry for this. I *warn* you!'

Well – it might be Catherine, it might be Gwen or Maureen, and it might be Bridget. It probably *wasn't* Alicia – because these letters came from a coward, and nobody could call Alicia that!

Who *did* write those beastly letters? And how could they ever find out?

Things happen

All sorts of things happened that week. At the next rehearsal there was another flare-up between Alicia and Moira – a really bad one that ended in Alicia resigning from the show! Betty promptly resigned, too, as co-producer.

It was a terrible blow to Sally and Darrell. 'We *can't* do without you, Alicia,' wailed Darrell. 'We'll never, never get a demon king like you – and all your wonderful juggling and conjuring and leaping about, too. You'll ruin the whole thing if you resign.'

'*If* I resign! I *have* resigned!' said Alicia, looking calm and unruffled, but inwardly seething with anger, disappointment and misery at seeing Darrell so upset. 'I'm sorry it affects you too – but I'm not working with Moira any more. And nothing in the world will make me go back into the pantomime now – no, not even if Moira herself resigned and came and apologized.'

Darrell knew that Moira would never do *that*. She was as unbending as Alicia was obstinate.

'Talk about the immovable meeting the irresistible!' she groaned. 'Oh, Alicia – for *my* sake, withdraw your resignation. Why, it's only three weeks now till the pantomime is presented. I can't rewrite it, and cut out your parts – you come in so often.'

'Darrell, I'm honestly sorry,' said Alicia, looking harassed now. 'But you know I never go back on my word. It's my pride now that's in the way. Nothing in the world would make me knuckle under to Moira – and that's what I should be doing if I withdrew my resignation.'

Darrell stared hopelessly at Alicia. Defiant, obstinate, strong-willed Alicia – nobody could do anything with her once she had made up her mind. She turned away, amazed and furious to find sudden tears in her eyes. But she was so bitterly disappointed. Her lovely pantomime – and such a wonderful demon king – and all that juggling and conjuring out of it now. No one but Alicia could do that.

Sally went with Darrell, trying to comfort her. She, too, was bitterly disappointed, and sighed when she thought of all the rewriting there would be to do – and another demon king to find and train in such a short time. But Darrell felt it most. It was her first big job, the first time she had tried her hand at writing something worth while – and now it was spoiled.

Moira was obstinate too. She would not talk about the matter at all. Nor would she resign. 'All I can say is, I'm sorry it's happened, but it was Alicia who blew up and resigned, not me,' she said. And not one word more would she say about it.

It was Mam'zelle who created the next excitement. She sat down at her desk in Miss Potts's room one day, and announced her intention of turning it out.

'About time, too,' said Miss Potts, dryly. 'You'll probably find the year before last's exam papers there, I should think. I never saw such a collection of rubbish in anyone's desk in my life.'

'Ha, Miss Potts! You wish to be funny?' said Mam'zelle, huffily.

'No,' said Miss Potts. 'Merely truthful.'

Mam'zelle snorted, and took hold of about a hundred loose papers in her desk. She lifted them out and they immediately fell apart and slithered all over the floor. One booklet floated to Miss Potts's feet. She looked at it with interest, for there was a very brightly coloured picture on the cover, showing a conjuror doing tricks. 'New tricks. Old tricks. Tricks to play on your enemies. Tricks to play on your friends,' she read out loud. She glanced at Mam'zelle in astonishment. 'Since when did you think of taking up tricks to play?' she enquired.

'I do not think of it,' said Mam'zelle depositing another hundred papers on the floor. '*Tiens*! Here is the programme of the play the third-formers gave six years ago!'

'What did I tell you?' said Miss Potts. 'You'll probably find the Speeches made at the Opening of the First Term at Malory Towers if you look a little further into your desk.'

'Do not tizz me,' said Mam'zelle. 'I do not like being tizzed.'

'I'm not teasing,' said Miss Potts. 'I'm quite serious. I say – *where* did you get these trick and conjuring lists from? Look at this one – I'm sure it's got in it all the tricks

157

that Alicia and Betty ever played on you!'

Mam'zelle took the booklets. She was soon completely absorbed in them. She chuckled. She laughed. She said '*Tiens*!' and 'Oh, *là là*!' a dozen times. Miss Potts went on with her work. She was used to Mam'zelle's little ways.

Mam'zelle had never read anything so enthralling in all her life as these booklets that described tricks of all sorts and kinds. She was completely lost in them. She read of machines that could apparently saw people's fingers in half without hurting them – cigarettes with glowing ends that were not really alight – ink spots and jam-clots that could be placed on table-cloths to deceive annoyed mothers or teachers into thinking they were real.

The booklets blandly described these and a hundred others. Mam'zelle was absolutely fascinated. She came to one trick that made her laugh out loud. 'Ah, now listen, Miss Potts,' she began.

'*No*, Mam'zelle,' said Miss Potts, sternly. 'I've twenty-three *disgraceful* maths papers to mark that the first form have had the nerve to give in today – and I do NOT want to listen to your recital of childish tricks.'

Mam'zelle sighed and went back to the booklets. She read over again the thing that had so intrigued her. There were two photographs with the description of the trick. One showed a smiling man with ordinary teeth – the other showed the same man – with trick teeth! He looked horrible.

Mam'zelle read the description over again. 'These trick teeth are cleverly made of celluloid, and are shaped to fit neatly over the wearer's own teeth – but project forwards and downwards, and so alter the expression of the wearer's face considerably as soon as he smiles, giving a really terrifying and exceedingly strange appearance.'

Mam'zelle studied the photographs. She tried to imagine herself wearing teeth like that – and suddenly flashing them at the girls with a smile. Ha! They had dared her to do a trick on them! Mam'zelle had a very very good mind to write for this teeth trick. Perhaps she would wear them at a lacrosse match out in the field – or maybe take the girls for a walk, and keep showing her trick teeth.

Mam'zelle shook with laughter. Ha ha – so many 'treeks' had those bad girls played on her, it was time their poor old Mam'zelle played a 'treek' on them too. How they would be astonished! How they would stare. How they would laugh afterwards.

Mam'zelle scuffled about among her untidy papers and found her writing-pad. In her slanting French handwriting she wrote for the 'teeth trick' and sent a cheque with the letter. She was delighted. She would not tell even Miss Potts.

'No. I will not tell her. I will suddenly smile at her – like this,' said Mam'zelle to herself – and did a sudden fierce grin – 'and I shall look so strange that she will start back in fright at my horrible teeth.'

Mam'zelle finished the letter and then casually looked through the other trick booklets before throwing them away. And it was then she came across the note. It was written in capitals, very carefully. It was not a nice note. It was headed:

TO FELICITY,

YOU THINK YOU'RE SO GOOD AT GAMES, DON'T YOU? WELL, IT'S
ONLY BECAUSE DARRELL FAVOURS YOU THAT YOU'RE EVER PUT INTO
ANY GAMES. EVERYONE KNOWS THAT!

It was not signed at all. 'Here is a nasty little note,' said
Mam'zelle in disgust, and tossed it to Miss Potts. Miss Potts
recognized the printed letters at once – they were exactly
the same as those on the anonymous letters sent to Moira.

'Where did you get this?' she asked, sharply.

'I found it in this trick booklet,' said Mam'zelle, startled.

'Whose is the booklet? Where did you get it?'
demanded Miss Potts.

'I took it from that bad little June's desk,' said Mam'zelle.

'Very interesting,' said Miss Potts. She got up and went
to the door. She sent a girl to find Moira, Sally and Darrell.
They came, looking surprised.

'I think I've found the writer of those notes,' said Miss
Potts. 'But before I tackle her I want to know if she's any
reason to dislike you, Moira. It's June, in the first form.'

'*June*!' exclaimed everyone, amazed.

Moira looked at Miss Potts. 'Yes – I suppose she'd think
she had cause to dislike me,' she said. 'I ticked her off
because she was cheeky about not being put into the
Wellsbrough match. Told her she had no team-spirit. I
also made her apologize to me for daring to say in front
of me that Darrell had put Felicity into the match out of
favouritism, because she was her sister.'

Miss Potts nodded. 'Thank you. It *is* June, then, I'm

afraid. I'll see her now. Send her to me, will you. I'm rather afraid this is a matter for Miss Grayling. We are not pleased with June and it wouldn't take much to have her sent away from here. This is a particularly loathsome act of hers – to send out anonymous letters.'

June came, looking defiant but scared. She had not been told why she was wanted.

'June, I have called you here on a very very serious matter,' said Miss Potts. 'I find that you have been writing detestable anonymous letters. Don't attempt to deny it. You will only make things worse. Your only hope is to confess honestly. Why did you do it?'

June had no idea how Miss Potts knew all this. She went white, but still looked bold. 'I suppose you mean the ones to Moira?' she said. 'Yes, I did write them – and she deserved them. Everyone hates her.'

'That's beside the point,' said Miss Potts. 'The point we have to keep to is that there is a girl in this school, a girl in the first form, who is guilty of something for which in later years she could be sent to prison – a thing that as a rule rarely begins until a girl is much much older than you, because it is only depraved and cowardly characters who attempt this underhand, stab-in-the-dark kind of thing.'

She paused. Her eyes bored like gimlets into the petrified June.

'We call this kind of thing "poison-pen" writing, when the writers are grown up,' she went on, 'and they are held in universal loathing and hatred, considered the lowest of the low. Did you know that?'

'No,' gasped June.

'I would not talk to you in this serious manner if there were not also other things I dislike very much in you,' said Miss Potts, still in the same hard, driving voice. 'Your disobedience, your defiance, your aggressiveness, your total lack of respect for anyone. You may think it is admirable and brave and grand. It isn't. It is the sign of a strong character gone wrong – and on top of all that you have shown yourself a coward – because only a coward ever writes anonymous letters.'

June's knees were shaking. Miss Potts saw them but she took no notice. If ever anyone wanted a good shaking up it was June.

'This matter must go to Miss Grayling,' she said. 'Come with me now. You may be interested to know that it was because Mam'zelle found this note – to Felicity – that I discovered who was the writer of the other letters.'

June took a quick glance at the note to Felicity. 'I didn't give it to her,' she said. 'I meant to – and then I didn't. I must have left it somewhere in a book.'

'Our sins always find us out,' said Miss Potts, solemnly. 'Always. Now, come with me.'

'Miss Potts – shall I be – be – expelled?' asked June – a June no longer bold and brazen, but a June as deflated as when her balloons had been suddenly pricked that day in class.

'That rests with Miss Grayling,' said Miss Potts, and she got up. 'Come with me.'

The news went round the fifth form rapidly. 'The

letters were written by June – the little beast!'

'She's gone to see Miss Grayling. I bet she'll be expelled. She's no good, anyway.'

Alicia listened in horror. Her own cousin! She disliked June as much as anybody else – but this was her own cousin in terrible trouble and disgrace. She was very distressed.

It's a disgrace for our whole family, she thought. And what *will* June's people say? They'll never get over it if she's expelled. They'll think I ought to have kept an eye on June more – and perhaps I should. But she really is such a little beast!

Felicity came tearing up to the fifth-form common-room that evening. She was in tears. 'Darrell!' she said, hardly waiting to knock. 'Oh, Darrell – June's going to be expelled. She is really. Miss Grayling told her so. Oh, *Darrell* – I don't like her – but I can't bear her to be expelled. Surely she's not as bad as all that.'

Everyone in the fifth-form common-room sat up with a jerk at this news. Expelled! It was ages since anyone had been sent in disgrace from Malory Towers. And a first-former, too. Alicia sat silent, biting her lips. Her own cousin. How terrible.

Poor Felicity began to sob. 'June's got to go tomorrow. Miss Grayling is telephoning her people tonight. She's packing now, this minute. She's terribly, terribly upset. She keeps saying she's not a coward, and she didn't *know* it was so awful, she keeps on and on . . . Darrell, can't you do something? Suppose it was *me*, Darrell? Wouldn't you do something?'

The fifth form were aghast at all this. They pictured June packing, bewildered and frightened. Miss Grayling must have had very bad reports of her to make her go to this length. She must have thought there was no good in June at all not to give her one more chance.

'Darrell! Sally! Alicia! Can't you go and ask Miss Grayling to give her a chance?' cried Felicity, a big tear running down her nose and falling on to the carpet. 'I tell you, she's *awfully* upset.'

Moira had been listening with the others. So it *was* June! She looked round at Gwen, Maureen and Catherine, three of the girls she had suspected. It was a load off her heart that it wasn't any of them. It was an even greater relief that it wasn't Bridget, her sister.

But suppose it had been? It would have been Bridget who was packing then – Bridget who would have been so 'awfully upset'. It would have been her own parents who would be so sad and miserable because a child of theirs had been expelled.

Moira got up. '*I'll* go and see Miss Grayling,' she said. 'I won't let her expel June. I'll ask her to give her another chance. After all – I've been pretty awful myself this term – and it's not to be wondered at if a mere first-former hated me – and descended to writing those letters. There was quite a lot of truth in them! June deserves to be punished – but not so badly as that.'

She went out of the room, leaving behind a deep silence. Felicity ran with her, and actually took her hand! Moira squeezed it. 'Oh, Moira – people say you're hard and unkind – but you're not, you're not!' said little Felicity. 'You're kind and generous and good, and I shall tell every single person in the first form so!'

Nobody ever knew what happened between Miss Grayling, Moira and June, for not one of the three ever said. But the result was that June was sent to unpack her things again, very subdued and thankful, and that Moira came back to find a common-room full of admiration and goodwill towards her.

'It's all right,' said Moira, smiling round a little nervously. 'June's let off. She's unpacking again. She won't forget this lesson in a hurry.'

Alicia spoke in a rather shaky voice. 'Thanks most awfully, Moira. You've been most frightfully decent over this. I can't ever repay you – it means an awful lot to me to know that my cousin won't be expelled. I – er – I – want to apologize for resigning from the pantomime. If – if you'll let me withdraw my resignation, I'd like to.'

This was a very difficult thing for Alicia to do – Alicia who had said that nothing in the world would make her withdraw her resignation or apologize! Well, something *had* made her – and she was decent enough and brave enough not to shirk the awkwardness and difficulty but to say it all straight out in public.

Everyone went suddenly mad. Darrell gave a squeal of delight and rushed to Alicia. Sally thumped her on the back. Mavis sang loudly. Irene went to the piano and played a triumphant march from the pantomime. Bill and Clarissa galloped round the room as if they were on horseback, and little Mary-Lou thumped on the top of the table. Moira laughed suddenly.

What had happened to all the spite and malice and beastliness? What had happened to the squabbles and quarrels and worries? They were gone in an instant, blown to smithereens by Moira's instinctive, generous-hearted action in going to save June.

'Everything's right again,' sang Mavis, and Mary-Lou thumped the table in time. 'Everything's right, everything's right – HURRAY!'

Mam'zelle's 'treek'

Certainly everything was much better now. Alicia went to see June and addressed a good many sound and sensible words to that much chastened and subdued first-former. It would be a long time before June forgot them, if she ever did. She didn't think she ever would.

Moira was basking in a new-found admiration and liking, that made her much more amenable to the others' suggestions, and rehearsals became a pleasure. Even the sulky Bridget came smiling into the fifth-form common-room to say she was glad Moira had saved June. 'It makes me feel you might do the same for *me*, Moira!' she said.

'Well – I would,' said Moira, shortly, and Bridget went out, pleased.

Mam'zelle had been very shocked and upset about everything. 'But it is terrible! How could June do such a thing? And Moira – *Moira*, that hard Moira to go and save her like that! Miss Potts, never would I have thought that girl had a generous action in her! Miss Potts – it shocks me that I know so little of my girls!'

'Oh, you'll get over the shock,' said Miss Potts, cheerfully. 'And you'll have plenty more. Well, well – the girls have cheered up a lot – the fifth-formers I mean. They really were a worried, miserable, quarrelsome crew last week! I was seriously thinking of playing a trick on them to cheer them up!'

Mam'zelle looked at Miss Potts. In her desk were the trick teeth which had arrived that morning. Miss Potts must not play a trick – if a trick was to be played, she, Mam'zelle would play it. Ah yes – to cheer up the poor girls! That would be a kind act to do.

There was a house-match that afternoon – North Tower girls against West Tower. Mam'zelle decided she would appear as a spectator at the match – with her teeth!

Ah, those teeth! Mam'zelle had tried them on. They might have been made for her! They fitted over her own teeth, but were longer, and projected slightly forward. They were not noticeable at all, of course, when she had her mouth shut – but when she smiled – ah, how sinister she looked, how strange, how fierce!

Mam'zelle had shocked even herself when she had put in the extraordinary teeth and smiled at herself in the mirror. '*Tiens*!' she said, and clutched her dressing-table. 'I am a monster! I am truly terrible with these teeth . . .'

That afternoon she put them in carefully over her others and went downstairs to the playing-fields, wrapping herself up warmly in coat, scarf and hat. Darrell saw her first, and made room for her on the bench she was on.

'Thank you,' said Mam'zelle, and smiled at Darrell. Darrell got a tremendous shock. Mam'zelle had suddenly looked altogether different – quite terrifying. Darrell stared at her – but Mam'zelle had quickly shut her mouth.

The next one to get the Smile was little Felicity, who came up with Susan. Mam'zelle smiled at her.

'Oh!' said Felicity in sudden horror, and Susan stared. Mam'zelle shut her mouth. A desire to laugh was gradually working up inside her. No, no – she must not laugh. Laughing spoiled tricks.

She did not smile for some time, trying to conquer her urge to laugh. Miss Linnie, the sewing-mistress, passed by and nodded at Mam'zelle. Mam'zelle could not resist showing her the teeth. She smiled.

Miss Linnie looked amazed and horrified. She walked on quickly. 'Was that *really* Mam'zelle?' she wondered. 'No, it must have been someone else. What awful teeth!'

Mam'zelle felt that she must get up and walk about. It was too cold to sit – and besides she so badly wanted to laugh again. Ah, now she understood why the girls laughed so much and so helplessly when they played their mischievous tricks on her.

She walked along the field, and met Bill and Clarissa. They smiled at her and she smiled back. Bill stood still, thunderstruck. Clarissa hadn't really noticed.

'Clarissa!' said Bill, when Mam'zelle had gone. 'What's the matter with Mam'zelle this afternoon? She looks *horrible*!'

'Horrible? How?' asked Clarissa in great surprise.

'Well, her *teeth*! Didn't you see her teeth?' asked Bill. 'They seem to have changed or something. Simply awful teeth she had – long and sticking-out.'

Clarissa was astonished. 'Let's walk back and smile at

her again,' she said. So back they went. But Mam'zelle saw their inquisitive looks, and was struggling against a fit of laughter. She would not open her mouth to smile.

Matron came up. 'Oh, Mam'zelle – do you know where Gwen is? She's darned her navy gym shorts with grey wool again. I want her indoors this afternoon!'

Mam'zelle could not resist smiling at Matron. Matron stared as if she couldn't believe her eyes. Mam'zelle shut her mouth. Matron backed away a little, looking rather alarmed.

'Gwen's over there,' said Mam'zelle, her extra teeth making her words sound rather thick. Matron looked even more alarmed at the thick voice and disappeared in a hurry. Mam'zelle saw her address a few words to Miss Potts. Miss Potts looked round for Mam'zelle.

Aha! thought Mam'zelle, Matron has told her I look terrible! Soon Miss Potts will come to look at my Smile. I shall laugh. I know I shall. I shall laugh without stopping soon.

Miss Potts came up, eyeing Mam'zelle carefully. She got a quick glimpse of the famous teeth. Then Mam'zelle clamped her mouth shut. She would explode if she didn't keep her mouth shut! She pulled her scarf across her face, trying to hide her desire to laugh.

'Do you feel the cold today, Mam'zelle?' asked Miss Potts anxiously. 'You – er – you haven't got toothache, have you?'

A peculiar wild sound came from Mam'zelle. It startled Miss Potts considerably. But actually it was only

Mam'zelle trying to stifle a squeal of laughter. She rushed away hurriedly. Miss Potts stared after her uncomfortably. What *was* up with Mam'zelle?

Mam'zelle strolled down the field by herself, trying to recover. She gave a few loud gulps that made two second-formers wonder if she was going to be ill.

Poor Mam'zelle felt she couldn't flash her teeth at anyone for a long time, for if she did she would explode like Irene. She decided to go in. She turned her steps towards the school – and then, to her utter horror, she saw Miss Grayling, the Head Mistress, bearing down on her with two parents! Mam'zelle gave an anguished look and hurried on as fast as she could.

'Oh – there's Mam'zelle,' said Miss Grayling's pleasant voice. 'Mam'zelle, will you meet Mrs Jennings and Mrs Petton?'

Mam'zelle was forced to go to them. She lost all desire for laughter at once. The trick teeth suddenly stopped being funny, and became monstrosities to be got rid of at once. But how? She couldn't spit them into her handkerchief with people just about to shake hands with her.

Mrs Jennings held out her hand. 'I've heard so much about you, Mam'zelle Dupont,' she said, 'and what tricks the naughty girls play on you, too!'

Mam'zelle tried to smile without opening her mouth at all, and the effect was rather peculiar – a sort of suppressed snarl. Mrs Jennings looked surprised. Mam'zelle tried to make up for her lack of smile by shaking Mrs Jennings's hand very vigorously indeed.

She did the same with Mrs Petton, who turned out to be a talkative mother who wanted to know *exactly* how her daughter Teresa was getting on in French. She smiled gaily at Mam'zelle while she talked, and Mam'zelle found it agony not to smile back. She had to produce the suppressed snarl again, smiling with her mouth shut and her lips firmly over her teeth.

Miss Grayling was startled by this peculiar smile. She examined Mam'zelle closely. Mam'zelle's voice was not quite as usual either – it sounded thick. As if her mouth is too full of teeth, thought Miss Grayling, little knowing that she had hit on the exact truth.

At last the mothers went. Mam'zelle shook hands with them most vigorously once more, and was so relieved at parting from them that she forgot herself and gave them a broad smile.

They got a full view of the terrible teeth, Miss Grayling, too. The Head stared in the utmost horror – *what* had happened to Mam'zelle's teeth? Had she had her old ones out – were these a new, false set? But how TERRIBLE they were! They made her look like the wolf in the tale of Red Riding Hood.

The two mothers turned their heads away quickly at the sight of the teeth. They hurried off with Miss Grayling, who hardly heard what they said, she was so concerned about Mam'zelle's teeth. She determined to send for Mam'zelle that evening and ask her about them. Really – she couldn't allow any of her staff to go about with teeth like that! They were monstrous, hideous!

Mam'zelle was so thankful to see the last of the mothers that she hurried straight into a little company of fifth-formers going back to the school, some to do their piano practice and some to have a lesson in elocution.

'Hallo, Mam'zelle!' said Mavis. 'Are you coming back to school?'

Mam'zelle smiled. The fifth-formers got a dreadful shock. They stared in silent horror. The teeth had slipped a little, and now looked rather like fangs. They gave Mam'zelle a most sinister, big-bad-wolf look. Mam'zelle saw their alarm and astonishment. Laughter surged back into her. She felt it swelling up and up. She gasped. She gulped. She roared.

She sank on to a bench and cried with helpless laughter. She remembered Matron's face – and Miss Grayling's – and the faces of the two mothers. The more she thought of them the more helplessly she laughed. The girls stood round, more alarmed than ever. What *was* the matter with Mam'zelle? What was this enormous joke?

Mam'zelle's teeth slipped out altogether, fell on to her lap, and then to the ground. The girls stared at them in the utmost amazement, and then looked at Mam'zelle. She now looked completely normal, with just her own small teeth showing in her laughing face. She laughed on and on when she saw her trick teeth lying there before her.

'It is a treek,' she squeaked at last, wiping her eyes with her handkerchief. 'Did you not give me a dare? Did you not tell me to do a treek on you? I have done one with the

173

teeth. They are treek teeth. Oh, *là là* – I must laugh again. Oh my sides, oh my back!'

She swayed to and fro, laughing. The girls began to laugh, too. Mam'zelle Rougier came up, astonished to see the other French mistress laughing so much.

'What is the matter?' she asked, without a smile on her face.

Irene did one of her explosions. She pointed to the teeth on the ground. 'Mam'zelle wore them – for a trick – and they've fallen out and given the game away!'

She went off into squeals of laughter again, and the other girls joined in. Mam'zelle Rougier looked cold and disapproving.

'I see no joke,' she said. 'It is not funny, teeth on the grass. It is time to see the dentist when that happens.'

She walked off, and her speech and disapproving face sent everyone into fits of laughter again. It was altogether a most successful afternoon for Mam'zelle, and the 'treek' story flew all through the school immediately.

Mam'zelle suddenly found herself extremely popular, except with the staff. 'A little *undignified*, don't you think?' said Miss Williams.

'Not a thing to do *too* often, Mam'zelle,' said Miss Potts, making up her mind to remove the trick booklets from Mam'zelle's desk at the first opportunity.

'Glad you've lost those frightful teeth,' said Matron, bluntly. 'Don't do that again without warning me, Mam'zelle. I got the shock of my life.'

But the girls loved Mam'zelle for her 'treek', and every

class in the school, from top to bottom, worked twice as hard (or so Mam'zelle declared) after she had played her truly astonishing 'treek'!

A grand show

The end of the term was coming near. The pantomime was almost ready. Everything had gone smoothly since the Big Row, as it was called.

Moira had softened down a lot, pleased by the unstinted admiration of the girls for her act in going down to the Head to speak for June. Alicia was back as demon king, as good as ever, complete with eerie chant. Betty was back as co-producer. Everyone knew her part perfectly.

Belinda's scenery was almost finished. She had produced all kinds of wonderful effects, helped by the properties 'Pop' had out in the barn – relics of other plays and pantomimes. She painted fast and furiously, and Pop had helped to evolve a magnificent coach which they had somehow managed to adorn with gilt paint.

'It looks marvellous,' said Clarissa, in awe. 'I suppose Merrylegs couldn't pull it, Belinda? He'd be awfully good, I know.'

'I dare say – but if you think I'm going to have Thunder and Merrylegs galloping about madly all over my precious stage, you can think again,' said Belinda, adding a final touch of gilt to a wheel.

All the actors knew the songs, both words and music.

The costumes were ready. Janet had done well, and everyone had a costume that fitted and suited the wearer perfectly. Cinderella looked enchanting in her ball-gown – a dress whose full skirt floated out mistily, glittering with hundreds of sequins patiently sewn on by the first-formers in the sewing-class.

The whole school was interested in the pantomime because so many of them had either helped to paint the scenery or make the 'props' or sew the costumes. They were all looking forward tremendously to the show the next week.

Gwen and Maureen looked enviously at Mary-Lou in her ball-gown. How they wished they could wear a frock like that. How beautiful they would look!

Catherine gazed at little Mary-Lou, too. She had got very fond of her. Mary-Lou was gentle and timid and always grateful for anything that Catherine did for her. She didn't call her a doormat or laugh at her self-sacrificing ways. She didn't even call her Saint Catherine as the others did.

Catherine had stopped being a doormat for the form. She had felt angry and sore about it. But she somehow couldn't stop waiting on people – and Mary-Lou didn't mind! So she fussed over her, and altered her frock, and praised her, and heard her words; and altogether she made life very easy for Mary-Lou, who was really very nervous about taking the principal part in the show.

Now the days were spinning away fast – Friday, Saturday, Sunday, Monday – two more days left, one more day . . .

'And now it's THE DAY!' cried Darrell the next morning, rushing to the window. 'And it's a heavenly day, so all the parents will get down without any bother. Gosh, I feel so excited I don't know what I'm doing.'

'Well, you certainly don't know the difference between my sponge and yours,' said Sally, taking her own sponge away from the excited Darrell. 'Come on – get dressed, idiot. We've got a lot to do today!'

The parents arrived at tea-time. Tea was at four. The pantomime was due to begin at half-past five, and went on till half-past seven. Then there came a Grand Supper, and after that the parents went – some to their homes, if they were within driving distance, some to hotels.

The tea was grand and the first – and second-formers scurried about with plates and dishes, helping themselves to the meringues and eclairs whenever they could. The fifth-formers slipped away to dress at half-past four. Darrell peeped at the stage.

How big it looked – how grand! It was already set for the first scene, with a great fire-place for Cinderella to sit by. Darrell felt solemn. She had written this pantomime. If it was a failure she would never never write anything again – and you never knew – it might be a terrible flop.

Sally came up. She saw Darrell's solemn face and smiled. 'It's going to be a terrific success,' she said. 'You just see! And you'll deserve it, Darrell – you really have worked hard.'

'So have you,' said Darrell, loyally – but Sally knew that the creative part had all been Darrell's. The words and the songs had all come out of Darrell's own imagination. Sally hadn't much imagination – she was sensible and sturdy and stolid. She admired Darrell for her quick creativeness without envying her.

The school orchestra were in their places, tuning up. They had learned all Irene's music, and she was going to conduct them. She looked flushed and pleased.

'Are you nervous?' asked Belinda.

'Yes. *Now* I am. But at the very first stroke of my baton, at the very first note of the music, I'll forget to be nervous. I just won't be there. I'll be the music,' said Irene. Belinda understood this remarkable statement very well, and nodded gravely.

The actors were all dressed in their costumes. Mary-Lou had on her ragged Cinderella frock and looked frightened. 'But it doesn't matter you looking pensive and scared,' Moira told her. 'You're just right like that – Cinderella to the life!'

Alicia looked simply magnificent. She was dressed in a tight-fitting glowing red costume that showed off her slim figure perfectly. It was glittering with bright sequins. Her eyes glittered, too. She wore a pointed hood and looked 'positively *wicked*,' Betty said.

'And don't you drop any of your juggling rings, and discover your rabbit isn't in your hat after all, or something,' she said to Alicia. But Alicia knew she wouldn't. Alicia wasn't nervous – she was cocksure and confident and brilliant-eyed, and leaped about as if she had springs in her heels.

'Shhhhhhh!' said somebody. 'The orchestra's beginning. The audience are all coming in. Shhhhh!'

The orchestra played a lively rousing tune. Lovely! Darrell peeped through the curtains and saw Irene standing up, conducting vigorously. What did it feel like to conduct your own music? Just as good as it would feel to see your own play acted, no doubt. She shivered in excitement.

A bell rang behind stage. The curtains were about to swing open. The chorus got ready to go in. The pantomime had begun!

When the chorus danced off the stage, Mary-Lou was left by the fire as Cinderella. She sang – and her small sweet voice caught Irene's lilting melodies, making everyone listen intently.

The Baron came on – Bill, stamping around in riding-boots, roaring here and roaring there.

'It's BILL!' shouted the delighted school and clapped so much that they held up the pantomime for a bit. The two Ugly Sisters brought down the house too. They were perfectly hideous, perfectly idiotic and perfectly wonderful. And how they enjoyed themselves! Gwen even found herself wishing she might have been one of them! Ugly or not, it must be wonderful to have a comic part like that. But Gwen was only a servant in the chorus, unseen and almost unheard!

Mrs Lacey hardly caught sight of her at all. But for once she didn't mind – she was so enraptured with the pantomime.

Then the Prince came – tall, slender Mavis, looking

shy and nervous until she had to sing – and then what a marvel! Her voice broke on the startled audience like a miracle, and there was not a single sound to be heard while she sang.

Mothers found their eyes full of tears. What a wonderful voice! What a good thing it had come back to Mavis. Why, one day she would be a great opera singer, perhaps the greatest that ever lived. Mavis sang on and on like a bird, her voice pure and true, and Irene exulted in the tunes she had written so well for her.

There was such a storm of clapping that again the pantomime was held up. 'Encore!' shouted everyone. 'Encore! ENCORE!'

Darrell was trembling with excitement and joy. It was a success. It WAS a success. In fact, it looked like being a SUPER success. She could hardly keep still.

Alicia was excellent. She leaped on magnificently, with her eerie chant. 'Oooooh!' said the lower school, deliciously thrilled. 'The demon king. It's Alicia!'

Without a single mistake Alicia juggled and tumbled, did cartwheels and conjured as if she had been doing nothing else all her life. Fathers turned to one another and exclaimed in astonished admiration.

'She's good enough to be on the London stage. How on earth did she do *that* trick?'

So the show went on, and everyone clapped and cheered madly at the end of the first act. The actors rushed to Moira and Darrell when the curtain came down at the end of the act.

'Are we doing all right? I nearly forgot my lines! Isn't the audience grand? Oh, Darrell, aren't you *proud*? Moira, we're doing fine, aren't we? Aren't we?'

The second act was performed. Now the audience had time to appreciate the lovely costumes and marvel at them. They marvelled at the scenery, too – and applauded the gilt coach frantically, especially the lower school, some of whom had helped to paint it.

And then at last the end came. The final chorus was sung, the last bow made. The curtain swung back once – twice – three – four times. The audience rose to its feet, cheering and shouting and stamping. It was the biggest success Malory Towers had ever had.

The audience sat down. A call came that grew more and more insistent.

'Author! *Author*! AUTHOR!'

Someone gave Darrell a push. 'Go on, silly. They're calling for you. You're the author! You wrote it all!'

Blindly Darrell stepped out in front of the curtain. She saw Felicity's excited face somewhere. She searched for her father and mother. There they were – clapping wildly. Mrs Rivers found tears running down her face. Darrell! Her Darrell! How wonderful it was to have a child you could be proud of! Well done, Darrell, well done!

'Speech!' came a call. 'Speech! Speeeeech!'

'Say something, ass!' said Irene, from the orchestra.

There was suddenly silence. Darrell hesitated. What should she say? 'Thank you,' she said, at last. 'We – we did love doing it. I couldn't have done it by myself, of course.

There was Irene, who wrote all the lovely music. Come up here, Irene!'

Irene came up beside her and bowed. She was clapped and cheered.

'And there was Belinda who designed everything,' went on Darrell, and Belinda was pushed out from behind the curtain, beside her. 'And Sally helped me all the time.' Out came Sally, blushing.

'Moira and Betty were co-producers,' said Darrell, warming up a little. 'Here they are. Oh, and Janet did all the costumes!'

They appeared, beaming, and got a large share of claps and cheers.

'And Mavis ought to come, too, because she helped so much with the singing – and trained the chorus,' said Darrell. Mavis sidled out shyly, and got a tremendous ovation.

'Oh – and I mustn't forget Pop!' said Darrell – and much to everyone's delight out came the handyman in waistcoat and green apron looking completely bemused and extremely proud. He bowed several times and then disappeared like a jack-in-the-box.

And then it was really all over. One last long clap, one last long shout – it was over.

I wish I could hold this moment for ever and ever, thought Darrell, peeping through the curtains once again. My first play – my first success! I don't want this moment to go!

Hold it then, Darrell, while we slip away. It's your own great moment. There'll never be another quite like it!

Last Term at

Malory Towers

Contents

First day

My last term! thought Darrell, as she got ready to go downstairs. My very last term! I shall be eighteen on my next birthday – I'm almost grown-up!

A yell came from below, 'Darrell! Aren't you *ever* coming? Daddy says do you mean to leave today or tomorrow?'

'Coming!' shouted back Darrell. She snatched up her tennis-racket and her small suitcase and fled down the stairs, two at a time as usual.

Her young sister Felicity was there, waiting for her. Both were dressed in the orange and brown uniform of Malory Towers – dark brown coat and skirt, white blouse, orange tie, straw hat with orange band.

'It's the very last time I shall go off with you in the same uniform,' said Darrell, rather solemnly. 'Next term you'll be going alone, Felicity. How will you like it?'

'Not a bit,' said Felicity, quite cheerfully. 'Still, you'll be having a wonderful time yourself, going off to the University. Don't look so solemn.'

'Last times are always a bit horrid,' said Darrell. She went out to the car with Felicity. Their father was just about to begin a fanfare on the horn. Why, oh why was he always kept waiting like this? Didn't they *know* it was time to start?

'Thank goodness you've appeared at last,' he said. 'Get in. Now, where's your mother? Honestly, this family wants a daily shepherd to round up all its sheep! Ah, here she comes!'

As Mrs Rivers got into the car, Felicity slipped out again. Her father didn't notice her, and started up the car. Darrell gave a shriek.

'Daddy, Daddy! Wait! Felicity's not in!'

He looked round in astonishment. 'But I saw her get in,' he said. 'Bless us all, where's she gone now?'

'She forgot to say good-bye to the kitten, I expect,' said Darrell, grinning. 'She has to say good-bye to everything, even the goldfish in the pond. I used to do that too – but I never wept over them all like Felicity!'

Felicity appeared again at top speed. She flung herself into the car, panting. 'Forgot to say good-bye to the gardener,' she said. 'He promised to look after my seedlings for me, and count how many strawberries come on my strawberry plants. Oh dear – it's so horrid to say good-bye to everything.'

'Well, don't then,' said Darrell.

'Oh, but I like to,' said Felicity. 'Once I've done a really *good* round of good-byes, I feel that I can look forward to school properly then. I say – I wonder if that awful Josephine is coming back! She kept saying something about going to America with those frightful people of hers, so I hope she has.'

'I hope she has too,' said Darrell, remembering the loud-voiced, bad-mannered Josephine Jones. 'She doesn't fit into Malory Towers somehow. I can't imagine why the Head took her.'

'Well – I suppose she thought Malory Towers might tone her down and make something of her,' said Felicity. 'It's not many people it doesn't alter for the better, really. Even me!'

'Gosh – has it done that?' said Darrell, pretending to be surprised. 'I'm glad to know it. Oh dear – I wish it wasn't my last term. It seems no time at all since I was first setting out, six years ago, a little shrimp of twelve.'

'There you go again – coming over all mournful,' said Felicity, cheerfully. 'I can't think why you don't feel proud and happy – you've been games captain of one or two forms, you've been head-girl of forms – and now you're head-girl of the whole school, and have been for two terms! I shall never be that.'

'I hope you *will*,' said Darrell. 'Anyway, I'm glad Sally and I are leaving together and going to the same college. We shall still be with each other. Daddy, don't forget we're calling for Sally, will you?'

'I hadn't forgotten,' said her father. He took the road that led to Sally Hope's home. Soon they were swinging into the drive, and there, on the front steps, were Sally and her small sister of about six or seven.

'Hallo, Darrell, hallo, Felicity!' called Sally. 'I'm quite ready. Mother, where are you? Here are the Riverses.'

Sally's small sister called out loudly: 'I'm coming to Malory Towers one day – in six years' time.'

'Lucky you, Daffy!' called back Felicity. 'It's the best school in the world!'

Sally got in and squeezed herself between Felicity and Darrell. She waved good-bye and off they went again.

'It's the last time, Darrell!' she said. 'I wish it was the first!'

'Oh, don't *you* start now,' said Felicity. 'Darrell's been glooming all the journey, so far.'

'No cheek from you, Felicity Rivers!' said Sally, with a grin. 'You're only a silly little second-former, remember!'

'I'll be in the third form next term,' said Felicity. 'I'm creeping up the school! It takes a long time, though.'

'It seems a long time while it's happening,' said Sally. 'But now it's our last term, it all seems to have gone in a flash.'

They talked without stopping the whole of the journey, and then, as they drew near to Malory Towers, Sally and Darrell fell silent. They always loved the first glimpse of their lovely school, with its four great towers, one at each corner.

They rounded a bend, and the eyes of all three fastened on a big square building of soft grey stone standing high up on a cliff that fell steeply down to the sea. At each corner of the building stood rounded towers

– North Tower, East, West and South. The school looked like an old castle. Beyond it was the dark-blue Cornish sea.

'We're nearly there!' sang Felicity. 'Daddy, go faster! Catch up the car in front. I'm sure Susan is in it.'

Just then a car roared by them, overtaking not only them but the one in front too. Mr Rivers braked sharply as it passed him, almost forcing him into the hedge.

'That's Josephine's car!' called Felicity. 'Did you ever see such a monster?'

'Monster is just about the right word,' said her father, angrily. 'Forcing me into the side like that. What do they think they are doing, driving as fast as that in a country lane?'

'Oh, they always drive like that,' said Felicity. 'Jo's father can't bear driving under ninety miles an hour, he says. He's got four cars, Daddy, all as big as that.'

'He can keep them, then,' grunted her father, scarlet with anger. He had just the same quick temper as Darrell's. 'I'll have a word with him about his driving if I see him at the school. A real road-hog!'

Felicity gave a squeal of delight. 'Oh, Daddy, you've hit on *just* the right name. He's exactly like a hog to look at – awfully fat, with little piggy eyes. Jo is just like him.'

'Then I hope she's no friend of yours,' said her father.

'She's not,' said Felicity. 'Susan's *my* friend. Here we are! Here's the gate. There's June! And Julie and Pam. Pam, PAM!'

'You'll deafen me,' said Mrs Rivers, laughing. She turned to her husband. 'You won't be able to get near the steps up to the front door today, dear – there are too many cars, and the school coaches have brought up the train girls too.'

The big drive was certainly crowded. 'It's as noisy as a football crowd,' said Mr Rivers with his sudden smile. 'It always amazes me that girls can make so much noise!'

Darrell, Felicity and Sally jumped out, clutching their rackets and bags. They were immediately engulfed in a crowd of excited girls.

'Darrell! You never wrote to me!'

'Felicity, have you seen Julie? She's been allowed to bring back her pony, Jack Horner! He's wizard!'

'Hallo, Sally! How tanned you are!'

'There's Alicia! Alicia, ALICIA! Betty! I say, everyone's arriving at once.'

A loud-voiced man, followed by a much overdressed woman, came pushing through the crowd, making his way to the enormous American car that had forced Mr Rivers into the hedge.

'Well, good-bye, Jo,' he was saying. 'Mind you're bottom of the form. I always was! And don't you stand any nonsense from the mistresses, ha ha! You do what you like and have a good time.'

Darrell and Sally looked at one another in disgust. No wonder Jo was so awful if that was the way her father talked to her. And what a voice!

Jo Jones's father was obviously very pleased with himself indeed. He grinned round at the seething girls, threw out his chest, and clapped his fat little daughter on the back.

'Well, so long, Jo! And if you want any extra food, just let us know.'

He caught sight of Mr Rivers looking at him, and he nodded and smiled. 'You got a girl here too?' he enquired, jovially.

'I have two,' said Mr Rivers, in his clear confident voice. 'But let me tell you this, Mr Jones – if I hadn't swung quickly into the hedge just now, when you cut in on that narrow lane, I might have had no daughters at all. Disgraceful driving!'

Mr Jones was startled and taken aback. He glanced quickly round to see if anyone had heard. He saw that quite a lot of girls were listening and, after one look at Mr Rivers's unsmiling face, he decided not to say a word more.

'Good for you, Daddy, good for you!' said Felicity, who was nearby. 'I bet nobody ever ticks him off – and now *you* have! Jo's just like him. Look, there she is.'

Jo scowled back at Felicity and Mr Rivers. She hadn't heard what Felicity said about her, of course, but she had heard Felicity's father ticking off her own, and she didn't like it a bit. Never mind – she would take it out of Felicity this term, if she could.

'We must go, darlings,' said Mrs Rivers, leaning out of

the car. 'Have you got everything? Good-bye, Darrell dear – and Felicity. Good-bye, Sally. Have a good term! The summer term is always the nicest of all!'

The car sped away. Felicity plunged into the milling crowd and was lost. Sally and Darrell went more sedately, as befitted two sixth-formers.

'It's nice to be at the top,' said Darrell. 'But I can't help envying those yelling, screaming lower-form kids. Just look at them. What a crowd!'

Arrivals old and new

Darrell and Sally went up the steps, and into the big hall. 'Let's go up to our study,' said Darrell. 'We can dump our things there and have a look round.'

They went up to the small, cosy room they shared between them. The sixth-formers were allowed to have these studies, one to every two girls, and both Sally and Darrell loved their small room.

They had put down a bright rug that Mrs Rivers had given them, and each had a favourite picture on the walls. There were some old cushions provided by both mothers, and a few ornaments on the mantelpiece – mostly china or wooden horses and dogs.

'I wonder who'll have this room next term,' said Darrell, going to the window and looking out. 'It's one of the nicest.'

'*Quite* the nicest,' said Sally, sinking down into one of the small armchairs. 'I suppose one of the fifth-formers will have it. Lucky things!'

The sixth-formers had a common-room of their own, as well as studies. In the common-room was a radio, of course, a library, and various cupboards and shelves for the use of the girls. It looked out over the sea and was full of air and light and sun. The girls loved it.

'Better go down and report to Matron,' said Darrell, when they had unpacked their night-bags, and set out two clocks, three or four new ornaments, and Darrell had put a little table-cloth into a drawer, which she had brought back to use that term. It would look nice if they gave a tea-party, as they often did!

'Got your health certificate?' asked Sally. 'I wonder if Irene has got hers. She has remembered it faithfully for the last three or four terms. I'd love her to forget it just this last time.'

Darrell laughed. Irene's health certificate was a standing joke in the school. 'I've got Felicity's certificate with mine,' she said. 'I'd better give it to her. Come on, let's go down.'

They went down and found Matron, who was standing in the middle of a mob of girls. They were handing out health certificates to her and, in the case of the lower-formers, handing over their term's pocket-money too.

A voice greeted Darrell and Sally. 'Hallo! Here we are again!'

'Irene!' said Darrell and Sally at once. Irene grinned at them. She looked very little different from when Darrell had seen her the first time, six years back – older and taller, but still the same old untidy scatter-brain. But her looks belied her. Irene was a genius at music and brilliant at maths – it was only in ordinary things that she was a feather-head.

'Irene!' called Matron, who had been in despair over the girl's health certificate almost every term. 'Am I to isolate you this term, because you've forgotten your certificate again – or have you condescended to remember it?'

'Here you are, Matron!' said Irene, and handed an envelope to her. She winked at Darrell and Sally. Matron opened it. Out fell a photograph of Irene in a swimming-costume!

'Irene! This is a photograph!' said Matron, annoyed.

'Oh, sorry, Matron. Wrong envelope,' said Irene, and handed her another. Matron tore it open, and glared at Irene.

'Is this a joke? This is a dog's licence!'

'Gosh!' said Irene. 'So that's where old Rover's licence went! Sorry, Matron. *This* must be the right envelope!'

Everyone was giggling. Alicia had now joined the mob round Matron, her bright eyes enjoying the joke. Matron opened the third envelope. She began to laugh.

It was a cleverly drawn picture of herself scolding Irene for forgetting her health certificate. Belinda, Irene's friend, had drawn it, and the two of them had pushed it into the third envelope for a joke.

'I shall keep this as a memento of you, Irene,' said Matron. 'It shall be pinned up in my room as a warning

11

to all girls who have bad memories. And now – what about the real thing, please?'

The 'real thing' was produced at last, and Matron pronounced herself satisfied. 'I suppose you *had* to keep up the tradition of losing your certificate for the last time,' she smiled. 'Now, June, where's yours – and you, Jo?'

Felicity came up and Darrell gave her her certificate to hand in. Then she went off with Alicia and Sally to see who was back.

'I bet that's Bill!' said Darrell, suddenly, as she caught the sound of horses' hooves up the drive. 'I wonder how many brothers are with her this time!'

Wilhelmina, Bill for short, had seven brothers, all of whom were mad on horses. Some of them accompanied her to school each term, which always caused a great sensation! The girls ran to the window to see.

'Yes – it's Bill – but there are only three brothers with her,' said Sally. 'I suppose that means another one's gone into the army, or into a job. Look, there's Clarissa too. She must have come with Bill on Merrylegs, her little horse.'

'*And* there's Gwen!' said Alicia, with malice in her voice. 'How many many fond farewells have we seen between Gwen and her mother? Let's feast our eyes on this one – it will be the last!'

But Gwen was on her guard now. Too often had the girls imitated her weeping farewells. She stepped out of the car, looking rather solemn, but very dignified. She kissed her mother and Miss Winter, her old governess, and wouldn't let them be silly over her. But she didn't kiss her father good-bye.

He called after her. 'Good-bye, Gwen.'

'Good-bye,' said Gwen, in such a hard voice that the girls looked at one another in surprise.

'There's been a row!' said Sally. 'I expect her father's ticked her off again for some silly nonsense. It's a jolly good thing for Gwendoline Mary that there's *one* sensible person in her family!'

Gwen's mother was now dabbing her eyes with her handkerchief. The car swung round, went down the drive and disappeared. Gwen came into the room behind the others.

'Hallo!' she said. 'Had good hols?'

'Hallo, Gwen,' said Darrell. 'Did you?'

'Fair,' said Gwen. 'My father was an awful nuisance, though.'

The others said nothing. Gwen never *could* understand that it just wasn't decent to run down your parents in public.

'Mother had fixed up for me to go to Switzerland to a simply marvellous finishing school,' said Gwen. 'Frightfully expensive. All the best people send their girls there. Lady Jane Tregennton's girl's going there, and . . .'

The same old Gwen! thought Darrell and Sally, feeling sick. Conceited, snobbish, silly. They turned away, feeling that nothing in the world would ever teach

Gwen to be an ordinary decent, kindly girl.

Gwen didn't in the least mind talking to people's backs. She went on and on. 'And then, when it was all fixed, Dad said it was too expensive, and he said it was all nonsense, and I ought to get a job – a *job*! He said . . .'

'I don't think you ought to tell us all this,' said Darrell, suddenly. 'I'm sure your father would hate it.'

'I don't care if he would or not,' said Gwen. 'He's tried to spoil everything. But I told him what I thought of him. I got my own way. I'm going!'

Sally looked at Darrell and Alicia. This was Gwen's last term. She had spent six years at Malory Towers, and had had many sharp lessons. Yet it seemed as if she had learned nothing of value at all!

She probably never will now, thought Darrell. It's too late. She walked out of the room with Sally and Alicia, all of them disgusted. Gwen scowled after them resentfully. People so often walked out on her, and she never could stop them.

Just as I was going to tell them some of the things I said to Dad, thought Gwen. I'm glad I hardly said good-bye to him. I'm his only daughter, and he treats me like that! Well, now he knows what I think of him.

She was so full of herself and her victory that she quite forgot to be mournful and homesick, as she usually pretended to be. She wandered off and found little Mary-Lou – a much bigger Mary-Lou now, but still shy and ready to think that most people were much better and more interesting than she was.

Mary-Lou always listened to everyone. Gwen began to tell her again all she had told the others. Mary-Lou stared at her in disgust. 'I don't believe you said anything *like* that to your father!' she said. 'You can't be as beastly as all *that*!'

And little Mary-Lou actually walked off with her nose in the air! Gwen suddenly began to realize that she wasn't going to be at all popular in her last term if she wasn't very very careful.

When supper-time came, the girls could see who was back and who wasn't. They could see the new girls in their Tower and they could see any new mistresses. Each Tower had its own common-rooms and dining-rooms. North Tower, where Darrell and her friends were, overlooked the sea, and was supposed to be the best Tower of all – though naturally the girls in the other Towers thought the same of theirs!

Darrell was sure there would be no new girls at all in the sixth. It was rare for a new girl to come so late to Malory Towers. She was very much surprised to see two new faces at the sixth-form table!

One girl was tall and sturdy and rather masculine looking, with her short cropped hair, and big legs and feet. The other was small, beautifully made, and had small hands and feet. As soon as she spoke, Darrell realized that she was French.

Mam'zelle Dupont introduced the girl, with one of her beaming smiles.

'Girls! This is Suzanne! She is niece to Mam'zelle Rougier who is in South Tower, but there is no room there for her, so she has come to me here. She will be in the sixth form – and she must learn the language well. Eh, Suzanne?'

'*Certainement*, Mam'zelle Dupont,' answered Suzanne, in a demure voice. She flashed a quick look round at the sixth-formers with bright black eyes, then lowered them again. Darrell felt a sudden liking for her.

'*Ah non* – you must not say one word of French, you bad girl!' scolded Mam'zelle. 'You must say "Certane-lee", not "*certainement*"!'

'Zer-tane-leee,' drawled Suzanne, and the girls laughed. Darrell nudged Sally.

'She's going to have some fun with Mam'zelle,' she said, in a low voice. 'And *we're* going to have some fun with Suzanne!'

Future plans

Mam'zelle then turned to the other new girl. 'And this is – how do you call yourself?' she asked the sturdy newcomer. 'Amanda Shoutalot?'

The girls laughed. The new girl gave Mam'zelle a rather contemptuous look. 'No – Amanda Chartelow,' she said, in a loud voice.

'Ah – that is what I said,' protested Mam'zelle. 'Amanda Shoutalot. Poor Amanda – her school has been burned down by fire! *Hélas* – it exists no longer!'

Nobody quite knew what to say. Amanda took some more bread, and ignored Mam'zelle. Gwen entered headlong into the gap in the conversation.

'Oh dear – what a dreadful thing! Did anyone get hurt?'

'No,' said Amanda, helping herself to more salad. 'It happened in the holidays. You probably read about it in the papers. It was Trenigan Towers.'

'Gosh, yes – I did read about it,' said Sally, remembering. 'Trenigan Towers! That's about the most famous school for sport in the country, isn't it? I mean – you win every single match you play, and you win all the tennis shields and lacrosse cups?'

'That's right,' said Amanda. 'Well, it's gone. There wasn't time to find another building in a hurry, so we all had to scatter, and find other schools. I don't know how long I'll be here – maybe a term, maybe longer. You haven't much of a name for sport, have you, at Malory Towers?'

This was rather too much from a new girl, even if she *had* come into the sixth form, and had arrived from a famous sports school. Darrell stared at her coldly.

'We're not too bad,' she said.

'Perhaps you'd like to give us a little coaching,' said Alicia in the smooth voice that most of the girls recognized as dangerous.

'I might,' said Amanda, and said no more. The girls glanced at one another. Then they looked at Amanda and saw how strong she must be. She was a great hefty girl about five foot ten inches tall. How much did she weigh?

Must be thirteen stone, I should think! thought Darrell, comparing Amanda with the slim, elegant French girl. Goodness – have we got to put up with her all the term? I shall find it hard to squash *her*!

Sally was thinking the same. She was games captain for the whole school, a most important position. What Sally said had to be taken notice of, from the sixth form down to the first. Sally was a first-rate tennis player, a first-rate lacrosse player, and one of the finest swimmers Malory Towers had ever had. Nobody but Darrell could beat her at tennis, and that very seldom.

She took another look at the stolid, rather scornful-looking Amanda. It was going to be very very difficult to give orders to her – especially as Amanda might easily prove to be a better tennis player and swimmer than even Sally herself. Sally was not as hefty as Amanda, though she was strong and supple.

'You were lucky to be able to find a place at Malory Towers,' gushed Gwen.

'Was I?' said Amanda, coldly, staring at Gwen as if she didn't like her at all. Gwen blinked. What a horrible girl! She hoped Alicia would be able to deal with her. Alicia could deal with anybody – her sharp tongue was quicker and more cutting than anyone else's in the school.

'I suppose you'll be going in for the Olympic Games,' said Alicia, meaning to be sarcastic. 'They're held next year in . . .'

'Oh yes. I should think I shall go in for about five different events,' said Amanda, calmly. 'My coach at Trenigan said I ought to win at least two.'

The girls gasped. Alicia looked taken aback. It had never entered her head that her scornful remark could be true. She looked so discomfited that Irene grinned.

'We ought to feel very honoured to have you here, Amanda!' she drawled.

'Thanks,' said Amanda, without looking at her.

'Amanda is such a beeg, beeg girl,' began Mam'zelle, mistaking Amanda's ungraciousness for shyness. 'She will be so marvellous at tennis. Sally, perhaps she will be in the Second Team, *n'est-ce pas?*'

Nobody replied to this. Sally merely grunted. Mam'zelle pushed on, under the impression that she was putting 'this great beeg Amanda' at her ease.

'How tall are you, Amanda?' she asked, feeling that the girl must be at least seven feet tall; she had made plump little Mam'zelle feel so short when she had walked in beside her! 'And how many – er – how do you say it – how many pebbles do you weigh?'

There was a squeal of laughter from the table. Even Amanda deigned to smile. Mam'zelle gazed round indignantly.

'What have I said?' she demanded. 'Is it not right – pebbles?'

'No – *stones*, Mam'zelle,' chorused the girls, in delight. 'Our weight is measured by stones, not pebbles.'

'Stones – pebbles – they are the same,' said Mam'zelle. 'Never, never shall I learn this English language.'

The bell rang for the meal to end. All the girls got up, laughing. Dear old Mam'zelle – her mistakes would fill a book.

Darrell and her friends went up to her study to talk and gossip. There were the usual crowd – Sally, Alicia, Belinda, Irene, Mary-Lou, Bill and Clarissa. Mavis was not there.

'It seems strange without Mavis,' said Sally. 'She's gone to train as a singer now. Perhaps we shall all crowd into her concerts one day!'

'I miss quiet old Janet too,' said Darrell. 'She is training as a dress designer. She ought to be jolly good at it! Do you remember the marvellous dresses she made for us when we gave that pantomime in the fifth form?'

'Catherine has left too,' said Alicia. 'Thank goodness! I never knew such a door-mat in my life. No wonder we called her *Saint* Catherine!'

'She wasn't so bad,' said Mary-Lou, loyally. 'It was only that she did like doing things for people so much.'

'She did them in the wrong way, that's all,' said Bill. 'She always made herself such a martyr. What's she going to do?'

'She's going to stay at home and help Mama,' said Alicia, rather maliciously. 'It'll suit her down to the ground. Mama thinks herself a bit of an invalid, I gather – so Catherine will really enjoy herself, being a saintly little daughter.'

'Don't be unkind, Alicia,' said Mary-Lou. 'Catherine was kind underneath her door-mat ways.'

'I take your word for it,' said Alicia, smiling at Mary-Lou. 'Don't get all hot and bothered. This is only a good old gossip! What are *you* going to do when you leave next year, Mary-Lou?'

'I'm leaving sooner than that,' said Mary-Lou. 'I've made up my mind what I'm going to be, and I'm going off to train in September. I'm going to be a hospital nurse – a children's nurse. I never wanted to be anything else, really. I'm going to train at Great Ormond Street Hospital. It's all settled.'

The others looked at quiet, loyal, idealistic Mary-Lou. Immediately each one of them saw that she had chosen the right career for herself. Nursing was a vocation – something you felt you *had* to do, for the sake of other people. It was absolutely right for Mary-Lou.

'I can't imagine anything you'd love better, Mary-Lou!' said Darrell, warmly. 'It's exactly right for you, and *you're* exactly right for it! Lucky children who have you to nurse them!'

Mary-Lou looked pleased and embarrassed. She looked round at the others. 'What are we all going to do?' she said. 'Belinda's easy, of course.'

'Yes. I've *got* to be an artist,' said Belinda. 'I always knew that. It's easy, of course, when you've got a gift. You can't do anything else but use it.'

'And Irene will study music,' said Sally. 'That's easy too. Bill – what about you – and Clarissa? You are both so mad on horses that I can't imagine you taking a job unless it's on horseback.'

Clarissa looked at Bill. She grinned. 'You've hit the nail on the head,' she said. 'Our job *will* be on horseback. Won't it, Bill?'

Bill nodded. 'Yes. Clarissa and I are going to run a riding school together.'

'You're not!' exclaimed the others, amazed and interested.

'Yes, we are. We decided it last hols,' explained Clarissa. 'I was staying with Bill, and we heard there were some stables for sale. We thought we'd like to get them, take our own horses, buy a few more, and begin a riding school. Actually it's not very far from here. We did wonder if we could get Miss Grayling to let us have some Malory Towers girls for pupils.'

'*Well*!' said Alicia, in deep admiration. 'If you two aren't dark horses!'

There was a yell of laughter at this typical Alicia joke. Bill grinned. She never said very much but she was a most determined young person. Nobody had any doubt at all but that the Bill–Clarissa riding school would be very successful indeed.

'I'll see that all my children are your pupils, when they come to Malory Towers,' promised Alicia, with a grin. 'Fancy you two thinking all this out and never saying a word!'

There was a short silence. It seemed as if most of them knew what they were going to do when they left school – and had chosen rightly.

'Well, Sally and I are going to college,' said Darrell. 'And so is Alicia – and Betty is coming too. We're all going to St Andrews up in Scotland, and what a good time we'll have!'

'You'll feel funny at first – being the youngest again, instead of the oldest,' said Belinda. 'I suppose you'll take Arts, Darrell, and eventually be a writer?'

23

'I don't know,' said Darrell. 'It's what I'd like to be. But, you see, Sally and I are not as lucky as you and Irene, Belinda. We haven't a gift that sticks out a mile – or a vocation like Mary-Lou. We've got to find what we're best fitted for, and we can do that at the University. We'll jolly well have to use our brains there, too. We'll be up against some brilliant people.'

Sally got up. 'Where did we put those biscuits, Darrell?' she said. 'Talking always makes me hungry. That's one thing that still makes me think we're not really very grown-up, even though we sometimes think we're getting on that way – we always feel so *hungry*. Grown-ups never seem to feel like that!'

'Long live our appetites!' said Alicia, taking a biscuit. 'And may our shadows never grow less!'

In Miss Grayling's room

Next day everyone awoke to the sound of the loud clang of the dressing-bell. New girls sat up in bed, startled, unused to the loud morning bell. Second-formers grunted and rolled over for another snooze. They were a notoriously lazy form that year. Darrell was always teasing her second-form sister, Felicity, about it.

'Lazy lot of kids,' she said. 'Always rushing down to breakfast with your ties half-knotted and your shoes undone. I wonder Miss Parker doesn't deal out punishments by the hundred!'

'Oh, old Nosey does!' grinned Felicity. 'Was she as bad in your time, Darrell, always nosing into this and that?'

'Never you mind,' said Darrell, remembering how she herself as a second-former had scrambled down to breakfast once with only one stocking on. 'How's that awful Josephine getting on?'

'Oh, throwing her weight about as usual,' said Felicity. 'Susan and I don't take much notice of her. It's when she comes up against June that she gets it hot! June simply *pulverizes* her! Serves her right.'

Darrell was quite sure that June would be able to

'pulverize' anyone, as Felicity called it. June was Alicia's young cousin, a very tough and aggressive young person, only slightly mellowed so far by her stay at Malory Towers. She was very like Alicia, and had Alicia's quick tongue and sharp humour. She also had Alicia's love of tricks, and everyone who taught her had learned to keep a very sharp eye indeed on June.

Except Mam'zelle Dupont! Anyone could play a joke on her and get away with it. But it was getting more difficult now, since Mam'zelle had discovered that there were actually booklets and leaflets sent out by firms, describing their jokes and tricks. She had made an intensive study of these, and was now much more on the alert.

'Do you remember when Mam'zelle played a trick on *us*?' said Felicity, giggling as she remembered. 'She bought a set of false celluloid teeth and fitted them over her own – do you remember? And everyone she smiled at had a fit, she looked so monstrous!'

'Yes, I shall never forget,' said Darrell. 'Dear old Mam'zelle. I do wish she'd play a "treek" this last term. That's her one and only so far.'

One or two girls still hadn't come back, because of illness or some good reason. Moira in the sixth form was due back that day. She and Sally worked well together over the games time-tables and matches – but otherwise Moira was still not very likeable.

'She's always so jolly sure of herself – so determined

to be cock-of-the-walk!' complained the girls. 'Never in the wrong, mustn't be contradicted – the great high-and-mighty Moira!'

Darrell caught sight of Amanda, the new sixth-former, going past. Something in the determined, confident walk reminded her of Moira. She smiled to herself.

'How will Moira like Amanda? It'll be funny to watch them together. There'll be some battles this term! Well – it's always more interesting when things happen. I wouldn't want my very last term to be dull.'

She went to the common-room after breakfast to find the others in her form. Sally was there, and Mary-Lou and Belinda.

'The bell for the first class will soon go,' said Darrell. 'I suppose we'd better go down.'

Someone knocked at the door. 'Come in!' called Darrell. A scared-looking second-former put her nose round the door. 'Please,' she began.

'Come *right* in,' said Belinda. 'We like to know the face has got a body. We shan't eat you!'

The second-former inserted her body into the room too. 'Please,' she said, 'Miss Grayling says will one of you take the new girls to her. She says not the new sixth-former, but any others in North Tower. She's waiting now.'

'Right,' said Darrell. 'Buzz off. Are the girls waiting in the hall, as usual?'

'Yes, please,' said the scared one, and buzzed off thankfully.

'I'll take the kids in,' said Mary-Lou, getting up. New girls always had to go to the Head on the morning of the second day. Miss Grayling liked to give them an idea of what was expected of them at Malory Towers and, as a rule, no girl forgot those few grave words. Darrell had never forgotten them.

She remembered them now and suddenly put out a hand to stop Mary-Lou.

'Mary-Lou – let *me* take them in. It's my job, anyway – and I just feel I'd somehow like to hear Miss Grayling talk to the new girls as she once talked to us. *I'll* go!'

'Right,' said Mary-Lou, understanding at once. She sat down again. Darrell went out of the room and into the hall. The new girls were there, five of them. Three were first-formers, one was a second-former and one a third-former. They all looked uncomfortable and rather scared.

'It's the head-girl!' hissed the third-former. 'Mind your Ps and Qs.'

Nobody had any intention of not minding them. The little first-formers looked with wide eyes at this big, important sixth-former. Darrell remembered how scared she had been of sixth-formers too, six years back, and she smiled kindly at them.

'Come along, kids. I'll take you in. Don't look so scared. You've come to the finest school in the world, so you're lucky!'

Darrell took the five girls to the Head Mistress's room,

and stopped outside a door painted a deep cream colour. She knocked.

A low, familiar voice called out, 'Come in!'

Darrell opened the door. 'I've brought the new girls to you, Miss Grayling,' she said.

'Thank you, Darrell,' said the Head. She was sitting at her desk, writing, a grey-haired, calm-faced woman, with startlingly blue eyes and a determined mouth. She looked at the five trembling girls standing in front of her, her blue eyes going from one to the other, considering each girl closely.

What did she see in them? Darrell wondered. Did she see the bad – and the good? Did she see which girls could be trusted and which couldn't? Did she know which of them would accept responsibility and do well in the school, and which would be failures?

Miss Grayling spoke to each girl in her low, clear voice, asking their names and forms. Then she addressed them all gravely. Darrell listened as intently as the youngsters, remembering the words from six years back.

'I want you all to listen to me for a minute or two. One day you will leave this school and go out into the world as young women. You should take with you eager minds, kind hearts and a will to help. You should take with you a good understanding of many things and a willingness to accept responsibility, and show yourselves as women to be loved and trusted. All these things you will be able to learn at Malory Towers – if you *will*.'

She paused, and every girl looked at her intently, listening hard.

'I do not count as our successes those who have won scholarships and passed exams, though these are good things to do. I count as our successes those who learn to be good-hearted and kind, sensible and trustable, good, sound women the world can lean on. Our failures are those who do not learn these things in the years they are here.'

Darrell wished she could see into the faces of the five listening girls. What were they thinking, these newcomers? Were they making up their minds, as she had once done, that they would each be one of Malory Towers' successes? The five girls hardly breathed as they gazed at Miss Grayling and listened.

'Some of you will find it easy to learn these things, others will find it hard,' went on Miss Grayling. 'But, easy or hard, they must be learned if you are to be happy after you leave here, and if you are to bring happiness to others.'

Miss Grayling stopped. She looked across at Darrell, who was listening with as much attention as the youngsters.

'Darrell,' said Miss Grayling. 'Do you remember my saying these words to you, when you first came here?'

'Yes, Miss Grayling,' said Darrell. 'And you said something else too. You said, "You will all get a tremendous lot out of your time at Malory Towers.

See that you give a lot back." '

'I did say that,' said Miss Grayling. 'And now I must add to it. Girls, six years ago I said those words to Darrell. She is one who *has* got a great deal out of her time here – and there is no one who has given more back than Darrell has.'

The five girls looked in awe at Darrell, their head-girl. They couldn't imagine her standing as a twelve-year-old in front of Miss Grayling, hearing those same words. But Miss Grayling remembered very well.

'You may go,' said the Head, pleased with the look of the five new girls. They were good stuff, she thought – likely to be the heads of forms and captains of games – and possibly head-girls of the future.

Darrell turned to go too. 'Wait a moment, Darrell,' said Miss Grayling. 'Shut the door.'

Darrell shut the door and came back to the desk. She felt herself blushing, she had been so pleased at Miss Grayling's words about her. She looked shyly at the Head.

'You are one of our successes, Darrell,' said Miss Grayling. 'One of our biggest successes. Sally is another, and so is Mary-Lou. I think there is only one sad failure, *real* failure, in your form. And she has only this one term to change herself. You know who it is I mean.'

'Yes,' said Darrell. 'Gwendoline.'

Miss Grayling sighed. 'You know her perhaps better than I do,' she said. 'Can you do anything with her at all? I have had a most unpleasant interview these holidays with Gwendoline's parents about her future. Her mother wanted one thing, her father another. Her father, of course, is right. But I hear that he has had to give way in the matter. Darrell, if you possibly can, I want you to try and influence Gwendoline so that she will come round to her father's point of view. Otherwise the family will be split in half, and there will be great unhappiness.'

'I'll try,' said Darrell, but so doubtfully that Miss Grayling knew there was little hope of success. 'I know all about it, of course, Miss Grayling – Gwen has seen to that! But it's impossible to move Gwen when she's determined to get her own way.'

'Well, never mind,' said the Head, smiling suddenly. 'I can put up with twenty Gwens so long as I have a few Sallys and Darrells!'

5

In Miss Oakes's class

Darrell went out of the room, feeling so proud and pleased that she could have sung out loud. She was one of the successes! She had always longed to be – but she had made mistakes, been unkind sometimes, lost her temper more times than she liked to remember – and had ruefully come to the conclusion that although she wasn't a failure, she wasn't a howling success either.

But Miss Grayling seemed to think she was, so she must be. Darrell held her head high, and went swinging along to the sixth-form classroom. She opened the door and went in quietly.

'I'm sorry I'm late, Miss Oakes,' she said. 'I took the new girls to Miss Grayling.'

'Yes, Mary-Lou told me,' said Miss Oakes. 'We were just talking about the work this term, Darrell. Those of you who are taking Higher Certificate are to work in one group, taking only a few odd lessons with the rest of the form. You have been working hard for the last two terms, so you should not find this term unduly hard – but you will have to keep at it!' Darrell nodded. She badly wanted to pass the Higher well. She felt sure

Sally would. As for Alicia and Betty, their quick brains and excellent memories would make success certain. She glanced round at the other girls from the other Towers, who would also be taking Higher. Yes – they would probably all pass. They were a keen, hard-working lot.

'I'm glad *I'm* not taking Higher,' said Gwen. 'Anyway, I suppose I could always take it at my school in Switzerland, couldn't I, Miss Oakes?'

Miss Oakes was not interested in Gwen's future school, any more than she was interested in Gwen.

'You are not up to Higher standard, whatever school you happen to be in,' she said coldly. 'I can only hope that you will work a little better this term than you have worked for the last two terms, Gwendoline. Would it be too difficult to leave me with a little better impression of your capabilities than I have at present?'

Gwen squirmed. She looked round at Maureen for sympathy. She got none, for Maureen always delighted in seeing Gwen made uncomfortable. The others looked studiously into the distance, determined not to catch Gwen's eye or give her any chance of speaking about her future school. They felt certain they were going to get very very tired of hearing about it.

'Amanda, I understand that you were going to work for Higher, if your old school had not been destroyed,' said Miss Oakes, turning to the hefty, solid new girl. 'Do you wish to do so here? I hear that it has been left to you to decide, as you can take it next year if you want to?'

'I don't want to take it this term, thank you,' said Amanda. 'It would be muddling, having had the work with different teachers. I shouldn't do myself justice. I intend to work at my games instead. I hope to be chosen for the Olympic Games next year, anyway.'

Only the North Tower girls had heard this bit of news so far. The girls from other Towers gaped at Amanda's forthright assertion. Go in for the *Olympic Games*! She must either be mad, or else alarmingly good at games!

'Ah yes,' said Miss Oakes, calmly. 'I forgot you came from Trenigan Towers. Well, Amanda, you will find that the games side is very good here, fortunately for you – and very well run.'

Amanda looked disbelieving, but didn't say anything. It was, however, quite apparent to everyone that she was busy turning up her rather big nose at the games she might expect at Malory Towers. Sally felt annoyed and half-amused. Moira felt angry. She glared at Amanda, making up her mind to take her down a few pegs as quickly as possible!

And if she tries to interfere, I'll soon show that *I* don't stand any nonsense, even if Sally does! thought Moira, scowling so fiercely at her thoughts that Belinda's hand went instinctively into her desk for her sketch-book – the one the girls called her Scowl Book. It had a most wonderful collection of scowls – though the finest were undoubtedly Gwen's!

How Gwen wished she could get hold of that horrible book of Belinda's! But Belinda guarded it jealously and had such a fine hiding-place for it when she took it out of her desk that Gwen had never been able to make out where it was.

'No, Belinda,' said Miss Oakes, who had already learned to recognize the Scowl Book when she saw it. 'We will have no Scowl Sketches in this session, please. And, Irene, could you stop tapping out that tune, whatever it is, on your desk?'

'Oh, sorry,' said Irene, stopping the tapping at once. 'I just can't help it when a new tune comes into my head. It's the way the wind blows in those trees over there, Miss Oakes – shusha, shusha, shusha – like that, it goes. And it made me . . .'

'You're tapping *again*, Irene,' said Miss Oakes, impatiently. She was never quite certain if Irene really *did* get as lost in her 'tunes' as she said she did, or if she acted like this to make a diversion and cause laughter.

But Irene was quite serious about it. She lived half in a world of music and half in the world of ordinary things – and when one world clashed with the other, she was lost! She was quite capable of writing out a tune in French *Dictée* instead of a word of French – and quite capable, too, of handing it in! Mam'zelle had often been amazed to find herself staring at pages of music notes, instead of lists of French verbs.

The French girl, Suzanne, had sat with her eyes

half-closed through the talk so far. Miss Oakes spoke to her suddenly and made her jump.

'Suzanne! Are you listening?'

'Police?' said Suzanne. Miss Oakes looked surprised.

'She means "Please?"' said Darrell, with a laugh. 'She *keeps* saying "Police?" whenever she doesn't understand anything. Don't you, Suzanne?'

'Police?' said Suzanne, not understanding a word. 'Police, Darrell, *je ne comprends pas*. I not unnerstand!'

'Well, Suzanne, you will have to listen with your ears *and* eyes open,' said Miss Oakes, 'or you will not learn a word of English while you are here. I understand that is why you have come – to learn to speak English fluently?'

'Police?' repeated Suzanne, again, her black eyes very wide open. 'I spik him bad.'

'What *does* she mean?' said Miss Oakes.

'She means she speaks English badly,' said Sally.

'She must have special coaching then,' said Miss Oakes, firmly.

'No, no. I not want zat,' said Suzanne, equally firmly.

'Ah – so you understood what I said *then*,' said Miss Oakes, beginning to be suspicious of this innocent-looking Suzanne.

'Police?' said Suzanne again, and Miss Oakes gave it up. She privately resolved to have a few words with Mam'zelle Rougier about her seemingly stupid niece. She began to give out instructions regarding the work to be done that term, what books were to be used, and what work was to be done by the girls on their own.

'I like old Oakey,' said Darrell, at break. 'But I've often wished she had more sense of humour. She never, never, never sees a joke. But she always *suspects* there may be somebody leading her up the garden path.'

'Yes. Like Irene and her tunes,' said Belinda, 'and actually Irene is perfectly serious about them. Look at her now – shusha, shush, shusha, shush, over by the window, with her eyes glued on the trees.'

Alicia grinned wickedly. She went up to Irene and tapped her on the shoulder. 'I say, Irene – can I play trains too? Shush, shusha, shush, shusha – come on, let's play trains.'

And before the surprised Irene knew what was happening, half the sixth-formers had formed a line and were playing 'trains' behind Irene, chuffing like engines.

Amanda watched disdainfully. What a school! she thought. Now if she were at Trenigan Towers, everyone would be out practising tennis strokes or something!

'Hold it, Amanda, hold it!' said Belinda, suddenly, spotting the unpleasant look on Amanda's large face. She had whipped out her Scowl Book, and was busy drawing. Amanda had no idea what she was doing. She was so new that she didn't even realize that Belinda could draw.

She saw in horror that Belinda had caught her face and expression exactly. She snatched at the book but Belinda dodged out of the way.

'I *didn't* look like that,' said Amanda, enraged. 'I just stood there thinking that if I were at my old school, we wouldn't be playing the fool like this, but out in the open air, practising strokes at tennis, or something sensible.'

'Really?' said Moira, coldly. 'I suppose it has escaped your notice that at the moment it is pelting with rain?'

Actually Amanda *hadn't* noticed. She had been too busy scorning the others at their fooling. She turned away, after giving Moira a most unpleasant look which Moira fully returned. Darrell thought there wasn't a pin to choose between the two looks!

Amanda turned off to the corner where the radio stood. She began to fiddle about with it and eventually managed to find a recording of some sporting event. The commentator was very excited, and his voice came loudly through the common-room, where the girls were having their break.

Nobody quite liked to tell her to turn it down a bit. Darrell nudged Sally and nodded to the window. It had stopped raining. Sally grinned.

She and Darrell made signs to the others to creep out of the room without disturbing Amanda. One by one they tiptoed out, and Darrell softly closed the door. They rushed to the cloakroom, found their lockers, slipped on tennis shoes, snatched up their rackets and ran out to the courts.

'Let's hope she sees us!' panted Moira.

Amanda did. The recording came to an end and she

switched off the radio. She was immediately struck by the quiet in the room, and swung round. It was empty. She heard the sound of voices outside, and the thud of tennis balls being struck, and went to the window. She scowled down. Beasts! They were just doing all that to annoy her!

The girls came back, laughing, when the bell went. 'Pity you didn't feel like a practice, Amanda!' called Moira. 'Never mind – better luck next time!'

6

Down in the pool

As usual the girls settled down very quickly for the new term. The summer term was always such a lovely one. There were so many things to do – and for those who liked swimming, the magnificent pool that lay in a great hollow of a rock down below on the shore was a source of the greatest delight.

Those who wished could go to swim before breakfast, and every morning, once the pool had been declared warm enough for swimming, girls ran down the steep cliff-path to the swimming-pool. They wore their swimming-costumes with a wrap round them.

Most of the girls loved the pool. A few didn't. Those who hadn't learned to swim were afraid. Those who didn't like cold water hated the pool. Gwen, of course, was one of these, and so was Maureen.

The new French girl also hated the very idea of the pool. She went to watch the girls there once, and squealed in fright if a splash of water so much as reached her toes!

'Suzanne! Don't be an idiot!' said Miss Potts, who happened to be in charge of the swimming that day. 'If you squeal like a silly first-former I shall make you strip off your clothes and go in. I can't think why Mam'zelle doesn't make you.'

Mam'zelle, of course, never would make anyone go into the pool if they didn't want to. She detested it herself, and so did the second French teacher, Mam'zelle Rougier, Suzanne's aunt. Neither of them understood the craze for games and sports of all kinds that they found in English schools.

'I go back,' announced Suzanne, at the next splash, and she turned to go up the sloping way to the cliff on which the school was built.

'Oh no, you don't,' said Miss Potts. 'You stay here. Even if you can't be persuaded to learn to swim, you can watch the others!'

'Police?' said Suzanne, with a blank expression on her face. Miss Potts wished fervently she had Suzanne in the first form under her for just one day. She was quite certain that Suzanne would never utter that infuriating word again!

Gwendoline and Maureen were made to swim, of course, though it still took them ages to make up their minds to get into the cold, clear water. They waited till everyone else was in, because it was simply extra-ordinary how many accidental pushes happened to them when Alicia or Moira or Betty came by. If there was one thing Gwen hated it was to enter the pool suddenly without warning!

The pool was always beautiful on blue sunny days. It shone a deeper blue than the sky, and after a few weeks of summer got really deliciously warm – till the tide came in, swamped the pool, and left cooler water there! Darrell loved the pool. Even when she was not swimming she used to take her books down beside it and dream there, looking over the brilliant blue water.

Moira was a very good swimmer. So was Sally. Darrell always had been. But the new girl, Amanda, surpassed them all!

She was a most magnificent swimmer. The first time she entered the water, everyone gasped. She streaked across the pool with the most powerful over-arm stroke the girls had ever seen.

'Gosh – what a swimmer!' said Darrell. 'I never saw anything like it. She *is* good enough for the Olympic Games. She could beat us hollow, Sally.'

Amanda was not content with the pool, big and deep though it was. She looked out to sea. 'I shall go and swim in the sea,' she said.

'You're not allowed to,' said Darrell, who was nearby, drying herself. 'There's a very dangerous current out there at high tide.'

'Currents aren't dangerous to a strong swimmer like me,' said Amanda, and flexed her arms to show Darrell her enormous muscles. She had great strong legs too. She was heavy in her walk, and not at all graceful in ordinary life – but when she was playing games or swimming, she had the strong grace of some big animal, and was most fascinating to watch. The lower forms gaped at her, and often came down to the pool when the word went round that Amanda was there – just to stand and stare!

'Would you like to give some of these youngsters a bit of coaching, Amanda?' Sally said one day. As head of school games, she was always on the look-out for likely youngsters to coach.

'I might,' said Amanda, looking bored. 'So long as it's not a waste of my time.'

'Oh well, if you feel like *that*!' said Moira indignantly. She was nearby, listening. Moira was not very likeable, but at least she did try to help the lower forms in their games, and was a great help to Sally.

'We never had to bother with the young ones at Trenigan Towers,' said Amanda, drying herself so vigorously that her skin came up bright red. 'We had plenty of coaches there. *They* looked after the youngsters. You seem to have too few games mistresses here.'

Darrell fumed inwardly at this criticism of Malory Towers. There were plenty of teachers for everything! Just because Malory Towers didn't make a religion of sport as Trenigan had, this great lump of an Amanda dared to look down her nose at it!

Sally saw Darrell's face, and nudged her. 'It's no good saying anything,' she said, as Amanda walked off. 'She's so thick-skinned, and so sure of herself and her future, that nothing we can say will make any impression. She must have been very upset when Trenigan went up in smoke – and she probably hates Malory Towers because it's new to her, and doesn't go in for the sport she adores as much as she'd like it to!'

'She's jolly lucky to *come* here,' snorted Darrell, still looking furious. Sally laughed. It was a long time since she had seen Darrell near to losing her famous temper. Once upon a time Darrell had lost her temper practically every term and had shocked the school by her rages – but now it very seldom showed, for Darrell had it well under control.

'Don't let her get under your skin,' said Sally. 'Believe me, she's much more likely to get under mine! She's infuriating over tennis – doesn't seem to think it's worth while even to have a game with us! She's got under Moira's skin all right – there'll be high words there soon.'

The second-formers came running down to the pool for their swim. The bigger girls heard the soft thud-thud of the rubber-shoed feet coming along, and turned. There was a yell from Felicity.

'Hallo, Darrell! Had a swim? What's the water like? Doesn't it look heavenly?'

'Wizard,' said Susan, her friend, and tried it with her toe as soon as she had taken off her shoes. 'Gosh, it's warming up already. Buck up, Felicity. The sooner we're in, the longer we'll have!'

Darrell had a few minutes to spare, and she stayed

with Sally and Moira to watch the younger ones. Now that Darrell was so soon leaving, she felt an intense desire to make sure that there were others who would carry on worthily the great traditions of Malory Towers – and in particular she wanted to be sure that Felicity, her sister, would.

She watched Felicity with pride. She and Susan dived in quickly, and with strong, graceful strokes swam across the great pool and back.

'That sister of yours is coming on,' said Moira to Darrell. 'She was good last year – she's going to be even better this. I think if she improves her back stroke, we might try her in one of the teams.'

'I hope so,' said Darrell, longing for Felicity to shine. 'Susan's good too – but not nearly so fast. Hallo – who's this porpoise?'

A fat and ungainly girl stood shivering on the brink of the pool. She was yelled at by some of the second-formers already in the water.

'Get in, Jo! Come on, Fatty! If you don't buck up, you'll have exactly two minutes in the water, and that's all!'

Even two minutes was too much for the fat and cowardly Jo. Bumptious and brazen in everything else, she was a coward over cold water. She had begged her father to get her excused from swimming, and he had rung up Miss Grayling and informed her that he didn't wish his daughter Jo to go in for swimming if she didn't want to.

'Why not?' asked Miss Grayling, coldly. 'Has the doctor forbidden it for her?'

'No. But *I* have,' said the loud-voiced Mr Jones, bellowing down the telephone. 'That's good enough, isn't it?'

'I'm afraid not,' said Miss Grayling, in her firm, decisive voice. 'Girls sent to Malory Towers follow the ordinary routine of the school, unless it is against doctor's orders. There is nothing wrong about swimming for Jo – she is merely afraid of cold water, so the games mistress tells me. I think you will agree with me that Josephine should conquer the cold water rather than that the cold water should defeat Josephine?'

Mr Jones had been about to say that *he* had always detested cold water, and he didn't see why Jo shouldn't do what he had done, and not go near it; but he suddenly thought better of it. There was something in Miss Grayling's cool voice that warned him. He put down the telephone abruptly. Miss Grayling might find there was no room for Jo at Malory Towers, if he persisted!

And so Jo, to her annoyance and surprise, had been told by her father that she'd got to put up with the swimming and get on with it. Every day she had to come down to the pool and shiver in dread on the brink, till she was inevitably pushed in or dragged in by a scornful second-former. Even the first-formers had been known to push Jo in!

Today it was Felicity who crept up behind, gave Jo an

enormous shove, and landed her in the pool with a colossal splash! Jo came up, gasping and spluttering, furiously angry. When she had got the water out of her mouth, she turned on the laughing Felicity.

'You beast! That's the second time you've done that. Just you wait, I'll pay you out. You're as bad as your father!'

'What's my father done?' asked Felicity, amused.

'He was rude to mine,' said Jo. 'About pushing your car into the hedge. *I* heard him!'

'Oh well – he pushed our car into the hedge – and now I've pushed you into the water!' cried Felicity. 'Tit for tat! We're quits! Look out – I'm coming to duck you!'

She dived under the water to get Jo's legs. Jo screamed and kicked. Her legs slid away from her and she disappeared under the water again. She came up, furious. She struggled to the side and called to Sally.

'Sally! Can't you stop Felicity playing the fool in the water? She's always going for my legs.'

'Learn to swim then,' said Sally. 'Get some coaching! You always slip out of any coaching. Look out – here comes somebody else after your legs!'

Poor Jo! However much she swaggered and boasted and blew her own trumpet out of the water, she was of less account than the youngest first-former when she was in the pool!

Darrell and Gwen

Darrell hoped that her last term would go very very slowly. So did Sally.

'I want to hold on to every moment, this last term,' said Darrell. 'I know quite well we'll have a wonderful time at St Andrews, when we leave here – but I do so love Malory Towers, and I want the time to go as slowly as possible. I want to go away remembering every detail of it. I never want to forget.'

'Well, we shall remember all the things we want to remember,' said Sally. 'We shall remember all the tricks we've ever played on Mam'zelle, for instance – every single one! We shall remember how the pool looks on a sunny day – and how the sea looks from the classroom windows – and what it sounds like when the girls pour out of school at the end of the morning.'

'And you'll remember dear Gwen and her ways,' said Alicia, who was nearby. 'You'll never forget those!'

'Oh, *Gwen*!' said Darrell, exasperated at the thought of her. 'I wouldn't mind forgetting every single thing about her. She's spoiling our last term with her silly behaviour!'

Gwen really was being very trying. She had never

liked Malory Towers, because she had never fitted in with its ideas and ideals. She was spoiled, selfish and silly, and yet thought herself a most attractive and desirable person. The only other girl in the form at all like her, Maureen, she detested. She could see that Maureen *was* like her in many many ways, and she didn't like seeing herself so often in a girl she disliked.

Gwen never stopped talking about her next and last school. 'It's in Switzerland, you know,' she said a hundred times. '*The* best school there. It's called a finishing school, and is very very select.'

'Well, I hope it will finish you off properly,' said Alicia. 'It's time something put an end to you!'

'That's not funny, Alicia,' said Gwen, looking dignified. 'Very first-formish.'

'You always *make* me feel first-formish,' said Alicia. 'I think of silly things like putting out my tongue and saying "Yah!" when you start talking about your idiotic school. Why you couldn't have gone this term, and left us to enjoy our last term in peace, I simply can't imagine.'

'I had an awful fight to go,' said Gwen, and the others groaned. They had already heard far too often about Gwen's 'fight'. Each time she told them, she related worse and worse things that she had said to her father.

'I bet she didn't say half those things,' said Alicia to Darrell. 'No father would stand it – and Mr Lacey has put Gwen in her place plenty of times before!'

However, it was true that Gwen had said some very

cruel things to her father during the last holidays, backed up by her mother. Mrs Lacey had been so set on sending Gwen to a finishing school where she could 'make nice friends', that she had used every single means in her power to back Gwen up.

Tears and more tears. Reproaches. Sulks. Cruel words. Mrs Lacey had brought them all out, and Gwen added to them. The old governess, Miss Winter, who adored Gwen and thought the world of Mrs Lacey, had been shocked.

Gwen related it all to her unwilling listeners. 'Miss Winter was an idiot. All she could say was, "Your father is tired, Gwendoline. He's not been well for some time. Don't you think it would be better not to worry him so much?" She's silly and weak – always has been.'

'Shut up,' said Sally. 'I'd hate to treat my father like that.'

'I said to my father, "Aren't I your only daughter? Do you grudge me one more year's happiness?"' went on Gwen, throwing herself into the part with all her heart. 'I said, "You don't love me. You never did! If you did, you would let me have this one small thing I want – that Mother wants too."'

'I said, shut up,' said Sally, again. 'We don't want to hear this. It doesn't reflect any credit on you, Gwen. It's beastly.'

'Oh, you're rather a prig, Sally, aren't you?' said Gwen, with her little affected laugh. 'Anyway, you wouldn't have the courage to stand up to your father, I'm sure.'

'You don't have to "stand up" to your parents if you pull together,' said Sally, shortly.

'Do go on, Gwen,' said Maureen, from her corner of the room. 'It's so interesting. You sound so grown-up!'

Gwen was surprised at this tribute from Maureen, but very pleased. She didn't see that Maureen was encouraging her to go on simply so that she might make herself a nuisance and a bore to everyone. Maureen could see how disgusted the others were. She was rather disgusted herself. Although she was very like Gwen, she did at least love her parents.

Let Gwen go on and on! she thought. Horrid creature! She's showing herself up properly!

And so Gwen went on, talking to Maureen, repeating the unkind things she had said to her father, exulting in the victory she had won over him.

'I went on till I got my way,' she said. 'I stayed in bed one whole day and Mother told him I'd be really ill if I went on like that. So Daddy came upstairs and said, "Very well. You can have your way. You're right and I'm wrong. You can go to Switzerland to school."'

Nobody believed that her father had said this. Nobody said anything at all except Maureen.

'What a victory, Gwendoline,' she said. 'I bet you were all over your father after that.'

'I would have been if he'd have let me,' said Gwen, looking a little puzzled. 'But he went all grieved and sad, and hardly spoke to any of us. Except sometimes to Miss

Winter. He was putting it on, of course, to make me feel awful. But I didn't. Two can play at that game, I thought, so I went cool too. I hardly even said good-bye to him when he drove the car away at the beginning of term. You've *got* to stand up to your parents when you get to our age!'

Darrell stood up suddenly. She felt really sick. She thought of her own father, Mr Rivers – kindly, hard-working surgeon, devoted to his wife and two daughters. How would he feel if she, Darrell, suddenly 'stood up' to him, and spoke cruel words, as Gwen had to her father?

He'd be heart-broken! thought Darrell. And I'm sure Mr Lacey felt the same. I expect he loves Gwen, even if she is beastly and selfish. How *could* she behave like that?

She spoke to Gwen, and the tone of her voice made everyone look up.

'Gwen, I'd like a few words with you,' said Darrell. 'Come on up to my study, will you?'

Gwen was surprised. What did Darrell want with her? She felt like refusing, and then got up. She was rather afraid of the forthright Darrell.

Darrell led the way to her study. She had remembered Miss Grayling's words. Could she possibly say something now, this very minute, to influence Gwen, and show her where she had gone wrong? Darrell felt that she might. She felt so strongly about the matter that she was certain she could make Gwen see her point.

'Sit down in that arm-chair, Gwen,' said Darrell.

'I want to say something to you.'

'I hope you're not going to preach at me,' said Gwen. 'You've got on that kind of face.'

'Well, I'm not going to preach,' said Darrell, hoping that she wasn't. 'Look here, Gwen – I can't help feeling terribly sorry for your father about all this.'

Gwen was amazed. 'Sorry for my *father*! Why? What's it to do with you, anyway?'

'Well, you've told us so often about this family row of yours, that I, for one, can't help feeling that it *is* something to do with me now,' said Darrell. 'I mean – you've made me share in all that bickering and rows and upsets, and I feel almost as if I've been a spectator.'

Gwen was silent for once. Darrell went on.

'I'm not going to say a word about who's right or who's wrong, Gwen,' said Darrell, earnestly. 'I'm not going to criticize anyone. I just say this. From what you've told me you've made that nice father of yours miserable. You've got what you want at the expense of someone else's peace of mind.'

'I've got to stand on my own feet, haven't I?' muttered Gwen.

'Not if you stamp on someone else's toes to do it,' said Darrell, warming up. 'Don't you love your father, Gwen? I couldn't possibly treat mine as you've treated yours. If you did say all those cruel things to yours, then you ought to say you're sorry.'

'I'm not sorry I said them,' said Gwen, in a hard voice.

'My father's often said unkind things to me.'

'Well, *you* deserved them,' said Darrell, beginning to lose patience. 'He doesn't. I've met him plenty of times and I think he's a dear. You don't deserve a father like that!'

'You said you weren't going to preach,' said Gwen, scornfully. 'How long are you going on like this?'

Darrell looked at Gwen's silly, weak face and marvelled that such a weak person could be so hard and unyielding. She tried once again, though she now felt sure that it was no use. Nobody in this world could make any impression on Gwen!

'Gwen,' she began. 'You said that your father said he couldn't *afford* to send you to Switzerland. If so, he'll have to go short of something himself, to let you go.'

'He was wrong when he said he couldn't afford it,' said Gwen. 'Mother said he could. He was just saying that as an excuse not to let me go. He was horrid about the whole thing. He said – he said – that I was s-s-silly enough without being made s-s-s-sillier, and that a good j-j-job would shake me out of a lot of n-n-nonsense!'

Stuttering with self-pity, Gwen now dissolved into tears. Darrell looked at her in despair.

'Couldn't you possibly go to your father and say you're sorry, you'll call the whole thing off, and do what he wants you to do, and get a job?' she asked, in her forthright way. It all seemed so simple to Darrell.

Gwen began to sob. 'You don't understand. I couldn't possibly do a thing like that. I'm not going to humble myself. Daddy would crow over me like anything. I'm *glad* I've made him miserable – it'll teach him a lesson!' finished Gwen, so maliciously that Darrell started to her feet.

'You're horrible, Gwen! You don't love your father or anyone else. You only love yourself. You're horrible!'

She went out of the room, and made her way straight to Miss Grayling's room. She had failed utterly and absolutely with Gwen. If Miss Grayling wanted to influence her she must try herself. It was beyond Darrell!

She told Miss Grayling everything. The Head Mistress listened gravely. 'Thank you, Darrell,' she said. 'You did your best, and it was well done. One day Gwen will meet her punishment, and it will, alas, be a terrible one.'

'What do you mean?' said Darrell, half scared by the foreboding tone in Miss Grayling's voice.

'I only mean that when someone does a grievous wrong and glories in it instead of being sorry, then that person must expect a terrible lesson,' said Miss Grayling. 'Somewhere in her life, punishment is awaiting Gwen. I don't know what it is, but inevitably it will come. Thank you, Darrell. You did your best.'

The magnet trick

Darrell would not let Gwen and her obstinacy spoil more than a day of her precious last term! She brooded over the interview in her study for a few hours, wishing she could have done better with Gwen – and then put it right out of her mind.

I know I can't do anything more, so what's the good of worrying about it? she thought, sensibly. She turned her thoughts to more interesting things – tennis matches – swimming matches – half-term, when her parents came down – and she also thought about a secret that Felicity had giggled out to her the day before.

'Oh, Darrell. Do listen! Susan's heard of a lovely trick from June. It's *so* simple, and *so* safe.'

Darrell grinned. It was good being high up in school, and an important member of the sixth form – but it did mean that tricks and jokes were no longer possible or permissible. It just wasn't *done* in the sixth, to play a trick on any mistress. The mere thought of playing one on the dignified, scholarly Miss Oakes was impossible.

But there was no reason why the younger ones shouldn't have their bit of fun, as they had in Darrell's own time. So Darrell grinned and listened, as Felicity poured out her bit of news in a secluded corner of the garden.

'June's getting a magnet,' she said. 'It's a very special one, treated in a special way to make it frightfully powerful. It's very small too, June says – small enough to be hidden in the palm of your hand.'

'Well? What do you intend to do with it?' asked Darrell. There didn't seem to be great possibilities in such an ordinary thing as a magnet.

Felicity began to giggle again. 'Well, you just listen, Darrell,' she said. 'You know how the two Mam'zelles wear their hair, don't you – in little buns?'

Darrell nodded, puzzled. She couldn't for the life of her see what buns of hair and a magnet had to do with each other.

'Mam'zelle Rougier has hers at the back, and Mam'zelle Dupont has hers near the top of her head,' said Felicity. 'And they both stick their buns full of hair-pins.'

Darrell stared at her young sister, and a light began to dawn. 'You don't mean – oh, I say, Felicity – you wouldn't *dare* to hold the magnet near either of the Mam'zelles' heads and make the hair-pins come out!' she said.

Felicity nodded, her eyes dancing. 'Yes. That's the idea,' she said. 'Oh, *Darrell*! Isn't it smashing? It's *super*.'

Darrell began to laugh. 'It's wonderful!' she said.

'Fancy us never thinking of such a simple trick as that. Felicity, when are you going to do it? Oh, I wish I could see it! I wish I could do it myself!'

'You can't. You're head-girl,' said Felicity, sounding quite shocked. 'But you *could* make some excuse, couldn't you, to come and see us play the trick? We thought we'd do it on Mam'zelle Dupont *and* on Mam'zelle Rougier just as many times as they'd stand for it, without getting suspicious.'

'I should think they'd jolly soon get suspicious,' said Darrell. 'Especially Mam'zelle Rougier. You'd better be careful of her, Felicity. She's not got the sense of humour that Mam'zelle Dupont has.'

'We'll be careful,' said Felicity. 'Well – *can* you make an excuse to pop into our classroom, if we tell you when we're going to do the trick?'

'I'll try,' said Darrell. But she felt sure she wouldn't be able to. Mam'zelle might be rather astonished if she kept appearing in the second-form room every time her hair-pins came out!

Darrell told the rest of the form, with the exception of Gwen and Maureen, whom nobody ever trusted enough to let into even the simplest secret. Amanda was there too, and to everyone's surprise, she suddenly guffawed. Like her voice, her laugh was very loud, and it made everyone jump. They hadn't heard the stuck-up Amanda laugh before – she was too busy looking down her nose at everything!

'That's great,' said Amanda. 'We did things like that at Trenigan, too.'

'*Did* you?' said Darrell, in surprise, and Trenigan went a little way up in her rather low estimation of it. 'What tricks did *you* play?'

For the first time Amanda opened out a little, and an animated conversation began about tricks – good ones and bad ones, safe ones and dangerous ones, ones likely to be too easily spotted, and ones that never were spotted. It was a most interesting conversation.

Amanda had to admit that Malory Towers was better at tricks than Trenigan had been.

'Oh well – it's because of Alicia, really, that we got such fine tricks,' said Sally. 'Alicia's got three brothers, and one of them, Sam, always used to send her good tricks he used himself. Alicia – do you remember the sneezing trick?'

'Oh *yes*,' said Alicia. 'It was a tiny pellet, Amanda, which we stuck somewhere near Mam'zelle – on the wall or anywhere, it didn't matter – and when you put a few drops of salt water on it, it sent off an invisible vapour that made people sneeze – and you should have HEARD Mam'zelle sneeze!'

'A-WHOOOOOOOSH-OOO!' said Sally, suddenly, and everyone jumped. Sally grinned. 'Just like that,' she said. 'And poor old Mam'zelle went on and on and on, till she was scared out of her life.'

'Oh dear – how we laughed. I envy those lower-form

kids,' said Alicia, putting on a comical look. 'No dignity to keep up, no responsibilities like ours, no necessity to set an example to the whole school. And that wonderful magnet trick to play!'

'Your young cousin June is certainly keeping up the family tradition,' said Mary-Lou. 'When are they going to do this absurd trick?'

It was fixed for a Thursday morning, at the end of the French lesson. This was the last lesson before break and after it the girls would be able to go out into the Court and laugh their heads off, if they needed to!

'Who takes the lesson? Mam'zelle Dupont or Mam'zelle Rougier?' asked Darrell, hoping it was the plump, jolly Mam'zelle Dupont.

But it wasn't. It was the thin, rather bad-tempered Mam'zelle Rougier. What in the world would she think when her hair fell down and her pins disappeared?

The second-formers planned it all carefully. They decided that June must not play the trick. All the teachers were suspicious of her. Somebody else must do the trick.

'Shall I?' said Felicity. 'Or what about Susan? Susan's always so good in class that nobody would ever suspect *her* of such a thing.'

'I'm *not* always good,' said Susan, quite hurt at this compliment. 'Anyway, I don't want to do the trick. I giggle too easily.'

'Nobody must laugh,' warned June. 'Once we laugh

we shall be suspected, and we shan't be able to play the trick again.'

'But how can we NOT laugh?' asked Nora, who was given to sudden snorts, like Irene's. 'I mean – laughing is like sneezing or coughing. You can't stop it coming, if it wants to.'

'Yes, you can,' said June, firmly. She had wonderful control over herself, and could keep a straight face during the most comical happenings. 'If you feel you are going to give the game away, you'd better go out of the room just before we do the trick. See?'

'Oh, I *couldn't*. I simply *couldn't* miss it,' said Nora. 'I won't laugh. I'll take three or four hankies and stuff them into my mouth.'

Thursday came. Lessons began. The French lesson came, and Mam'zelle Rougier walked into the room, her heavy tread sounding all the way down the corridor. June was holding open the door. A little snort came from Nora, whose pockets were bulging with handkerchiefs.

'Shut up!' said several people, in loud whispers. Nora looked round, ready to snort again, but met such fierce glares that she subsided.

Mam'zelle Rougier came in. '*Asseyez-vous*,' she said, in her sharp, crisp voice. The class obeyed, sitting down with much scraping of chairs. They looked at Mam'zelle Rougier, suspiciously bright-eyed.

But Mam'zelle Rougier was used to facing dozens of bright, laughing eyes. She snapped out her instructions.

'Page thirty-three. I hope you have prepared the lesson well.' She repeated it slowly in French. 'Nora, please begin.'

Nora was bad at French. She suddenly lost all desire to laugh, and stood up, stammering through the French translation. One by one the others followed. Mam'zelle Rougier was in a bad temper. Words of anger came from her more readily than words of praise that morning! The class felt very pleased she was going to have a trick played on her!

Just before the end of the lesson, Mam'zelle gave her usual order. 'Clean the blackboard, please.'

Susan stood up. She had the powerful little magnet inside the palm of her hand. It had already been tried out on many things, with most miraculous results.

Susan walked steadily to the board near Mam'zelle. Mam'zelle had opened her desk and was rummaging in it for a book. It was a wonderful chance to use the magnet at once!

Watched by twenty-three breathless second-formers, Susan held the magnet to the back of Mam'zelle's head. She held it about two inches away from the bun of hair on Mam'zelle's neck, as she had been instructed.

Before her delighted eyes, every one of the rather large hair-pins that Mam'zelle Rougier used for her bun flew out, and attached themselves firmly and silently to the magnet. Susan grinned at the class, went abruptly to the blackboard and cleaned it.

Mam'zelle had apparently noticed nothing. The bell

went, and she stood up. 'Dismiss!' she said, and the class dismissed, Nora stuffing one of her handkerchiefs into her mouth already. They went to the big hall to get biscuits and milk, watching for Mam'zelle to come too.

She came – and the second-formers gave a squeal of joy. 'It's coming down. The bun's all undone!'

So it was. Mam'zelle hadn't noticed it – but Miss Peters saw it at once. She tapped Mam'zelle on the shoulder and spoke to her. 'Your hair is coming down, Mam'zelle,' she said.

Mam'zelle put up her hand, and to her immense astonishment found that her bun was completely undone and hanging down her back! She groped about for the hair-pins to pin it up again.

There wasn't a single hair-pin in her head! This was not surprising, as they were all on the magnet, which Susan now had safely in her pocket! Mam'zelle Rougier felt frantically all over her head, and Nora gave a muffled snort. She stuffed her second hanky in her mouth.

Mam'zelle now began to feel down her neck, wondering if the hair-pins had disappeared down there. Miss Peters looked at her curiously.

'Lost a hair-pin?' she said.

'I have lost them *all*!' said Mam'zelle, filled with alarm and astonishment. She wondered if she could possibly have forgotten to do her hair that morning. Had she gone into her classes with her hair down her back? She blushed red at the thought. What *must* the girls have thought?

She caught sight of the laughing second-formers, and saw Nora stuffing her third hanky into her mouth. She turned hurriedly and almost ran from the hall.

'The girls were laughing! I *did* come into my classes without pinning up my hair,' said poor Mam'zelle to herself. 'What a thing to do! How could I have forgotten to pin it up? I haven't a single pin in my hair!'

She went to her room and did her hair very carefully indeed. She had no suspicion at all that a trick had been played on her. But if she could have seen the wicked little second-formers laughing and rolling on a secluded piece of grass under the trees in the grounds, she would have felt very suspicious indeed!

'When she groped down her neck for the pins that weren't there!' chuckled June. 'And oh, Miss Peters' face when she saw Mam'zelle's hair all down her back. I could have died.'

'Let's do it again,' begged Felicity. 'Do, do let's. It's one of the funniest tricks we've EVER thought of!'

9

Amanda makes a surprising suggestion

Darrell was working hard for her exam, and so was Sally. But they played hard too, and somehow found time to attend all the debates, the sing-songs, lectures and meetings that cropped up through the week. It was a happy, busy life, and one that Darrell enjoyed to the full.

She had now been six years at Malory Towers and had learned to work really well, so the exam work did not seem as difficult as she expected. Miss Oakes was pleased with her.

'Already you can work by yourself, Darrell, with just a little guidance,' she said. 'You are ready for college now. There, you will find that students can work as much or as little as they like. It is up to them! But you will always work well, and Sally too – you have the habit now.'

Privately Miss Oakes thought that Darrell and Sally would do much better at college than Alicia or Betty, although these two had quicker brains and better memories than either Sally or Darrell.

Being grown-up, and feeling free for the first time from bells and strict time-tables and endless classes, will go to Alicia's head, and Betty's too, thought Miss Oakes. They won't do a scrap of work at college! They'll be out to dances and parties and meetings the whole time – and in the end sound little Darrell and solid little Sally will come away with the honours that Alicia and Betty should find it easy to get – but won't!

At that moment Darrell and Sally were drawing up lists for the first tennis match of the season. Moira was there, giving excellent advice in her rather domineering way. However, Sally put up with that for the sake of her help. Moira knew what she was talking about when it came to games.

Amanda came up and looked silently over their shoulders. The others ignored her. Moira turned her back on her even more pointedly.

'I think for the third team we'll put in Jeanie Smithers, from the third form,' said Sally. 'She's got a very fine serve, and she's steady. She'll make a good couple with Tessie Loman.'

'Tessie's no good,' remarked Amanda. 'Never will be. Not until she gets rid of her peculiar way of serving. She loses half her power, the way she swings her racket.'

'I bet you don't even know which Tessie is!' said Sally.

'Oh yes, I do,' said Amanda, unexpectedly. 'I some-times go and watch those babies. You can *always* pick out the ones with promise.'

'Well, you're cleverer than we are, then,' said Moira. 'It's possible to pick out someone brilliant – and then find it's just a flash in the pan – they're no good at all.'

'I could always pick out the promising ones,' said Amanda, with conviction. 'I could tell you now who to put into the first team – that's easy, of course – and the second, third and fourth teams. But I wouldn't choose either Jeanie or Tessie for the third team. They'll go to pieces.'

The others felt annoyed. Why all this interference? How could Amanda, who had only been a few weeks at Malory Towers, possibly know anything about the sports capabilities of all the girls?

'Well, perhaps you'd like to tell us who will be the captain of school games three years hence,' said Moira, sarcastically. 'We're listening hard!'

'Yes, I can tell you,' said Amanda, without the least hesitation. 'If she had some coaching – proper coaching – and stuck to practising every minute she had, there's a kid in the second form who could be games captain of every form she's in, and far and away best at tennis, whatever form she's in.'

The other three turned and stared at Amanda. She sounded so very very certain.

'Who's the kid?' asked Moira, at last, after all three of them had searched their minds in vain for this elusive second-former. *Who* could it be?

'There you are – you can't even spot her when I've

told you she's outstanding, and told you what form she's in,' said Amanda, walking away. 'Why, at Trenigan Towers she would have been spotted the second day she was at school! But you could have a world champion here and never know it!'

'Amanda! Don't go!' ordered Moira. 'Now you've aired your opinions so freely, let's hear a few more. Who's this wonderful second-former?'

'You go and watch them playing, and find out,' said Amanda, in a bored voice. But Moira flew to the door and shut it just as Amanda had opened it to go out. 'No, Amanda,' she said. 'You tell us before you go – or we'll think you're just talking through your hat, and that there isn't any wonderful kid!'

'I don't waste my breath like that,' said Amanda, scornfully. 'And don't glare at me in that way, Moira – you can order the others about as much as you like, and talk to them as if they were bits of dirt – they're used to it! I'm not, and I won't have it. If there's any talk of that sort to be done, *I'll* do it!'

Sally came to Moira's defence, though secretly she was pleased to find someone who could stand up to the opinionated Moira, and fight her on her own level.

'You're a new girl, Amanda,' she said. 'But you seem to forget it. You can't talk to us like that, and you *must* realize that Moira knows more than you do about our girls, even if *I* don't!'

'She doesn't,' said Amanda, contemptuously. 'All

right. I'll tell you the kid, and you'll see I'm right. It's June.'

'June!' said the other three, amazed. June, the defiant, aggressive, daredevil cousin of Alicia's! Well, who would have thought of June?

'She never bothers even to listen when she's being coached,' said Sally.

'She only plays when she wants to,' said Darrell, 'and more often than not she plays the fool! She's no good.'

'June's always been like that,' said Moira. 'Ever since she's been here – she could run faster at lacrosse and tackle better than anyone if she tried – but we have never been able to put her into a team. She could swim like a fish if she didn't always fool about – she's fast when she wants to be. But you can never depend on June.'

'Look,' said Amanda, with conviction in her voice, 'I tell you, if June was coached properly and soundly, at tennis and swimming – I don't know if she's any good at lacrosse, of course – I tell you that kid would be the finest player and swimmer you've ever had. Oh, I know she fools about, I know she's a dare-devil and doesn't care a rap for anyone – but my word, once she finds out she can be superlative at something, well – watch her! She'll go to the top like lightning!'

This was all very surprising – and somehow, spoken in Amanda's loud, very sure voice, it was remarkably convincing. Darrell looked at Sally. Could Amanda be right? Had their dislike and disapproval of the cheeky, don't-care June prevented them from seeing that she had the promise of a first-class games-player?

'Well,' said Sally, doubtfully, thinking of June's tennis, and remembering the way she had watched her playing the fool on the court the week before, 'well, I don't know. She's wonderfully quick and supple, and she's very strong – but her character is against her. She won't *bother*.'

'She just wants someone to take an interest in her and encourage her,' said Amanda. 'I bet it's a case of "give a dog a bad name and hang him", with June. If I had the handling of her, I'd soon make something of her!'

'Well, why don't you?' said Moira, rather disagreeably. She had suddenly seen that Amanda was right. June *was* a natural games-player – she had a wonderful eye, and a beautiful style. She's cheeked me so often that I just couldn't see her good points, thought Moira, grimly. She put her question to Amanda, and stood waiting for the answer. 'Well, why don't you?'

'Oh, Amanda can't be bothered to coach *any*one, can you, Amanda?' said Sally, slyly. She felt sure that by appearing doubtful about Amanda's wish to help she would make the big, aggressive girl volunteer to do so. Clever Sally!

Amanda fell into the trap at once. 'I *can* be bothered to coach if the person is worth it,' she said, shortly. 'Well, I'm glad you seem to agree with me, anyway. I'll take on June and, what's more, I'll have her in the second tennis team and second swimming team before the term's finished!'

She walked out, shutting the door loudly, in her usual way. The three left in the room looked at one another. Darrell rubbed her nose as she always did when surprised and taken aback.

'Well! She's right, of course. June *could* be and *would* be a wonder at games if she wanted to. She's like Alicia – brilliant, but unstable. A wonder so long as she's doing something she wants to do, and something she's determined to do well – but no good otherwise.'

'*I* shouldn't care to take that little wretch of a June on,' said Moira. 'She's rude and ungrateful, and she fools about all the time. I wish Amanda joy of her!'

'She's certainly taken on a handful,' said Sally, picking up her games lists. 'But if she *does* help June's game, it'll be something! Anyway, thank goodness we've got Felicity to depend on, Darrell. She's going to follow in your footsteps all right!'

Darrell glowed with pleasure. Yes, Felicity was all right. Felicity would make good – and yet, June would be twice as good as even Felicity, if she only took the trouble!

'Well – it will be interesting to see what happens,' said Moira. 'Very, very interesting. The confident cocksure Amanda – and the confident cocksure June. My word, how I do dislike them both!'

Amanda and June

When Amanda had made up her mind to do something, she did it immediately. As soon as she had got outside the door she looked out for a second-former, and she saw Susan.

'Hey, you – what's your name – Susan!' she called. 'Go and find June, tell her I want her, and send her up to my study.'

Susan sped off, wondering what June had done. As a rule the second-formers were only sent for when they needed lecturing about something. She found June and delivered the message.

June was surprised. Amanda, as far as she knew, hadn't even bothered to know her name, though she had seen the big sixth-former watching the lower-form tennis practice and swimming several times. She looked at Susan.

'I'm sure it's not me she wants,' she said. 'It's someone else. Anyway, I haven't done anything wrong – and if somebody was going to tick me off, it wouldn't be Amanda. It would be Sally or Darrell. I'm not going. I don't like Amanda.'

'But you *must* go,' said Susan, shocked at the idea of June disobeying a sixth-form order. 'Even if it's a mistake, you ought to go and find out.'

'I'm busy,' said June. 'Leave me alone. I'm the one that will get into trouble for not going, not you. But I shan't, don't worry! Amanda meant someone else, not me.'

Susan went off. All right – let June disobey Amanda if she wanted to. Susan had delivered the message. It was just like June's silly obstinacy. She hated being ordered about by the bigger girls.

Amanda went to her study and waited. She had no real interest in June beyond the fact that she had certainly noted June's decided gift for games. She just wanted to coach her to prove her point. She sat and waited for the second-former to come.

She waited five minutes, patiently, knowing that it might take Susan a little time to find her. Then, most impatiently, she waited another five minutes. She got up, annoyed, and went to the door to see if by any chance June was there and had knocked, and she hadn't heard her.

The passage outside was empty. Amanda went to the window and looked. Down in the garden she saw June, walking with two or three others, talking animatedly. She yelled out of the window.

'June! Come here! Didn't Susan give you my message?'

June pretended not to hear. Amanda yelled again. The others nudged June and pointed to the shouting

Amanda. June reluctantly detached herself and went under the window.

'Come up to my study at once,' ordered Amanda. 'I've already been waiting ten minutes and more!'

The other second-formers laughed at June's annoyed face. 'Now you're for it!' called Katherine. 'What have you been up to, June? You're in for a good old wigging!'

June couldn't think of *any*thing she had done. She had hated being hauled indoors in front of all the others. She went in sulkily and stood outside Amanda's door. She knocked sharply. Amanda had expected a soft, apologetic knock and she jumped.

'Come in,' she said. June went in and shut the door too loudly. She would show Amanda she didn't stand in awe of sixth-formers, however high and mighty they thought themselves!

It was not a good beginning for any co-operation between them. Amanda was annoyed, June was cross.

'I suppose Susan didn't give you my message?' said Amanda.

'Yes, she did,' said June.

'Then why on earth didn't you come?' demanded Amanda.

'I thought you'd made a mistake,' said June. 'I didn't know you even knew my name.'

'What a feeble excuse!' said Amanda and, indeed, it did sound rather feeble, even to June, as she said it.

June scowled. She waited to hear what she had done

wrong. She half expected to see a Punishment Book ready on the table, but there was none. All the sixth-formers had Punishment Books, in which they wrote down any punishment they meted out to lower-formers who had offended in some way. Usually the punishment was lines to learn and repeat.

I wish she'd tell me what I've done, thought June, eyeing Amanda aggressively. Actually Amanda, finding June so exasperating, was debating whether or not to change her mind about offering to coach her. She decided to go on with it. She couldn't bear the idea of Moira sneering at her if she didn't.

'Look here, June,' she began, abruptly. 'I've been watching you.'

June was startled. '*Watching* me!' she said, on the defensive at once. 'What for? I'm not aware that I've been worth watching – I've been fairly harmless lately.'

'Don't talk in that silly way,' said Amanda. 'I've been watching you at tennis and swimming. You could be good. In fact you could be better than anyone in the second form *or* the third form. And if you worked at your games, instead of playing the fool, you'd soon beat anyone in the fourth form too.'

June gaped. This was so very extraordinary and unexpected that she couldn't think of a word to say.

Amanda went on.

'So I propose to coach you myself, June. I've told Sally and Darrell and Moira my views about you, and

I've said I could make you good enough to put you in the second tennis team and second swimming team before the end of the term. I want to prove that I'm right.'

Still June stared at Amanda, overcome with astonishment. She couldn't understand Amanda picking her out like this. June had no illusions about herself – she knew she could be outstanding if she tried – but it was too much trouble to try! Still, it was very very flattering to be told all this!

'Well?' said Amanda, impatiently. 'Why don't you say something? I propose to begin coaching you right away – this afternoon, if possible.'

June hesitated. She was torn between two alternatives. She disliked Amanda, and wanted to throw her offer back in her face, because it had something hard and condescending about it. On the other hand – what fun to lord it over the other second-formers, and tell them that Amanda, from the great sports school, Trenigan Towers, had actually picked *her* out from all the other lower-formers – and considered it worth while to spend a great deal of time on her!

'All right,' said June, at last. 'Did Sally say I could have special coaching from you?'

Amanda gave a snort. 'Don't be silly. And I think you might at least show a spark of gratitude. I'm going to give up a lot of my time to you.'

'Well – you're really only doing it to prove yourself right, aren't you?' said June, with her devastating sharpness. 'Not because you're really interested in *me*? I don't mind. It suits me, if it suits you!'

Amanda restrained her tongue with an effort. It wouldn't do to put this cheeky youngster in a hostile mood at the beginning, or there would be no co-operation between them, and no good results. But how she did dislike her!

'Very well,' said Amanda, crisply. 'We'll have the whole thing on a business basis. *I* want to prove I'm right, and *you* want to be in the second school teams. At least, I imagine you do. It would be a tremendous thing for a second-former.'

'All right,' said June, in her maddeningly casual way.

'But there's just one thing you must understand,' said Amanda, 'or the whole thing's off. You have jolly well got to come at the times I set for coaching in swimming and tennis. Got that?'

'That's fair enough,' said June. And so the bargain was struck between them, a cold sort of bargain with no liking or real interest on either side. June went off jauntily. What a shock for the other second-formers to hear her news!

As soon as she appeared in the second-form common-room the others called out to her.

'What was it, June? What did she want you for?'

'How many lines have you got to learn *this* time?'

'Did you cheek her? What did you say?'

'She sent for me because she said she wanted to coach me in tennis and swimming,' announced June.

This was so astonishing to the others that they were struck into silence. Felicity gasped.

'Amanda – coaching *you*, June! Whatever for?'

'Well, she appears to think I could be in the second tennis team and the second swimming team by the end of the term if I want to,' said June, airily.

'You couldn't. You always fool about too much,' said Susan at once.

'Right. *Amanda* appears to think so, I said,' answered June. 'I've no doubt your opinion is more correct, though, Susan.'

'Look – don't be so exasperating,' said Felicity. 'Tell us what really happened.'

'I've told you,' said June. 'Amanda wants to coach me every day, and I've agreed. That's all.'

There was another silence. The second-formers found it all very hard to believe. But they knew June was speaking the truth. She always did.

'Well, all I can say is, I wish you joy of being coached by that awful, loud-voiced creature,' said Susan. 'She'll order you about like anything.'

'She'll have to mind her Ps and Qs,' said June, smoothly. 'I don't take kindly to being ordered about. If she wants to prove she's right, and get me good enough for the second teams, she'll have to go about it the right way.'

'You're a pair,' said Harriet. 'A real pair! I shall come and watch the coaching.'

'I don't want you to,' said June, hastily.

'Oh, but we *must*,' said Felicity, winking at the others. 'After all – with coaching marvellous enough to push you into the second teams so soon, even *we* might pick up a few hints.'

'Just a few crumbs from the rich man's table!' giggled Susan. 'Well – what a bit of news!'

On the tennis court and in the pool

The news about the special coaching soon flew round the school. The games-mistress looked a little doubtful when she heard it. Too much special attention devoted to any one lower-former was not really good.

On the other hand, June *could* be brilliant at games if she was interested enough. Perhaps this offer of Amanda's would really jerk her into working hard at tennis and swimming. If she only worked hard at *some*thing it would be a help to her character!

'She's a maddening child,' Miss Parker, the second-form mistress, remarked to Mam'zelle. 'All that ability of hers for practically everything – and she's just not interested enough to take the trouble to shine. Except at making the others laugh.'

'Yes – she is too good at that,' agreed Mam'zelle, who had suffered from this ability of June's far too often.

'She's superlative at playing the donkey,' said Miss Potts, who had had June in the first form. 'She's about the only child I've ever had in my form that I really would have liked to see the back of!'

They laughed. 'Well, if Amanda can make her keep her nose to the grindstone, it will be very interesting,' said Miss Parker. 'We'll see!'

Amanda drew up a most intensive time-table for June. June gasped when she saw it. A time was set aside every single day for coaching in swimming *and* in tennis. June wondered whether she should protest or not. No – if Amanda was as much in earnest as all that, all right. June would keep her part of the bargain too.

The coaching began. An interested crowd of first- and second-formers came to watch. Amanda was astonished to see the crowd, and June didn't like it at all. She didn't want to be laughed at, or barracked all the time.

'What's all this?' said Amanda, waving her hand towards the onlookers sitting round the court on the grass.

'They've come to watch us,' said June. 'They would, of course.'

Amanda addressed the crowd at once.

'If you've come to pick up hints, all right. If not, clear off. Anyone who interrupts the coaching, or disturbs it in any way, can think again. I've got my Punishment Book with me as usual.'

This was greeted by a dead silence, and then, as Amanda turned away, a low and discreet murmur arose. Amanda was decidedly not popular. She was even less popular than the domineering Moira. A few of the girls got up and went away. They had only come to call out funny things to June. Now that it meant their names going down in the Punishment Book, there didn't seem much point in staying. June wished fervently that *every*one would go. To her great annoyance and surprise she found that she was nervous!

Amanda began with playing pat-ball, keeping a sharp eye on June's returns and placing. She noted that June used her head as well as her hands. She watched the way she swung her racket right back, and kept her eye on the ball. She took in every single detail. There really wasn't much that Amanda didn't know about tennis! She had already played in school-girl championships, and she was a born teacher as well as a born player.

'I say – how long's this going on for?' complained June at last. 'This pat-ball, I mean.'

There was a ripple of laughter from the onlookers. They sat up, hoping that June would begin to be funny.

Amanda didn't answer. She sent another ball over to June. June pretended to miss it, almost fell over and, by a seemingly miraculous recovery, hit the ball from behind her back, and stood up again. This was the kind of clowning she did superlatively well.

There was a wave of laughter from the watchers. 'Go it, June!' called Harriet.

Amanda caught the ball in her hand and swung round to the lower-formers. 'One more shout and off you'll all go,' she announced. 'I can tell you straight away now that there is nothing whatever I can teach

June in the way of playing the fool – she knows all the tricks there are – but she doesn't know much about playing real tennis, I'm afraid. Do you see how badly she plays a backhand ball? She goes like this – instead of like this! And did you notice her feet when she played those balls off the right-hand side? All wrong!'

June stood still, fuming. Why point out her faults to the audience? But she knew why, of course. It was Amanda's return for that bit of clowning. Every time she clowned, and a laugh came, Amanda would stop and point out other faults of June's!

The next time a ball went near where the spectators were, June spoke to them in a low voice.

'I wish you'd clear off. It's jolly difficult trying to concentrate with you all looking.'

But they didn't clear off, especially when Amanda stopped the pat-ball play and began to explain to June, in her loud, dominating voice, the few hundred things she did wrong. It was wonderful to see the don't-care June having to stand there like someone from the kindergarten and listen to all her tennis failings! The lower forms really enjoyed it.

June didn't enjoy it at all. If she had been a weaker character she would have made up her mind to call the whole thing off, and refuse to be coached again. But June was not weak – and besides, she couldn't help realizing that Amanda really did know what she was talking about. And Amanda also knew how to be patient and how to explain a thing simply and clearly.

June found herself looking at Amanda with unwilling admiration as she illustrated, by various swings of her racket and placing of her feet, exactly what she meant.

I've learned more in this one coaching than I've learned in a whole term, thought June. But she didn't tell Amanda that. She wasn't going to hand the loud-voiced Amanda any bouquets!

Amanda didn't hand June any bouquets either. She merely said, 'That's enough for today. You've plenty of things to think about, as you can see. Get some of them right for next time. And be down at the swimming-pool to the minute tomorrow morning. I've only ten minutes to give you, and I don't want a second wasted.'

June *was* down to the minute. Amanda was there exactly on time too. She put June through a very gruelling ten minutes, and found as many faults with her swimming as she had done with her tennis. Darrell, Moira and Mary-Lou happened to be there too, and they watched in silence.

'If June can stick it, this is going to do her a world of good,' said Darrell. 'My word – what a driver Amanda is – she never lets up for a moment.'

'June *can* stick it all right. The question is – will she?' said Mary-Lou. 'I have a feeling she'll get very tired of all this soon – not the coaching, but the way it's done. So ruthless, somehow.'

Three or four second-formers came down to swim,

among them Josephine, fat and pasty-looking, airing her opinions as usual. They weren't worth anything, of course. They never were. But, like her father, she loved hearing the sound of her voice, and if she could boast about anything, she did.

She had plenty to boast about. 'My father has a whole *fleet* of cars! My mother has a diamond necklace she never wears because it's too valuable. We've a dog at home worth five hundred pounds. My aunt's sending me five pounds for my birthday. My brother's got . . .'

These were the items of family news that Jo continually talked of. There was no doubt at all that they were true.

'Miss Parker is an old nosey! I meant to get out of swimming this morning, and of course she must come and poke her nose in and send me out. I told her what I thought of her. I said . . .'

'Shut up,' said Amanda, who was shouting instructions to June in the water. 'Shut up, and get into the water. I'm coaching someone.'

Jo gave a giggle. She hadn't at first recognized Amanda in her swimming-costume. 'Oh, it's Amanda. Oh, do let's watch this. It'll be as good as the tennis.'

She happened to get in Amanda's way, and impatiently Amanda gave her a push. Into the water went Jo with an agonized squeal. The others yelled with laughter.

But Jo had gone into a deep part, and she couldn't swim. She came up, gasping and terrified, trying to feel the bottom with her feet. But there was no bottom to feel. She went under again.

'Look – quick – Jo's in the deep water!' yelled Darrell. 'She can't swim.'

June swam up to the struggling Jo, and began to life-save her. But Jo was now completely out of control, and so terrified that she clutched hold of June and dragged her under too. She was fat and heavy, and June could do nothing with her.

There was a splash as Amanda dived neatly in. In a moment she was by Jo and had gripped her. 'Let go, June!' she ordered. 'I'll manage her!'

Jo clutched blindly at Amanda, who saw there was only one thing to be done. She must bring Jo back to her senses immediately – and she could only do that by giving her a sharp shock. Otherwise it would take ages to get the terrified girl to the edge of the pool.

She raised her hand and slapped Jo very sharply on the right cheek. The slap echoed round the pool. Jo gasped and came to her senses at once, very angry indeed.

'That's right. Now you listen to me,' ordered Amanda, sharply. 'Don't clutch. I've got you all right. Lie still and I'll take you to the edge.'

It was only a few seconds before Amanda had got Jo to the edge, and Moira and Darrell and Mary-Lou were hauling her up.

Jo collapsed. She wailed. She howled. 'I nearly drowned. You hit me! I'll write to my father and tell him you pushed me in, you big bully!' she wailed. 'I feel awful. I nearly drowned. Oh, my cheek does hurt where you slapped me!'

'Don't be silly,' said Moira. 'You didn't nearly drown. You just lost control of yourself. You didn't even *try* to swim though you've been having lessons!'

'Amanda got you out all right,' said Mary-Lou, gently, seeing that Jo had been really frightened. 'She didn't know you couldn't swim or she wouldn't have pushed you in.'

'She's a bully,' wept Jo. 'I'll tell my father.'

'Tell him,' said Amanda. 'The only thing that's wrong with you is that you're a little coward. I'll give *you* special coaching too, if you like – I'll have you swimming like a fish in a couple of lessons!'

That was the last thing Jo wanted. She dressed and, still weeping and uttering threats, went back to the school. The others laughed.

'Poor Jo! She doesn't fit in at Malory Towers,' said Mary-Lou. 'What a little idiot she is!'

The days go by

Jo got very little sympathy from anyone except a small first-former called Deirdre. Deirdre met her as she was coming up from the pool, still weeping.

'Oh! What's the matter, Jo?' asked Deirdre, in distress. 'Have you hurt yourself?'

'I've been practically *drowned*,' said Jo, more tears springing out. 'That brute of an Amanda pushed me into the deep end, though she *knew* I couldn't swim. She slapped me too – look! I shall tell my father.'

'Oh, I should,' said Deirdre, flattered at the way this second-former was talking to her, a first-former. Deirdre couldn't swim either, and she could quite well understand what fear Jo had felt when she had been pushed into the deep end of the pool. 'How wicked of Amanda. Nobody likes her and I'm not surprised.'

Jo sat down on a ledge of rock, halfway up the cliff. She wiped her eyes with her hand. 'I don't feel well,' she said. 'I feel beastly. I'm sure I'm chock-full of sea water. I shan't be able to eat anything at all today.'

This seemed dreadful to Jo, and almost as dreadful

to Deirdre, who had a very good appetite. She ventured to feel Jo's arm.

'You're shivering,' she said. 'You'd better go in. Shall I fetch Matron for you?'

'Oh goodness, no,' said Jo, at once. She had no more love for Matron than Matron had for Jo. Matron had too often seen through Jo's pretences and evasions. One of them was a bad headache on the afternoons when a long walk was prescribed!

'Funny,' Matron had said. 'Long walk – headache. The two always go together with you, Jo. Well, you can take your headache on the long walk. It'll do it good!'

So Jo certainly didn't want any attention from Matron on the morning when she had been 'practically drowned'. All Jo wanted was sympathy and a lot of it.

But the only sympathy she got was from the little first-former, Deirdre. Everyone else laughed at her.

'Practically *drowned*!' said Susan, scoffing. 'You just went under and got a mouthful of water, Jo.'

'I'll hold you under for a lot longer if you *really* would like to know what being "practically drowned" is like,' offered June, when she had heard Jo's laments about six times.

'Jo's been practically drowned at least twelve times,' said Dawn. 'I can't think why she doesn't *try* and learn to swim. Then she wouldn't keep on getting "practically drowned"!'

'I don't know why you're so mean to me,' said Jo,

looking pathetic. 'Don't I share my sweets and cakes and everything with you? Didn't I tell you I'd just got twenty-five pounds from my aunt to spend on a birthday feast? You know we'll have a jolly good time on my money. Don't I always . . .?'

'Be quiet,' said Felicity, crossly. 'Don't we *all* share our things with one another? You're not the only one!'

'Yes, but I get so many *more* things,' said Jo. 'Look at that enormous cake I had last week – it lasted our table two days. And look at . . .'

'Don't keep on pushing your riches down our throats!' said June, exasperated. 'And keep your cakes and sweets to yourself in future. I don't want any. You keep on and on reminding us of them. Eat them all yourself!'

Jo's eyes filled with tears. 'You're mean,' she said. 'You're all horrid. One of these days I'll run away!'

'Do,' said June. 'It would be too wonderful for words to wake up one morning and find your bed empty. What a relief!'

Jo sniffed dolefully and went in search of Deirdre again. She knew Deirdre would be sympathetic. And so she was – especially when Jo produced a big box of chocolates that had come the day before, and which, so far, she hadn't shared with anyone.

'I shan't give the second-formers one single chocolate,' Jo declared. 'We'll have them all, Deirdre. Go on – take half the box back with you. And when my next cake comes I'll give you a quarter of it!'

Deirdre had no mother to send her any cakes or sweets. She had only a father, who was at sea, and an old aunt who didn't realize that little girls liked parcels at boarding school. So she was very thrilled with the chocolates indeed. They were magnificent ones too, as Jo's always were.

'My family never get anything but the best,' Jo said. She found that she could boast as much as she liked to Deirdre, who drank it all in. 'I wish you could see my bedroom at home, Deirdre – it's all red and gold – and I've got a little bathroom of my own too, done in red and gold.'

This was perfectly true. Jo's father was rolling in money. Jo once boasted that there wasn't anything her father couldn't buy. June had enquired whether he had enough money to buy himself a few hundred Hs. Jo had never forgiven June for that. For the first time she had realized that her father's loud-voiced remarks were made all the worse by the way he continually dropped his Hs, and by his curious lapses in grammar.

Amanda actually came after Jo one morning to ask her if she *would* like her to coach her in swimming. She had felt rather guilty about pushing Jo in, and had kicked herself for not finding out first if she could swim. Jo turned her back rudely on Amanda.

'No thanks,' she said curtly. 'It's a good thing for you I *didn't* write and tell my father. Anyway I wouldn't be put through what you're giving June for anything in the world. No, *thank* you!'

Sally was with Amanda. She swung Jo round by the shoulder. 'Now, just apologize to Amanda for your rudeness,' she said. 'Go on, quick!'

'No,' said Jo, seeing the admiring Deirdre nearby.

'Very well,' said Sally, whipping out her little Punishment Book. 'You can learn any piece of poetry in your French poetry book, so long as it's not shorter than twenty lines. And say it to me before Wednesday next.'

'I apologize,' said Jo, sulkily. French was not one of her best subjects.

'Too late,' said Sally. 'The punishment stands. And take that scowl off your face.'

'No. Hold it!' said Belinda's voice from the back, and out came her sketch-book. 'It isn't often I get such a nice fine *fat* scowl! Aha – see yourself, young Jo!'

Jo gazed in anger at the caricature of herself – wickedly like her at her most bad-tempered. She turned on her heel and slouched off, Deirdre following her like a faithful little dog.

'That kid wants taking in hand,' said Sally. 'I hear from Felicity that she gets parcels practically every day from home – really extravagant ones too. And the money she gets! If I catch her flinging it about I shall confiscate it or send her to Matron. Those lower-formers have got to stick to the rules where money is concerned. It isn't fair to the others, who only have a couple of pounds a term to spend. She's a pest, that kid.'

The interest in Amanda's coaching of June soon died

down. June stuck it, though sometimes with a bad grace. Amanda never praised – that was the worst of her. She found fault dozens of times, but even when June really did produce an ace of a serve, Amanda's only comment would be, 'Well, it's pleasant to see a good serve at last!'

Amanda herself soon proved to everyone that she was far and away the best in the school at tennis and swimming. She was put automatically into the first team for swimming and diving and the first tennis team too. It was a joy to watch her swim or play. Darrell never ceased to marvel at the grace of her great hefty body on the tennis-court or in the pool.

Moira and Amanda had many squabbles, especially over helping the younger ones. Moira was very good about this, but Amanda took no interest at all.

'Tessie's got to learn how to place her balls better,' she would say. Or, 'Lucy would be better if she stopped yelling about at swimming and practised a bit more. She'd be good then.'

'Well – what about telling Tessie, and showing Lucy what she should do?' Moira would say, impatiently. 'You always see what's wrong – but you never never want to put it right. Except for June. She's the only one.'

Amanda didn't answer. She didn't seem to be listening and this always annoyed Moira more than anything.

'That's right. Look away in the distance and think of the wonderful days when you'll win everything at the Olympic Games,' sneered Moira, going out of the room.

Moira would have liked to be as good as Amanda was at games. They were her greatest interest, much to the French girl, Suzanne's, perpetual astonishment.

'This Moira, this Amanda,' she said to Mam'zelle Dupont *'elles sont très drôles*!'

'Speak in English, Suzanne,' Mam'zelle would say, severely. 'How many times must I tell you this?'

'Police?' said Suzanne.

'You heard me,' said Mam'zelle. 'Now – say what you said – in English, please.'

'This Moira, this Amanda – they – are vairy piggy-hoo-learrr!' said Suzanne, earnestly.

Mam'zelle stared at her. '*What* was that word?' she asked, astonished.

'Piggy-hoo-learrrrrr!' repeated Suzanne. 'It is a true word, Mam'zelle Dupont. Darrell tiched it me.'

'Darrell taught you?' said Mam'zelle. 'Ah, I must ask her what it is.'

It turned out to be 'peculiar', of course, and for some time after that everything odd was referred to as 'piggy-hoo-learrrr'! Alicia took it upon herself to teach Suzanne a few more words, which also astonished poor Mam'zelle very much.

She taught the unsuspecting Suzanne such words as 'fiddlesticks!', 'piffle', and 'scrumplicious', which, of course, was a mixture of scrumptious and delicious.

Suzanne liked the words very much, and used them whenever she could. She described Mam'zelle's new lace collar as 'scrumpleeeecious!' and amiably told her that in her opinion swimming was 'peefle' and 'vairy feedle-steecks' and didn't Mam'zelle agree with her?

'What is this "peefle" and "feedlesteecks"?' Mam'zelle asked suspiciously. 'They are not words. Alicia, have you ever heard of them, tell me truly?'

'Oh yes, Mam'zelle,' said Alicia, gazing innocently at Mam'zelle. She caught sight of a hair-pin coming out of Mam'zelle's bun, and the sight made her remember the wonderful magnet. Had June used it again? She must find out.

'Peefle,' muttered Mam'zelle, feverishly searching through the dictionary for it. 'Peefle. He is not here, this peefle. Suzanne, take this dictionary and look through it carefully for me.'

'Police?' said Suzanne, politely. Mam'zelle exploded.

'Yes – look up your everlasting "police", too!' she cried. 'See what it means. One day they will be after you – the POLICE! Ah, you foolish girl. Never will you learn to spik the English as he should be spoke.'

A shock — and a nice little plot

Alicia remembered to ask June about the magnet. June grinned at her, put her hand into the pocket of her navy-blue gym skirt and pulled out the neat, powerful little magnet.

Alicia took it. It was very heavy. She slid it along the desk. A large pencil-sharpener appeared almost to leap through the air and fasten itself on the magnet. Then a compass came, and two or three paper-clips.

'We played the trick on Mam'zelle Rougier again,' said June. 'Harriet did it that time. We did it a bit differently, and it was just as funny.'

'What happened?' asked Alicia.

'Well, the hair-pins came out again, of course,' said June, smiling broadly. 'And Harriet quickly took them off the magnet, and dropped them by the door when she went back to her place. Mam'zelle Rougier felt her hair going down her back and put up her hand to see, of course. She couldn't find a single pin and looked absolutely horrified.

'Then Felicity put up her hand and said she had seen some hair-pins down by the door, and were they Mam'zelle's by any chance?

'Mam'zelle simply couldn't understand how they had got there. We offered all kinds of explanation. I said Mam'zelle must have dropped them coming in. Harriet said she didn't think they could be Mam'zelle's, and how lucky it was that somebody else had dropped hair-pins in our classroom, and . . .'

'Mam'zelle Rougier will be smelling rats if you offer too many explanations,' said Alicia, with a laugh.

'I think she does smell a rat, actually,' said June. 'She keeps on and on putting up her hand to her hair to see if it's still up, and she fingers her hair-pins all day long to make sure they're still there! And she looks frightfully suspiciously at us now!'

'I wish I could see it played on Mam'zelle Dupont,' sighed Alicia. 'She's the one that would be the funniest.'

'Yes. It's a pity sixth-formers are too high and mighty to play a little joke,' said June. 'I hope I'm not like that if ever I get into the sixth.'

'You won't be much good if you aren't,' said Alicia. 'Well – it's a good trick. I'd like to have had it when *I* was in the second form. I think I'd have used it to more effect than you appear to have, though!'

She went off. June looked after her. Now how would Alicia have used it to better effect? It couldn't be done! June put the magnet back slowly into her pocket, her quick mind going over all that Alicia had said.

She sought out Felicity and Sally, and the three of them put their heads together. Jo came into the room and saw them. She went over, all agog at once.

'What's the secret? What's up?' she said.

'Nothing,' said June.

'You *might* tell me,' said Jo, offended. 'I do think you're mean. I'm always kept out of everything. *I* always share things. I'm planning to have a first-class feast next week. Look – I've got twenty-five pounds!'

For about the fourth time that day she took the notes out of the pocket of her tunic to show the others. She did not dare to keep them in her drawer in case Matron found them and removed them.

'We've seen them too many times already,' said Felicity, bored. 'What's your father going to send you for your birthday? A Rolls-Royce? Or a string of race-horses? Or will he be too mean for words and only send you a real pearl necklace?'

Jo turned away angrily. How was it she never never could learn not to show off? Felicity wondered. Did she take after her parents so closely that she had all their mannerisms and habits too?

A most unfortunate thing happened to Jo just after she had left the common-room. The pocket of her tunic wore through – and it happened to be the one in which she kept her money! No doubt much pulling in and out of notes had weakened it. Anyway, it quietly frayed, and Jo didn't know it.

She wandered down the corridor, feeling the familiar sensation of being left out in the cold. What had those three been mumbling about? *Why* didn't they tell her? She determined to go and find Deirdre and talk against the second-formers once more. Deirdre was always a willing listener, and a more than willing sharer of Jo's many goodies.

Matron came out of her room just as Jo had passed. She was most astonished to see a five pound note lying on the floor. She picked it up. It had fallen out of Jo's pocket, of course, and Jo hadn't noticed it. Matron stuffed it into her pocket and went on again. She came across a second five pound note, lying in the middle of the corridor. How very extraordinary!

Matron became suspicious. Were they real notes – or was this somebody's joke? Were there bright eyes watching her pick them up? Matron glanced round, but there was no one to be seen at all. She looked at the notes. They certainly seemed genuine enough.

She was really amazed when she came across the third one. It was just round the corner, and lay there, flapping a little in the draught of the corridor. Matron picked it up thoughtfully. Surely they couldn't belong to any of the girls? Nobody had so much at once!

'Fifteen pounds,' she said to herself. 'Fifteen pounds – and not given in to me! And HOW did they come to be here, lying around like this?'

The last two notes lay together in a corner of the corridor near the garden door. Matron pounced on them. 'Twenty-five now! Well, well, well – somebody very rich has been walking along here – but why cast away so much money?'

Matron looked out of the door. She saw two figures in the distance – Deirdre and Jo, talking together earnestly.

A light dawned on Matron. Of course! Jo! Some of her wealthy relations had been providing her with illicit pocket-money again. But twenty-five *pounds*! How foolish Jo's people were. They were ruining her with their silly, extravagant ideas!

Jo must have dropped them. Matron stood by the door and frowned. Had Jo any more money than this? She should, of course, have given it in to Matron – that was the strict rule. She saw Jo pull at her tunic and slip her hand into her pocket. Ah – so that was where the money was kept!

And then, of course, Jo found the hole – and no notes! She gave a cry of horror and alarm.

Matron disappeared. She went back to her room. She put the money into her safe and wrote out a notice in her firm, clear handwriting.

Meantime Jo looked at Deirdre in horror when she discovered her money was gone. 'Look – there's a hole in my pocket! I must have dropped the notes. Come on, quickly – we must look for them! They can't be far away.'

But, of course, the money was gone. Not a penny could poor Jo find. She wept in dismay, and Deirdre tried to comfort her.

Jo met June, Felicity and Susan coming down the

corridor, looking very pleased with themselves. They had made a very nice little plan, with the magnet as the centre of it! Jo rushed up to them.

'I've lost my money – all of it! Do you know if anyone's found it?'

'There'll soon be a notice put up on the big board, if anyone has,' said Felicity, and the three went on, not at all inclined to let Jo weep on their necks.

'Beasts! Unkind beasts!' said Jo. 'Why did I ever come here? Deirdre, you're the only decent person in the school – the only one I can depend on. I've a good mind to run away!'

Deirdre had heard this many times before. 'Oh no,' she said comfortingly. 'You mustn't do that, Jo, dear. Don't say things like that!'

Felicity and the others laughed to see Jo on her knees in the corridor, still searching for the notes, when they came back. They had already seen Matron's notice on the big board. What a shock for Jo when she knew who had found her money!

'Look on the notice board,' said June. 'Someone has found your money, Jo, you'll be glad to know. You can get it back in two minutes!'

Thankfully Jo got to her feet and rushed off with Deirdre to read the notice. June laughed. 'I wonder what Matron will say to Jo,' she said. 'That is – if Jo dares to go and ask for the money!'

But Jo didn't interest them for more than a minute.

They were too pleased with their plot to forget it for long. They had been looking for Nora to tell it to. Nora would be sure to laugh her head off!

They found her at last. 'Listen, Nora,' said June. 'You know my cousin Alicia? Well, she saw our magnet today and she said if *she* had had it she would have played a much better trick than we did – and she was moaning and groaning because she's in the sixth and they're too priggish to play tricks any more.'

'So we decided we'd give the sixth form a treat,' broke in Felicity. 'And one of us is going to appear in their room with a message to Mam'zelle Dupont, when she's taking a lesson there – and extract all her pins, and then go!'

'And Mam'zelle will think one of *them* has been up to something,' said Susan. 'They simply won't know what to do!'

'We thought we might do it twice or three times, just to show the sixth we play our tricks as well as they could,' said June.

Nora went off into squeals of laughter. 'Oh, let me be the one to go,' she begged. 'Do, do, do! I swear I won't giggle. It's only when I'm with the second form I keep wanting to laugh, and can't stop. I'll be as solemn as a judge if you'll let me go.'

'Well, we thought we *would* choose you,' said June. 'Mam'zelle might suspect *us* – we've played tricks on her before – but she'd never suspect you – you're one of her favourites too, so she'll be quite pleased to see you.'

Nora was the fluffy-haired big-eyed type that Mam'zelle always loved. She twinkled at the three plotters. 'I'll do it!' she said, with a chuckle. 'I'll do it three times if you want me to!'

'Oh no – somebody else must do it next,' said June. 'We don't want Mam'zelle to get suspicious – and she would if you kept on appearing!'

'Especially if her hair fell down each time,' giggled Susan. 'Golly, I wish I was going to be there!'

'Here comes Jo!' whispered June. 'My word, she looks petrified!'

Jo *was* petrified! She had gone to the notice board and had seen Matron's notice at once.

Will the person who dropped twenty-five pounds in five pound notes along the corridor please come to me?
Matron

Jo could have dropped through the floor. *Matron*! Now whatever was she to do? If there was one person poor Jo really dreaded, it was Matron!

Problems for Amanda

Poor Jo lamented loud and long to Deirdre about her bad luck. To think that *Matron* had the money! How in the world could she explain to Matron that she had had twenty-five pounds – *twenty-five pounds* – and not handed it in for safe custody as usual?

'Jo, you'll just have to go and tell her,' said Deirdre, anxiously. 'If you don't, you might not get the money back, ever. If Matron doesn't know who it belongs to, how *can* she give it back?'

'Well, I suppose I'd better,' said Jo. But she had no sooner got to the door than she came back. 'I can't,' she said to Deirdre. 'I daren't face her. Don't think me a coward, Deirdre, but honestly I shake at the knees when Matron puts on that face of hers and says the most awful things.'

Timid little Deirdre had never had any awful things said to her by Matron, but she knew she would feel the same as Jo if she had. She stared at Jo. How were they to get out of the difficulty?

'Jo – I suppose you couldn't slip into Matron's room when she's not there, and just see if the money is lying anywhere about, could you?' she said, in a half whisper. 'After all – it's yours. You would only be taking what belongs to you!'

Jo's little eyes gleamed. 'Yes!' she said. 'I might be able to do that – if only Matron *has* got the money somewhere loose. I know I've seen some tied up in neat packages on her table sometimes – petty cash, I suppose. She might have put mine there, too, ready to hand out to the loser.'

'She wouldn't hand it out,' said Deirdre. 'You know that. She'd keep it and dole it out. All the lower-formers have their pocket-money doled out to them. You'd probably get just a bit of it each week, and the rest would be handed back to you when you go home for the holidays.'

Jo frowned. 'I meant to spend that money on a terrific feast,' she said. 'It's my birthday soon, you know. I simply *must* get it somehow.'

'Shh,' said Deirdre. 'Someone's coming.'

It was Felicity. She poked her nose round the door and grinned. 'Got your money back yet, Jo?' she said. 'Or are you going to make a present of it to Matron? I know *I* wouldn't care to go and own up to having twenty-five pounds – especially if I had been careless enough to lose it too! What an ass you are.'

'Shut up, Felicity,' said Jo. 'I've had enough of people getting at me all the time. I can't think why you're all on to me every minute of the day. Anyone would think I wasn't fit to be at Malory Towers.'

As this was exactly what most of the second-formers did think, Felicity made no reply. Jo never would fit, she was certain. If she had had parents who would have backed up the school, and helped Jo, there might have been a chance for her.

But they laugh at the rules of the school, they tell Jo not to bother to keep any rule if she doesn't want to, they send her parcels of things she's not supposed to have, and far too much money, thought Felicity, going off to practise serving at tennis. Her father keeps saying she's only to enjoy herself, and not to bother to work hard – *he* was always at the bottom of the form, and yet now he's rolling in money – so he thinks it doesn't matter if Jo's at the bottom too!

It was puzzling that some parents backed up their children properly, and some didn't. Surely if you loved your children you *did* try to bring them up to be decent in every way? And yet Jo's father *seemed* to love her. It puzzled Felicity. If he really did love her, how could he encourage her to break rules, to be lazy, to do all the wrong things? How could he laugh when he read disapproving remarks on Jo's reports?

Jo said he clapped her on the back and roared with laughter when he read what Miss Parker had written at the bottom of her report last term, remembered Felicity. What was it she wrote, now? 'Jo has not yet learned the first lesson of all – the difference between plain right and wrong. She will not get very far until she faces up to this lesson.' Gosh – if I'd had that on my report, Daddy would have been broken-hearted, and I should have got the most awful rowing. But Jo's father only laughed!

Felicity found Susan, who was going to take her practice serves. Soon they were on a court, and Felicity was lamming the balls hard at the patient Susan. Amanda wandered up after a time and watched. Felicity redoubled her efforts at serving well.

Since Amanda had taken on June and was training her so well, every lower-former hoped to be singled out for a little attention from the big sixth-former. Felicity sent down one or two fast serves, and Susan called out to Amanda.

'She's good, isn't she, Amanda?'

'So-so,' said Amanda, and turned away, not appearing in the least interested.

'Beast!' said Susan, under her breath. 'Moira would at least have said yes or no – and if Felicity was doing something wrong she'd have set her right, and if she was doing well, she would have praised her.'

Actually Amanda had hardly noticed Felicity's play. She was thinking hard about something. About two things, in fact. She was worried about June – not about her progress, which was, in fact, amazing. Amanda knew how and what to teach, and June was a very able and quick pupil – but June was getting tired of Amanda's strictness and lack of all praise. She was becoming annoyed with the sharp commands and curt orders. It had never been easy for June to knuckle under to anyone, and to be ordered about by someone she really disliked was getting a little too much for her.

She had said so to Amanda the day before. Amanda had taught her a fast new swimming-stroke, and had insisted on her thrashing her way up and down the pool, up and down. Then she had gone for June because she hadn't paid attention to some of her shouted instructions.

'You deliberately swam all the way up the pool using your legs wrong,' she said. 'I yelled at you, but you went on and on.'

'Do you suppose I can hear a word when water is in my ears, and my arms are thrashing over my head like thunder?' demanded the panting June. 'It's true that even the school could probably hear your voice, and no doubt they could even hear it at the post-office, a mile away – it's always loud enough! But I *couldn't*, so you'd better get a megaphone. Though I grant you your voice is better than *any* megaphone, at any time, in any place. Why, even at church . . .'

'That's enough,' said Amanda, angrily. 'I don't take cheek from a second-former.'

'And I'm beginning to feel I won't take orders from a sixth-former,' said June, drying herself with a towel. 'I've had almost enough. So I warn you, Amanda –'

Amanda was about to say something really cutting, but stopped herself. She had begun to be very proud of

June. June was a most marvellous pupil, although un-friendly and usually silent. It would be a pity to stop the coaching now that June was almost as perfect as she could hope to be at tennis and swimming. She was quite good enough for the second team now, and Amanda meant to ask to have her tried out for it in a week or two's time.

So Amanda turned away, fuming inwardly, but trying not to show it. June grinned to herself. She knew quite well that Amanda didn't want to give up the coaching now that June was proving her right in what she had said to the others. All the same, thought June, I'm getting tired of it. This is a most unpleasant term, slaving like this. Do I really, honestly, care enough about being in the second team to go through all this? I'm not sure that I do!

That was June all over, of course. If she took enough trouble, and cared enough, she could shine at anything. But there seemed to be a flaw in her strong character that caused her not to care enough about things.

June was one of the problems that occupied Amanda's mind. The other was her own swimming. Swimming was perhaps her most magnificent achievement in the sports line. To see Amanda hurtle across the pool was a sight in itself. Nobody could swim even one half as fast. Even the small first-formers stopped their chattering when Amanda took to the water.

And what Amanda was thinking hard about was her

swimming. The pool wasn't enough for her. She wanted to swim right out to sea. How could she get enough practice for really long-distance swimming if she didn't swim in the sea? The pool was wonderful – wide and long and deep – but after all, it was only a pool. Amanda wanted to swim for at least a mile! Two miles, she thought, exultantly, three miles! I am strong enough to swim the Channel, I really do believe.

At Trenigan, where her old school had been, the sea coast was safer than the treacherous Cornish coast at Malory Towers, with its strong currents, and vicious rocks on which great waves pounded day and night. But Amanda was sure she could overcome even a strong current.

No one was allowed to swim right out to sea at Malory Towers. That was an unbreakable rule. Anyone wanting real sea-swimming from the shore could go in a party to another beach some way along, and swim in safety from there. But no one was allowed to swim out from the shore at Malory Towers.

No one even wanted to! Enormous waves ran up the rocks to the pool. Even on a calm day, the blue water surged and heaved, and swept with great force over the rocks. Amanda, who loved the strength of water, longed to battle with the fierce sea here. She was quite fearless in all physical things.

She had hardly seen Felicity's tennis, as she stood by the court, idly following the ball with her eyes. Should she take a chance, and go swimming out to sea some time? She didn't much care if she got into a row or not. She wasn't going to stay very long at Malory Towers, and the rules didn't frighten *her*! She suddenly made up her mind.

I *will* go swimming out to sea, she decided. I've talked to Jack the fisherman, and he's told me what currents there are. If I went down to the edge of the rocks at low tide, I could dive off into deep water, and avoid the worst currents by swimming to the west, and then straight out. I should be all right.

The thing was – when could she do this unnoticed? Not that she *minded* getting into a row – but it was silly to do that if it could be avoided. Amanda turned the matter over in her mind.

Early morning would be best, she thought. *Very* early morning. Nobody would be about then. I could have about an hour and a half's real swimming. It would be heaven!

Having settled that, Amanda felt happy. She wished she could settle the June business as easily. But that didn't altogether rest with her! She wasn't going to give in to June's ideas as to how she should be coached, and if June chose to be rude and make things difficult, then there might be a serious row.

'I don't *want* one!' said Amanda to herself. 'But if June provokes one, perhaps it will clear the air, and let her know where she stands. I'm certainly not going to put up with any nonsense, and I think if it came to the point, June wouldn't be idiot enough to throw away her chance of being put in the second school teams.'

15

Half-term

Half-term came and went. It was brilliant weather and the parents thoroughly enjoyed themselves wandering over the school grounds and down by the sea.

The enclosed garden, set in the hollow square in the middle of the four-towered building, was very popular. It was crammed with hundreds upon hundreds of rose-bushes, and the sight and scent of these filled the fathers and mothers with delight.

'I'm glad Malory Towers is at its very best my last half-term,' Darrell said to her mother, as she took her to see the roses. 'I shall always remember it like this. Oh, Mother, thank you a thousand times for choosing this school for me. I've been so happy here.'

Her mother squeezed her arm. 'You've done very well indeed at Malory Towers,' she said. 'All the mistresses have been telling me how much they will miss you, and what a help you've always been. They are glad you have a sister to follow in your footsteps!'

Gwen went by with her mother and Miss Winter. 'My last half-term!' she was saying. 'Fancy, my next half-term will be in *Switzerland*. I'm sure I shall be much happier there than I've ever been here.'

Gwen's father had not come. Gwen was glad. 'I was afraid he might come and spoil everything,' she said to her mother. 'He was so horrid to us last holidays, wasn't he?'

'He would have come,' said Miss Winter. 'But he's not well. He hasn't really been well for some time, Gwen. You should have written to him this term, you know. I really do think you should.'

'It's not your business,' said Gwen, coldly. 'Honestly, you can't always tell whether Daddy isn't well, or is just bad-tempered, can you, Mother? Anyway, we shan't miss him today.'

'Where's Maureen?' asked Mrs Lacey. Maureen, so like Gwen, with her fluffy golden hair and big, pale-blue eyes, was quite a favourite with Mrs Lacey and the old governess. But Gwen wasn't going to have anything to do with Maureen that day! Maureen 'sucked up' to Gwen's people and they just loved it.

'Maureen's got her own people here today,' she said. 'Poor Maureen – I'm sorry for her, Mother. *She's* not going to a finishing school, or even to college of any sort. She's just going to take a secretarial course, and go into somebody's office!'

Jo's people came by, with Jo hanging on to her father's arm. The big, loud-voiced, vulgar man could, as usual, be heard all over the place.

'Not a bad little rose-garden this, Jo, eh?' he said. 'Course it's not a patch on ours. Let's see, Ma, how many roses have we got in our rose-garden?'

'Five thousand,' said Mrs Jones, in a low voice. She was always rather overawed by the other parents, and she was beginning to wish that her husband wasn't quite so loud and bumptious. She had caught sight of a few astonished glances, and a few sly smiles. She wondered if she had put on too much jewellery?

She had. She 'dripped with diamonds', as June said to Susan. 'I'm only surprised she doesn't have a diamond nose-ring, as well as all the rest,' said June. 'I've a good mind to suggest it to Jo. She could pass on the idea, perhaps.'

'No, don't,' said Susan, afraid of June's unkind wit. 'She can't help having such parents. Oh, isn't her father dreadful this time?'

He really was. He had cornered Miss Parker, Jo's form mistress, and was blaring at her in his fog-horn voice.

'Well, Miss Parker – how's our Jo getting along? Naughtiest girl in the form as usual? Ah, well – they're always the most popular, aren't they? The things *I* used to do as a boy. My name's Charlie, so they called me Cheeky Charlie at school! The things I said to my teachers! Ha ha ha!'

Miss Parker made no reply. She merely looked disgusted. Jo felt frightened. She knew that face of Miss Parker's. She had a feeling that Miss Parker might say something that even Cheeky Charlie wouldn't like.

Her father went blundering on. 'Well, you haven't

said a word about our Jo. She's a card, isn't she? Ha ha – I bet she calls you Nosey Parker!' And he actually gave Miss Parker a dig in the ribs!

'I have nothing to say about Jo except that she apparently takes after her father,' said Miss Parker, scarlet with annoyance. She turned away to speak to Darrell's mother, who had come to her rescue. Everyone always hoped to be rescued from Mr Jones!

'Daddy! You shouldn't have said that,' said Jo, in great distress. 'That was *awful*. You made her angry. Please don't say things like that.'

'Well, I like *that*!' said Mr Jones, tipping his hat back on his head and scratching the top of his forehead. 'What did I say? Oh – I was being old Cheeky Charlie again, was I? Well, you do call her Nosey Parker, don't you? My word, there's your Head. I must have a word with *her*!'

Jo tried to pull him back, and cast an agonized glance at her mother. Jo was beginning to realize that her father hadn't very good manners. Why, why, why did he shout so, why did he *always* have such a bright red shiny face, why did he poke people in the ribs and tell silly jokes? Why did he barge in on people when they were talking together, and interrupt them?

He was doing that now. Jo hadn't been able to prevent him from going right up to the little group in which the Head Mistress stood, talking to three or four parents. Her mother was blushing red. She too knew that 'Cheeky Charlie' was not at his best.

117

'Hallo, hallo, hallo!' said Mr Jones, walking right into the middle of the group, and holding out a great red hand to Miss Grayling. 'You're like the Queen of England today, aren't you – holding court, with us poor parents as subjects! Ha ha ha!'

Mr Jones was so pleased with this brilliant remark that he was quite overcome, and beamed round, expecting much approval and admiration.

He got none. Miss Grayling shook hands politely and then dropped Mr Jones's great paw immediately. 'How do you do?' she murmured, and turned back to the parent she was speaking to. Not one of them looked at Mr Jones, but Cheeky Charlie had a very thick skin and didn't notice things like that.

'I hope our Jo's a credit to her school,' he began again. 'Her pa wasn't! He was a naughty boy, he was – always at the bottom of the form, wasn't he, Ma? Well, the school's looking fine, Miss Grayling!'

'Thank you,' said Miss Grayling. 'I'm afraid I must ask you to excuse me for a few minutes, whilst I finish my talk to Dr and Mrs Leyton.'

Mrs Jones pulled at his arm. 'Come away, Charlie,' she begged, thinking that her husband must really have got a touch of sunstroke. He always did behave like this, of course, and shout and boast – but somehow it didn't show so much at home, among his own friends. Here it suddenly seemed very vulgar and out of place.

Mr Jones was about to address a few hearty words to

Dr Leyton, when he caught an extraordinarily icy look in that distinguished-looking gentleman's eye. It reminded Cheeky Charlie of one of his old headmasters who had once told him exactly what he thought of him. Mr Jones backed away, mumbling something.

Miss Grayling sighed with relief. 'I'm sorry,' she said to the other parents. 'It was an experiment, taking Jo – but I'm afraid it's not an experiment that's going to work out well. We've had other experiments before, as you know – taking girls that don't really fit in, hoping they will, later. And so far they always have done, in a marvellous way. I think Jo would too, if only she got a little backing from her parents. But her father always undoes any good we do here for Jo!'

'Let's go to another part of the grounds,' said one of the other parents in the group. 'I feel it would be safer!'

Jo was relieved to see the Head going off in another direction. Oh dear – she really would have to take her father in hand and tell him a few things. She looked rather downcast and her father squeezed her arm. 'What's up, old lady?' he said, in a kindly voice. 'Cheer up! I don't like to see my little Jo not smiling. Her old dad would do anything in the world for her!'

Jo cheered up at the love in his voice. Blow Miss Parker and Miss Grayling and everyone else! It was half-term and nobody should spoil it. She pulled at her mother's arm.

'Mother! Can I ask Deirdre, my friend, to come and be

with us today? Her father's at sea and she's got no mother. So she's alone today.'

'Yes, you ask her,' said her father in his booming voice, before her mother could answer. 'We'll give her a slap-up time. I'm glad you've got a friend at last, Jo! You never seemed to have one before.'

So Deirdre was asked to join the Jones's, and was pleased to have someone to go out with, though Mr Jones really scared her with his loud, booming voice and jovial ways.

'So you're my Jo's friend, are you?' he boomed at her. 'Well, you stick by my Jo, she's worth it, my Jo is. What's your name? Deirdre? Well, we'll send you some stunning parcels, won't we, Ma? You stick by Jo, Deirdre!'

'Yes,' stammered Deirdre, almost deafened.

'What about that money Auntie sent you the other week?' enquired Mrs Jones, as soon as she could get a word in. 'We never heard if you got it. Have you got it safe?'

Jo hesitated. She was afraid to tell her mother that she had dropped it, and that Matron had it, and that she, Jo, hadn't dared to go and get it back. If her father knew that, he would go right up to Matron and demand the money then and there, for his precious Jo! That was simply unthinkable.

'It's quite safe,' muttered Jo, and racked her brains to think how to change the subject.

'Oh well – if you've got that money untouched, I

won't give you any more at present,' said her mother. 'Twenty-five pounds is enough to keep in your drawer, or wherever you keep it. You can write if you want any more.'

Jo didn't know what to say. She had hoped her mother would give her more money – then she wouldn't need to go poking about in Matron's room for hers. Poor Jo hadn't screwed up her courage even to peep inside Matron's room yet. She had no money at all except for a few coins left from her week's pocket-money – handed out by Matron.

Half-term flashed by. The parents departed by car and train, except for Bill's father and mother, who came and went on horseback, much to Bill's delight and Clarissa's. Their half-term had been spent in riding over the cliffs, the horses enjoying the half-term as much as anyone!

'My last half-term gone,' mourned Darrell. 'Now I'm facing my very last few weeks!'

'Cheer up!' said Alicia. 'A lot can happen in a few weeks.' She was right. A lot did happen – and most of it was really very unexpected!

A row – and a trick

The first thing that happened was the row between June and Amanda. Most people had thought the two would blow up sooner or later, and they did!

It was over quite a simple thing. Amanda was coaching June at tennis, sending her fast serves to take – so fast and hard that June was half scared of some of them! But she slammed them back valiantly, pleased at being able to handle such terrific serves.

'June! Use your head!' shouted Amanda, stopping her serves for a minute. 'What's the good of returning these fast serves if you don't put the ball somewhere where I've got to run for it! Or even somewhere that I can't reach! All you do is to put them back right at my feet.'

'It's as much as I can do to take the serves, let alone *place* the return ball,' answered June. 'Give me a chance! Also, the court is a bit bumpy this end, and the ball doesn't bounce true. It puts me off when that happens.'

'Don't make excuses,' said Amanda.

'I'm not!' yelled June, indignantly. But Amanda was already throwing the ball high in the air for her next serve.

The ball flew like lightning over the net to June. Again it bounced on an uneven bit and swerved a little to the right. June lashed at it wildly.

It flew straight up into the air, and then swerved right over the netting round the court, landing in the middle of a watching group, who fell all over themselves trying to catch the ball, shrieking with laughter.

'If you fool about, June, we'll stop,' said Amanda, honestly thinking that June had hit the ball wildly on purpose. Something immediately went 'ping' inside June, as it always did when she lost her temper.

She didn't lose it outwardly at first. She merely collected up the balls round the court, and then sent them all flying over the surrounding netting into the watching girls, one after another.

'I'm finished,' she announced to Amanda. 'It's impossible to work with you. I shan't turn up for this sort of thing any more. It's not worth my while. So long!'

And under the admiring eyes of the watching girls, June strolled off the court, whistling softly.

Amanda called to her. 'Don't be a fool, June. Come back at once.'

June took no notice. She whistled a little more loudly, and began throwing her racket up into the air and catching it deftly as it came down. She did a few imaginary strokes with it, and then began to fool. The watching girls laughed.

Amanda strode after June. 'June! I told you to come

back. If you don't, I'll see you're not chosen for even the third team.'

'Don't want to be!' said June, throwing her racket up into the air again and catching it. 'You go and find some other second-former to bawl at and chivy round. Don't waste that nice kind nature of yours, Amanda.'

And this time she really did go off, having given Amanda a look of such scorn and dislike that Amanda was shocked. The little group of spectators were scared now. They dispersed, whispering. What a bit of news to spread round the school. What a row. And wasn't June MARVELLOUS! 'Honestly!' whispered the first- and second-formers. 'Honestly, she doesn't care for anyone, not even Amanda!'

Amanda told Sally, Darrell and Moira the news herself. 'June flew into a temper and the coaching is off,' she announced. 'I'm not giving up any more of my time to that ungrateful little beast. I'm sorry I gave her any now. But she would have been well worth it.'

'Oh, what a pity!' said Sally. 'We had arranged to watch June swimming tomorrow, and playing tennis the next day, to see if she could go into the second team, as you suggested. She's already good enough for the third. She could have been in all the matches!'

'Well, she can't be,' said Amanda, and then she spoke spitefully. 'She's gone off her game this week. She doesn't deserve to be in the third team either.'

Alicia spoke to June about it. 'What happened?' she

said. 'Couldn't you have stuck it for a bit longer? We were going to come and watch you swimming and playing tennis this week – meaning to put you into the second teams, so that you could play in the matches.'

'I'm not going to be chivied about by anyone,' said June. 'Least of all by Amanda. Not even for the sake of shining in the second teams with the fourth- and fifth-formers!'

'But, June – aren't you rather cutting off your nose to spite your face?' asked Alicia. 'Don't you *want* to play in the matches? They're important, you know. We do want to win them this year. We lost the tennis shield last year, and were only second in the swimming matches.'

June hesitated. She *did* want to play in the matches. She *would* have liked to bring honour and glory to the teams – and yes, to Malory Towers too. June was really beginning at times to see that one should play for one's side and not always for oneself.

'Well,' she said at last, 'I'll be honest with you, Alicia. Yes, I *was* looking forward to playing in the matches, and I was pretty certain I'd be chosen. But Amanda is a slave-driver and nothing else – she made me slave and she got good results – but she's so absolutely in*human*. I couldn't stick her one moment more, even if it meant giving up the matches.'

'Although you knew you might help the school to get back the tennis shield and win the swimming?' said Alicia.

There was a pause. 'I'm sorry about that,' said June,

with an effort. 'I didn't think enough about that side of the question, I'm afraid. But look, Alicia – it's done now, and I'm not going back on my word. I'm fed up to the teeth with tennis and swimming. I don't want to touch a racket again this term, and if I go into the pool, I shall just fool about.'

'You'll fool about all your life, I expect,' said Alicia, getting up. 'All you think about is yourself and your own feelings. I'm sorry about it, June. You're my cousin, and I'd like to have cheered myself hoarse for once, watching you do something fine – like Darrell cheers Felicity.'

She walked off and left June feeling rather small and uncomfortable. But nothing, nothing, nothing would make June go to Amanda again. Nothing in this world. June gritted her white even teeth and swung an imaginary racket into the air and caught it. Finish! No more coaching!

Nora came running up. 'Was that Alicia? You didn't tell her we were going to play the magnet trick on Mam'zelle Dupont today, did you?'

'Don't be an ass,' said June, scornfully. 'Do you suppose I'd split after we said we wouldn't say a word?'

'Oh. Well, you seemed to be having such a confab,' said Nora. 'I came to ask if I could have the magnet. I've been waiting ages to ask you. Was Alicia rowing you?'

'No,' said June, shortly. 'Don't be so jolly inquisitive, and mind your own business. Here's the magnet.'

Nora took it, beaming. She felt proud of being chosen

by the second-formers to play the trick up in the grand sixth form. She had planned everything very carefully, with Felicity's help.

'I popped into the sixth form and took one of the exercise books off the desk,' Felicity had told Nora. 'All you've got to do is to walk into the room, apologize, and ask Mam'zelle if the book belongs to a sixth-former. You can do the trick whilst she's examining it.'

It sounded easy. Nora was thrilled when the time came that afternoon. The second-formers were free, but the upper forms were busy with work. Nora sped up to the sixth form with the book.

She heard the drone of someone reading aloud in French as she got there. She knocked at the door. Mam'zelle's voice came at once. '*Entrez*!'

Nora went in with the book. 'Excuse me, Mam'zelle,' she said, holding out the book. 'But does this belong to one of the sixth-formers?'

Mam'zelle took the book and looked at it. 'Ah – it is Mary-Lou's missing book,' she said. Behind her Nora was holding the powerful little magnet two inches away from Mam'zelle's neat little bun of hair.

Alicia's sharp eyes caught her action and she stared, hardly believing her eyes. All Mam'zelle's hair-pins at once attached themselves to the magnet. Nora withdrew it hastily, said 'Thank you, Mam'zelle' and shot out of the room before she burst into laughter. Alicia felt sure she could hear the little monkey snorting in the corridor as she fled back to the second-formers.

Mam'zelle seemed to have felt something. She usually wore more pins in her hair than Mam'zelle Rougier, and probably she had felt them all easing their way out! She put up her hand – and immediately her bun uncoiled itself and flapped down her back!

'*Tiens*!' said Mam'zelle, surprised. The girls all looked up. Alicia felt like a first-former again, longing to gulp with laughter. Mam'zelle patted her hand over her head to find her hair-pins. She could find none.

'*Que c'est drôle, ça*!' said Mam'zelle. 'How strange it is!'

She stood up and looked on the floor, wondering if, for some extraordinary reason, her pins had all fallen down there. No, they hadn't. Mam'zelle grovelled on hands and knees and looked under her desk to make certain.

The girls began to laugh. Alicia had quickly enlightened them as to what had happened. The sight of poor Mam'zelle groping about on the floor for hair-pins that were not there, her hair hanging over one shoulder, was too much even for the staid sixth-formers.

Mam'zelle stood up, looking disturbed. She continued her frenzied hunt for the missing pins. She thought possibly they might have fallen down her neck. She stood and wriggled, hoping that some would fall out. She groped round her collar, her face wearing a most bewildered expression.

She saw the girls laughing. 'You are bad wicked girls!' she said. 'Who has taken my hair-pins? They are gone.

Ah, this is a strange and puzzling thing.'

'Most piggy-hoo-leeearrrr,' said Suzanne's voice.

'But nobody could have taken your pins, Mam'zelle,' said Darrell. 'Why, not one of us has come up to your desk this afternoon.'

'*Ça, c'est vrai*,' said Mam'zelle, and she looked alarmed. 'That is true. This is not a treek, then. My pins have vanished themselves from my hair. Girls, girls, can you see them anywhere?'

This was the signal for a frantic hunt in every ridiculous nook and cranny. Darrell was laughing helplessly, unable to keep order. For three or four minutes the sixth-formers really might have been back in the second form. Irene produced several explosions, and even the dour Amanda went off into fits of laughter.

'Girls, girls! Please!' Mam'zelle besought them. 'Miss Williams is next door. What will she think?'

Miss Williams thought quite a lot. She wondered what in the world was happening in the usually quiet sixth form. Mam'zelle got up. 'I go to make my bun again,' she said, and disappeared in a dignified but very hurried manner.

17

Jo and Deirdre

The girls laughed and laughed. 'It was that little monkey of a Nora,' said Alicia, again. 'I saw the magnet in her hand. The cheek of it – a second-former coming right up into our room.'

'Terribly funny, though,' said Clarissa, wiping her tears away. 'I haven't laughed so much for terms. I wish Nora would do it again, with me *looking*!'

'Poor Mam'zelle – she was absolutely bewildered,' said Mary-Lou.

'*Ah ça – c'est très très* piggy-hoo-leeeearr,' said Suzanne, enjoying the joke thoroughly. 'Vairy, vairy, piggy-hoo-leeeearrrrr. Most scrumpleeeeecious!'

Mam'zelle had shot into the little workroom she shared with Miss Potts, the first-form mistress. Miss Potts was mildly surprised to see Mam'zelle appear so suddenly with her hair down her back – not more than mildly though, because in her years with Mam'zelle Miss Potts had become used to various 'piggy-hoo-leeeearrr' behaviour at times from Mam'zelle.

'Miss Potts! All my pins have went!' said Mam'zelle, her grammar going too.

'Pins? What pins?' said Miss Potts. 'You don't mean your hair-pins, do you? How could they go?'

'That I do not know,' said Mam'zelle, staring at Miss Potts with such tragic eyes that Miss Potts wanted to laugh. 'One moment my bun, he is there on top – the next he is all undone. And when I look for his pins, they are gone.'

This sounded like a trick to Miss Potts, and she said so.

'No, no, Miss Potts,' asserted Mam'zelle. 'Not one girl left her place to come to me this afternoon, not one.'

'Oh well,' said Miss Potts, dismissing the matter as one of the many unaccountable things that so often seemed to happen to Mam'zelle, 'I expect you didn't put enough pins in, so your bun just came down.'

Mam'zelle found some pins and pinned her bun up so firmly that it really looked very peculiar. But she wasn't taking any risks this time! She went back to the classroom, with her dignity restored.

Nora recounted what she had done, when she got back to the second-formers. They laughed. 'I bet the sixth got a laugh when Mam'zelle's bun descended!' said June. 'It's a pity you couldn't stay and see.'

The first sixth-former they saw was the French girl, Suzanne. She came hurrying up to them, smiling.

'Ah, you bad Nora!' she cried, and went off into a stream of excited French. Susan, who was good at French, translated swiftly, and the second-formers laughed in delight at the vivid description of Mam'zelle's astonishment and dismay.

'Clarissa said she wished you would do it again, when she was looking,' said Suzanne, in French. 'We would like to see it done. Me also, I would like it very much. *We* are too big and old and prudent to do tricks – but we do not mind watching *you*!'

This was very naughty of Suzanne. No sixth-former would be silly enough to encourage the younger ones to come and play tricks in their room as much as they liked – which was what Suzanne was telling them to do! But Suzanne was French. She hadn't quite the same ideas of responsibility that the British girls had.

She was often bored with lessons, and longed for 'peefle' of some kind. If the second-formers would provide some, that would be '*Magnifique*! *Superbe*!'

'Right,' said June at once. 'If that's what you want, it shall be done. I'll think up a little something for the entertainment of the sixth.'

June was bored now that she had practically given up playing games or swimming properly. She was in the mood for wickedness and mischief of some kind – and what better than this? She set her sharp brains to work at once.

Jo was aggrieved at not having been told that the hair-pin trick was to be played by Nora in the sixth form. 'You *might* have told me,' she said. 'You always leave me out.'

'You tell everything to that first-form baby – what's her name? – Deirdre,' said June. 'That's why we don't let you into our secrets.'

'I've a good mind to share my parcel that came today with the first form, instead of with *you*,' said Jo.

'Do,' said June. 'Probably you can buy their liking and their friendship with food. Unfortunately you can't buy ours. A pity – but there it is!'

Jo was miserable. She *was* beginning to understand that heaps of money and sweets and food didn't in the least impress the girls. But perhaps if she gave a most wonderful midnight feast on her birthday, and asked them all to it and was very modest and friendly herself, they might think she was not too bad after all?

But how could she buy a grand feast without money? She brooded over the money that Matron had of hers. She still hadn't claimed it.

'And if I do, she won't give it to me,' Jo wailed to Deirdre for the twentieth time. 'I *must* screw up my courage, snoop into her room, and see if I can spot where she's put my money.'

A most unexpected opportunity suddenly came. Matron sent a message by Susan to say she wanted Jo.

Jo went pale. 'What for?' she asked.

'Don't know,' said Susan. 'Probably you've mended your red gloves with blue wool again. You must think Matron's colour blind when you keep doing things like that!'

Jo went off dolefully. She felt absolutely certain that Matron was going to ask her if the twenty-five pounds was hers. She felt it in her bones!

She found the door of Matron's room open, and went in. There was nobody there. From far down the corridor she could hear yells. Somebody must have fallen down and hurt themselves and Matron had rushed off to give first aid. Jo took a quick look round the familiar room. Ugh, the bottles of medicine!

There was no money to be seen anywhere – but suddenly Jo saw something that made her stand stock-still.

Matron had a small, heavy safe in the corner of the room, into which she locked what money she had – the girls' pocket-money, the doctor's fees, and so on. To Jo's enormous surprise, the safe door was a little open, the keys hanging from the keyhole! Obviously Matron had just been about to open or shut the safe when she had heard the agonized yells. She had rushed out, forgetting the keys left in the safe door.

Jo ran to the door and peered out. Not a soul was there. She ran back to the safe and opened the door. There was a pile of notes on one shelf, and a pile of silver on the next. Jo grabbed some notes, stuffed them into her pocket and fled!

No one saw her go. Not a soul did she meet as she raced back. She went to find Deirdre and they shut themselves into one of the bathrooms and locked the door.

'Look,' said Jo, pulling the money out of the pocket. 'Nobody was in Matron's office. I've got my money back.'

'But Jo – there's more than twenty-five pounds there!' said Deirdre.

So there was. There were nine five pound notes, all new and clean.

'Gosh – I didn't think there were so many,' said Jo. 'Never mind. I'll borrow the extra four! I can easily get Daddy to send me four fivers when I next write to him, and then I'll put them back.'

'Wouldn't it – wouldn't it be called stealing if we don't put them back at once?' asked Deirdre, scared.

Jo was so frightened that Deirdre might ask her to return them to Matron's room, that she pooh-poohed this suggestion at once. She felt sure she would be caught if she went to put them back!

'No, of course not,' she said. 'Don't be silly. I've always plenty of money. I don't need to *steal*, do I? I tell you, twenty-five pounds of this is my own money and four fivers I've just borrowed – and I'll pay them back next week.'

Deirdre cheered up. 'Shall we go and buy things for the feast now?' she asked. 'Gosh, what a lot we can get! We'll go over to the town, shall we, next time we're allowed out, and buy stacks of things!'

Jo was very cock-a-hoop now. She felt she had done a very fine and daring thing. She got two safety-pins and pinned the notes safely in the pocket of her blouse, afraid that she might lose them again.

The two of them set out the next day to go shopping. 'Where shall we hide the stuff?' said Jo. 'I daren't put it anywhere in the dormy, and the common-room's not safe.'

'Well, it's very fine weather. We could really hide it under a hedge somewhere,' said Deirdre.

They bought a great many things. Packets of biscuits, tins of Nestlé's milk, tins of sardines, chocolate bars by the dozen, bags of sweets, tins of peaches and pears! They staggered out with half the things, promising to go back for the others. They had kit bags with them, but these didn't hold half the goods.

They found a good place in a field to hide the food. An old tree stump had fallen down, covering a hollow beneath it. The girls stuffed everything into the little hollow, which was perfectly dry. They went back for the rest of the things.

They paid the bill – twenty-five pounds! Deirdre could hardly believe her ears. It was more money than she had had to spend in five years!

'We've got good value for the money, though,' said Jo, as they staggered off again, laden with tins and packages. 'There's enough and more for every one of the twenty-three girls in the form!'

They hid the second lot of food, strewed ivy strands over the opening to the hollow, and went back to school, well pleased with themselves. They had decided to ask a dozen or so of the second-formers to go with them to retrieve the food later on. They were sure they could never manage to take it all the way to school without falling by the wayside!

But, before anyone could be told about the exciting array of goods, Jo got into trouble. She was supposed to go out for walks only with another second-former or with someone of a higher form. The first-formers only went for walks accompanied by a sixth-former or by a mistress, though the rule was sometimes disregarded. Jo had broken it by taking a first-former out – and she had also brought Deirdre back an hour too late for her prep.

So that evening Miss Parker, the second-form mistress, gave Jo a shock. She rapped on her desk, after a note had been brought in to her, and everyone looked up from their prep.

'I have here a note,' said Miss Parker. 'It informs me that Deirdre Barker, of the first form, was taken out this afternoon by a second-former – which is against the rules – and did not return until an hour after prep was started in the first form. Deirdre has not given the name of the second-former. I must therefore ask her to stand up so that I may see who it is.'

Everyone knew it was Jo, of course. They had seen her go off with Deirdre, and even if they hadn't they would have guessed it was Jo, Deirdre's friend. One or two looked at Jo expectantly.

And Jo was afraid of owning up! She was afraid of

having to say where they had been, and what they had bought, and where the money had come from. She trembled in her seat, and kept her eyes down. Her cheeks grew crimson. Miss Parker waited for two minutes in silence.

'Very well,' she said. 'If the culprit will not own up, I must punish the whole class. The second form will not go swimming for three days.'

Running away

Still Jo did not stand up. She couldn't. Oh, the girls didn't understand! It wasn't just owning up to taking Deirdre out without permission, it was all the other things that might be found out – that forty-five pounds for instance!

Forty-five pounds. FORTY-FIVE POUNDS. It suddenly began to loom bigger and bigger and bigger. Why had she taken it? Just to get her own money back, and out of bravado too – to impress Deirdre. Jo kept her head down for the rest of prep, but she was quite unable to do any work at all.

The storm broke in the dormy that night.

'Jo! What do you mean by not owning up?' demanded June. 'You go down and own up immediately. Go on!'

'It wasn't me with Deirdre,' said Jo, feebly.

'Oh, JO! You're worse than ever. How can you tell lies like that?' cried Felicity. 'Go down and own up. You don't really mean to say you're going to have the whole form docked of its swimming for three days? You must be mad!'

'All right, I'm mad, then,' said Jo, feeling like a

hunted animal when she saw all the angry, accusing faces turned towards her.

'You're not fit to be at Malory Towers,' said Susan, in a cutting voice. 'I can't think why you ever came. You're getting worse instead of better.'

'Don't,' said Jo, her eyes filling with tears.

'That's right – cry!' said Katherine. 'You deserve to. Now, for the last time, are you going to own up or not?'

'I wasn't with Deirdre,' repeated Jo, obstinately.

'We shall send you to Coventry,' said June. 'We shall not speak to you, any of us, or have anything to do with you for three whole weeks. See? That's the kind of punishment that is kept specially for people who behave like you, Josephine Jones – people who let others be punished for what they have done themselves, and then are too cowardly to stop it. We shan't speak to you for three weeks!'

'But – it's my birthday soon – and I've got a feast for everyone!' cried Jo, wildly.

'You'll be the only one at your feast,' said June, grimly. 'Unless you like to ask that drip of a Deirdre. Now it's understood, isn't it, everyone? From this moment Jo is in Coventry!'

Jo hadn't heard of being sent to Coventry before. It was new to her. It meant that not a single person spoke to her, answered her, or even looked at her. She might not have been there for all the notice they took of her that night. Jo cried in bed. *Why* hadn't she given up that money to Matron as soon as she had had it from her aunt? That was when all the trouble had begun.

She waited till the others were asleep and then went to find Deirdre. The two crept together into the corridor to whisper. 'Deirdre – I can't stand it,' wept Jo. 'I shall run away. I want to go home. Everyone's so unkind to me here. Except you.'

'I shouldn't have come shopping with you,' whispered Deirdre. 'I'm the cause of all the trouble.'

'Oh, Deirdre – will you come with me if I run away?' asked Jo, sniffing. 'I'd be afraid to go alone. Please, please say you'll come with me.'

Deirdre hesitated. The idea of running away scared her – but she was very weak and easily led. Jo was much the stronger of the two and Jo had been very generous to her.

'All right. I'll come too,' she said, and immediately Jo cheered up. They began to plan.

'I tell you what we'll do,' said Jo. 'We'll take all that food of ours to that shack we passed on a long country walk we went on last term – do you remember? The first- and second-formers went together and we all played in the shack. It was in a very lonely place. We'll take the food there, and we can stay there a day or two before trying to find the way home.'

This seemed rather a delightful adventure to Deirdre. She agreed at once. 'We'd better get up early tomorrow,' she said, 'and go and take the stuff to and fro. It will take us two journeys at least, and it's quite a long way to that shack.'

Jo felt quite cheerful now. What would the second-formers feel like when they knew that sending her to Coventry had made her run away? Jo didn't think of the worry she would cause the school and her parents by disappearing suddenly. She was completely selfish, and soon began to view the whole thing in the guise of a wonderful escapade.

Somehow or other she managed to wake the next morning very early. She dressed and woke Deirdre, whose bed was fortunately beside the door in her dormy. The two set off quietly. They came at last to the hollow where they had hidden their goods, and then began the long trek to and fro to the shack. It took them longer than they imagined. The shack was a good place to hide in. It was a long long way from any road, and only a bridle path led anywhere near it. No one, except for a few hikers, usually came near it.

'There,' said Jo, pleased, putting down the last tin of peaches. 'We must remember to bring a tin-opener. We've really got enough food to last for weeks, Deirdre.'

'We ought to get back quickly,' said Deirdre, looking at her watch. 'We'll be awfully late for breakfast – and whatever we do we mustn't be seen coming in together again.'

'Nobody's spotted us at all so far,' said Jo. 'We're lucky.'

It was true that nobody had recognized them. But

somebody had seen them, far away in the distance! Bill, on her horse Thunder, and Clarissa, on Merrylegs, were out for one of their early-morning rides, and had followed a bridle path not far distant from the shack. Bill's sharp eyes caught sight of two figures going into the shack.

'Funny!' she said. 'That looks like two Malory Towers girls – same uniform. Perhaps it's two out for an early-morning walk.'

'Probably,' said Clarissa, and thought no more about it. They galloped on, and had a wonderful ride, getting back just before Jo and Deirdre – who were careful to slip in at different gates.

They had planned to run away that night, when all the others were asleep in bed. The second-formers were surprised at Jo's behaviour that day. They had expected her to be miserable and subdued, because being ignored completely was a very hard punishment – but instead Jo was bright-eyed and cheerful, seeming not to care in the least about being sent to Coventry.

'She's a thick-skinned little beast,' said June to Felicity. June was doing a double dose of ignoring. She was not only ignoring Jo, she was ignoring Amanda! It so happened that they met quite a number of times during those few days and June took great delight in turning her back on Amanda in a very marked manner.

That night, when the girls in the second-form dormy were fast asleep, Jo got up and dressed very quietly. She took the rug off her bed, and then stole into Deirdre's dormy. Deirdre was awake, half afraid now that the time had come. For two pins she would have given up the idea entirely!

But Jo had no idea of giving it up or of allowing Deirdre to either! It wasn't long before both of them were stealing down the moonlit corridor, each with their rug over their arm. It was easy to open the garden door and go out into the grounds.

'I'm glad it's moonlight,' said Deirdre, with a half-scared laugh. 'I wouldn't like to go on a dark night. Oh, Jo – you're sure it's all right? You're sure your people won't mind my turning up with you?'

'Oh no. They'll welcome you as my friend,' said Jo. 'And they'll laugh at our adventure, I know they will. They'll think it's wonderful!'

They got to the shack at last. All their food was still there. They spread the rugs on the floor and lay down to sleep. It was quite warm, but for some time neither of them could sleep. In the end Jo broke open a packet of biscuits and they munched steadily. Deirdre fell asleep first, and then Jo found her eyes closing.

What would the girls think tomorrow? They'd be sorry they'd driven her away! thought Jo. Miss Parker would be sorry for the nasty things she had said. So would Mam'zelle. So would . . . But Jo was now fast asleep, and never even heard a little hedgehog scuttling across the floor of the shack.

Nobody took any notice of the girls' empty beds in the

morning. It was quite usual for someone to get up early for a walk or a swim. The first- and second-formers clattered down to breakfast, chattering as usual.

But before long, the news went round the school. 'Jo's gone! Deirdre's gone! Nobody knows where they are. They've hunted everywhere for them!'

The second-formers couldn't help feeling rather guilty. Had their punishment sent Jo off? No – she had so very very often said she would run away! All the same – perhaps she had run away because she couldn't stand being sent to Coventry – and taken weak little Deirdre with her. What would happen? Where on earth had they gone to?

The police were told. Miss Grayling rang up Mr Jones and informed him that his daughter was missing, but they hoped to find her, and also a girl she had taken with her, at any moment. They couldn't have gone far.

Miss Grayling was amazed at Mr Jones's reception of her news. She had expected him to be upset and worried, perhaps to reproach the school for not taking more care of Jo. But down the telephone came a bellow of laughter.

'Ha, ha, ha! If that isn't exactly like our Jo! She's just like me, you know. The times I played truant from school! Don't you worry about our Jo, Miss Grayling. She knows how to look after herself all right. Maybe she's on her way home. I'll telephone you if she arrives.'

'Mr Jones – the police have been informed,' said Miss

Grayling, disgusted at the way Jo's father had taken her news. 'I will try to keep it out of the papers as long as I can, of course.'

'Oh, don't you bother about *that*,' said the surprising Mr Jones. 'I'd like to see our Jo hitting the headlines in a spot of adventure. Great girl, isn't she?'

He was surprised to hear the click of the receiver being put down firmly at Miss Grayling's end. 'What's the matter with *her*?' he wondered. 'Cutting me off like that. Hey, Ma – where are you? What do you think our Jo's done?'

A very disturbing piece of news came to Miss Grayling that morning. It came from the police sergeant who had been told of the missing girls. After Miss Grayling had spoken about them and given their descriptions, the sergeant cleared his throat and spoke rather awkwardly.

'Er – about that other matter you reported a short while ago, Miss Grayling,' he said. 'The notes that were stolen from your Matron's safe. You remember Matron knew the numbers printed on the notes – they were in a sequence. Well, we've traced them.'

'Oh,' said Miss Grayling. 'Do you know who the thief is, then?'

'Well, Mam, yes, in a way we do,' said the sergeant. 'Those notes were given in at two shops in the town, by a Malory Towers girl. She came in with another girl and bought a whole lot of food – tins and tins of it.'

Miss Grayling's heart sank. She covered her eyes. Not

a *Malory Towers* girl! Could there possibly be a thief like that among the girls?

'Thank you, sergeant,' she said at last. 'I will make enquiries as to which girls they were. Good morning.'

19

A dreadful morning for Jo

It was soon quite clear that it was Jo and Deirdre who had done the shopping. Everything came out bit by bit. Matron told how she found the five pound notes and knew that they belonged to Jo. Jo had never claimed them.

The second-formers related that Jo meant to buy food for a birthday feast. Miss Parker added the bit about Deirdre going out with a second-former, and how she had not been able to make that second-former own up. 'But,' she said, 'there is no doubt at all but that it was Jo.'

'Yes,' said Miss Grayling, seeing the whole miserable story now. Jo had gone to Matron's room to get back her own money and had taken more than she meant to – and then had been too afraid to put it back. Then trouble had come, and fear and misery had caused Jo to run away. Silly, ill-brought-up, spoiled little Jo!

'Mostly her parents' fault, of course,' said Miss Grayling to Matron. 'Nothing to be done there, I'm afraid. They're no help to her.'

There was a knock at the door. Bill and Clarissa were outside.

They had remembered the two figures they had seen

near the old shack the morning before. Could they have been Jo and Deirdre?

'Quite likely,' said Miss Grayling. 'They may have hidden their food there, and be camping out. Do you know the way?'

'Oh *yes*,' said Bill. 'We often ride out there. We thought it would really be quickest for us to ride out on Thunder and Merrylegs, Miss Grayling, and see if the two girls *are* there.'

'Miss Peters can go too, on her horse,' said Miss Grayling. 'If the girls are there, she can bring them back.'

So the three riders set off, and rode over the fields and hills till they came to the bridle path that led near the shack. Jo and Deirdre, sitting inside the shack, having their fourth 'snack' that morning, heard the hooves. Deirdre peeped out.

'It's Bill and Clarissa,' she said, darting back, looking scared. 'And Miss Peters.'

'They can't guess we're here,' said Jo, in a panic.

But they *had* guessed, of course, and very soon the three of them dismounted, and Miss Peters walked to the shack. She looked inside. She saw Jo and Deirdre, looking very dirty and untidy and frightened, crouching in a corner.

'So there you are,' she said. 'What a pair of idiots. Come out, at once, please. We've had enough of this nonsense.'

Like two frightened puppies, Jo and Deirdre crept out of the shed. Bill and Clarissa looked at them.

'So it *was* you we saw yesterday,' said Bill. 'What are you playing at? Red Indians or something?'

'Bill! Shall we get into awful trouble?' asked Deirdre, looking rather white. She had not enjoyed the night in the shack. A wind had blown in, and she had felt cold in the early morning. She had awakened and had not been able to sleep again. Also there seemed to be rather a nasty smell of some sort in the shack – perhaps it was mice, thought Deirdre, who was terrified of them.

Bill looked at the pale Deirdre and felt sorry for her. She was only a first-former, just thirteen years old, and a timid, weak little thing – just the type that Jo *would* pick on to boast to, and persuade to do wrong.

'Look, Deirdre – you've been an idiot, and you might have caused a lot of worry and trouble, if it hadn't happened that Clarissa and I spotted you the other day, when you were here,' said Bill. 'It's a mercy it hasn't got into the papers yet. The best thing you can do is to be absolutely straight and honest about it, and to be really sorry, and promise to turn over a new leaf. Then I dare say you'll get another chance.'

'Shall I be expelled?' asked Deirdre, panic-stricken at the thought. 'My father would be awfully upset. I haven't got a mother.'

'I shouldn't think you'd be sent away,' said Bill, kindly. 'You've not got a bad name, so far as I know. Come on now. You can get up on Thunder, behind me.'

Deirdre was frightened of horses, but she was even

more frightened of disobeying Bill, and getting into further trouble. She climbed up on Thunder, and Jo was taken on Miss Peters' horse. Miss Peters said only a few words to the dirty, bedraggled Jo.

'Running away from things is never any good,' she said. 'You can't run away from difficulties. You only take them with you. Remember that, Jo. Now hang on to me and we'll go.'

They got back just about break-time. The sound of hooves was heard as they came up the drive, and the girls ran to see if Jo and Deirdre were being brought back. They looked in silence at the dirty, bedraggled, sorry-looking pair!

The two were taken straight to Miss Grayling. Deirdre was now in a state of utter panic. However *could* she have gone with Jo! What would her father say? She was all he had got, and now he would be ashamed and sorry because she had brought disgrace on the fine school he had sent her to.

Tears streamed down her cheeks, and before Miss Grayling could say a word, Deirdre poured out all she was feeling.

'Miss Grayling, I'm sorry. Don't tell my father, please, please, don't. He trusts me, and I'm all he's got. Miss Grayling, don't send me away. I'll never, never do such a thing again, I promise you. I can't think why I did it. If only you'll give me another chance, I'll do my best. Miss Grayling, please believe me!'

Miss Grayling knew real repentance when she saw it. This was not someone trying to get out of trouble, it was someone shocked by what she had done, someone thinking now of the effect it might have on somebody she loved – someone with an earnest desire to turn over a new leaf!

'I'll show you that I mean what I say,' went on Deirdre, beseechingly, rubbing away her tears with a very grubby hand, and streaking her face with dirt. 'Give me all the hard punishments you like, I'll do them. But please don't tell my father. He's a sailor, and he would *never* run away. He'd be so ashamed of me.'

'Running away never gets us anywhere,' said Miss Grayling, gravely. 'It is the coward's way. Facing up to things is the hero's way. I shall think what I am to do with you, and tell you later on in the morning. I am sure that whatever I decide you will accept, and face bravely.'

She turned and glanced at Matron, who was sitting quietly knitting in a corner of the big room.

'Will you take Deirdre now?' she said. 'She wants a bath, to begin with, and clean clothes. Don't let her go into class this morning. Give her some job to do with you, will you? When she's in a calmer state of mind I'll talk to her again.'

Matron, calm, kindly and efficient, put her knitting into her bag. 'Come along, my girl,' she said to Deirdre. 'I'll soon deal with you. I never did see such a grubby first-former in my life. A hot bath and clean clothes will make you feel a lot better. And after that you can help me to tidy out my linen cupboard. That'll keep you busy! Keep you out of mischief too!'

She took the girl's arm in a kindly way, and Deirdre heaved a sigh of relief. She was always scared of Matron, but suddenly she seemed a real rock, someone to lean on – almost like a mother, thought Deirdre, who had missed a mother very much indeed. She kept close to Matron as she hurried her away. She longed to ask her if she thought the Head would expel her, but she was afraid of the answer. Poor Deirdre. She was not meant for escapades of any sort.

Jo had been standing silent all this time, fearful of saying a word. Miss Grayling looked at her. 'I am expecting your father in ten minutes' time,' she said, 'or I would send you to have a bath too. But it would be better to wait now, till he comes.'

Jo's heart lifted. So her father would soon be here. *He* wouldn't be cross about this. It would tickle him. He would laugh and joke about it, and tell all his friends about the latest thing his Jo had done. He would put things right!

Jo heaved a sigh of relief. 'Sit down,' said Miss Grayling. 'We will discuss this miserable affair with your father when he arrives. I sent for him as soon as I heard from Bill and Clarissa that they knew where you were hiding.'

Miss Grayling began writing a letter. Jo sat still. She

wished she didn't look so dirty. She had a great hole in her tunic, and her bare knees were filthy.

In ten minutes' time an enormous car roared up the drive. Daddy! thought Jo. He hasn't been long! The car came to a stop with a screeching of brakes. Someone got out and the car door was slammed loudly.

Soon Mr Jones appeared at the sitting-room door. He came in, beaming. 'So you found that rascal, did you?' he said. 'Why, here she is! Just like you, Jo, to go off like that. She's a scamp, isn't she, Miss Grayling?'

'Won't you sit down?' said Miss Grayling, in a remarkably cool voice. 'I want to discuss this matter with you, Mr Jones. We take a serious view of it, I am afraid. It is fortunate that it did not get into the papers.'

'Yes, but look here – what's so serious about it?' exploded Mr Jones. 'It was just a bit of fun – Jo's a high-spirited girl – nothing wrong about her at all!'

'There is a lot wrong,' said Miss Grayling. 'So much so, Mr Jones, that I want you to take Jo away with you today – and I regret to say that we cannot have her back. She is not a good influence in the school.'

Mr Jones had never in his life had such a sudden and unpleasant surprise. He sat with his mouth falling open, hardly able to believe his ears. Jo – Jo expelled! They wanted him to take her away and not bring her back? Why? WHY?

Jo was shocked and horrified. She gave a gulp and stared at her father. He found his voice at last.

He began to bluster. 'Yes, but look here, you can't do that – you know it was only a bit of fun. I grant you Jo shouldn't have done it – caused a lot of trouble and all that – and she shouldn't have taken the other kid with her either. But – but you can't *expel* her for that, surely!'

'We could, Mr Jones, if we thought she was an undesirable influence,' said Miss Grayling. 'It doesn't often happen, of course – in fact, very, very rarely. But in this case it *is* going to happen. You see – it isn't only the running away – it's a little matter of the taking of some money.'

Jo covered her face. She could have dropped through the floor. So Miss Grayling knew all about that too! Her father looked dumbfounded. He stood up and looked down at Miss Grayling, and his voice shook.

'What do you mean? You can't say my Jo is a thief! You can't! I don't believe it. She's always had *heaps* of money.'

Miss Grayling said nothing. She merely indicated Jo, who still sat with her face covered, bending forward with tears soaking between her fingers. Her father stared at her, aghast.

'Jo,' he said, in a voice that had suddenly gone hoarse. 'Jo – you didn't, oh you didn't! I can't believe it!'

Jo could only nod her head. That awful, awful money! There was still the rest of it pinned in her blouse. She could feel it rustling when she moved. She suddenly pulled it out. She put it in front of Miss Grayling. 'That's all that's left,' she said. 'But I'll pay the rest back.'

'Let me pay everything, everything – I'll double it!' said Mr Jones, in the same hoarse voice. 'To think of Jo – my Jo – taking money!'

Both the bold brazen Jo and the once blustering bumptious man looked at Miss Grayling miserably and humbly. She was sorry for them both.

'I think there is no need to say any more,' she said, quietly. 'I don't want any explanations from Jo. You can get those from her, if you wish. But you will see, Mr Jones, that I cannot keep Jo here any longer. She had a fine chance at Malory Towers, and she didn't take it. And I think I should say this to you – her parents are partly to blame. You didn't give Jo the backing-up and the help that she needed.'

'No, you didn't, Dad!' cried Jo, sobbing. 'You said it didn't matter if I was bottom of the form – YOU always were! You said I needn't bother about rules, I could break them all if I liked. You said so long as I had a good time, that was the only thing that mattered. And it wasn't, it wasn't.'

Mr Jones stood still and silent. He turned suddenly to Miss Grayling. 'I reckon Jo's right,' he said, in a voice that sounded astonished. 'And I reckon, Miss Grayling, that you might have given Jo another chance if you'd thought *I'd* see things the right way – and I didn't. Come on, Jo – we've got to get things straight between us – come on home, now.'

He held out his hand, and Jo took it, gulping.

Mr Jones held out his hand to Miss Grayling and spoke with unexpected dignity.

'Good-bye, Miss Grayling. I reckon I'm the one that's really at fault, not Jo. You won't spread this matter about, will you – for Jo's sake? About the money, I mean.'

'Of course not,' said Miss Grayling, shaking hands. 'And Mr Jones – however much you make a joke of the escapade to your friends, and gloss over the fact that Jo has been expelled – I do beg of you not to make a joke of it with Jo. This is a serious thing. It may be the turning-point in her life, for good or for bad – and she has a right to expect that her parents will show her the right road.'

In a few minutes' time the big car roared off down the road. Jo was gone – gone for ever from Malory Towers. One of the failures, who perhaps in the future *might* be a success, if only her parents backed her up.

How important parents are! thought Miss Grayling. Really, I think somebody should start a School for Parents too!

Amanda goes swimming

Deirdre was not expelled. Her real fault had been weakness, and that could be dealt with. When she heard that she was to stay on, she could have sung for joy. She was shocked about Jo, but secretly relieved to be free of her strong, dominating influence.

The whole school was shocked too. It was so very rare for any girl to be expelled – but everyone agreed that Jo was impossible.

'Poor kid,' said Mary-Lou. 'Who could be decent with idiotic parents like that – throwing money about all over the place, boasting, thick-skinned, trying to make Jo as bad as themselves. Well – it was one of Malory Towers' experiments that went wrong.'

'I must say I'd rather have a generous parent like Jo's than a mean one like mine, though,' put in Gwen. 'Jo's father would never have grudged her an extra year at a finishing school.'

'You've got a bee in your bonnet about that,' said Alicia. 'And let me tell you, it buzzes too loudly and too often. Your father's worth ten of Jo's – oh, not in money, but in the things that matter!'

'That was a very nasty business about Jo,' said Darrell. 'I'm glad it's over. Now perhaps we'll have a bit of peace without any more alarms and excursions!'

This was, of course, a foolish thing to say. Things began to happen almost immediately!

Amanda had decided that the tide would be right for her swim out to sea the next morning. She was looking forward to it eagerly. A good long swim at last!

She was in a small, sixth-form dormy, with only three others. All the others were very sound sleepers – Moira, Sally and Bill. She could easily creep out without waking them. She didn't mean to tell any of them what she was going to do, or what she had done, when she had had her long swim! They were so keen on rules being kept – but such rules, thought Amanda, really didn't apply to a future Olympic swimmer!

She got up at half-past four in the morning. It was dawn, and the sky was full of silvery light. Soon it would change to gold and pink as the sun came up. It would be a heavenly day!

She went quietly out. There wasn't a sound to be heard in the whole of the school. Amanda was soon standing by the pool, stripping off her clothes. She had on her swimming-costume underneath. She had a dip in the pool first – lovely! Her strong arms thrashed through the water, and her strong body revelled in it. She turned on her back for a few minutes and dreamed of the next year, when she would win the swimming at the Olympic

Games. She pictured the crowds, she heard the roar of cheering and the sound of hundreds of people clapping.

It was a very pleasant picture. Amanda enjoyed it. Then she climbed out of the pool and made her way down to the edge of the rocks. The waves came pounding in there, although further out it was very calm. Amanda looked out to the brilliant blue sea and sky. She dived cleanly into a deep pool and swam through a channel there, and was suddenly out in the open sea.

At last! she thought, as her arms cleaved the water and her legs shot her steadily forward. At last I am really *swimming* again!

She went in the direction she had planned. The sun rose a little higher in the sky and shone down. It was going to be a hot day. Little sparkles came on the water, and Amanda laughed for joy. Splash, splash, splash – she swam on and on, part of the sea itself.

Nobody had seen her go. She planned to be back before anyone came down for an early-morning swim. At the earliest that would be seven o'clock. She had plenty of time.

But someone came down *before* seven o'clock that morning. June woke up early and could not get off to sleep again. The sun shone right on her face. She glanced at her clock. Six o'clock. Gosh – ages before the dressing-bell went. She sat up and pulled her dressing-gown towards her.

I'll go down and have a swim, she thought. A real

swim in the pool, not just fooling about, like I've been doing since I had that row with Amanda. I'll see if I've remembered all her rules.

She went softly down the stairs and out into the sun-drenched grounds. She was soon down by the pool, and went to find her swimming-costume, which she had left there to dry. She pulled it on. Then into the pool she went with a neat dive.

It was glorious there – and lovely to have it all to herself. Usually it was so crowded. June floated lazily. Then she began to swim. Yes – she had remembered everything that Amanda had taught her. She shot through the water at top speed, her lithe body as supple as a fish. Up and down she went, up and down, till she was tired out.

She climbed out to have a rest and sit in the sun. She decided to go down to the edge of the sea, and let the waves splash her as she sat on the rocks. So down she went, and found a high shelf of rock to sit on, where waves could just splash over her legs.

She gazed idly out to sea. What a marvellous blue – a kind of delphinium blue, June decided. And then her eyes suddenly fastened on a little black bob, some way out to sea. Could it be a buoy, fastened there to show a hidden rock? June had never noticed it before.

Then she saw what looked like a white arm raised. She leaped to her feet. Goodness gracious – it was a swimmer! Out there, caught by the current, someone was swimming desperately to prevent themselves being forced on to the rocks some way along.

June stood still, her heart suddenly beating fast. She watched intently. It *was* a swimmer, though she couldn't make out whether it was a man or a woman. Did he or she *know* the current had caught him, and was dragging him to the rocks, where waves were pounding high?

Yes. Amanda knew. Amanda felt the strong, swift current beneath her. How could she ever have laughed at it? It was stronger than ten swimmers, than twenty swimmers! It pulled at her relentlessly, and no matter how she swam against it, it swept her in the opposite direction.

Amanda was very tired. Her great strength had been used for a long time now against the treacherous current of water. She saw with panic that she was being taken nearer and nearer to the rocks she had been warned against. She would have no chance if one of those great waves took her and flung her on them – she would be shattered at once!

June saw that the swimmer was trying to swim against the current. She knew it was hopeless. What could she do? Had she time to run back to school, warn someone and get them to telephone for help? No, she hadn't.

There's only one thing to do, thought June. Just one chance! The boat! If I can get to the boat-house in time, drag out the boat, and cut the swimmer off before he gets on the rocks, I might save him. Just a chance!

She tore off to the little boat-house in her swimming-costume. It was some way along the shore, in a place free of rocks and pounding waves. June found the key, unlocked the door and tried to drag out one of the little boats the girls sometimes used, when old Tom the boatman could be persuaded to take them for a row.

Even this little boat was heavy. June tugged at it and pushed – and at last it reached the water, and took off on a wave. June sprang in and caught up the oars. She began to row at top speed, but soon had to slacken, because she was so out of breath. She glanced round to spot the swimmer.

There he was – no, it must be a she, because it had longish hair, wet and draggled. What an idiot! June pulled strongly at the oars, horrified to see that the swimmer was being swept very near the rocks now.

The sea was calm, fortunately, so the waves that pounded the rocks were not so tremendous as usual. June yelled to the swimmer.

'AHOY THERE! AHOY!'

The swimmer didn't hear. Amanda was almost spent. Her arms were now hardly moving. She could fight against the current no longer.

'AHOY!' yelled June again. This time Amanda heard. She turned her head. A boat! Oh, what a blessed, beautiful sight! But could she possibly get to it, or it to her, in time?

The boat came on. A wave suddenly took Amanda

strongly in its grasp, swelled up and flung her forward. A hidden rock struck her leg, and she cried out in agony.

Gosh – she's almost on the rocks, thought June, in a panic. She rowed wildly, and at last reached the swimmer, who was now allowing herself to float, unable to swim a stroke.

June reached out to her over the side of the boat. It's Amanda! she realized, with a shock of amazement. Well, who would have thought she'd be such an idiot?

Miraculously the swell subsided for a minute or two, and June pulled at Amanda. 'Come on – help yourself up!' she shouted. 'Buck up!'

How Amanda ever got into the boat she didn't know. Neither did June. It seemed impossible, for Amanda had a badly hurt leg and arm. But somehow it was done, and at last she lay in the bottom of the boat, exhausted, trembling, and in pain. She muttered thanks, but beyond that could not utter a word.

June found that she now had to pull against the current. She was tired already and soon realized it was impossible. But help was not far off. Some early-morning swimmers in the pool had spotted the boat, and one bright fourth-former had fetched a pair of binoculars. As soon as it was seen that the boat was in difficulties, old Tom was sent for – and now here was his small outboard motor-boat chugging along to rescue the two exhausted girls!

They were soon on shore. Matron had been fetched,

as soon as June had been recognized through the glasses. No one had spotted Amanda at first, as she was in the bottom of the boat. The girls crowded round, and cried out in horror.

'Oh, look at Amanda's leg and her poor arm! Oh, isn't it *terrible*!'

Amanda makes plans

Again the news flew round the school like wildfire! 'Amanda went swimming out to sea and got caught in the current! June went down to swim in the pool and saw her. She got the little boat and rescued her – but Amanda's badly hurt.'

'Fancy *June* rescuing her bitter enemy!' said the lower-formers. 'Good old June! She's collapsed, Matron says. They are both in the san.'

June soon recovered. She had been completely exhausted, and that and the panic she had felt had knocked her out for a few hours. Then she suddenly sat up and announced that she felt quite all right, could she get up, please?

'Not yet,' said Matron. 'Lie down. I don't want to speak severely to such a brilliant life-saver, but I might, if you don't do what you're told! You certainly saved Amanda's life.'

'How *is* Amanda?' asked June, shivering as she remembered Amanda's terrible leg and arm – bruised and swollen and cut.

'She's not too good,' said Matron. 'Her arm isn't so

bad – but the muscles of the leg have been terribly torn. On a rock, I suppose.'

June lay silent. 'Matron – will it – will this mean Amanda can't swim or play games any more this term?'

'It may mean more than that,' said Matron. 'It may mean the end of all swimming and games for her – unless those muscles do their job and heal up marvellously.'

'But – Amanda was going in for the Olympic Games next year,' said June. 'She was good enough, too, Matron.'

'I know all that,' said Matron. 'It's a bad thing this, June. When a person has been given strength and health and a wonderful gift for games, and throws it all away for an hour's forbidden pleasure, it's a tragedy. What that poor girl is thinking of, lying there, I don't like to imagine.'

June didn't like to imagine it, either. How terrible for Amanda! And to think she had brought it on herself too – that must be even more terrible.

'Can I go and see Amanda?' she asked Matron, suddenly.

'Not today,' said Matron. 'And let me tell you this, June – I know about your clash with Amanda, and I don't care who's right or who's wrong. That girl will want a bit of help and sympathy, so don't you go and see her if you can't be generous enough to give her a bit. You saved her life – that's a great thing. Now you can do a *little* thing, and make it up with her.'

'I'm going to,' said June. 'You're an awful preacher,

Matron. I can't imagine why I like you.'

'The feeling is mutual!' said Matron. 'Now, will you please lie down properly?'

June found herself a heroine when she at last got up and went back to school! There were cheers as she came rather awkwardly into the common-room, suddenly feeling unaccountably shy. Susan clapped her on the back, Felicity pumped her right arm up and down, Nora pumped her left.

'Good old June!' chanted the girls. 'Good – old – JUNE!'

'Do shut up,' said June. 'What's the news? I feel as if I've been away for ages. Played any tricks up in the sixth form yet?'

'Good gracious, no! We've been thinking and talking of nothing else but you and Amanda!' said Felicity. 'We haven't once thought of tricks. But we ought to now – just to celebrate your bravery!'

'I wish you wouldn't be an ass,' said June. 'I happened to be there, and saw Amanda in difficulties, that's all. It might have been anyone else.'

But the second-formers would not hide their pride in June. Alicia was pleased and proud too. She came down to clap her small cousin on the back.

'Good work, June,' she said. 'But – it's jolly bad luck on Amanda, isn't it? Out of all games for the rest of the term – and maybe no chance for the Olympic Games next year either.'

No one said, or even thought, that it served Amanda right for her conceit, and for her continual boasting of her prowess. Not even the lower-formers said it, though none of them had liked Amanda. Her misfortune roused their pity. Perhaps the only person in the school who came nearest to thinking that it served Amanda right was the French girl, Suzanne, who had detested Amanda for her brusque ways, and for her contempt of Suzanne herself.

But then Suzanne could not possibly understand *why* Amanda had gone for that long swim, nor could she understand the bitter disappointment of being out of all games for so long.

June was as good as her word. She went to see Amanda as soon as she was allowed to, taking with her a big box of crystallized ginger.

'Hallo, Amanda,' she said, 'how's things?'

'Hallo, June,' said Amanda, who looked pale and exhausted still. 'Oh, I say – thanks for the ginger.'

Matron went out of the room. Amanda turned to June quickly. 'June – I'm not much good at thanking people – but thanks for all you did. I'll never forget it.'

'Now *I'll* say something,' said June. 'And I'll say it for the two of us and then we won't mention it again. We were both idiots over the coaching, *both* of us. I wish the row hadn't happened, but it did. It was fifty-fifty, really. Let's forget it.'

'You might have been in both the second teams,' said Amanda, regretfully.

'I'm going to be!' said June. 'I mean to be! I'm going to practise like anything again – and will you believe it, Moira's offered to time me at swimming each day, and stand and serve me balls at tennis each afternoon!'

Amanda brightened at once. 'That's good,' she said. 'June – I shan't mind things quite so much – being out of everything, I mean – if you *will* get into the second teams. I shan't feel I'm completely wasted then.'

'Right,' said June. 'I'll do my best.'

'And there's another thing,' said Amanda. 'I'm going to spend my time coaching the lower-formers when I'm allowed up. I am to have my leg in plaster and then I can hobble about. I shan't be able to play games myself, but I shall at least be able to see that others play them well.'

'Right,' said June again. 'I'll pick out a few winners for you, Amanda, so that they'll be ready for you when you get up!'

'Time to go, June,' said Matron, bustling in again. 'You'll tire Amanda with all your gabble. But, dear me – she looks much brighter! You'd better come again, June.'

'I'm going to,' said June, departing with a grin. 'Don't eat all Amanda's ginger, Matron. I know your little ways!'

'Well, of all the cheeky young scamps!' said Matron, laughing. But June had gone.

Matron was pleased to see Amanda looking so much brighter. 'June's just like Alicia, that wicked cousin of hers,' she said. 'Yes, and Alicia is just like her mother. I had her mother here, too, when *she* was a girl. Dear,

dear, I must be getting old. The tricks Alicia's mother used to play too. It's a wonder my hair isn't snow-white!'

She left Amanda for an afternoon sleep. But Amanda didn't sleep. She lay thinking. What long long thoughts come to those in bed, ill and in pain! Amanda sorted a lot of things out, during the time she was ill.

Nobody pointed out to her that pride always comes before a fall, but she pointed it out a hundred times to herself. Nobody pointed out that when you had fallen, what really mattered was not the fall, but the getting up again and going on. Amanda meant to get up again and go on. She meant to make up for many many things.

And if my leg muscles never get strong enough for me to play games really well again, I shan't moan and groan, she thought. After all, it's courage that matters, not the things that happen to you. It doesn't really matter *what* happens, so long as you've got plenty of pluck to face it. Courage. Pluck. Well, I *have* got those. I'll be a games-mistress if I can't go in for games myself. I like coaching and I'm good at it. It will be second-best but I'm lucky to *have* a second-best.

And so, when she got up and hobbled around, Amanda was welcomed everywhere by the lower-formers, all anxious to shine in her eyes, and to show her that they were sorry for her having to limp about. Amanda marvelled at their short memories. They've forgotten already that I never bothered to help anyone but June, she thought. She gave all her extra time to the

171

eager youngsters, the time that normally she would have had for playing games herself, if it hadn't been for her leg.

'She's really a born games teacher!' the games-mistress said to Miss Peters. 'And now she's taken June on again, and June is so remarkably docile, that kid will be in the second teams in no time!'

So she was, of course, unanimously voted there by Moira, Sally and Darrell. Amanda felt a prick of pride – but a different kind of pride from the kind she had felt before. This time it was a pride in someone else, not in herself.

'And now, my girl,' said Alicia to June, '*now* you can show the stuff you're made of! We had hoped that Amanda might win us all the inter-school shields and cups that there *are* – but she's out of it. So perhaps *you'll* oblige, and really get somewhere for a change!'

A most successful trick

The next thing that happened was a good deal pleasanter. The Higher Certificate girls had sat for their exam and at last had got it behind them. They had gone about looking harassed and pale, but made a miraculous recovery immediately the last exam was over.

'And now,' said Alicia, 'I feel I want a bit of relaxation. I want to be silly and laugh till my sides crack! What wouldn't I give to be a second-former just now, and play a few mad tricks on somebody.'

And then the tricks had happened. They were, of course, planned by the irrepressible second-formers, particularly June and Felicity, who had both been sorry for Darrell and Alicia during their hard exam week.

These two had put their heads together, and had produced a series of exceedingly well-planned tricks. They told the other second-formers, who giggled helplessly.

'These tricks all depend on perfect timing,' said June. 'One we already know – the hair-pin trick – the other is one I've sent for, that I saw advertised in my latest trick booklet.' June had a perfect library of these, and although they were always being confiscated, they were also being continually added to by the indefatigable June.

'We didn't think the hair-pin trick was quite played out, yet,' said Felicity. 'It still has possibilities. But we thought we'd combine it with another trick, which will amaze the sixth-formers as well as Mam'zelle.'

'Good, good, good!' said the eager listeners. 'What is it?'

June explained lucidly. 'Well, listen. See these pellets? They are perfectly ordinary pellets till they're wetted – and then, exactly a quarter of an hour after they're wetted, they swell up into a kind of snake-thing – and they hiss!'

'Hiss?' said Nora, her eyes gleaming. 'What do you mean – hiss?'

'Well, don't you know what "hiss" means?' said June. 'Like this!' And she hissed so violently at Nora that she shrank back in alarm.

'But how *can* they hiss?' she asked.

'I don't know. It's just part of the trick,' said June, impatiently. 'They're wetted – they swell up into funny white snakes – and as they swell, they hiss. In fact, they make a remarkably loud hissing noise! I've got one wetted ready on that desk, so that you can see it working in a few minutes.'

'Oooh,' said the second-formers, in delight.

June went on: 'What I propose to do is to send one of us into the sixth form when Mam'zelle is taking it, and withdraw her hair-pins with the magnet,' said June.

'She'll miss them and rush out to do her hair again. In the meantime, up the chimney there will be one of these pellets, ready wetted – and by it will be a tiny pin-cushion. But instead of pins, it will have hair-pins – just like Mam'zelle's – stuck into it!'

'I see the trick, I see it!' said Katherine, her eyes dancing. 'By the time Mam'zelle has come back and is settled down, the pellet-snake will come out, and began to hiss like anything – and everyone will hear it . . .'

'Yes,' said Felicity, 'and when they go to hunt for the hissing noise, just up the chimney they will find – the little cushion stuck full of Mam'zelle's hair-pins!'

'But won't they see the snake?' asked Nora.

'No – because it falls into the finest powder when it's finished,' said June. 'It can't even be seen. That's the beauty of it. They'll take down the cushion, and won't they gape! I can see my cousin Alicia wondering what it's all about!'

'That's not all,' said Felicity. 'There's still some more. One of us goes into the room again and takes out Mam'zelle's *second* lot of hair-pins – she'll have done her hair again you see – and we'll slip another wetted pellet just behind the blackboard ledge – with another little cushion of hair-pins!'

The second-formers shrieked at this. Oh, to be up in the sixth form when all this happened!

'And the snake will come out, hidden behind the blackboard, on the ledge, and will hiss like fury,' said

June. 'And when the hissing is tracked there, they'll find a hair-pin cushion *again*!'

'Priceless,' said Harriet.

'Smashing!' said Nora.

'It's really quite ingenious,' said June, modestly. 'Felicity and I thought it out together. Anyway it will be a real treat for the poor old jaded sixth form, after their week of exams.'

They found out when Mam'zelle was taking a French lesson in the afternoon again. It had to be a time when the second-formers were free, or could go swimming or play tennis. It would be easy to arrange to slip up at the correct times then.

'Wednesday, a quarter to three,' reported June, after examining the time-tables of her form and the sixth. 'Couldn't be better. Nora, you can go in first with the magnet. And, Felicity, you're going in next, aren't you?'

'*I'll* go in first,' said Felicity. 'Who will wet the pellet and put it up the chimney before the class begins?'

'I will,' said June. So, when Wednesday afternoon came, there was much excitement and giggling among the second-formers. Miss Parker wondered what they were up to now. But it was so hot that she really couldn't bother to find out.

June disappeared upstairs just before a quarter to three with the wetted pellet and the little cushion of pins. There was a tiny shelf a little way up the chimney and she carefully placed the pellet at the back and the cushion just in front. Then she fled.

The class filed in a few minutes later. Mam'zelle arrived. Then Felicity entered, panting. 'Oh please, Mam'zelle, here is a note for you,' she said, and put the envelope down in front of Mam'zelle. The name on it had been written by June, in disguised handwriting. It said 'Mam'zelle Rougier'.

'Why, Felicity, my child, do you not know by now that my name is Mam'zelle Dupont, not Rougier?' said Mam'zelle. 'This is for the other Mam'zelle. Take it to her in the fifth form.'

Felicity was a little behind Mam'zelle. The class looked at her suspiciously. Why the enormous grin on the second-former's face? They soon saw the magnet being held for a few seconds behind Mam'zelle's head. Then Felicity hid the magnet – and its hair-pins – in her hand, took the note, and departed hurriedly.

It was done so quickly that the sixth form gaped. Mam'zelle sensed almost immediately that something was wrong with her hair. She put up her hand, and gave a wail.

'Oh *là là*! Here is my hair undone again!'

And once again she searched in vain for her hair-pins. Knowing from her experience the first time that she would probably not find a single one, she left the room to do her hair, puzzled and bewildered. What was the matter with her hair these days – and her pins too?

Mam'zelle seriously considered whether or not it would be advisable to have her hair cut short!

She rushed into her room, did her hair again and stuffed her bun with hair-pins, driving them in viciously as if to dare them to come out! Then she rushed back to the class, patting her bun cautiously.

The hissing began just as she sat down. Up the chimney the wetted pellet was evolving into a sort of snake, and giving out a loud and insistent hissing noise.

'Ssss-ssss-SSSSSSSS-sss!'

The sixth-formers lifted their heads. 'What is this noise?' asked Mam'zelle, impatiently. 'Alicia, is it you that heesses?'

'No, I don't heess,' said Alicia, with a grin. 'It's probably some noise outside, Mam'zelle.'

'It isn't,' said Moira. 'It's in this room. I'm sure it is.'

The hissing grew louder. 'SSSSSSSSSSSSS!'

'It sounds like a snake somewhere,' said Darrell. 'They hiss just like that. I hope it's not an adder!'

Mam'zelle sprang up with a scream. 'A snake. No, no. There could not be a snake in here.'

'Well, what on earth is it, then?' said Sally, puzzled. They all listened in silence.

'SSSSS-sssss-sss-SSS,' said the pellet, loudly and insistently, as the chemicals inside it worked vigorously, pushing out the curious snake-like formation.

Alicia got up. 'I'm going to track it down,' she said. 'It's somewhere near the fireplace.'

She went down on hands and knees and listened. 'It's up the chimney!' she exclaimed in surprise. 'I'll put my hand up and see what's there.'

'No, no, Alicia! Do not do that!' almost squealed Mam'zelle, in horror. 'There is a snake!'

But Alicia was groping up the chimney, pretty certain there was no snake. Her hand closed on something and she pulled it down the chimney.

'Good gracious!' she said, in an astounded voice. 'Look here – your hair-pins, Mam'zelle – in a cushion for you!'

The sixth-formers couldn't believe their eyes. How could Mam'zelle's hair-pins appear miraculously up the chimney, when nobody had gone near the chimney to put them there? And what had made the hissing noise?

'Anyone got a torch?' said Alicia. 'Hallo – the hissing has stopped.'

So it had. The pellet was exhausted. The snake had fallen into the finest of fine powder. When Alicia switched on the torch and shone it up on the little chimney-shelf, there was absolutely nothing to be seen.

Mam'zelle was very angry. She raged and stormed. 'Ah, *non, non, non*!' she cried. 'It is not good of you, Alicia, this! Are you not the sixth form? *C'est abominable*! What behaviour! First you take all my hair-pins, then you put them in a cushion, then you hide them up the chimney, and you HEEEEESS!'

'We didn't hiss, Mam'zelle,' protested Darrell. 'It

179

wasn't us hissing. And how *could* we do all that without you seeing us?'

But Mam'zelle evidently thought they were quite capable of doing such miraculous things, and was perfectly certain Alicia or someone had played her a most complicated trick. She snatched at the pin-cushion and threw it violently into the waste-paper basket.

'Abominable!' she raged. 'ABOMINABLE!'

The door opened in the middle of all this and in came Nora, looking as if she could hardly control herself. She was just in time to hear Mam'zelle's yells and see her fling the pin-cushion into the basket. She almost exploded with joy and delight. So the trick had worked!

'Oh, excuse me, Mam'zelle,' she said, politely, smiling at the excited French mistress, 'but have you got a book of Miss Parker's in your desk?'

Mam'zelle was a little soothed by the sight of one of her favourites. She patted her bun to see if it was still there, plus its hair-pins, and tried to control herself. 'Wait now – I will see,' she said, and opened the desk. As June had carefully put a book of Miss Parker's there, in readiness, she had no difficulty in finding it.

And Nora, of course, had no difficulty in holding the magnet close to Mam'zelle's unfortunate bun! The sixth form saw what she was doing and gasped audibly. The cheek! Twice in one lesson! And had the hissing and the cushion been all part of the same trick? Alicia's mind began to work furiously. How had they done it, the clever little monkeys?

Nora had plenty of time to slip the little wetted pellet on the ledge that held the blackboard against the wall, and to place the tiny pin-cushion in front of it, well hidden behind the board. She managed to do this without being seen, as the lid of the desk hid her for a moment, when Mam'zelle opened it to look inside.

Nora took the book thankfully and fled, bursting into gulps and snorts of laughter as she staggered down the corridor. Miss Potts met her and regarded her with suspicion. *Now* what had Nora been up to?

Nora had hardly shut the door when a familiar sensation came over Mam'zelle's head – her hair was coming down. Her bun was uncoiling! In horror she put up her hand and wailed aloud.

'Here it is again – my pins are vanished and gone – my bun, he descends!'

The girls dissolved into laughter. Mam'zelle's face of horror was too comical for words. Suzanne laughed so much that she fell off her chair to the floor. Mam'zelle rose in wrath.

'You! Suzanne! Why do you laugh so? Is it you who have played this treek?'

'*Non*, Mam'zelle, *non*! I laugh only because it is so piggy-hoo-leeEEEARR!' almost wept Suzanne.

Mam'zelle was about to send Suzanne out of the room, when she stopped. The hissing had begun again! There it was. 'Sssssssssss-ssss!'

'This is too much,' said Mam'zelle, distracted, trying in vain to pin her bun up without any pins. 'It is that snake again. Alicia, look up the chimney.'

'It's not coming from the chimney this time,' said Alicia, puzzled. 'Listen, Mam'zelle. I'm sure it's not.'

They all listened. 'SSSSSSSSSSS!' went the noise merrily. The girls looked at one another. Really, the second-formers were jolly clever – but how *dared* they do all this? Darrell and Alicia grimly made up their minds to have quite a lot to say to Felicity and June after this.

'Ssss-SSSS-sss!'

'It's coming from behind you, Mam'zelle, I'm sure it is,' cried Moira, suddenly. Mam'zelle gave an anguished shriek and propelled herself forward so violently that she fell over the waste-paper basket. She quite thought a snake was coming at her from behind.

Alicia shot out of her seat and went to Mam'zelle's desk, while Darrell and Sally helped Mam'zelle up. 'It's somewhere here,' muttered Alicia, hunting. 'What *can* it be that hisses like that?'

She tracked the noise to the ledge that held the blackboard. Cautiously she put her hand behind – and drew out another little cushion full of pins! The sixth form gaped again! Mam'zelle sank down on a chair and moaned.

'There are my pins once more,' she said. 'But who took them from my bun, who put them in that cushion?

There is some invisible person in the room. Ahhhhhhh!'

There was nothing to be seen behind the blackboard at all. Once more the snake had dissolved into fine powder, and the hissing had stopped. The girls began to laugh helplessly again. Moira hissed just behind Mam'zelle and poor Mam'zelle leaped up as if she had been shot. Suzanne promptly fell off her chair again with laughing.

The door opened and everyone jumped. Miss Potts walked in. 'Is everything all right?' she enquired, puzzled at the scene that met her eyes. 'Such peculiar noises came from here as I passed.'

Suzanne got up from the floor. The others stopped laughing. Alicia put the pin-cushion down on the desk. Mam'zelle sat down once more, trying to put up her hair.

'You don't mean to say you've lost your hair-pins *again*, Mam'zelle!' said Miss Potts. 'Your hair's all down.'

Mam'zelle found her voice. She poured out an excited tirade about snakes filling the corners of the room and hissing at her, about cushions appearing full of pins, about hair-pins vanishing from her hair, and then returned to the snakes once more, and began all over again.

'You come with me, Mam'zelle,' said Miss Potts soothingly. 'I'll come back and deal with this. Come along. You shall put your hair up again and you'll feel better.'

'I go to have it cut off,' said Mam'zelle. 'I go now, Miss Potts. This very instant. I tell you, Miss Potts . . .'

But what else she told Miss Potts the sixth-formers didn't know. They sank down on their chairs and laughed again. Those wicked second-formers! Even Alicia had to admit that they had done a very, very clever job!

A black day for Gwen

Nobody ticked off the second-formers after all. The sixth agreed that they had had such a wonderful laugh that afternoon that it wasn't really fair to row them. 'It was just what I needed, after that nightmare week of exams,' said Darrell. 'Poor Mam'zelle. She's recovered now, but those wicked little second-formers hiss whenever they walk behind her – and she runs like a hare.'

'They're worse than we ever were,' said Alicia. 'And I shouldn't have thought that was possible!'

Now the term began to slide by very quickly indeed. Darrell could hardly catch at the days as they went by. Matches were played and won. Swimming tournaments were held – and won! Moria, Sally and Darrell played brilliantly and swam well – but the star was June, of course. She was in the second teams for swimming and tennis, the youngest that had ever played in them or swum.

Amanda, still hobbling about, was very proud of June. 'You see! I picked her out, and I told you she was the most promising girl in the school!' she said, exultantly, to the sixth-formers. 'She'll pay for watching and training, that child. She's marvellous!'

Sally and Darrell looked across at one another. What a different Amanda this was now. It had been decided that as she couldn't possibly be allowed to train for any games or sports for at least a year, she should stay on at Malory Towers. And now that Amanda could no longer centre her attention on her own skill and prowess she was centring it on June, and other promising youngsters. Already she had made a great difference to the standard of games among them.

'I shall be able to keep an eye on June, and on one or two others,' went on Amanda, happily. 'I'm sorry you're all leaving, though. It'll be strange without you. Won't you be sorry to go?'

'Gwen's the only one who will be glad to leave Malory Towers,' said Darrell. 'None of the others will – even though we've got college to go to – and Belinda's going to a school of art, and Irene to the Guildhall.'

'And Bill and I to our riding school,' said Clarissa, 'and Moira . . .'

'Oh dear,' said Darrell, interrupting. 'Let's not talk about next term yet. Let's have our last week or two still thinking we're coming back next term. We've had a lot of ups and downs this term – now let's enjoy ourselves.'

They all did – except for one girl. That was Gwen. A black afternoon came for her, one she never forgot. It came right out of the blue, when she least expected it.

Matron came to find her in the common-room.

'Gwen,' she said, in rather a grave voice, 'will you go to Miss Grayling's room? There is someone there to see you.'

Gwen was startled. Who would come and see her so near the end of term? She went down at once. She was amazed to see Miss Winter, her old governess, sitting timidly on a chair opposite Miss Grayling.

'Why – Miss Winter!' said Gwen, astonished. Miss Winter got up and kissed her.

'Oh, Gwen,' she said, 'oh, Gwen!' and immediately burst into tears. Gwen looked at her in alarm.

Miss Grayling spoke. 'Gwen. Miss Winter brings bad news, I'm afraid. She . . .'

'Gwen, it's your father!' said Miss Winter, dabbing her eyes. 'He's been taken dreadfully ill. He's gone to hospital. Oh, Gwen, your mother told me this morning, that he won't live!'

Gwen felt as if somebody had taken her heart right out of her body. She sat down blindly on a chair and stared at Miss Winter.

'Have you – have you come to fetch me to see him?' she said, with an effort. 'Shall I be – in time?'

'Oh, you can't see him,' wept Miss Winter. 'He is much, much too ill. He wouldn't know you. I've come to fetch you home to your mother. She's in such a state, Gwen. I can't do anything with her, not a thing! Can you pack and come right away?'

This was a terrible shock to Gwen – her father ill – her mother desperate – and she herself to leave in a hurry.

187

Then another thought came to her and she groaned.

This would mean no school in Switzerland. In a moment her whole future loomed up before her, not bright and shining with happiness in a delightful new school, but black and full of endless, wearisome jobs for a hysterical mother, full of comfortings for a complaining woman – and with no steady, kindly father in the background.

When she thought of her father Gwen covered her eyes in shame and remorse. 'I never even said good-bye!' she cried out loudly, startling Miss Winter and Miss Grayling. 'I never – even – said – good-bye! And I didn't write when I knew he was ill. Now it's too late.'

Too late! What dreadful words. Too late to say she was sorry, too late to be loving, too late to be good and kind.

'I said cruel things, I hurt him – oh, Miss Winter, why didn't you stop me?' cried Gwen, her face white and her eyes tearless. Tears had always been so easy to Gwen – but now they wouldn't come. Miss Winter looked back at her, not daring to remind Gwen how she had pleaded with her to show a little kindness and not to force her own way so much.

'Gwen, dear – I'm very sorry about this,' said Miss Grayling's kind voice. 'I think you should go and pack now, because Miss Winter wants to catch the next train back. Your mother needs you and you must go. Gwen – you haven't always been all you should be. Now is your chance to show that there is something more in you than we guess.'

Gwen stumbled out of the room. Miss Winter followed to help her to pack. Miss Grayling sat and thought. Somehow punishment always caught up with people, if they had deserved it, just as happiness sooner or later caught up with people who had earned it. You sowed your own seeds and reaped the fruit you had sowed. If only every girl could learn that, thought Miss Grayling, there wouldn't be nearly so much unhappiness in the world!

Darrell came into the dormy as Gwen was packing. She was crying now, her tears almost blinding her.

'Gwen – what's the matter?' said Darrell.

'Oh, Darrell – my father's terribly ill – he's not going to live,' wept Gwen. 'Oh, Darrell, please forget all the horrible, horrible things I've said this term. If only he'd live and I had the chance to make up to him for the beast I've been, I'd do everything he wanted – take the dullest, miserablest job in the world, and give up everything else. But it's too late!'

Darrell was shocked beyond words. She put her arm round Gwen, not knowing what to say. Miss Winter spoke timidly. 'We really must catch that train, Gwen dear. Is this all you have to pack?'

'I'll pack her trunk and see it's sent on,' said Darrell, glad to be able to offer to do something. 'Just take a few things, Gwen, in your nightcase.'

She went with Gwen to the front door, miserable for her. What a dreadful way to leave Malory Towers! Poor Gwen! All her fine hopes and dreams blown away like smoke. And those awful words – too late! How dreadful Gwen must feel when she remembered her unkindness. Miss Grayling saw her off too, and shut the door quietly after the car had gone down the drive.

'Don't be too miserable about it,' she said to Darrell. 'It may be the making of Gwen. Don't let it spoil your last week or two, Darrell dear!'

Darrell gave the surprised Miss Grayling a sudden hug, and then wondered how in the world she dared to do such a thing! She went to tell the news to the others.

It cast a gloom on everyone, of course, though many thought secretly that Gwen deserved it. Gwen had no real friends and never had had. She had grumbled and groaned and wept and boasted her way through her years at Malory Towers, and left only unpleasant memories behind. But Sally, Darrell, Mary-Lou and one or two others tried to think kindly of her, because of her great trouble.

Soon other things came to make the girls forget Gwen. Darrell and Sally won the school tennis match against the old girls. Moira won the singles. Someone had a birthday and her mother sent such a magnificent cake that there was enough for everyone in the school! It was delivered in a special van, and carried in by two people!

Then news came of Jo. It came through Deirdre. She received a parcel from Jo and a letter.

Here's some things for you I got myself [wrote Jo]. And I've packed them myself too. I don't know what I'm going to do yet. Dad says he won't be able to get me into a school as good as Malory Towers, I'll have to go to any that will take me. But I don't mind telling you I'm not going to be idiotic again. Dad's been a brick, but he's awfully cut up really. He keeps saying it's half his fault. Mother's fed up with me. She shouldn't have kept boasting I was at Malory Towers. She says I've let the family name down. All I can say is, it's a good thing it's only 'Jones'.

I'm sorry I got you into a row, and I'm awfully glad they didn't expel you too. I wish you'd do something for me. I wish you'd tell the second-formers (go to Felicity) that I apologize for not owning up that time. Will you? That's been on my conscience for ages.

I do miss Malory Towers. Now I know I'm not going back again I see how splendid it was.

Hope you like the parcel.

Jo

Deirdre took the letter to Felicity, who read it in silence and then handed it back. 'Thanks,' she said. 'I'll tell the others. And – er – give her best wishes from the second-formers, will you? Don't forget. Just that – best wishes from the second-formers.'

News came from Gwen too – news that made Darrell

heave a sigh of relief. Gwen's father was not going to die. Gwen had seen him. It hadn't been too late after all. He would be an invalid for the rest of his life, and Gwen would certainly now have to take a job – but she was trying to be good about it.

It's mother who is so difficult [she wrote]. She just cries and cries. Well, I might have grown like that too, if this hadn't happened to me. I shall never be as strong-minded and courageous as you, Darrell – or Sally – or Bill and Clarissa – but I don't think I'll ever again be as weak and selfish as I was. You see – it wasn't 'too late' after all. And that has made a lot of difference to me. I feel as if I've been given another chance.

Do, do, do write to me sometimes. I think and think of you all at Malory Towers. I know none of you think of me, but you might just write occasionally.

All the best to the form and you.

Gwen

Darrell did write, of course. She wrote at once. Darrell was happy and had a happy future to look forward to, and she could well afford to spill a little happiness into Gwen's dull and humdrum life. Sally wrote too and so did Mary-Lou. Bill and Clarissa sent photographs of the stables they meant to set up as a riding school in the autumn.

And now indeed the last term was drawing to an end. Tidying up of shelves and cupboards began. Personal belongings from the sixth-form studies were sent home.

Trunks were lugged down from the attics. All the familiar bustle of the last days of term began once more. Belinda drew her last 'scowl', and Irene hummed her last tune. The term was almost finished.

24

Last day

'Last day, Darrell,' said Sally, when they awoke on the very last morning. 'And thank goodness it's sunny and bright. I couldn't bear to leave on a rainy day.'

'Our last day!' said Darrell. 'Do you remember the first, Sally – six years ago? We were little shrimps of twelve – smaller than Felicity and June! How the time has flown!'

The last-day bustle began in earnest after breakfast. Matron was about the only calm person in the school, with the exception of Miss Grayling, whom nobody had ever seen flustered or ruffled. Mam'zelle was as usual in a state of beaming, bewildered good temper. Miss Potts bustled about with first-formers who had lost this, that or the other.

The trunks had most of them gone off in advance, but those being taken by car were piled up in the drive. Pop, the handyman, ran about like a hare, and carried heavy trunks on his broad shoulder as if they weighed only a pound or two. The first car arrived and hooted in the drive. An excited third-former squealed and almost fell down the stairs from top to bottom when she recognized her parents' car.

'*Tiens*!' said Mam'zelle, catching her. 'Is this the way to come down the stairs? Always you hurry too much, Hilary!'

'Come down to the pool, Sally,' said Darrell. They went down the steep path and stood beside the gleaming, restless pool, which was swept every now and again by an extra big wave coming over the rocks. 'We've had fun here,' said Darrell. 'Now let's go to the rose-garden.'

They went there and looked at the masses of brilliant roses. Each was silently saying good-bye to the places she loved most. They went to all the common-rooms, from the first to the sixth, remembering what had happened in each. They peeped into the dining-room, and then into the different form-rooms. What fun they had had!

And what fun they were *going* to have! 'We'll have a good look backwards, today, then we'll set our eyes forward,' said Sally. 'College will be better fun still, Darrell – everyone says so.'

June and Felicity caught sight of the two sixth-formers wandering around. June nudged Felicity. 'Look – they're saying a fond farewell. Don't they look solemn?'

June caught up with the sixth-formers. 'Hallo,' she said. 'You've forgotten something.'

'What?' asked Sally and Darrell.

'You've forgotten to say good-bye to the stables and the wood-shed, and . . .'

'That's not funny,' said Darrell. 'You wait till it's your last day, young June!'

'June's got no feelings at all, have you, June?' said Alicia, appearing round the corner. 'I feel a bit solemn myself today. Here, you two youngsters, this can jolly well be a solemn day for you too!'

To June's intense surprise she took her by the shoulders and looked into her eyes. 'Carry on for me,' she said. 'Carry the standard high! Do you promise, June?'

'I promise,' said June, startled. 'You – you can trust me, Alicia.'

'And I promise, Darrell,' said Felicity, equally solemnly. 'I'll never let Malory Towers down. *I'll* carry the standard high too.'

Alicia released June's shoulders. 'Well,' she said, 'so long as we've got *some*one to hand on the standard to, I'm happy! Maybe our own daughters will help to carry on the tradition one day.'

'And have riding lessons on Bill's and Clarissa's horses,' said Felicity, which made them all laugh.

There was more hooting in the drive. 'Come on. We shan't be ready when our people arrive,' said Alicia. 'That sounds like my brother Sam hooting. He said he'd come and fetch me today.'

Into the seething crowd they went. Mam'zelle was shouting for someone who had gone long since, and Suzanne was trying to explain to her that she wasn't there. Miss Potts was carrying a pair of pyjamas that had apparently dropped out of someone's nightcase. Matron rushed after a small first-former anxiously, nobody could imagine why. It was the old familiar last-morning excitement.

'Darrell! Felicity!' suddenly called Mrs Rivers' voice. 'Here we are! Where on earth were you? We've been here for ages.'

'Oh, that was *Daddy's* horn we heard hooting,' said Felicity. 'I might have guessed. Come on, Darrell. Got your case?'

'Yes, *and* my racket,' said Darrell. 'Where's yours?'

Felicity disappeared into the crowd. Mr Rivers kissed Darrell and laughed. 'Doing her disappearing act already,' he said.

'Good-bye, Darrell! Don't forget to write!' yelled Alicia. 'See you in October at St Andrews.'

She stepped back heavily on Mam'zelle's foot. 'Oh, sorry, Mam'zelle.'

'Always you tread on my feet,' said Mam'zelle, quite unfairly. 'Have you seen Katherine? She has left her racket behind.'

Felicity ran up with her own racket. 'Good-bye, Mam'zelle. Be careful of snakes these holidays, won't you?'

'Ahhhhhhh! You bad girl, you,' said Mam'zelle. 'I heeeess at you! Ssssssss!'

This astonished Miss Grayling considerably. She was just nearby, and got the full benefit of Mam'zelle's ferocious hiss. Mam'zelle was covered with confusion and disappeared hurriedly.

Darrell laughed. 'Oh dear – I do love this last-minute flurry. Oh – are we off, Daddy? Good-bye, Miss Grayling, good-bye, Miss Potts, good-bye, Mam'zelle – good-bye, Malory Towers!'

And good-bye to you, Darrell – and good luck. We've loved knowing you. Good-bye!